MU

A Click Your Poison book

by
James Schannep

The eAversion Version

First Print Edition

This is a work of fiction. The actions depicted are neither real nor based on real events. The actual locations and businesses in this book are all used in conjunction with fictional and fictionalized elements; their inclusion is for literary effect only and was done without permission or consent. Any similarity between characters in the book and actual persons is purely coincidental and unintentional. Nothing in the book is intended to convey or imply facts about any businesses, persons, elements or events.

Certain details in this book that could be construed as negative impressions of Brazil and Brazilians are merely the intended plot and story elements germane to a murder mystery, in order to portray a "noir" feel. The same is true of US Foreign Service members herein depicted within.

Author's note: The factual elements of this book were garnered from many hours of research, including travel guides, documentaries, travel blogs, and my personal experiences abroad. You might find mistakes in the text; some are based on my taking creative liberties, while others are intentional misinformation given by the characters in the story. However, as I'm not a native Brazilian, you may find unintentional errors. If you do, please contact me at www.jamesschannep.com so I can revise the text for future editions.

Print Edition

Library of Congress Cataloging-in-Publication Data
Schannep, James, 1984—
MURDERED: a Click Your Poison book / James Schannep

1. International Mystery & Crime—Mystery & Detective—Fiction.
2. Crime—Thrillers—Fiction. 3. Noir—Fiction. I. Title

COVER ART BY NIKKI JANSEN

This book has been modified from its original version. It has been formatted to fit this page.

ISBN-10: 1494443309
ISBN-13: 978-1494443306

How it works: *MURDERED* is a novel unlike any other. YOU, Dear Reader, are the main character of this story. Solve the mysteries found within, or let the killer(s) get away with murder, based solely on the merit of your own choices. Do not read this book front to back. Instead, follow the choices at the end of each chapter to the next section. The story evolves based on your decisions, so choose wisely. Could YOU solve a murder?

Click Your Poison books

INFECTED—*Will YOU Survive the Zombie Apocalypse?*
MURDERED—*Can YOU Solve the Mystery?*
SUPERPOWERED—*Will YOU Be a Hero or a Villain?*
PATHOGENS—*More Zombocalypse Survival Stories!*
MAROONED—*Can YOU Endure Treachery and Survival on the High Seas?*
SPIED (coming in 2019)—*Can YOU Save the World as a Secret Agent?*

** More titles coming soon! **

Sign up for the new release mailing list at: http://eepurl.com/bdWUBb
Or visit the author's blog at www.jamesschannep.com

"Once you eliminate the impossible, whatever remains, no matter how improbable, must be the truth."
—Sherlock Holmes, by Sir Arthur Conan Doyle

"Great deeds are usually wrought at great risks."
—Herodotus, *The Histories,* Book 7

Acknowledgments

Special thanks to my friend Chris Boyes, and my wife Michaela, your notes were an invaluable addition. A big thanks to Special Agents "Carnahan" and "Hobbs" of the Diplomatic Security Service for the inspiration and technical base for the book. Thanks also to Mike Beeson and Richard Young for Beta testing, and to Damon Bosetti for your technical expertise. To Kelli Mears for letting me bounce ideas day after day.

To my copyeditor: Linda Jay Geldens, cover artist: Nikki Jansen, and to Paul Salvette and the team at BB eBooks. Thank you all for your generosity and professionalism.

And to my friends and family, for your unyielding encouragement, enthusiasm and support.

MURDERED

You're in Rio de Janeiro, Brazil, in the days before *Carnaval.* You've only just arrived, less than three hours ago, but any travel weariness is replaced by the rush of Rio nightlife. You're here on vacation with friends, ready for The Biggest Party on Earth, but right now you're alone.

It might still be four days until the giant flotillas re-imagined as hummingbirds or jaguars parade down the street, covered in exotic, scantily-clad dancers like an infestation of glamorous fleas. It might be less than a week until the party *really* begins, but right now you can't tell the difference. If this is merely part of the pre-festivities, this raucous, impromptu street party, you can scarcely imagine the pandemonium of full-blown *Carnaval.*

In four days, the whole country will cut loose, but already the streets are packed with singing and dancing crowds, like a cultural flashmob unconcerned with cameras or irony. They're here for the *samba* and for the *caipirinha*—sugarcane liquor with lime and more sugar. You've had some already, but thankfully, you're far from drunk. Otherwise you might not be concerned that the crowd has swept you up in their current and dragged you away from your friends.

There's not a familiar face in sight.

In fact, all you see are Brazilians. Either gaunt, hard-workers, temporarily enraptured by the glee of *Carnaval*; or those who live for the party and so tonight is simply another Monday. Black descendants of former slaves freed into lives of poverty and revelers with Portuguese heritage mixed with a flourish of native Amazonian tribesmen—their traditions now intermingled into one novel culture.

You snap a picture—the scene is amazing. Still, you look around for your friends, scanning each face, and appearing very much like the hopelessly lost tourist that you are. Maybe for the rest of the week you should tie a rope around the lot of you; anchor yourself together as if you were summiting Mt. Everest.

Now the avalanche of humanity takes you further down the street, the relentless drumbeats threatening to set you dancing. You seek shelter in an alleyway, catching your breath, wiping sweat off your brow, and taking a moment to get your bearings. The ground in the alley is typical of these concrete passages, speckled with black tar-patches of gum and other residue, and cracks in the pavement sealed with collective detritus. A bird's nest of telephone and electrical wires hangs overhead, nearly within reach. It's much cooler here in the alley, away from the pulsing heat emitted from the dancers in the street proper. The alley walls are claustrophobically close, and stretch way down around the corner; they're red brick, lacquered with teal green everywhere an arm could reach. Your camera rises as a reflex action; you take a picture.

In the preview on the LCD screen, you notice there's the beginning of a graffiti mural sticking out from the adjoining alley. You peek around the corner to see the full image. It's an angel, larger than life and in stunning detail. His hair is long and his face is placid, much like a beardless Christ. Yet this is a dark angel; his wings, not feathered, are formed from two AK-47 machine guns divided in broad symmetry. Two snakes wrap around his legs, originating from behind his ankles and enveloping his lower half like the caduceus, their heads biting his wrists and spreading his arms. A nuclear mushroom cloud which serves as his halo bursts forth from behind his flowing mane. In stylized calligraphy, the caption above reads, "*Vou testemunhar.*"

Just as the shutter clicks on your camera, a wooden *slam* from behind injects you with a shot of adrenaline. You turn and, seeing only a door flapping loosely in the cross-breeze, let out a sigh of relief. But as the door swings wide once more, you find your spine tingling.

There's someone lying there, recumbent on the floor. Another tourist, passed out from too much *caipirinha,* perhaps? The opening to the doorway glimmers crimson under the streetlights.

As you step forward, your unease gives way to a newfound terror—there's blood, and lots of it. You lean inside the porthole and snap a picture of the room, just to be certain.

From your vantage point in the doorway, a woman's shoe is illuminated, and a pale foot with painted toenails; that's all you can see from this angle. Trembling, you step forward into the dark recesses of the room, careful not to tread in the blood. You want to call out, to ask if she's okay, but right now concentrating on your breathing is the only thing fending off all-out panic.

And so you move forward in silence, teeth gritted and heart pounding. She's not okay, you soon discover, not okay at all. More blood is spattered on the wall behind her. She is lying on the floor, facing away from the door, her blood pooled in a greater quantity than you realized was inside a human body.

When you come around in front of her, you see that her face has completely caved in under the force of some great trauma. You cover your mouth in horror at her injuries and quickly turn away.

Atop a large crate opposite the woman rests a snub-nosed, blue-metal revolver and a note that reads:

"PICK ME UP."

- Pick up the gun. Go to page 7
- Leave it. Go to page 15

Action-oriented

The battle rages on, gunshots pinging off the armored car as if lamenting their own inefficiency. At this point, it's a stalemate. Elite Squad is pinned down, yet perfectly secure in their armored *caveirão*. The drug traffickers, although unable to harm the special police, remain in relative safety within the recesses of homes and atop buildings.

It looks like the situation might be favoring the police, who can take their time, aim, and expertly engage their targets, whereas the traffickers aren't able to do much more than blind-fire. One of the Elite Squad troops lands a shot on a gang member standing on the rooftop across from yours; he slumps before tumbling down onto the street in a limp heap. Is this how it works—Elite Squad goes in, like a stick jabbing into a termite mound, then waits for the drug lords to come crawling out one by one, outgunned and outmatched?

A young drug trafficker steps out of a house and hurls something at the vehicle. It's a quick movement, and he's safely back inside again before the police can shoot him. What was that, a rock? You squint, trying to get a better look. Dear God, it's a *grenade*. Okay, perhaps the traffickers aren't outmatched.

The grenade explodes, rocking the vehicle back and forth and scarring the pavement beneath. The Elite Squad members duck back inside their protective fortress. After the dust settles, it appears the *caveirão* is unharmed. Not even the tires are punctured; this thing is a beast.

And now it's angry.

The tires screech as the thing darts forward under full acceleration. Since the front end is reinforced, covered with an extra-thick cattle guard, the vehicle doesn't feel much when it *smashes* into the building head-on and punches a hole through the poorly constructed brick and mortar. Pulling back with equal force, the vehicle retreats away from the damaged home as the roof collapses.

All right, maybe outgunned and outmatched *is* the right description after all. If we're sticking with termites as the image, it looks like Elite Squad can stamp out the entire mound with those steel-toed work boots whenever they please.

Then, as if to prove you wrong, movement on the rooftop across the way catches your eye. There's another trafficker coming out, holding an RPG—the guy has a fucking *rocket launcher*! So…maybe they're not outgunned either.

He crouches down on one knee, takes aim, and prepares to fire. Irma stands up, hurriedly removing a pistol from her leg holster to take him out. But she's not fast enough. Instead, the top of the armored car flips open, and an Elite Squad member bursts forth from the cylindrical hatch, firing his rifle as he emerges.

No time to take aim, yet incredibly, he hits the RPG-wielding gang member. Only winged, the trafficker fires a wild shot; the rocket-propelled grenade flies off, spiraling straight toward you.

You jump out of the way and Irma hits the deck. In its corkscrew trajectory, the missile rises off the rooftop with just enough clearance not to destroy the building. Instead, it burrows deep into the next home in the *favela*, showering you with debris from the explosion.

Emerging like a dulled protest from your ringing ears, you hear shouts and more gunfire from the street. Elite Squad, plus Agent Danly, pours out of the armored car. They chase several drug traffickers down an alley opposite your position. The man who held the RPG has been killed. It appears that the tide has now fully turned in the police's favor, but they don't want the criminals to escape.

A lone figure runs out of one of the homes. Rather than wearing a tank top or going shirtless like the other drug traffickers, this man is well-dressed and has a backpack. Rather than sporting a homemade mask, this man has on glasses. And when he looks up over his shoulder, you can see his piercing blue eyes.

It's the man from the warehouse crime scene.

Though you're dazed and only see his face for an instant, you're certain of it. The suspect sprints into a different alley, pursued by a lone Elite Squad member.

- "Irma, it's *him,* let's go!" Go to page 108
- "I've got to go find Danly!" Go to page 363

Ain't Nobody Got Time for That

Bertram silences the phone and you keep running through the sugarcane. Soon the sound of shuffling leaves and your huffing breaths are overpowered by a loud chugging. Setting his course for the unmistakable growl of a diesel engine, Agent Bertram dashes through the sugarcane and out to a dirt road.

There, standing next to an idling jeep, a man holds a machete. He's clothed head to toe in gray cloth, like a padded ninja, a turtleneck pulled up over his face and a boonie hat pulled so low that only his eyes are visible. They're open wide, frightened at the sight of Agent Bertram's assault rifle.

The man in the driver's seat considers fleeing, but Bertram's persuasive Portuguese convinces him to stay.

"Let's move, Hotshot," Bertram says, loading up into the jeep.

He finds a shotgun resting in the back, hands it to you, and adds, "Keep an eye out for our friend, will ya?"

Holding the weapon, you sit, appropriately, in the front passenger seat. Just like in the stagecoach days of the Wild West. The four of you jump in the vehicle and flee quickly from the Man in Black. Finally safe, Bertram makes his call.

"Agent Bertram," he says into the phone. "Negative, I'm still on scene."

You can't hear the caller's words over the roar of the engine, but you can hear the angry tone.

"Sir, all due respect, that's bullshit. I haven't even—"

He grits his teeth.

"Yes, sir… yes, sir." He hangs up and says, "We've got to go back."

"What? Why?"

"The official investigation team landed this morning. We're off the case."

"But we haven't even—" you start to say. His glare silences you.

"Do you still have that helicopter pilot's card? We need to get back so I can debrief."

"I think so," you mumble as you check your pockets.

Agent Bertram speaks to the men in Portuguese, but they shake their heads. He tries to emphasize his point by chambering a round in his pistol. The *click* of the slide springing into action sends a chill into your bones, but the men continue shaking their heads.

"Goddammit," Bertram growls. "They're taking us to the plantation. To see the Sugar King, the Big Man. Mateo Ferro is the Governor of this territory, and the largest sugarcane ethanol producer in the world."

Whoa, you think. That would make Ferro one of the richest people on the planet.

"He's *here*?" you ask.

"Apparently. I told them—just bluffing, mind you—that I'd kill them if they took us there. Didn't matter. I can only imagine what they're afraid of. The standard crime lord threat seems to be 'I'll kill your family,' but they might do something even worse than that."

"Can't wait to meet him," you say sarcastically.

➢ *Proceed to the plantation.* Go to page 270

The American

You casually stroll up to the guard shack, smooth back your hair, straighten your shirt and stand tall. Cool…yet relaxed. With your winningest grin and your charm turned up to eleven, you look through the glass panel.

It's set up like a bank or a movie theater concession stand, with a six-inch slit at the bottom for passing documents and a circular grate in the center for communication.

A local Brazilian hired as outer-layer security, the guard seated behind the glass has the same Kevlar body armor as those stationed outside the bullet-proof sentry station and even wears his "on-duty" hat. He's maybe twenty years old and lowers his pop-culture magazine when he sees you standing there.

"Good morning," you say, leaning toward him. "How are you this fine day? Getting excited for *Carnaval?"*

The guard eyes you with suspicion. "Can I help you?" he asks impatiently.

- "This is a little awkward, but I left my ID badge in my car in the garage. Mind if I run in and grab it real quick?" Go to page 89
- "So…I met somebody at a club last night, but didn't get a phone number. All I have is the license plate. Can I give you $100 to leave a note on the car for me?" Go to page 295
- "Hi! I'm a journalist late for an interview with the Consul. Is this where I sign in?" Go to page 341

Armed and Dangerous

You pick up the revolver, the carbon steel glinting cold and black under the flickering fluorescent lights, to examine it closer. A compact weapon with a snub nose, it's the same size as the open palm of your hand, but it's heavy.

There's nothing too complex about the revolver; you pull back the hammer and the cylinder rotates in response. Five cartridges dance like musical chairs toward the chamber, each cartridge pristine, save for the one already dented by the firing pin. The one whose bullet most likely killed the woman lying on the floor.

All you have to do is squeeze the trigger and the weapon will kill for you too.

But as you look up from the revolver, you realize you're not alone. A man stands before you, at a door opposite yours, staring at the woman's body. His expression is odd, a mix of horror and confusion. Shock, perhaps.

You get a good look at him: like any other local Brazilian, his skin is olive-tan, but he carries himself like a European. Thin, clean-shaven, high cheekbones, looking like he recently had a haircut. Atop his swooping nose sit silver-colored, professorial-looking spectacles.

When he looks up at you, that's when you see the rage. His eyes are very unusual for a Brazilian—icy-blue. With a muscular twitch, his jaw sets and he takes a step forward, but then stops in his tracks when he spots the revolver in your hand.

He turns to run away.

- Let him go. Go to page 17
- It's the killer! Shoot him in the back! Go to page 38

Antitrust

Let's face it, too much competition is bad for the black market, right? Irma Dos Santos' eyes grow wide as you shoot her repeatedly with the assault rifle. Is it shock at your evident betrayal? Or is it simply surprise that you managed to get her first? You—a simple tourist—are getting a one-of-a-kind travel experience. Pretty sure "Kill Slumlords and a Rio Cop" won't be on the tour guide.

Still, you don't want to be around when this crime scene gets investigated. You've already learned that lesson. You leave the four bodies on the floor and venture back into the alleys. Looking carefully for more drug traffickers, you jog through the concrete labyrinth until….

What's that smell? Liver, rare. And the taste in your mouth? It stings like copper. You're in the street when an Elite Squad member draws down on you with his assault rifle, the barrel smoking.

Is that what that *crack* sound was? You fall to your knees, then face down onto the dusty street.

When somebody comes running at these guys with an AK-47, they don't think, they just react. They're the best. Agent Danly's gonna have a hell of a lot of paperwork to write up on you.

THE END

Ask Around

Viktor starts by asking Isis, but her posture turns defensive. "*Não, não, não,*" she says over and over, her palms raised and her head shaking.

"She refuses to get involved with the traffickers," Viktor tells you. "I'm willing to bet she's had some bad experiences in the recent past."

You notice for the first time the ever-so-faint outline of a healing bruise around her left eye. The skin there is yellowed, with a few mottled pink spots. Viktor pays her for her trouble and she seems to calm down. She thanks him and leaves.

Viktor is about to say something to you, but one of the male pickers comes to take her place, swooping in like one of the opportunistic seabirds that raid the garbage mound underfoot. The man offers to help, looking for a similar reward to what Viktor just gave Isis.

"He says he has a cousin who's a trafficker and another who's a prostitute. He's willing to arrange a meeting with either of them."

- "Straight to the source. Trafficker it is." Go to page 211
- "I'm less afraid of a prostitute than I am a drug lord. So…ladies first, that's my vote." Go to page 72

Askew

You knock the gun just as she pulls the trigger, sending the shot wide. The bullet ricochets wildly off the brick wall, but doesn't hit anyone. Viktor drops the bomb, reflexively ducking and raising his hands in surrender. It *clinks* harmlessly against the pavement.

Excruciating pain shoots through the right side of your chest just beneath the ribs, and suddenly you can't breathe. At first you think you've been shot, that maybe the ricochet hit you, but when you look down, there's a knife in your chest and Irma is holding the handle.

As she pulls the blade out, your lung collapses.

"I really wish you hadn't made me do that," she says. "I liked you."

You try to respond, but you can't draw in enough air to speak.

Viktor's blue eyes are like saucers. Irma turns and shoots him. As he crashes to the ground, she shoots him again. She walks over to his body and shoots him once more, for good measure, then places the knife in his hand.

You fall to one knee, incredibly weak now.

"I wish I could just put you out of your misery," she says, "but Viktor only stabbed you once, see? Then I was able to shoot him, bringing the killer to justice and solving the case."

You try to call out for help, but you can't. The strain weakens you further and you fall down. You lose consciousness, but regain it sometime later. You can't be sure how long it's been.

Just barely, over the sound of your own wheezing, you hear footsteps approaching. From the shadows, the Rio chief of police emerges.

"Well done, Detective," the man says.

He examines the scene, then notices you're still alive. He removes a handkerchief from his pocket and kneels down next to you.

"We must finish the job here," he says, "on the off-chance that the American would recover in the hospital. Understand?"

"Yes, sir."

He presses the handkerchief over your nose and mouth. Slowly, everything goes black.

THE END

At the Copa, Copacabana

The government SUV pulls up to the city's most famous hotel, the Copacabana Palace. Only three miles up the road from your old hostel in Ipanema but three times the price for a room, you're greeted with all the pomp and circumstance of a visiting rock star. The white façade is something out of the 1920s, and to be quite honest, it looks more like a presidential home than a hotel.

"The Secretary of State was set up to be here during the Energy Summit but got called away, so the suite is available for the night. Enjoy," Agent Bertram says, a warm smile breaking through his beard.

"Try and get some sleep," Danly says, exiting the car.

Your room is so opulent, it borders on the obscene. More a luxury apartment than a hotel room, the tiled floors glimmer under soft white lamps. The main room has furniture made of a dark, jungle wood. Several vases of fresh, locally exotic flowers await you. The curtains are open to your own private balcony, inviting a cool sea breeze from the ocean, so close you can practically feel the spray from the waves.

You sit on the bed, pick up the phone, and dial your room at the hostel, but no one answers. As you're leaving a message to let your friends know you're okay, a sinking feeling creeps over you. They're probably just still out partying, right?

With this optimism in mind, you lie down to ponder the implications. Before you know what's happened, you've melted into the 80,000-thread-count sheets and fallen deeply asleep, the day's events unable to touch you on your luxurious perch.

The next morning you enjoy a cup of steaming, delicious coffee—courtesy of your own private butler—on the balcony. It's large enough for deck chairs, and you lounge under the warm embrace of the morning sun, admiring joggers starting their day along the white sandy beach.

When you try to call your friends once more, they answer this time and you spend the next hour regaling them with tales of adventure and a near-horrific end. Promising to meet up soon, you hang up and head down to the main floor in search of breakfast.

In the lobby, the American agents are reading the morning paper in comfortable leather chairs. Upon recognizing you, their papers are folded and returned to the end tables. The pair rises in greeting. With routine familiarity, they button their suit jackets as they stand up.

"Good morning, gentlemen," you offer.

"I trust everything was in order?" Danly asks.

"Oh, in spades," you reply, in the pageantry of elegance.

"Join us for breakfast," Bertram says, pointing an open hand to the hotel's restaurant.

It's on a terrace near an enormous swimming pool, where many guests have already claimed a spot with a mixed drink and a good book. The busboy delivers three glasses of water and soon after, your waiter appears.

"The Embassy isn't footing the food bill," Danly says dryly.

The three of you order, the waiter leaves, and as you look out over the pool, Bertram says, "It's been confirmed. Our Jane Doe is now Jane Nightingale, an Office Management Specialist at the Rio consulate. I didn't know her."

Danly shakes his head; neither did he.

Agent Bertram continues, "She didn't hold a significant position—they're the ones that do the secretarial work—so we don't think the killing was politically motivated, but we won't rule out a terrorist attack until we know for sure."

"Most likely she was separated from the crowd, just like you, and it was a mugging turned sour. Who knows, you may owe the woman your life. It could have been you in there."

"It's even possible this is a serial killer—he's the right demographic, based on that sketch you provided—and you probably interrupted him during his rituals," Bertram says.

"I doubt it," Danly says. "Serial killers are extremely rare."

"In America, maybe. But with no extradition laws, Brazil is like a retirement community for criminals."

"And this guy has come out of retirement?" you ask.

"I don't buy it," Agent Danly says. "This was a first-time job, too sloppy to be a pro. Regardless, this is going to be a total shitstorm. We haven't had an American murdered in the Foreign Service since the Sixties, and that was at the hands of a coworker. So an American killed outside the line of duty by a foreign national? Shitstorm. Within 48 hours, a team will be dispatched by HQ, and in a couple of days this place will be crawling with feds from Arlington."

"But we know the first 48 hours are the most important, and we've been cleared to start the investigation."

"What about the local police?" you ask.

"It's their job," Danly says. "We're just going to do it for them."

Agent Bertram spreads his arms magnanimously. "Look, we're just going to do what we can before the trail goes cold, and the reason we're telling you is because we want your help. You're the only one who knows what the suspect looks like."

"What do you want from me?"

"Come with us and ID the subject. Help us find the goddamn murderer," Agent Danly says, leaning back and folding his arms over his chest.

- "Uh, no thanks. I'm here on vacation… I don't want to drag you guys down. Good luck." Go to page 353
- "I'm in. Do I get a gun and a badge? Or a pipe and a magnifying glass, at least?" Go to page 61

Bad Cop

The professor folds his arms across his chest and squints. "Is this some kind of joke?"

"I assure you it's not, but the investigation is still ongoing," Bertram says, raising his palms in a gesture of peace.

"But your buddy is our primary suspect. Have much of a temper, did he?"

"Viktor never hurt a fly. As far as I know, he and his fiancée were quite happy together."

"And how well did you know Viktor?" Bertram asks, removing a notebook from his suit pocket. "When did you first meet?"

"Not very well. He does a visiting lecture here every now and again. First time was maybe… two years ago?"

"What was his area of expertise?"

"Engineering."

You sit in silence, wondering if the professor will elaborate, but he doesn't move a muscle. The man glowers at you, and you know you hit a nerve. He's feeling the need to protect a suspected murderer—but why? Does this go beyond academic trust and professional courtesy?

"What's the sentence for aiding and abetting a murderer in this country?" you ask.

"Cool the jets, Hotshot," Bertram says.

Professor Tavares-Silva rises from his chair and says, "If you'll excuse me, I'm a very busy man."

"I'm sorry, we'll play nice," Bertram says. "Just a few more questions, please."

"The University keeps a lawyer on retainer. You may direct any further inquiries to our legal department. Good day."

Bertram stands up and buttons his suit jacket. Exiting, he says to you, "You may want to let me ask the questions in the future, asshole."

➢ *Whatever, that guy was about to crack. To Viktor's apartment!* Go to page 166

Balls (or Ovum) of Steel

The street lights flicker on and you wait for the corrupt policeman to arrive, your *ovos* tingling in anticipation. Soon he does, but it's not what you expected. First, he isn't alone. The man is in plainclothes, but he keeps two uniformed officers as his escort. Second, he knows you are.

In an instant, you recognize the cop. Incredibly, it's Detective Lucio Muniz, the bleach-blond policeman who interviewed you on the night you were detained. Is he the one you're going to bribe?

"*You?*" he says.

"We're looking for the truth," you say coolly. "If you can help us, we can help you."

"You're the ones that called?"

Viktor nods.

Detective Muniz smiles. "Well, then, we're all friends here. Let's get down to business. What information would you like to buy?"

"The murder I stumbled upon, what do you know?" you ask.

"More than you could imagine," he smirks.

Viktor steps forward. "Do you know who's responsible? Who the killer is?"

Muniz carefully considers the question, then smiles and rubs his fingers together in the universal sign for money. Clearly, he's waiting for his bribe.

"Ah, one second," you say, stepping behind Viktor and opening his backpack. "I believe this will help loosen your tongue."

Detective Muniz's smile drops instantly. When you step back out, you're brandishing the sub-machinegun.

All three cops go for their handguns.

You fire into the air, a quick burst, then level the gun at the men. They stop, hands raised. Viktor moves out and takes their three pistols, tossing them into a gutter sewer grate.

"You're dead—*dead*! Do you hear me?" Detective Muniz shouts.

"I do," you say. It's almost as if the words are coming out on their own. "You're hardly the first man to want us gone, but if you don't want to join us in the grave, I'd start talking."

"*Vai po calarho,*" Muniz curses.

Viktor pistol-whips the detective. One of the police officers steps forward, but you check his move with the muzzle of your weapon. Muniz spits blood.

Icy-cold, Viktor says, "Please, give me a reason to do that again."

Detective Muniz's jaw sets and he says, "Find the Shadow Chiefs gang and talk to an informant named Falador."

"See? That wasn't so hard," you say.

"If you don't kill me, I will fuck your corpse."

"Let's just go," Viktor says.

- "No, he has a point." Gun down the three policemen. Go to page 324
- Get out of here, quick. Go to page 294

Bare-handed

As you look up from the revolver, you realize you're not alone. A man stands before you, at a door opposite yours, staring at the woman's body. His expression is odd, a mix of horror and confusion. Shock, perhaps.

You get a good look at him: like any other local Brazilian, his skin is olive-tan, but he carries himself like a European. Thin, clean-shaven, high cheekbones, looking like he recently had a haircut. Atop his swooping nose sit silver-colored, professorial-looking spectacles. His eyes are very unusual for a Brazilian—icy-blue.

He turns to run away.

- Let him go. Go to page 30
- It's the killer! Grab the gun and shoot him in the back! Go to page 38

Bathrooms

You round the corner to arrive at the *Banheiros,* and as soon as you see a male figure on one door and a female figure on the other, both marked with a "WC," you realize that you've arrived at the restrooms.

Probably should've known that one as a tourist in Brazil… but then again, your "Pork and Cheese" (Portuguese) was never very good. Still, you could duck in there and give Agent Danly the slip.

- Don't stop. Check out *Salas de Conferências.* Go to page 46
- Keep going, this time try left—*Apoio.* Go to page 311
- Duck in the bathroom, then double back to *Imprensa.* Go to page 252
- Wait until Danly's gone, then try *Auditório Principal.* Go to page 193

Behind

What the hell did you just stumble upon? It's possible, in your shock, that you just let the murderer escape. Damn, should've snapped a picture. It won't do much to exonerate you or help the police, but you won't soon forget the man's face. Or those crystalline, piercing eyes. The kind of eyes that look like they were carved from an ice cave or lifted from a lightning-infused Norse god.

"Stay where you are," a woman's voice commands from behind.

"Turn around slowly, hands where we can see them," a man adds.

Both have thick Brazilian accents. You turn slowly, keeping the revolver close to your chest as if you were protecting some dangerous secret, ready to face whoever it might be.

The woman is thin, tall, with skin like soy milk and shimmering raven hair pulled back in a bun. She looks professional, like an American businesswoman, save for her oversized hoop earrings and long, lustrous eyelashes. The other is an average-looking man, skin bronzed, hair bleached to match.

They both wear suits, but the man's shirt is shimmering silk, teal green like the walls in the alley.

Both hold revolvers, and both weapons are aimed at you. Their eyes blaze as they see the revolver in your hands.

"*Arma*!" the man calls out.

The woman yells at you in Portuguese, then, noticing your confusion, adds in English, "Drop the weapon!"

- "You drop yours! Don't make me use this thing!" Go to page 59
- Drop the gun, hands raised. Go to page 80

Bête Noire

You sprint after the assassin, who in turn chases the prime suspect in the murder of Jane Nightingale. You shove your way through dancing revelers, ignoring their shouts of protest, trying desperately to keep up with the two men.

The crowd parts like a school of fish evading a predator.

There before you is a brick wall with nothing more than a locked door. The bespectacled man finds himself at a dead end with nowhere else to go. He slams into the door three times with his shoulder, to no avail, then turns back to face his fate.

The devil-costumed assassin pulls the two handguns off his pitchfork, as the center rod falls to the ground with a *clang*. His prey's blue eyes follow the rod to the asphalt. It hits hard against the ground and bounces before finally coming to a rest. The man looks back up at the assassin—but not before flicking his eyes over to you in the briefest moment of recognition.

With two shots from the left handgun and one from the right, the assassin kills the man, gunning him down right there in the public street. Women scream and the crowd pushes further away from the murder.

Suddenly, you feel very naked and alone. You look around and realize there's a large bubble of empty space on the street, with you smack in the middle.

Before you can run, the devilish assassin turns around. The teeth painted atop his lips part to reveal the real teeth beneath them. With an impish grin, his handguns come up and you go down.

THE END

Better Left Unsaid

Agent Danly turns progressively more red as you explain your previous night's escapades. The vein on his forehead is ready to burst. You can't be sure if he's even heard what you're saying—about the new information you've uncovered—because there's never even a glimmer of hope that he's happy with you.

He crushes his coffee cup in his hand, sending the scalding liquid pouring over his knuckles without his so much as acknowledging it. When you're finished speaking, the only sound is the grinding of his teeth.

"That's it. You're off the case."

"Did you even hear what I said?" you plea.

"This was Bertram's *stupid* idea to begin with, and now this is the last straw. You're endangering your own pathetic life, but worse, you've endangered the investigation."

"But!—"

"I don't care what you saw or what you *think* you saw; did you honestly believe any of this would be admissible in court? Or that we could use it in our reports? You've jeopardized everything. Now let's go. I'm taking to you the consulate, turning you over to Security there, and putting you on the first plane back to the States—and you better pray I never see you again."

THE END

Big Oil

Though it's getting later in the afternoon, both companies are able to meet with you. Bertram drops you off and tells you to have your contact's secretary call him when you're ready to be picked up.

The office at BP's headquarters is modern, clean, and reeks of money. Your contact comes out to meet you—an American businesswoman in a smart blazer and knee-length skirt. She's in her forties. Her curly, auburn, almost maroon-color hair bounces lightly on her shoulders as she walks toward you on clicking high heels, her hand outstretched.

"Marilyn Margaret," she says. "We've got a conference room set up, if you'll come with me."

You follow her to the glass-walled meeting room and help yourself to a cheese danish at the coffee bar (you haven't had a proper lunch yet). It's just the two of you, and she waits until you're ready.

"So, Ms. Margaret, you're an American running the Brazilian branch of British Petroleum?"

"Oh, I don't run the branch. I'm the American liaison, and please call me Marilyn. We represent interests in most developed nations, and what we do here in Brazil attracts the attention of many shareholders. Now then, how can I help you?"

- "Do you know why Viktor Lucio de Ocampo was blacklisted? Did BP have anything to do with it?" Go to page 280
- "Can you tell me what BP hopes to gain by attending the Energy Summit?" Go to page 40

Blindfire

The assault rifle kicks to life in your hands as you shoot with the weapon placed phallically at waist height. The drug traffickers who enter are greeted with a roaring audience to the lead-inspired *samba* they now dance. There were two of them, both now dead and bullet-riddled at your feet.

You keep the weapon trained on the door but no one else enters. There's a long silence, with no movement save for the wisp of smoke coming off your gun barrel and blood pooling from the bodies on the floor.

"Nice work," Irma says. She stands, nonchalantly shoots the boy on the couch, and watches as he dies. Then she turns to you, her revolver not quite pointed at you, but not quite pointed away. "Give me the rifle."

- Give it to her. Go to page 330
- Shoot her. Go to page 8

Blind Pursuit

Using your best mix of stealth and urgency, you shimmy away from the rooftop's edge, scale down the back of the building, and sprint off in the direction you think the suspect might've gone. Irma rushes behind you, but soon you find you're covering the same ground over and over again. Streets and alleys crisscross with no sign of him.

A taxicab rushes by and crosses in front of another cab. The man could be anywhere by now.

"Damn it," you say.

"We'll get him," Irma says, putting a hand on your shoulder. "It doesn't have to be tonight. But we will get him. Give me the revolver. I'll take you back to your hotel."

- "You're right. Let's go." Go to page 300
- "No. Let's go back and see what else Detective Muniz might be up to." Go to page 356

A Bond Moment

"You aren't going to join your friends? Check out my surprise in the chapel?"

You shake your head, eyeing him cautiously.

"You are the smart one; I mean that." He meanders over toward the edge of the precipice, stopping at one of the viewpoints of the city. "Beautiful, isn't it? I love my city."

"What about the local police?" you ask. "Did you go to them for help?"

"Corruption," he says matter-of-factly. Then, looking at his watch, he adds, "I don't imagine they'll be much longer in the church. It's not a very good surprise. Is it okay if I spoil it for you?"

"Sure..."

He puts his hands together, palms flat, as if he's in prayer. "The surprise is..." he says, opening his hands to reveal nothing. "There's no surprise. I just needed them to go away while I make my exit. I'm not going in for questioning, not yet anyway. Now, if you'll excuse me, I have a train to catch."

You move to block his path, looking over your shoulder to the train turnaround station, only to see the tail of the red train car leaving for the base. He's missed the train, but you're sure he doesn't intend to wait for it to return.

The two agents emerge from the chapel, spotting the pair of you on the viewing platform and rush back just as Viktor steps up onto the stone ledge serving as a barrier against the sky.

Overlooking the city, he spreads his arms like the statue of Christ. Then, turning his head back to you, he says, "*Boa sorte, e velocidade de Deus.* Good luck on the case."

Then he jumps.

You lunge forward in shock, your stomach swirling with vertigo, but he's gone. You lean over the wall, fully expecting to see the man plunge down the mountainside to his doom—but instead he lands atop the red train car, having perfectly timed its departure.

He waves up to you, and you just stare. The agents finally make it to your side, just in time to see him slip into one of the open windows of the train car, and the entire train disappear behind the bend of the mountain trail.

"Goddammit, one of us should've stayed back here," Danly says.

"No shit, Sherlock. I expected you to back me up while I checked it out," Bertram growls.

"Back *you* up? You think you're lead on this investigation? That's rich."

"Blow me, Stuart."

"Ummm, guys?" you say, interrupting.

The whole mountain crowd stares at the scene they're making.

"All right," Danly says, composing himself. "Let's forget that crackpot; we've got work to do."

"That work includes looking into this guy. He's obviously a sociopath. His fiancée hasn't even been buried yet and the guy's all smiles."

"We follow the evidence, and if it leads to him, so be it."

"No way. We need to put this nut behind bars before he hurts someone else."

"Bertram, seriously, do I need to ask the RSO to officially assign one of us as lead?"

"You might."

"This might just be a naïve rookie talking," you say, "but couldn't you guys split up and cover more ground?"

They both look at you, blinking. Then they say in unison, "Yes."

"Okay," Bertram says, "Let's split up. I'll follow the fiancé, you work with the local police."

"Fine with me. Just make sure you file your reports so we can cross-reference one another's findings."

"You want some cab fare to get back to the garage?" Agent Bertram asks. "The car's checked out in my name, so…"

"I'll be fine," Danly says.

They linger for a moment, staring at one another, before Bertram offers to shake hands. "Good luck, and I mean that," he says.

"Don't shoot anybody," Danly counters, managing a slight smirk. "The paperwork involved is worse than death."

- "And I'll come with you, Agent Danly. I've always wanted to go behind the scenes of an investigation." Go to page 322
- "The fiancé might not be the guy I saw last night, but maybe he can lead us to him. Let's do it, Agent Bertram!" Go to page 320

The Boogeyman

You leap out of the car, arms raised high over your head, shouting gibberish, letting your tongue waggle in the wind for good measure. All in all, you think you're pretty terrifying.

But the kids don't.

They roar in laughter, their starved little bellies shaking in delight. All smiles and amusement, they come closer while you stand there, dumbfounded that your plan didn't work. Before you realize what's going on, the two with the spray paint cans begin to unleash their art form on your pant legs. You squirm away, but that's like a scared mouse running from a kitten. These feral children laugh again and start to chase you.

Out of panic for some way to fight back, you grab the lead kid's soccer ball, run two steps, and on the third step, you *punt* the ball far over the wall. All six watch in surprise and despair as the ball sails out of view. That'll teach the bastards! Now you're the one who's smiling.

Instead of playful grins, they now look at you with glowering hatred. The lead kid reaches down to the ground and picks up a chunk of brick about the size of an apple. He tosses it up and down, catching it in his hand. And now he's smiling again. The other boys get his meaning and pick up their own rocks from the ground.

You want to run back to the car, but you won't make it in time. Instead, you stand your ground and utter one of the six Portuguese words you know: *desculpe*—sorry.

The lead kid winds up for a big pitch; you raise your hands to protect your face. When a giant *CRACK* pierces the air, you start to search yourself for blood or a wound. But when you open your eyes, you see the kid still has his rock.

Agent Danly and Detective Muniz are back; the detective has his handgun pointed into the air, smoke curling away from the barrel. The boys run away while Muniz aims his revolver at them and shouts something in Portuguese.

"What the hell, Rookie? I leave you for five minutes, and…" Danly says.

Shaken, trying not to look like an idiot, you say, "Did you find anything out there?"

"No. Asshole here took us to a pacified slum," he says. Then responding to your puzzled look, he adds, "That's a slum that's been cleaned up. Christ, those kids would've had guns in any other slum. Come on, we're headed back to the station."

➢ *Return to the station.* Go to page 221

You form up, weapons drawn, so that each of you take a third of the 360 degrees of sugarcane surrounding you. Looking at your third, you keep the shotgun level and your finger on the trigger, watching as the leaves rustle and the cane sways. A loud *slop-slap-slop* announces a man trudging through the mud in your direction.

He's holding a hunting rifle and when he sees you, he starts to aim. But with a blast from the shotgun, you find out you're quicker than he is. Gunfire erupts from behind you as both Agent Bertram and Maria engage their own batch of *grileiros*. You pump another shell into the breach and scan the sugarcane for further threats.

With a guttural scream, Maria falls into you, disrupting the triangle formation and nearly knocking you over. Both you and Agent Bertram instinctively swing your respective weapons around and engage the two men shooting at Maria.

In another two seconds, you've killed the rest of the *grileiros*, but it's too late. There are six bodies bleeding into the muddy pools around the sugarcane. Five men, and Maria, the pilot.

Bertram falls to the earth on one knee, ready to use his first aid and buddy care training. You look for more threats from the sugarcane, but the crop is silent.

"She's dead," he says, rising slowly.

Her mouth is parted slightly and her lifeless eyes stare up to the heavens. You hunker down and close her eyelids, shutting them for all time.

"Come on," Bertram says. "They'll have left us a truck and we're gonna pay this Sugar King a visit."

"What about the callback?" you ask.

He shrugs. "What's an hour more? Besides, I got the call after we'd already visited, remember?"

You'd like to smile, but with Maria dead at your feet, all you can do is trudge silently towards the road.

Bertram was right. The men left a pickup truck waiting on the dirt road. Checking his GPS one more time, he drives you to the plantation and in just ten minutes, you've arrived at the main house.

You half-expected something out of the pre-Civil War Southern states, like a giant manor from *Gone With the Wind*, but you're greeted with a much more utilitarian structure. This isn't a place where people live, it's a place where people work.

Still, it's a massive set of buildings. A cafeteria, several barracks for workers, washing and refining stations, and of course, the main house of the plantation.

Bertram slings his rifle over his shoulder and climbs the steps. "Come on, Hotshot. Let's see if this devil's home."

➢ *Meet the king of this underworld.* Go to page 270

Break-dance Fighting

These men don't look like any farmworkers you've ever seen. They wear loose-fitting dojo pants with no shirts, showing off their toned musculature that hasn't an inch of fat. Already their bodies glimmer with sweat—they've been warming up for your arrival.

The arena, if you could call it that, is simply an empty room where the performers stand on the periphery. The Sugar King and his Security team lean against a wall, and seeing as you've got nowhere else to go, you join him, along with Maria and Bertram.

Maria leans in and whispers, "*Capoeira* is an ancient art, dating back to the time of slaves. It was illegal to practice martial arts, so the slaves disguised their combat as a tribal dance. It was handed down secretly for generations until only in the modern era it became known."

The Governor snaps his fingers and the show begins. Their movements are lightning-fast and incredibly precise. In an expertly timed display, the men flip and kick at one another, moving into a dodge at the same time their partner moves in for an attack, so that they fluidly "dance" together as one unit. They both kick at the same time, windmilling across each other's bodies; if the timing was off by even a millisecond, both performers would be seriously injured.

If you were an arts fan, you'd be reminded of *Cirque du Soleil*. If you were a videogame fan, you'd be reminded of Eddie Gordo in *Tekken*. If you were a nature buff, you'd be reminded of eagles diving through the air in courtship.

Whatever it reminds you of, you're blown away by this presentation. Truly, you wouldn't have expected such a show from the Sugar King. If anything, you had a feeling of dread as you entered this room, but now you see only power and beauty.

Until the guards lock the door.

"What the hell is going on?" Maria demands.

"You're to be a part of the show," the Governor, Mateo Ferro, says. "It will be more fun that way."

"Like hell—" Bertram starts, only to be cut short when a flying kick comes at his face.

Instinctually, he brings his arms up so his forearms block the force of the kick. The federal agent has had his own unarmed combat training, which now comes to the fore. You swing a fist at one of the men, but he dodges it with preternaturally fast reflexes, almost anticipatory in speed.

Maria tries to kick at one of the fighters, but he does the same windmill move—only faster. He batters the pilot across the side of her torso, knocking the breath out of her and sending her to the ground, possibly breaking a rib.

Agent Bertram moves full into action and deftly dodges one man's kick only to deliver a blow to a second performer. He slams the meat of his palm into the man's nose, crushing it up into his skull in a fatal blow.

Now the *capoeira* artists are furious. Seeing Bertram as the most immediate threat, they concentrate on him and rightly so. Still, a DSS agent is trained in many different disciplines, and while his unarmed combat skills might defeat the average criminal with ease, a martial arts master is a different beast altogether.

As they congregate upon him, Bertram has no chance.

"What are you doing?" you scream at the Sugar King. "This isn't a game!"

The man simply smiles. "Sure it is. You're my plaything. Don't you realize you're already dead? Your helicopter crashed and no one has heard from you! Beating you to death isn't only fun, but it will be consistent with the injuries expected from someone who fell from the sky in a metal box. Enjoy your last few minutes of life."

You turn back to see both Maria and Agent Bertram lying lifeless on the floor. The fighters all look to you. Gritting your teeth, you raise your fists. You don't stand a chance, but you don't go down without a fight.

THE END

Bug Out

You turn and run back the way you came, in spite of the shouted protests from the Elite Squad member behind you. You flee, praying he's going to stay and guard the vehicle. Your legs windmill beneath you from pure adrenaline, and eventually you emerge from the alley into another wide street like the one where the armored car battle took place. Looking down each side of the road, you see several Elite Squad figures blocking each egress route. If those are traffickers bearing down behind you, you're about to get stuck in another gun battle.

"What now?" you ask in desperation.

She looks around, equally frightened. Then something catches her eye. She points ahead at a graffiti sign reading, *Albergue.*

"It's a hostel!" she cries. "Come on!"

➢ *Flee to the hostel.* Go to page 187

Bye-Bye

What the hell did you just stumble upon? It's possible, in your shock, that you just let the murderer escape. Damn, should've snapped a picture. It won't do much to exonerate you or help the police, but you won't soon forget the man's face. Or those crystalline, piercing eyes. The kind of eyes that look like they were carved from an ice cave or lifted from a lightning-infused Norse god.

"Stay where you are," a woman's voice commands from behind.

"Turn around slowly, hands where we can see them," a man adds.

Both have thick Brazilian accents. You turn slowly, ready to face whoever it might be.

The woman is thin, tall, with skin like soy milk and shimmering raven hair pulled back in a bun. She looks professional, like an American businesswoman, save for her oversized hoop earrings and long, lustrous eyelashes. The other is an average-looking man, skin bronzed, hair bleached to match.

They both wear suits, but the man's shirt is shimmering silk, teal green like the walls in the alley.

Both hold revolvers, and both weapons are aimed at you.

"You an American?" the woman asks with a scowl.

"Are you guys cops?" you return.

"Lucky for you," the man answers. "Now why don't you tell us what the hell you're doing here?"

"I—I don't know. I was lost and….Look, I just want to leave," you say. "My friends will be wondering where I am."

"So will hers," the woman continues, indicating the body on the floor. "And I'm guessing once the consulate hears of this, you'll have some questions to answer. Muniz, call it in."

Muniz—the man with the teal shirt—nods, holsters his pistol, and takes out a cell phone. He steps out into the alleyway as he dials. Your heart sinks and you feel as though you might vomit.

The woman picks up on your distress, holsters her own weapon, and produces a badge. "I'm Detective Irma Dos Santos and that was my partner, Lucio Muniz. If you didn't do anything wrong, you should have nothing to worry about. Now, please, step outside so we can take you to the police station. We don't need you contaminating the crime scene further."

"You think I'm innocent?"

"We'll see."

➢ *Get escorted to the police station.* Go to page 65

Can You Hear Me Now?

"Agent Bertram," he says into the phone.

You hold the pistol, scanning the cane for any signs of movement.

"Negative, I'm still on scene."

It should be pretty easy to spot someone in here, what with the large gaps in the rows.

"Sir, all due respect, that's bullshit. I haven't even—"

You spot something. Far down the line of sugarcane, a shadow drops to the ground.

"Yes, sir… yes, sir." He hangs up.

You squint to see the shadow. The thing would be impossible to hit from this range with the pistol, but….

You fall onto your back, with a tremendous pain in your chest, unable to breathe. You've been shot. Bertram crouches to help you, but then suddenly falls dead from a rifle shot. Lesson learned, too little too late: using a pistol against a sniper rifle is a bit like bringing a knife to a gunfight.

Damn, that guy is good.

THE END

"Good choice, Rookie," Danly says. "There may be hope for you yet."

"Before you go, I've got a joke," Bertram says.

"Okay…" you reply.

"How do you spell *Carnaval*?"

You think about it for a moment, then say, "What, like with an 'i' or an 'a'? This some kind of spelling test?"

"You're overthinking it. Just—how do you spell *Carnaval*?"

"C-A-R-N—"

"Nope, wrong," Bertram interrupts. "It's spelled T-N-A."

He grins. Finally, Danly jumps in. "As in, tits and ass."

"Because that's what *Carnaval* is all about. Good luck, Hotshot! Take lots of pictures."

You share one more toast with the agents, then head outside. The massive parade flotillas will go through the *Sambadrome* arena, but since you don't have a several-hundred-dollar ticket, you're left to the streets. Still, the party is ubiquitous and extreme.

Inside every bar, restaurant, and hotel, costume balls are held, all of them spilling out noisily onto the streets, and free open-air concerts pump *samba* into the night air. Drinking, dancing, and revelry pervade the entire city, without a bore or nudnik to be seen.

People dance, grind, and sweat. Drunken, smiling women grope and kiss strange men. Half the populace wears costumes or body paint. Some men dress like women, some women dress like men, and some you can't tell how they started or where they end.

Someone hands you a drink. Sure, why not? Tastes like more of that sugar-cane liquor. Soon the streets swell and buzz and the bright lights swirl about you. People pair off into alleyways, looking to feel alive together after the end of the restrictions of Catholic Lent. That's what this five-day party is kicking off, after all.

A group of three women draw your eye. They have peacock feathers attached to the back of elaborately designed corsets, as well as peacock "eyes" painted over their own. The look is finished by peach, skin-toned string bikinis complete with nipples. Wait, those are tan lines. There are no bikinis.

These women wear nothing other than feathers, body paint, tiny corsets, and a smile. And they wear them proudly. This place is insane! You snap some pictures of the street and the crowd with your digital camera.

Carnal, that's what you should have told Agent Bertram. C-A-R-N-A-L, as in, sex. Because that's what *Carnaval* is all about.

Another costume catches your attention: it's a devil. A hulking man in glimmering black body paint, his body firm and muscular like an MMA champion fighter's. His face is painted white over black, like a bleached skull (the only color on his otherwise black painted body) and his shaved head is topped with long, twisted ram's horns. A thick scar covers his chin. The paint is all-encompassing, and with his carved frame and intricate costume, you'd think he would be at the *Sambadrome,* leading an underworld team.

Then his eyes move in two different directions.

Is it—could it be—is this the *Jamanta*? There, you see it again! His eyes move independently and catalog separate information on their own. They move briefly over you, quickly scanning your details before they continue their search. Thankfully, you seem to blend in with the enormous crowd.

The devil turns to reveal a back covered with black feathers in a nightmarish blending of raven and hedgehog. He holds a pitchfork, and when you step forward to get a better look, you see that the two outer prongs on the pitchfork are actually handguns, long and slender, with silencers on the barrels.

Without a doubt, this is the *Jamanta,* the Devil Ray.

You raise your camera to take a picture, but in a blur he starts to move—fast. Your eyes dart ahead to see who he's following. You're even more blown away now: it's the suspect, the man from the beginning, the bespectacled "perp" with the icy-blue eyes, and he's sprinting through the crowd.

The assassin picks up to a run in hot pursuit. Why is he chasing the man he's supposed to be protecting? Is he fleeing from the assassin or chasing someone else?

You shake your head free of the alcohol and party buzz, willing yourself to be lucid enough to think. How long have you been out here? An hour? Two? More? Is it worth chasing them down? How far have you come? Do you have time to get the agents?

Your head swirls, but you have to make a decision.

- Go get the agents! Go to page 335
- Follow the assassin! Go to page 18

"Maybe you're right," he says. "Too risky… but if all the cops are *here,* then maybe we can return to the warehouse where you—"

Found her body. He can't even say it.

"Okay, good idea."

Viktor nods, then slowly backs away from the apartment complex, remaining invisible to the policeman just ahead.

The alley looks completely different in the light of day. You stop at the graffiti mural that held your attention only the night before, but now the colors seem washed out under the brilliant summer sun. Still, the dark angel has a severity in his features surprisingly lifelike for a two-dimensional image. Again, his caption speaks out to you and says, "*Vou testemunhar.*"

"What does that mean?" you ask.

Viktor, who has been looking in the alley's detritus for some kind of clue, now examines the mural. In his hand, he holds a scrap of paper. "In this context, something like, 'I shall bear witness.' Life here is a cruel existence for the impoverished people of my country, and many of them turn to God for their justice—if not in this world, then in the next. It's hard to tell if this fresco is speaking with cynicism or sincerity, but the pain of society's abandonment is there nonetheless. I had hoped to give the people of Brazil something special with my work, but now…only God knows if that will come to pass."

"What's that?" you say, indicating the paper.

"It was on the ground here. It's probably nothing; a bilingual tourist cheat-sheet. See? It has common phrases with their English translations and you can point to various questions like 'What is in this dish?' or 'How much does this cost?' in Portuguese and then waiters can point to the answer. It wouldn't have belonged to my Jane. Her Portuguese is—was—almost as good as my English."

He glowers and tosses the paper back into the alley trash. You can't imagine how he must feel inside, pining over his lost love and forced to relive the tragedy at the very spot of her death. Without any words to comfort him, you head into the warehouse.

Police tape cordons off the entrance and no one is here. The room is dark and cold, an urban cave in the midst of heat and oppression. Dried blood still stains the floor and evidence cards mark the sepulcher—like flowers on a grave. You look around but don't see anything that wasn't here last night. You turn back to the entrance, where Viktor stands, looking aghast and nauseated.

"I can't do this!" he cries and flees back into the alley.

You rush out, but he's already vomiting in a trash bin.

"Please step back into the warehouse," says a gravelly voice behind you.

Shocked, you turn around. The man is tall, well-built, his black hair close-cropped like a combat soldier's. Clean-shaven, but there's a thick scar along the front of his chin like you'd expect to see on someone who flew over the handlebar of a motorcycle. He wears aviator-style shooting-range glasses and his face is as pale as a skull sun-bleached in the desert. He wears all black—combat boots, tactical cargo pants, a vest to match, and skin-tight long-sleeved under-armor. He holds dual-handguns and wears black motorcycle gloves.

In short, he's terrifying.

He keeps one pistol aimed on you and motions toward the door with the other pistol. His right eye follows his hand, looking off to the side, while his left eye stays staring at you. With hands raised, you sidestep gingerly toward the door.

You duck instinctively as a trash can flies past your head. The man fires into the bin while vomit curls around the alley in a wide arc that graciously misses you.

"Run!" Viktor shouts, shoving you inside.

You sprint back into the crime scene and out through the same back door Viktor used last night. A bullet slams into the doorway just as you pass through it. Back on the streets, you rush into traffic and crowds of pedestrians.

Viktor gets onto a bus and bids you to follow. With one final look back, you see your would-be assassin melt again into the shadows of the warehouse, his pistols still trained forward.

➢ *Get on the bus, quickly!* Go to page 95

Cocktail Hour of Need

Back at the hotel, he leaves you to your own devices, so you swim, shower, and then take a nap. Later that night, you head down to the hotel lobby bar to reconvene with both agents. The bar is modern and elegant, if a little small. There are a few tables, some Internet kiosk stations, and the bar itself. The counter is smooth and cool, with an illuminated trim that changes color in a pattern both soothing and psychedelic. Atop the bar is a mirrored bowl filled with chilling champagne—though it's just a bit premature for celebration.

You're the first to arrive, so you order a drink, pointing to the sign that reads "Happy Hour Special," followed by Portuguese words. The bartender nods and starts to prepare your libation. When it arrives, you're taken aback by its appearance. The glass, filled with a vibrant red punch, is large enough to double as a flower vase and is garnished with a skewered orange slice, a grape, and a cherry. When you draw in on the double-large straw, you're greeted with a sickly sweet surge of sugar and alcohol. You pay, then carry your drink to one of the Internet kiosks.

You've just signed in to your personal email account when the two agents arrive. Agent Danly heads to the bar to order. Bertram shows his badge to a table of Brazilian tourists and commandeers the table, saying, "*Negócios officiais*," which causes them to clear out.

Bertram then orders from the bartender simply by raising his pointer finger. Danly leaves a few bills on the bar, then comes to the table and sits across from Bertram. You sign off the computer and take a seat between them.

"Nice drink, Hotshot," Bertram scoffs.

Unfazed, you sip on your fruit punch while the bartender brings out their orders—a glass of port wine for Danly and *caipirinha* for Bertram. He takes the sugarcane liquor from the server and replaces it with a folded bill.

Sipping his drink, Bertram says, "How was your day, dear?"

"Didn't get too much, actually," Danly replies, ignoring the joke. "The Brazilian police, unsurprisingly, have fuck-all for intel—and the revolver found at the crime scene has no serial number."

"Of course."

The day apart appears to have done them well, and you hope alcohol won't spoil the camaraderie.

"One interesting tidbit, though," Agent Danly says. "Evidence shows Ms. Nightingale was brought into that room and left there—by multiple perps."

Bertram rubs his beard. "So our guy had help. Maybe the guy our Cooperating Witness spotted at the scene was an accomplice to the nutjob fiancé?"

"I think it's more than that. Detective dos Santos took me to Nightingale's apartment and we found a major stash of cocaine, but something was…off. It looks like the set of a Hollywood movie, or like what someone *imagines* a rich white-girl party should look like. The whole thing reads like a Potemkin Village, created to discredit someone."

"But why do that?" you ask.

"To cover your trail. If you kill someone in Rio, making it look like one of the drug gangs was involved is a pretty smart move," Bertram says.

You sip your drink, letting that sink in.

"Well, if the fiance's trying to make it look like a drug deal gone bad, hiding until the case is closed, he's doing a decent job," Agent Bertram says. "I'm not any closer to catching *Senhor* Lucio de Ocampo. There are traces of the guy in the city—he's got an empty apartment—but the real surprise is this *visitor* who was casing the place."

"How's that?"

"Guy looked like he was former military, maybe Spec-Ops. Dunno, he ditched as soon as I made him. Still, keep an eye out. If he's a mercenary, we might be in trouble. And if he was hired by our guy, that means I'm close."

"Could this mercenary be the killer?" you ask.

"Anything's possible," Danly says. "But if there's a pro involved, it's a clean-up team. The original crime scene looked anything but professional."

"Unless it's a *real* pro, who wanted it to look rushed," you say.

"Could be," Danly replies without umbrage.

Agent Bertram thumbs through the dossier he brought with him, sips his drink, then continues. "The background check came through about an hour ago. Viktor Lucio de Ocampo. No criminal record, no history of violence. He got his undergrad at the University of São Paulo, then went on to do his doctoral work at Harvard and MIT, earning top marks at each school, before he took an internship at Human Infinite Technologies in the States. Later worked for some German engineering startups, no doubt earning himself some spending money, which he then augmented with clean energy grants. He's been working independently for the last few years and he was set to be the keynote speaker at the Energy Summit, evidently with plans to share some kind of breakthrough, but he was recently blacklisted."

"Why?" you ask.

"That's my next move. Time to see if he might have some enemies, or at least if there's someone running this conference who can tell us more."

"I'm going into the *favelas*," Danly says suddenly.

Bertram nearly spits out his drink. "What? Why?"

"I'm fine with you looking into the fiancé angle, but I need to look into the drug angle. I think she was a warning sign for somebody, and I aim to find out who."

"I'm fine with you looking into *that*."

"Guys… keep it civil," you say.

"That means the Rookie stays with you," Danly adds. "The slums are no place for a civilian."

"I don't know, what if this Spec-Ops 'merc turns out to be a threat?"

Okay, you're being doubted. Time to prove you're more than just luggage. Or at least explain that you're willing to prove it, should the need arise.

"I'm here to ID the guy," you say. "You didn't think I knew there'd be danger when I signed on to help you catch a *murderer*?"

They both stare at you.

- "This drug angle seems the most plausible. Didn't the RSO say she failed a drug test? Agent Danly, I'm going with you." Go to page 275
- "The fiancé is some kind of scientist and the guy I saw was slim, wore glasses. Maybe they're connected? I'd like to stick with you, Agent Bertram." Go to page 125

Cold-blooded

Just before the man makes it away, the revolver erupts into a deafening roar, shaking the bones in your hand with the recoil. The man drops dead on site. Spinal shot. Smoke rises from the muzzle and blood pools around the man's still body.

A man shouts at you in Portuguese from behind.

- Turn and shoot! Go to page 51
- Drop the gun; you've been bested. Go to page 60

Colonel Mays

The entire room empties back into the waiting area: Paul, the assistant, Agent Danly, Agent Howard and his two partners, and finally, the Ambassador himself. The man looks exactly like his picture from the Rio consulate, right down to the sharp suit and power tie.

With a practiced smile and a tone that makes you feel like some sort of visiting dignitary, he says, "Well, this must be our Cooperating Witness—your nation thanks you for all your help on this case. I'm sure Howard here will want to pick your brain later."

You shake hands and the Ambassador says, "Paul, do we have room on the plane for these two?"

"Six open seats, Colonel."

"Perfect. Come on, we leave for Rio in an hour. The Energy Summit starts tonight, and I don't want to be late."

Danly shakes his head. "It's fine, sir. We can drive."

"Why the hell would you do that?" the Ambassador asks. "I'm not just being polite, we'll need you for added security. Let's go!"

"Yes, sir," Danly says.

The duration of the flight is just shy of two hours. Most of the time, Agent Danly stares out the window while the Ambassador and Howard swap Army stories. Paul, the assistant, manages paperwork while the two other agents nap. After you land and deplane, the Ambassador excuses himself and gets into a private car.

Once he's gone, Agent Howard says, "Okay, see you two around. Enjoy the sites in Rio. *Carnaval* starts tonight; try not to get into too much trouble. And watch the news the next few days—you should see us wrap up this case in no time."

"Don't worry, I'll drop my notes off right now," Danly says. "Come on, Rookie."

With a burst of laughter, the three men parrot "Rookie" and slap one another on the back. Danly just walks away.

Once out of earshot of the others, Danly says, "I need to spend a few hours at the consulate. Can you take a taxi back to the hotel? Take a shower, maybe a nap—I'll check on Bertram and ring your room when I get back."

"Sure thing," you reply.

➢ *Back to Rio…* Go to page 219

"The same thing everyone wants," she says with a shrug. "The newest, best ideas. Technology has proven to be a worthy investment as production costs go down and efficiency goes up. We're hoping to be blown away by some of the presenters and then entice them to join our team."

"People like Viktor Lucio de Ocampo, the ex-keynote speaker?"

"Yes, we were looking forward to what he had to say. His new programs were set to push clean energy forward by at least a decade. Of course, BP wanted to be at the forefront. We have a generous slush fund prepared for those who 'wow' us at the Energy Summit."

"Are you thinking of buying up their patents so you can sit on them? Let oil remain king?"

"The opposite, actually. We've just invested heavily in ethanol, so the next logical step would be to invest in its successor. The kind of topic the doctor was supposed to present on."

- "What exactly was Viktor going to present on?" Go to page 186
- "Tell me more about BP's ethanol developments." Go to page 195
- "I've heard enough. Thank you for your time." Go to page 98

You watch as father and son continue loading the ship, preparing to cast off after the other crew members return. Neto notices your glance as he carries an open crate full of green, spiny fruit. After unloading, he takes one of the fruits and bids you to follow him.

Once you make it to the top deck of the ship, the boy holds the fruit up to you for inspection. "*Graviola*," he says. "Sometimes we call it 'Soursop' in English. It's good, you should try!"

Before you can respond, he pulls a knife seemingly from thin air and cuts the fruit lengthwise, offering half of it to you. The inside is white, but glistens yellow, slick with juice; black seeds dot the meat of the fruit.

Not wanting to be rude, you take it, watching as Neto scoops out the pulp, and then follow suit. It's pleasantly sweet, though the juices run stickily over your hands and mouth.

"I hope you like," he says.

"Where did you learn English?"

"Ehh, there are many sailors who speak little. I know them and I speak them so I learn. One day I go to America!"

"Oh, yeah? What do you want to do over there?"

"I will be famous movie star—like Will Smith!"

You can't help but smile. The ship's engine roars to life, churning the river and sending you away from port. Suddenly, Bertram is beside you.

"All right, Hotshot. Wake me if there's trouble. I'll be in the mid-deck cabin they set aside, swaying in a hammock. Enjoy your riverboat tour!"

When he leaves, you look back at the boy, Neto, who's more than ready to play tour guide for you.

"This is a pretty big river," you say. "Have you ever been on the Amazon?"

"No, never. That is far north of here and does not connect to *Rio Fingido*."

A monkey's ululating howl comes from somewhere in the treetops and branches sway in reaction to movement that can't be seen from beneath the thick canopy. A nesting family of egrets calls out as a fledgling egret loses its balance and falls into the river below. The bird is quick to come to the surface but, not yet able to fly, it squawks and flails its wings in a panicked swim.

The river suddenly explodes in a cacophony of fish and churning water so powerful that the bloody spindrift hits the boat. The egret doesn't have a chance against the piranha feeding frenzy and you watch in awestruck terror as the bird disappears in only a matter of moments.

"Do not worry; the piranha don't eat people. They can take a finger, but he is what you need to be careful for: *Camen*."

You follow Neto's outstretched finger toward the far bank, where a crocodilian animal at least ten feet long slips into the river and silently swims toward the commotion, which is over before it gets there.

"They eat people?" you ask.

"They drown people."

"Noted," you say.

"Sample any fruits you like," Neto says, stepping away from the rail. "I must go see if father wants help."

You look down at the newly placid water, knowing that a dangerous ecosystem lurks beneath, with offenders far worse than piranhas. A feeling of vertigo overcomes you and you quickly take a step away from the edge. Shaking it off, you look at the other crates.

The first crate to catch your eye has bananas, which were harvested bright and yellow—unlike in America where they ripen on the journey to the grocery store—which means the fruit should be exceptionally rich and sweet. Bonus: you could toss the peel overboard and watch it get attacked.

You opt for the banana, but when you go to pick one up, you're in for a surprise. A large spider leaps out of the crate, barely missing your hand; its compact body is two inches long but its spindly brown legs extend to a full six inches.

The frightsome arachnid raises its forelimbs in a defensive display, boasting banded leg-stripes and large, ruddy fangs. Then, suddenly aggressive, the spider charges forward. You back away, trying to distance yourself from it, and slam against the back railing. The river is behind you; the spider keeps coming at you.

You shimmy against the rail, hoping desperately to reach the stairs, but the spider cuts you off. It's almost as if the beastie is hunting you. Your brain muted by panicked adrenaline, you're either about to scream, leap over the rail of the boat, or both, but just in time a knife slams into the spider, killing it instantly. Its legs curl around the blade.

"Did you get bite?" Neto asks.

You shake your head no, your sweat instantly turning cold.

"Good. This is *armadeiras*, called 'wanderer,'" he says, sliding the knife against the boat's edge and dropping the spider into the water below. "Most deadly in world. Bite from a big one, no more heartbeat, understand?"

You nod, still stunned at how close you came to death.

"Come, it is time to eat."

Waiting for you in the kitchen is a large pot boiling over with the most wonderful smell. The chef ladles out generous helpings of some kind of stew and hands you a bowl when you enter. A picnic table with attached benches serves as the kitchen table.

"*Feijoada*," Neto says. "Black bean, pork, and cow."

You look down at the stew, which was poured over a bed of rice, and your mouth waters. It's warm, rich, and flavorful, and the whole crew eats heartily without so much as saying a word. After the meal, Bertram bids you good night and you head off to bed for your one big chunk of sleep.

The next morning you wake up with the sun in a small, single-window room as hazy light filters through a linen curtain. You are floating in a hammock above cleaning supplies and crates. All in all, you had a pretty decent night's sleep.

When you make it back out to the deck, you find a tired Agent Bertram sitting with his assault rifle cradled in his lap. The deck is wet, and beads of water stand atop anything that isn't soaked through. You must have slept through quite a rainstorm.

"Good morning, Hotshot! Welcome back to the land of the living."

"Did I miss anything?" you ask.

"Nah, the pirates never showed."

"Pirates?"

"Yeah, river pirates are a big thing here. Didn't want to worry you. How'd you sleep?"

"Just fine," you say, knowing that that might not have been the case had you been thinking about pirates.

"Well, I'd like to do the same. Wake me when we're pulling into port."

With that, he disappears below decks.

➢ *Wait out the arrival to port.* Go to page 344

Company Man

"Oh?" he says. "I wasn't aware of any inspections that are scheduled."

"That's what makes it a *pop* inspection. Anyway, the guys we have upstairs are doing most of the work—checking the books and what-have-you—I'm just zeroing in on one thing specifically."

You smile, impressed with your own silver tongue.

His smile drops. "You have people upstairs?"

"Yes, undercover. It's an internal affairs kind of thing."

He blinks, dumbfounded.

You put a finger up to your lips. "Shhh. You're not supposed to know." Then, with a wink, you continue, speaking low like he's your confidant. "So, what's the progress on erasing Viktor Lucio de Ocampo from the program lineup?"

"What?" He's still got that deer-in-the-headlights look.

"Have we successfully ended the doctor's involvement?"

"I… the only thing I know about it is that he was removed by the Energy Summit. Are you saying it's bigger than that?"

"Isn't it?" you bluff.

"Wh—what?"

The man is terrified. Maybe it's time to let him off the hook.

"That was just a test. Well done," you say convincingly.

"So… we weren't involved?"

"Were we?"

"No," he says, shaking his head.

You give him a wink and a smile. "Please call my ride."

- *Go wait for Agent Bertram.* Go to page 98

Computing

You walk around to the back of the assistant's desk, where you find a three-hole punch, a candy bowl, and a picture of Paul with his parents. On the computer screen, there's a desktop background picture of a formation of fighter jets screaming across a blue sky with a gigantic, translucent eagle superimposed in parallel to their trail. Minimized on the task bar is his Outlook email program, and another called "LOTUS Forms Viewer."

Out of sheer curiosity, you click the LOTUS program and find none other than Jane Nightingale's drug report open in edit mode. The contents aren't very elucidating, but after poring over the form, you learn that she was given "counseling" after testing positive for cocaine use. She claimed it was a coca-leaf tea, which was deemed plausible for the level of the narcotic found in her urine. A subsequent test showed the drug to be nearly out of her system. Extra computer-based anti-drug courses were recommended.

Switching over to the email system, you see the Ambassador's calendar, which includes the current meeting with the new investigation team. Next up, a phone meeting with "RP Resource," then another phone conference with the Energy Summit Security committee. After that, it's lunch, and then….

The door to the Ambassador's office starts to open. You quickly minimize the programs, dig your hand into the candy bowl, and act like nothing ever happened.

➢ *Time to meet The Colonel.* Go to page 39

Conference Rooms

This hallway is short and ends in a T before splitting again. The sign shows "*Salas de Conferências* 1-14" to the left and "*Salas de Conferências* 15-28" to the right.

You quickly peer into the nearest conference room; a woman in a lab coat is setting up an overhead projector for a classroom of about 50 people—the stadium-style seats are currently empty.

In another conference room, a male professor is preparing his lecture hall. He sees you looking in and smiles in response. The third conference room you check is dark and empty.

This is where the Energy Summit presenters will show off their discoveries. After the opening ceremony, individual talks on specific aspects of energy consumption and/or preservation will be given, according to the program brochure and the week's schedule.

But it's not where you want to be, not now. You've got to hurry while all the attendees are still together.

- Don't stop. Check out *Banheiros*. Go to page 16
- Keep going, this time try left—*Apoio*. Go to page 311
- Duck in the empty conference room, then double back to *Imprensa*. Go to page 252
- Wait until Danly's gone, then try *Auditório Principal*. Go to page 193

Confused

Agent Danly scowls. "Actually, that would be *you* who has me confused with a dumbass. Put your face against the wall!"

You stare at him, dumbfounded. To make himself perfectly clear, he grabs you by the shoulder, slams you against the wall, and cuffs your hands behind your back.

"I don't know where the fuck you've been, but I don't have time for this shit. You better hope to hell you're not an accomplice on this thing or so help me God, I will see you *rot.*"

Holding you prone against the wall, he removes a radio and calls for backup.

Security soon arrives and Agent Danly instructs the cop to "keep an eye on" you. Later, when Viktor is killed "making an attempt on the Ambassador's life" and Jane mysteriously disappears, Agent Danly will make good on his promise.

You'll be tried and found guilty of treason. The rest of your life will not be pleasant.

THE END

Consolation Pizza

The restaurant's red flag sails above the entry to hail your arrival. You find Viktor in a rear booth, waiting for you. The building's exterior walls are all glass, giving a panorama of street life while saving you from the sounds of traffic and the smell of the street vendors' food offerings.

You sit down across from Viktor, feeling the smooth pleather/vinyl seat beneath you, its surface polished by a thousand rear ends. The waiter gives you a menu and a glass of water, then leaves.

"How did it go on your end?" Viktor asks.

You shake your head. "I was a little too late. A couple of guys showed up, looking like the Mafia in the movies, and… sorry, no laptop."

"Cleanup crew. You made it out okay?"

You shrug. "How'd your side go?"

He leans back. "'Money talks'—isn't that how the American saying goes? The note was deposited, I wasn't seen, and the agents should be on their way up to the statue."

"So what's next?" you ask.

"Lunch. Take a look at the menu; everything's good here. I recommend the Gino's Combo if you're torn."

The waiter returns and you order a pizza. After a moment, you ask the burning question in your mind. "So who do you think killed her, and why?"

He looks around. "I'm sorry, Tourist, I can't say just yet. The people we're dealing with… Later, I'll tell you later."

You nod but say nothing.

Viktor continues, "I must confess—I had one of my students follow you today—because I wasn't sure if you'd go through with your end. I thought maybe you'd get cold feet… I'm sorry I doubted you; I won't again. Still, I cannot tell you any more here. If I had you followed, it's possible we're not alone."

"Okay… then, aside from eating pizza, what are we doing?"

"Nothing," he says, his brow raised. "Have to eat, don't you? But after…."

He clears his throat, then downs the rest of his beer. "Afterward, I think we might find something at Jane's apartment, but we're not going to get it with those agents prowling nearby. André will send me a text when they've arrived, far out of our way."

He holds up a disposable cell phone, showing it off just as the waiter arrives with your pizza. The crust is thick and doughy, the cheese perfectly melted and browned, and the aroma makes your mouth water. You dig in, enjoying the pizza with Viktor, but after you pick up your second slice his phone buzzes.

After checking it, he looks up to you. "Finish up, it's time."

➢ *Follow Viktor to the evidence.* Go to page 169

Cookies, Milk, and Storytime

Over the hum of the engine, Viktor and Jane's quiet conference lulls you to sleep. Guess you were pretty tired after all. You awaken just as the plane begins its descent. You're back in Rio before sunset and presently look out the window towards Rio's enormous crowds forming for *Carnaval* and the Energy Summit.

Viktor turns to you and says, "This is it, Tourist. The grand finale. Thanks to André, the police are looking for him rather than myself, and they think Jane here is dead, so we should be able to sneak in undetected."

"What about me?" you ask.

"You're still anonymous. After tonight, win or lose, the world will know who you are."

"Unless…" Jane says.

You look from Viktor to Jane and back again.

"Unless you're ready to retire," Viktor says. "You've done so much for us. This—tonight—is our fight. You don't need to risk your life any further."

"Look for us on the news," Jane says. "There should be live coverage. I'm going to upload the evidence onto the Energy Summit computer system and project it on the main screen during the opening ceremonies. Then Viktor will arrive on stage, proclaim his innocence, and condemn these two evil Kings while everyone is there to see it."

- "Okay… Good luck. I'll want to meet for champagne after you're successful." Go to page 263
- "Seriously? So close to the finish line? No way you're leaving me here!" Go to page 309

Covered

"Don't move. We'll be there in five," Agent Bertram said the moment you called.

Now you're walking down to the beach, the two agents carefully tailing you, trying not to make their presence known and thereby spoil the rendezvous. The neighborhood lights of Ipanema and Rio de Janeiro reflect off the surf down by the shoreline. Couples walk hand-in-hand, exploring the romance of the beach outside popular bars and hotels. Still, the crowd is nothing like it is in the daytime.

You carry your shoes, trying to play casual, looking for the man so ingrained in your memory. You scan every face for those terrible blue eyes, but he never shows.

Eventually, the two agents approach you on the beach.

"Looks like he got cold feet," Danly says, running his tired hand over a day's stubble.

"All right, you're staying with us. No ifs ands or buts this time," Bertram says with a firm hand on your shoulder, leading you back away from the sea.

➢ *Continue to the Embassy's Hotel.* Go to page 11

Cowboy, Baby

You spin around, already squeezing the trigger as you turn. The hammer falls back and the chamber rotates in time—you shoot the man behind you before you even see him. His gun is already drawn, but you catch him off-guard. The shot is a wild one, though you're close enough to make accuracy irrelevant. He grabs his gut, drops his handgun, and coughs up a spurt of blood.

Then the woman next to him shoots you.

You didn't even know he had a partner, her gun drawn as well, ready to back the man you just killed. That's two men dead at your hand, and the woman on the floor will most likely be blamed on your tourist-gone-mad rampage. As your life seeps away, you realize this is how you'll be remembered—as a murderer.

Mom would be proud.

THE END *

* *Hold the phone. This book is called, "MURDERED" not "MURDERER." Solving mysteries is a thinking game; if you want brash action, maybe go read "INFECTED." Still, congrats on finding this book's only Easter egg—now go try again!*

Crossroads

The next morning the boat is slick with rain. There was a downpour all night, though you wouldn't have known it from your private cabin. You slept fitfully on the small, hard mattress, but after the rain-drenched glares from the other passengers on the barge, you feel lucky to have had a room to call your own.

Viktor finds coffee and sweetbreads for breakfast, which you share and finish just as the barge pulls into port. The two of you slip off the boat without much fuss or fanfare and disappear into the surrounding market.

Mostly the vendors are just selling fish; some of the traveling merchants offer their wares at the port market before ferrying them further into the interior. At the fringe, you see a three-toed sloth for sale; sad and manacled to a post, its hair is matted and dirty.

Viktor slips into a taxicab just outside of the fish market and you join him. The cabbie drives fast over the hard-packed dirt road, the car bobbing up and down over the inlaid grooves. There are expansive, muddy fields as far as the eye can see.

"So… where are we going?" you ask Viktor after he tells the driver in Portuguese.

Viktor smiles through pensive eyes. "We're going to 'the source.' The place that inspired my life's work. You see all of this around you? Only ten years ago this was dense jungle. There wasn't even a port here. Now we drive along the Sugarcane Highway, an illegally made road through illegally cleared rainforest. This is all farmland now, Tourist. The jungle has been slaughtered for the sake of sugarcane plantations, to harvest enough crop for the ever-rising ethanol demand. I wanted to change that. With your help, maybe I still can…"

He looks out the window and you ride in silence. After some time, the cab pulls up to a field just outside a small village. Viktor pays the driver and exits the car. When you get out of the cab, you stare at the muddy embankment, surprised at what lies ahead.

An ocean of wooden crosses, each one handmade and individually painted white or red, cover the field before you. Nearly a thousand crosses, each one about four feet high and two feet across. The variation in the rise and swell of the land makes the crosses off-kilter and inconsistently tilted, a rather jarring effect.

"A cemetery?" you ask.

"A memorial," he says. "The red ones represent those living under death threats from land-thieving criminals. *Grileiros*. The white ones are for those who were killed because they stood in the way of the *grileiros*."

Almost all the crosses are white.

He continues, "There was a nun here who stood up to the land thieves, and in broad daylight they murdered her in cold blood. This memorial was started for her. Jane and I saw this when we were traveling, vacationing and exploring the country. It was a shock just how uninvolved we were. Laughing and loving amidst such pain and chaos. We couldn't go back to our normal lives.

"That's when I knew I could use my background, my education and the work I'd done to create a new kind of fuel. An ethanol that could use waste, and not food. We could feed our people and our industry with the same technology—if only I could succeed where so many others had failed."

"All these people died protecting the land?" you ask, looking over the sea of crosses.

He nods. "They weren't all environmental activists, not hardly. Most were simple farmers who cleared small patches and lived in harmony with the jungle. They were descendants of the natives who lived off the land for thousands of years."

Viktor sighs, then adds, "You know, I had hoped my Jane would be here. That she'd be waiting and would just throw her arms around me as soon as I'd stepped out of that cab. It was her idea, you know. To change the world; to do some good. She wanted to get the Embassy to help—to usher in a new era of cooperation between our nations, but she didn't count on the King. The Governor here has his own sugarcane empire and wasn't ready to abdicate the crown. Pity what rich men will do for more money…."

You turn, suddenly aware you're being watched. Three naked boys approach, a tattered note held by their leader. He offers it to you, then opens his palm. Paying the boy a *real,* Viktor accepts the letter. On the envelope is written,

"To be given to the outsider."

Viktor unfolds the paper and reads it aloud: "I know it is you, my love. No other outsiders come to this field. No tourists visit to see pain and suffering. Can you come a little further? There is a tribe nearby that no outsiders visit either. Your treasure is safe there."

He lowers the note, his fierce eyes glinting with emotion. He shakes his head, unable to speak.

"Come on," you say. "Let's go find that evidence. When does the Energy Summit start?"

He thinks for a moment, then laughs. "Tonight. You're right, we must be quick!"

You move into the nearby village, looking for transportation and a guide who knows what tribe Jane might be describing.

"Without any money or anything to trade, how will we find help?" you ask.

"God will provide," Viktor says, absentmindedly. Then, holding up the jar of candied sugarcane, he says with a smile, "Here's hoping the natives have a sweet tooth."

In the village, which consists of a main dirt road and half a dozen offshoots, you see merchants setting up their shops. It's still very early, you realize. A coffee vendor pushes his rolling cart and gestures you to try his product. You wave him off.

Viktor finds a man wearing a Che Guevara shirt and speaks to him in Portuguese.

"You are the one!" the man exclaims in English. "I will take you and your friend to the *Jamacão* tribe. Your passage has been paid for. There was a woman—"

"Jane!" Viktor cries. "Is she close?"

The man nods. "I will take you by canoe. One hour, maybe less."

In addition to your paid passage, you're provided with a water pot—ingeniously designed to keep the water held within it cool, despite the jungle heat. Viktor rides in the first canoe with your guide while you paddle the second, with the water pot for company.

The canoe is small, just barely wide enough to accommodate your hips, and every stroke of the paddle causes the vessel to shimmy back and forth, threatening to dump you into the river with whatever lurks beneath.

The next time you look up, you see two naked men on the riverbank. They each have a bone spur on their chin like some kind of tusk. Your guide calls to them in greeting and brings his canoe to the embankment.

When you follow and disembark, you see that the bone spur is actually sticking *through* their faces. One part of the tusk rests atop their bottom teeth and they have mutilated their skin so that the bone shoots through the lower lip and rests along the chin.

They hug the guide. You hug the pot in defense. Viktor nods at the men, but stays close to you. They escort you deeper into the jungle, pushing aside leaves the size of curtains, and in less than five minutes you're in so deep you'd never find your way back to the river alone.

"Wow," you say.

"*Wow*," echo twenty voices from above.

You look up to see a flock of parrots. You've never seen so many in your life, and you say so.

"These birds are social animals. They're not meant to be pets…."

You say nothing, just keep walking. The next sound is your own screaming as something bites you on the arm. Everyone looks back and you rub the source of the wound—it's already flushed and swollen.

"What was it?" Viktor asks with concern.

"I have no idea," you reply, "but it burns!"

The pair of native men turn back and approach you, and one removes a knife. You back away, but he doesn't cut at you. Instead, he slices across an ashen tree. Red liquid pours out of the tree's cut as if it was bleeding.

The second native man scoops the liquid onto the palm of his hand, smearing it against his skin with his thumb in a circular motion until the red turns pure white with froth. He then applies the white cream to your bite as the first man cleans his knife.

You watch as he next applies a shrub leaf to the cut on the tree. The tree's wound stops bleeding. Your bite stops burning.

"Thank you," you say, amazed.

The man with the bone spur sticking out of his chin nods, then turns back to continue into the jungle.

Soon you arrive at the village. The entire group of *Jamacão* Indians, maybe fifty or seventy-five people, are there to greet you. Every single villager is naked and has a tusk sticking through his or her face, with the exception of young children. Perhaps it's a coming-of-age ritual.

As you set down the water pot, the adults are suddenly all smiles. Viktor gives the children the jar of candied sugarcane and their faces light up too.

"Where is she? Where is the woman?" he asks with fervor.

"Right here," a woman's voice says.

You turn to see a woman in khaki pants and a pocketed shirt, both light and airy, smiling at you. She's in her mid-fifties; strands of white streak through her black hair, which is pulled back in a ponytail. It's not Jane Nightingale.

"You…paid our passage?" Viktor says. His voice cracks with emotion.

"Susan Brandon. It's a pleasure to finally meet you, Doctor. I'm a researcher myself. I've been staying with these people for nearly six months now."

"I see," Viktor says. "You'll have to forgive me. When I was told there was a woman here, I simply assumed…"

"I think you misunderstand," she says with a smile.

"I'm sorry?"

"You don't have to be sorry," another woman says.

You turn to see Jane Nightingale, her eyes full of tears and her smile shining brilliantly. The leaves in the trees dance as if in response.

"Jane told me much about you. When she said you'd be coming, I offered to pay your way."

Viktor rushes over to embrace his fiancée, grabbing her tightly and swinging her around. In-between kisses he says, "How? Why? When? Where?" and just about every other way to start a question.

"I thought if I stayed dead, they might leave you alone."

He shakes his head, his eyes welling with tears. "I thought I'd lost you."

"Yet here you are. And I have everything we need, my love."

"Forgive me," Viktor says, wiping the tears from his face and turning to you. "I forgot to introduce my companion."

"Thank you so much," she says, giving you a warm smile.

"Would you mind giving us a private moment?" Viktor asks you.

- "Yes, of course, take all the time you need." Go to page 134
- "There's no time. Let's grab the evidence and return. You can catch up on the way back." Go to page 283

Crowd Control

"Good luck," the two agents say in stereo.

You wish them the same, then watch as they dash into the halls of the Energy Summit conference grounds. Back outside, Irma scans the massive crowd of revelers for potential threats.

"You don't think he's inside yet?" you ask.

"The Energy Summit security is tight. It's possible he's in there, but it's more likely he's lying in wait somewhere near here. If his next target is one of the scientists, it's much easier to get the man on his way to or from the conference. Whenever there's an event of this scale, police resources are stretched so thin that crime skyrockets in other areas. Bank robberies will be up this week, simply because so many cops are busy here and with *Carnaval.*"

"I never thought of that," you say.

"Just ask your agent friends: the most dangerous part of protection is when the subject is on the move. Buildings are hardened, people are soft."

"Unless you hired an actor, so that the police are looking for the wrong guy."

"True," she says.

Without warning, the ground beneath your feet quakes and a loud boom comes from the Energy Summit. It's a dull, cavernous sound, like a cherry bomb going off in a bathtub full of water.

"*Bomba!*" she shouts, going for her service revolver and running toward the building.

A moment later, you see two men sprint out the back of the building. It's the blue-eyed suspect (the *real* Viktor) followed closely by Agent Bertram. You call out to Irma just as the detective is about to enter the front door.

She turns and follows as you sprint after the two men, trying desperately not to lose them in the crowd.

The telltale *crack* of gunfire rings out over the music and screams echo through the party-turned-nightmare. When the crowd parts, you see Agent Bertram lying on the ground, a devil-costumed man lying just beyond him.

Viktor stands on the periphery, his blue eyes glimmering behind his glasses. Then he turns and runs away.

"Did he just shoot Bertram?" you ask. "And some random civilian?"

"I don't know! Go see if Bertram is okay and I'll take care of Viktor."

- "No way! I'm coming with you. Let's nail the bastard." Go to page 210
- "Go! I'll make sure he gets to the hospital." Go to page 267

Dead Bastard

You stand, but have considerable difficulty breathing and significant burning in your chest. You raise your hands and wheeze out the words, "*Turista! Turista! Turista!*"

Irma goes with your move and draws, standing and pointing her pistol at him while he swings to meet her. Gunshots ring out, but neither from the AK nor from Irma's handgun. There's another shooter, up on the rooftop. He's tall, well-built, his black hair close-cropped like a combat soldier's. Clean-shaven, but there's a thick scar along the front of his chin like you'd expect to see on someone who flew over the handlebar of a motorcycle. He wears aviator-style shooting-range glasses and his face is as pale as a skull sun-bleached in the desert. He wears all black—combat boots, tactical cargo pants, a vest to match, and skin-tight long-sleeved under-armor. He has dual-silenced handguns pointed at you and he wears motorcycle gloves.

In short, he's terrifying.

He fires with both weapons simultaneously, expertly putting a round in Irma's chest, the subject's chest, and then yours. He returns, shooting each of you another time, with proficiency as exact as a computer simulation, before putting a bullet in each of your heads. The entire thing, nine shots, takes three seconds—one instant for each of you.

THE END

Dead End

The *KABOOM* of the revolver echoes through the alley, ending in a high-pitched ring that stays in your ears. The metal orb of the would-be bomb falls to the ground harmlessly with a *clink* and Viktor falls to the concrete in a heap.

She hit him directly in the forehead.

The whole alley is silent, save for the ringing in your ears. You can barely hear something off in the distance, maybe Irma calling for backup, but right now your senses are muted, as if you're floating in the ocean at night, deep, deep, far from the surface.

Irma Dos Santos shakes you. "Hey, are you okay?" she asks.

You nod. You look around, reassessing where you are. An evidence team moves through the alley, tagging the body, the bomb, the bullet casing, anything relevant. Time appears to have dilated in your state of shock.

"Well done," a man says. You turn to see it's the Rio Chief of Police. "You helped, yes? You are the American?"

You nod again. The man shakes your hand firmly, with prolonged eye contact.

"What about the agents?" Irma asks.

"They're fine," the Chief says. "They're on their way to the hospital as we speak. Both are stable and should have a full recovery."

"Okay, let's get you back to your hotel, huh?" she says to you.

"Sure," you say. "It's over…."

➢ Go to page 304

Dead to Rights

You raise the revolver, thinking you'll have some sort of standoff like they do on TV, where they shout, you shout, then slowly you'll all lower your weapons to the floor and talk this thing out like civilized people.

Nope.

As soon as you make like you're pointing the gun at one of them, both open fire, filling your chest with lead. You fall to the floor, dead before you even know what hit you.

THE END

Dead (Wo)Man Kneeling

The revolver clatters on the tile floor, cracking a piece of jungle-chic ceramic that was popular in the 1950s. You get a really good look at it as the man and his partner (there were two of them behind you, evidently) slam you to the ground and handcuff your arms behind your back.

Staring at the body of the man before you, your future becomes all too clear. You'll be tried for murder, and it doesn't look good. It's hard to claim self-defense when you shoot an unarmed man in the back. And the woman? They'll probably pin her death on you too. You think you've heard something about Brazilian prisons somewhere before, maybe on an episode of *Locked Up Abroad,* and your gut tells you this won't be an easy sentence.

You're not sure if this country has the death penalty, but you'll probably be begging for it once the locals get done with the tourist-gone-mad killer.

THE END

Deputized

"Firsts things first, Hotshot," Agent Bertram says, "We've got to get you vetted through the RSO."

Agent Danly then goes on to explain what an RSO is—a Regional Security Officer; basically, the head American Law Enforcement presence in Brazil. He's your new partners' immediate supervisor. And apparently it's necessary for you to meet with his approval before you can all work together.

"What about the trail getting cold? Let's get moving!" you protest.

"That's why we're not headed to the Embassy in Brasilia. It's north of a twelve-hour drive into the interior, but luckily for us, he's down here at the Rio Consulate," Danly says. "We've got to do things by the book if we want a conviction. There may be plenty of lawlessness in this country, but there is no law without regulation. Sorry, that's just how it works."

"Well, if I'm going to be working with you guys, I should probably check out of my hostel."

"Sounds good," Bertram nods. "Let's go get your stuff."

You head over to say a final goodbye to your friends, give them your blessing to continue their Brazilian vacation without you, and pack up the last of your belongings. After that, you're off to the *Consulado Geral Dos Estados Unidos*.

It's kind of an odd sight. In the middle of a busy downtown intersection there's an office building with majorly restricted access. Foot traffic is constantly scrutinized by men in Security uniforms and Kevlar vests. The road out front is blocked from any would-be kamikaze car-bombers by rows of concrete pylons and a guard shack allowing entry only to those with proper identification. Bertram shows his credentials and you're in.

The inside of the building is a little less extreme, though there are a few more security hoops to jump through. Mostly, it's just people in cubicles doing administrative work. A conference room is set up for you, and you're offered bottled water while the RSO is told of your arrival.

The room is essentially a large table surrounded by chairs, with a projector screen mounted on a wall opposite the doorway. To the left of the entry, a framed poster reads, "MISSION STATEMENT — The U.S. Mission in Brazil seeks to protect the well-being of U.S. citizens, represent U.S. interests, promote better bilateral relations, and foster friendship between the people of our two countries."

"Please, take a seat," a voice from behind booms over the rush of the door opening. You turn to see a man probably ten years older than the agents, his head shaved bald, adjusting his suit jacket in a manner that suggests he had just put it on. "I'd like to keep this brief."

He sits at the head of the table and pops open a manila file folder. While he rummages through the papers, the three of you sit down, Agents Danly and Bertram on either side of the table and you opposite the RSO. There's a moment of silence as the three of you watch the RSO read his dossier.

"Background check looks good; nothing out of the ordinary."

"Background check?" you parrot.

"Yes," the RSO says, looking up to you. "It's good to have some idea of whom I'll be partnering up my Junior RSOs with, wouldn't you say? A rush job just faxed over, but an essential formality."

He closes the folder. "So, you're to be a Cooperating Witness. Why's that?"

Without giving it much thought, you say, "I was asked to."

"Yes, but *why* did you agree?"

"Just seemed like the right thing to do," you say, giving the most Boy Scout answer you can muster.

"That it is." The RSO rises and, in a grand gesture, draws your attention to a photograph on the right-hand wall. It's a portrait of a man in his mid-50s, with a politician's warm smile, his graying hair neatly combed and short-cropped. He wears a navy blue suit, the red power-tie beaming with authority, and poses in front of an American flag overlapping its Brazilian counterpart.

"Ambassador Mays acts as the President of the United States for all affairs in this country. Right now, right here, I am his proxy. And now you, along with my Special Agents, will represent me. Meaning you directly reflect our President's will. That's not a responsibility you should take lightly, and I don't think you will. This is a brave thing you're doing, and your country thanks you for it."

He offers to shake hands. You accept, and then with a brief squeeze on your shoulder, he says, "I'll get somebody in here to give you a guest briefing. A little *howsitgoin* that we sometimes share with new visitors; tells you a brief background about the DSS and what we do."

The RSO drops his diplomatic smile and turning toward the two agents, hands them each a file. "Agent Bertram, you talk with Karen Atwood—she's the veteran OMS, she's seen the girl from hiring until present. Danly, you've got Tompkins. She's new, but according to the staff she's Nightingale's closest friend. Find me the bad guy, boys!"

With that, the man turns, rushing out to go take care of the rest of his day's agenda. Before he leaves, you blurt:

- "Thanks so much! Looking forward to learning more about the DSS and my time here!" Go to page 82
- "Actually, I'd prefer to sit in with Agent Bertram. I think I might learn more that way." Go to page 233
- "Would you mind if I joined Agent Danly instead? I'm ready to start the case." Go to page 360

Deputy Shift

You awaken in a small, single-window room as hazy light filters through a linen curtain. You are floating in a hammock above cleaning supplies and crates. How did you get here again? The grogginess soon fades, and with it your memory returns, but for an instant you don't understand why the world is swaying and what causes the humming that comes from the walls.

You're on the *Navio do Destino,* the fishing trawler Agent Bertram hired to ferry you to the sugarcane plantation. You recall the ship casting off, heading downriver toward the interior and into the jungle like in *Heart of Darkness,* and as the reptilian camens sank below the surface of the river, so too did you sink below deck and fall deeply asleep.

Rising with a stretch, you head out into the jungle air to check on the ship's crew and inform Bertram that the hammock is all his. The boy, Neto, grins and waves at you when you step out. The captain smokes a pipe while Bertram puffs away at another cigar, but the crewmen are nowhere to be seen.

"Did I miss anything?" you ask.

"Hey, Hotshot! Welcome back to the land of the living. Actually, yeah, there was a pretty intense piranha feeding frenzy when a baby bird dropped into the river. Other than that, calm seas and fair winds."

"And spider!" Neto adds.

"Oh yeah, we had one of those killer bugs on here. Nasty thing." Bertram tosses his spent cigar overboard. "Anyway, I think Cookie is whipping up some dinner down in the kitchen. After that, I'll leave you to it."

You stare out at the river; miles and miles of brown murk pass under the ship, with God-knows-what lurking beneath. The jungle is silent, save for a pair of toucans yelping to one another somewhere in the distance. You take the opportunity to snap a picture of Bertram, the Captain, and the passing jungle.

The Captain says something to Bertram in Portuguese, and you naturally turn to Neto. The boy seems excited to practice his English. "He's warning your boss for pirates."

"Pirates?" you gulp.

"Thieves come nighttime. Sometime kid with knife, sometime pirates with AK-47."

"Have you been robbed before?"

He smiles. "Not me. My father, yes. They kill his best friend and that is when I start sailing with him, yes? But I am like 'good luck,' I have many adventures and no pirates."

A bell rings below deck and everyone turns to head down to dinner.

"Pirates?" you say to Bertram.

"Don't worry too much, Hotshot. They might have guns, but they don't know how to shoot. I'll call their bluff."

"I feel better already."

Bertram laughs. "The captain says there are known dangerous stretches, and they usually turn out their lights when they go by. But the moon is bright and nearly full, so the risk of running aground is relatively low. C'mon, I'm starving."

Great, you think. This ought to be a fun night, standing guard unarmed while Bertram sleeps with his rifle. You briefly consider asking to borrow his flak jacket, but think better of it.

Waiting for you in the kitchen is a large pot boiling over with the most wonderful smell. The chef ladles out generous helpings of some kind of stew and hands you a bowl when you enter. A picnic table with attached benches serves as the kitchen table.

"*Feijoada,*" Neto says. "Black bean, pork, and cow."

You look down at the stew, which was poured over a bed of rice, and your mouth waters. It's warm, rich, and flavorful, and the whole crew eats heartily without so much as saying a word. After the meal, Bertram bids you good luck and heads off to bed.

The night passes slowly. But it also passes uneventfully. At the captain's insistence, the crew remains silent after dark and when they turn off the lights, it's a bit like being alone in an empty house, wondering if every creak is an intruder. If it weren't for the threat of pirates, it would have been a peaceful night, drifting under moonlight and listening to the songs of insects.

Just as it begins to rain, your shift ends. Once you're back in the hammock, the pleasant petrichor that accompanies the first downpour of the rainy season lulls you to sleep.

➢ *Arrive in port.* Go to page 344

Detained

You're taken to the local police station, a place overwhelmed with criminals waiting to be processed. You do your best to stay away from the drunks and drug-addled offenders slouched on the benches along the walls—but it's impossible to avoid their stench. Women shriek in Portuguese, men struggle in vain against handcuffs, and the accused are herded from section to section like unruly cattle.

The two Rio detectives leave you in the hands of a desk agent, giving him instructions in Portuguese, then quickly disappear into the recesses of the station without so much as a word to you. In what feels like the adult nightmare version of being a toddler dropped off at kindergarten, you look around at the ghastly surroundings through watery, uncertain eyes.

"Please," a man protests in English to a desk officer, his eyes red from tears and his cheeks pink from rubbing the tears away. "I know it's only been a few hours, but we always stay together. She's my *sister.* You have to help me."

That reminds you; your own friends are probably tearing the city apart trying to find you, tortured by your disappearance, and you've no way of letting them know you're here. Or, on second thought, they're probably all wasted, drunk and partying, yet to realize you're even gone. Hopefully it doesn't come to them finding you *here* tomorrow—still locked up. Hopefully the Brazilian police will allow you the standard one phone call, so you could at least leave a message for them at your hostel.

You try asking the policeman who escorts you, his arm gripped tightly around your bicep, but his English might actually be worse than your non-existent Portuguese. Going with the flow until someone will inevitably have to talk to you, you're fingerprinted and placed inside an interrogation room that looks like it was modeled after a US cop show.

A young man barely old enough to have graduated high school comes in to take your testimony. Turning on a digital recorder, he says, "Please recount tonight event."

Oh, boy. Please, God—*please* let them understand your English better than they speak it. Imprisonment due to a loss-in-translation is not your idea of a good time. Still, you spill everything, harping on your innocence, repeating the details several times, employing various synonyms, and hoping something will stick.

Once you finish your story, you freely give the information on your hostel and the room numbers of your friends, imploring the man to let them know you're okay.

A sketch artist is called in to depict the suspect you saw and the likeness that comes through isn't bad. His angular face, the through-line of his jaw, the thoroughbred's cheekbones, and his swooping nose all come across quite nicely. What's wrong is the eyes. They just look like ordinary, run-of-the-mill eyes. What's left out is the life, the blazing passion in his eyes. The man you saw had eyes more like a falcon's.

Then the men leave, and you're left to simmer in apparent guilt for the better part of two hours while they corroborate your testimony.

At length, the door opens and the two detectives who brought you here enter.

"Hello, I'm Detective Irma Dos Santos, and this is my partner, Lucio Muniz," she says, introducing herself once more. Her English is flawless, though there is a slight accent. "We'd like to hear your version, once more, before we let you go—if that's all right." When you hear the words, "let you go," you could reach over the table and kiss her. Instead, you nod.

All you can do is replay the events in that room. What was it, anyway? Some kind of drug dealer's meet-up spot? There were no decorations, no fixtures, just a tile floor, cracked plaster walls, poor lighting and a creepy-as-hell crate with a note inviting carnage. The woman's body—the detectives show photos of her gore-spattered face in order to gauge your reaction—was completely unharmed. She was shot point blank.

"Execution-style," Muniz says.

Detective Dos Santos closes her file folder. "We're going to let you go. The time stamp on your digital camera, as well as the series of pictures leading up to your discovery of the body, confirms your story and you're no longer a suspect." Her accent is thicker around hard Cs. 'Digital *Key*-mera' and '*Peek*-tures.'

"There were also no powder burns on your hands, so we know you didn't fire the weapon," Muniz adds.

"There's only one detail that doesn't add up," the woman says, rubbing an index finger over her full lips. "The revolver is in our evidence locker, but we found no such 'pick me up' note. The follow-up team didn't either."

"It was right there, on the crate!" you blurt.

She shrugs.

Once you are discharged from the police station, you head out to look wearily for a cab, only to find a pair of men waiting for you. They're in their mid-thirties, clean-cut, wearing tailored Ralph Lauren suits and stern grimaces. One is slightly taller, thinner, with razor burn on the creases of his neck. The other is broad-chested and has a trimmed, manicured beard.

The tall one says, "How'd it go?"

"Fine, I guess," you reply.

"I'm Special Agent Danly," the man continues, producing a badge, "and this is Special Agent Bertram. We're with the United States Diplomatic Security Service."

Bertram nods his thick, ruddy beard in greeting.

"You're here to help me because I'm American?" you ask.

"Yes and no," Danly says. "The murdered woman you stumbled upon was positively identified as an employee of the State Department. She worked at the Rio consulate, so we'll be launching our own investigation and we'd like to ask you a few questions."

You unconsciously let out a bone-tired sigh.

"But it can wait until morning," Bertram says.

"Thanks," you say, managing a slight smile.

Detective Dos Santos comes back out of the station, hurrying to catch you, and hands you a business card. "If you remember anything else, please call," she says, then adds a few words in Portuguese to the agents. It's lightning-fast, and utterly meaningless to you, but one word does jump out: *Testemunhar*—the word from the mural in the alley.

She smiles politely, then after a nod to the three of you, ducks back inside.

"What did she say?" you ask.

"They might need you as a witness, in case of a lineup," Agent Danly answers.

"Do you think they'll catch him? The murderer?"

"Not likely," the bearded Agent Bertram says. "Brazil has plenty of excesses, including their crime rate. And in Rio at the start of *Carnaval*? I'd be surprised if they even have a man dedicated to the case."

"Let me put it this way," Danly adds. "In order to clean up their public image for the Olympics, Rio now enjoys the lowest murder rate it's had in a decade."

"Isn't that a good thing?" you ask.

He nods. "Except that their 'unsolved missing persons' cases are the highest they've ever been. The fact that we have a body is a big red flag. It's a common tactic here to hide the body and claim ignorance."

"C'mon, we've got a car waiting," Agent Bertram says, starting to walk away. "We've got you set up in a new hotel for the night. Don't worry, DS will pay for it. You're the only person who can identify a suspected murderer, so it's worth lying low until he's brought into custody."

- "No, thank you. I'll be fine." Back to your hostel. Go to page 150
- "If you think that's best." Go to the new hotel. Go to page 11

"Fine, but don't touch anything. Wouldn't want you contaminating two crime scenes. You know what? Just keep your hands in your pockets."

This is it! Your chance to release your inner bloodhound. You've seen the crime shows, now let's see how observant you are. Hmmm, where to start…?

You walk past the gaggle of cops, around the cocaine, and into the kitchen. Everything is meticulously cleaned and organized. No perishable foods are out; no bread, fruits, nothing. You use the bottom of your shirt to open the refrigerator handle without leaving your fingerprints. Inside the fridge, it's a similar story. The kitchen seems very…unused. Like she might've spent more time at her fiancé's apartment than her own.

"Rookie, knock it off!" Danly calls.

You close the refrigerator and move on. Around the corner is an office nook. It's the kind of space-saving technique that an apartment like this, which can't be larger than 300 square feet, has to employ. You scan that area, but it doesn't look like Ms. Nightingale used that space much either. She doesn't have a computer, at least not here, and it seems like her main purpose for this nook was to display pictures. There's a graduation photo, an old pre-instagram-faded picture which is most likely her mother holding her as a baby, and of course, a picture of her up at the *Cristo Redentor* statue with her arms volant as if she's preparing to fly away. She smiles playfully in that last picture…. maybe her fiancé was the photographer? Oddly, there appear to be no portraits of him.

Moving on, you find your way to the bedroom. Following the theme of spartan décor, the bed is crisply made, like a newly rented hotel room or a military cadet's lodging. The room itself is only big enough to hold the bed, a nightstand, and a small bookcase. On the nightstand you find a pad of paper, but there's nothing written on it. You can see the impression made from previous notes now ripped off, so you decide to try the old shade-over-the-note-to-see-what-was-written-on-it trick.

She wrote with a firm hand, so you pick up several layers of text as you lightly brush the pencil diagonally across the page. Most of it is too overwritten to make out, but you can see a reminder to make a dental appointment. Hmmm, that doesn't tell you much. Still, you did learn one thing—hers wasn't the handwriting from the "Pick me up" note you found at the crime scene.

The last room in the house is the bathroom. Surprise, surprise, it's barren. There's not even so much as a toothbrush. You know what would be a good question? When did she move in here? You make a mental note to ask Danly. With a tissue pulled from a small Kleenex box, you grasp the handle and open the medicine cabinet. Inside is the standard cocktail: ibuprofen, over-the-counter allergy medicine, a packet of throat lozenges, and a bottle of Pepto-Bismol. You close the cabinet and head back into the living room.

Agent Danly looks up from the coffee table as you enter. "Come on, Rookie, I want to get back to the hotel and review Ms. Nightingale's files."

Then, looking to Irma Dos Santos, he adds, "Detective, I'll be by tomorrow to see about a trip into the *favelas*. We should get to the bottom of this drug angle."

"Okay, I'll see what I can do," she replies with a nod.

Danly puts his sunglasses back on as you leave the apartment. Once you're in the SUV and driving back, he says, "Listen, you're doing great, but I'm not sure you should stay with me. I aim to get to the bottom of this, even if that means coming head-to-head with the drug cartels in the *favelas*. You can't even imagine what it's like in there—gangsters dance in the clubs while shooting AK-47s in the air. Even the kids are armed and they won't hesitate to shoot you if they think it's worth a laugh. I can't put your life in jeopardy like that.

"Tonight we'll meet up with Agent Bertram and decide how to proceed."

➢ *Head to the DSS hotel.* Go to page 36

De-Tour

You rush forward and shout, "*Turista!*" the last syllable coming out in a cough of blood.

As you fall to your knees, you realize you've been shot. You manage a glance back, and see Irma lying dead on the ground, just as you fall onto your stomach. The Elite Squad member walks back to the armored vehicle without a second thought about ending your life.

This is one Brazilian experience your friends won't share.

THE END

The Devil Ray

Letting the suspect escape, you follow Irma away from the action. After you've jogged for another few minutes to a spot she's deemed as relatively safe, you stop to catch your breath.

"What is it, Irma?"

"That man… I know of that man."

"Who is he?"

"We call him *Jamanta*—The Devil Ray, but the word has a double meaning, it's also 'The Juggernaut' and both names apply to this man. He's the most dangerous assassin in all of Rio—in all of *Brasil.*"

The way she pronounces her country sounds like "Brass Seal." She shakes her head and continues, "We must go; once he sets his sights on you, you're as good as dead."

You dry-swallow the lump in your throat. You've never seen her so afraid like this.

"Who does he work for? The mafia? Elite Squad?"

"I don't know. I've never seen him before tonight… Let's go, I'm taking you back to your hotel."

➢ *Return to your hotel.* Go to page 300

Did You Say "Tapas" Bar?

It's not hard to find a prostitute in the slums. A fact you're quickly learning, the terms "legal" and "illegal" seem to have interchangeable meanings here. Back out into the *favela* proper, Viktor asks where to find the best action, and you're directed to one of the larger nightclubs in the shantytown.

At this time of day, the club is nearly deserted, but seems to be always open for business. There is only one reason to show up here before the nightlife hours begin, so the greeter at the entrance merely bids you to follow him without so much as a word.

He has a surprisingly young, pimpled face with tired eyes and gelled hair. He wears a black button-up, jeans, and angus cowboy boots. He leads you into the club, past the grand open-air *discoteca* dance hall, and into the VIP area. With a gesture of his hand, he offers you a seat at one of the tables.

Viktor takes out his money clip, setting it before him in such a way as to be obvious to the sordid cicerone. The man disappears back out into the club, leaving the two of you alone for a moment.

"What exactly are we doing?" you ask.

"Soliciting a hooker. We'll be paying for her companionship, but the only need she'll be fulfilling today is our desire for information. It should be a welcome break for the girl, who I imagine is mentally preparing to 'perform' as we speak."

Mr. Acne returns with a shrink-wrapped case of local Brazilian beer. He takes out a knife from his pocket and cuts through the red plastic that keeps the cans tethered together. As he works on this, three women arrive behind him: one with high-European Portuguese ancestry, her skin pale and her hair in ruddy curls; a bronzed, Amazonian type with straightened hair and glittering gold lipstick; and an Afro-Brazilian with curly hair to her shoulder, great hooped earrings and a studded nose ring. Apparently they give their clients the Neapolitan option here.

The man folds the knife, leaving the dozen beers for you, and then exits with a deferential nod and Viktor's money clip in his hand. Each woman wears heavy makeup and is clad in nothing other than high heels and a bedazzled jacket covering just below the cat's meow. One blue, one golden yellow, and one rosy pink, respectively.

"Ah, this is called a 'can-cup,'" Viktor says, claiming one of the beers, his back to the women.

The three graces try to gesture for you to choose one of them, but all you can muster is an embarrassed shrug. At length, they all point to the one closest to your own skin tone and you simply shrug again, shaking your head uncertainly, eyebrows raised to the ceiling. They all smile at your coyness.

"You see," Viktor explains, holding down the red and gold can, "You can peel off the entire top of the beer so it becomes a cup."

The three women peel off their jackets, revealing nothing beneath. At the same time, Viktor opens the can of beer, pulling back the entire top like a can of sardines, and the beer gives off a crisp hiss of carbonation. He slides the beer over to you and takes another for himself.

"It's marketed as 'reusable,' but really, it's just…what's the word? It's a…gimmick! Yes, that's all it is, is a gimmick."

With the woman you "chose" in the center, the other two pour massage oil on their hands and begin to rub down her nude form. She simply stands there with a smile, staring at you, her newly moist flesh glistening in the low light.

"Umm, Viktor?" you cough out. You grasp the beer, ready to take a drink.

"Ah, yes. *Saúde*!" he says, clinking his can to yours in a toast.

You guzzle the beer while the bizarre show goes on behind your companion. It's almost like they're *prepping* her, like you're witnessing the start of a cattle auction. It wouldn't be surprising if they opened her mouth to show off the quality of her teeth.

Viktor finally notices your gaze and turns to the women. "Oh, *nossa! Ta louco!*"

He rises and persuades the three women to put their coats back on. The two with oil only on their hands hurry out of the VIP lounge.

"What do you want?" the third asks in English.

"Please, sit."

She does so, arms folded across her chest, wary of your intentions.

"You speak English?" you say, confirming the obvious.

"Yes. I worked in clubs in Copacabana with many international clients."

"Then what are you doing working the *favelas,* and the day shift, no less?" Viktor asks.

She slips her hair behind her right ear, revealing a long, thick scar which runs from her temple down toward the bottom of the ear itself. "This happened last time a client paid for an *unusual* request."

You offer her a beer. "All we want to do is talk."

She hesitates, but takes the drink.

"Today is your lucky day, I promise," Viktor says. "Just tell us the name of the cop your boss bribes, or get a phone number for us, then we share a couple of drinks and relax until the time we paid for expires."

"That's it?" she asks, incredulous.

"I told you; your lucky day."

She shakes her head and smirks, "That's easy. We see cops all the time for dates. I can write the number down for you right now."

Viktor smiles at you.

- Finish the "date," then arrange a new one to meet with the cops. Go to page 224
- "As long as we're on the clock, why don't we have a little fun…?" Go to page 357

The Difference between Dirty and Corrupt

You move quickly; Detective Muniz has already left the station and you rush to catch up with him lest he throw you off for good. The sun sets in the sky as you ride in the passenger seat of Irma's personal vehicle. After all, you don't want to arouse suspicions by showing up in a squad car. Even so, she'll stick out like a sore thumb in her detective's pantsuit, but there wasn't time to change.

"According to his call sheet, he's on patrol," she says. "But what this really means is that he's out collecting bribes."

She lets that information sink in before continuing. "The police get their cut of petty crime: drugs, arms deals, that kind of thing. Cops have *shit* for pay, as you say, so the need to supplement our income is high."

"Even you?" you ask.

"I do not want you to think criminals get a free pass here, but we don't hold bake sales. If that money doesn't go to us, it just funds more crime. I tried keeping my nose out of it, but no one on the force trusts a cop who doesn't take bribes. Do you understand?"

You sit in silence, unsure how to respond.

She sighs. "Okay, how do I explain? Would you trust a butcher who is a vegetarian?"

You shrug.

"You just come from a different world, *Americano.* No one will admit it if you ask them, but everyone takes payoffs. Even the Chief."

"So why are *you* admitting it?"

She stares straight ahead. "I want to prepare you for what you're about to see. Ah, good, there's his car."

The detective pulls off onto the side street and parks the car under a streetlight just as it flickers on. She closes the door and without a word jogs off in the direction Muniz's car faces. You run to catch up.

Irma stops at the end of the road, and you soon hear why: voices come from the next intersection. Not daring to go out into the open, she instead stops and looks around the sides of the brick and concrete buildings that surround the small street. In a quick, athletic move, she climbs atop a crate, uses a rain gutter to stabilize herself, then steps atop and off a dumpster to arrive on the rooftop.

Trying to keep quiet, you make the same ascent. One you've scaled the building, you follow Irma Dos Santos on your hands and knees to the roof's edge. There, just below you, is Detective Lucio Muniz with two uniformed policemen. They speak in Portuguese, just loud enough that Irma can make it out. Muniz looks at his watch.

"They say the payoff is supposed to arrive just after the streetlights power on. They're wondering where he is," she whispers to you.

In the umber glow of the streetlight, their black uniforms look darker than ever. One of the cops lights a cigarette, the flint strike of his lighter the only sound in the still air. Smoke curls up towards the streetlight in a wisp. That's when the payoff arrives.

Even in the low orange light, his eyes glow blue.

It's the man from the warehouse! In a hushed but urgent voice, you say as much to Irma while the primary suspect walks toward the three policemen. She lays a calm hand on your wrist to hush you—she wants to see what they'll do next.

The bespectacled suspect wears a backpack over a light jacket (despite the summer heat), with his hands in his pockets. The police seem threatened by this. You can't tell what they're saying because none of it is in English, but the body language is clear enough. The three cops go for their handguns while Muniz shouts tersely.

The man with the icy-blue eyes takes his right hand from his pocket, revealing a wad of cash. Now Muniz laughs and the cops leave their weapons holstered. The detective makes a grand speech with arms spread wide.

"He commends this man for the size of his balls," she translates, "and asks what information he wants to purchase."

"He won't arrest him?"

She shakes her head.

"What information?"

"He says he wants to know what gang controls the territory where the girl was found. And he wants the name of an informant."

"Why? To make sure he's covered his tracks?"

She frowns, leaving your question lingering. The men continue talking while the suspect waves the money in the air, the tension from the moment seemingly gone. After a moment, the man tosses the cash towards the cops, seemingly satisfied, and then disappears down an alley.

"Where is he going? We've got to chase him!" you plead through hushed urgency.

She shakes her head. "We can't expose our position. If Lucio learns we know about this—consorting with a murderer is not a simple payoff—we'll be in grave danger. It's best if we stay hidden."

"Can't we slip off the back of the roof and go around?"

"We could, but we could also learn something here."

- "You're right, let's listen. What are they saying now?" Go to page 86
- "Let's go!" Go to page 22

Double Agent

Somehow you convince him that you'll work the agents for information, getting in their good graces, and then funnel all that knowledge back to him. In reality, you don't trust him. Obviously, the cops are the good guys—the mysterious note disappearance notwithstanding—and you'll help them bring this guy in.

On your way back to the hostel, you call Agent Bertram and set up a meeting for tomorrow. He suggests *Capricciosa*, a nearby pizza joint in Ipanema. Sounds just fine.

The next day, you ditch your friends and snake your way through the streets, turning a five-minute walk into fifteen minutes. Still, you can't help but feel you're being watched. When you finally arrive, the restaurant's red flag sails above the entry to hail your arrival. You find the pair of agents waiting for you inside.

The building's exterior walls are all glass, giving a panorama of street life while saving you from the sounds of traffic and the smell of the street vendors' food offerings. You sit down at the agents' table, right next to the window. The waiter presents you a menu, a round of water for all, then leaves you to decide.

"We already ordered," the bearded Agent Bertram says. "The thin-crust pepperoni here is fan-damn-tastic."

"So, you have something for us?" Danly asks.

"Do I?" you say with a grin. "The guy from yesterday found me. He wants me to help him."

"What? You talked with him?" Bertram asks in disbelief.

"Yep. He thinks I'm helping clear his name, says that he's been framed."

"They all say that," Danly says.

A teenager walks up to your table wearing clean, crisp, kitchen whites. He sets down a large tray covered in a room-service style serving dome—the kind usually reserved for gourmet restaurants. "Compliments of the chef," he says with a twinge of nervousness.

He bows slightly, and then leaves in an awkward hurry.

"First day?" you wonder aloud.

"The federal-agent-look has that effect on people," Bertram says.

"Probably a dopehead," Danly adds, lifting the dome off the tray.

Sitting there, where a fan-damn-tastic pepperoni pizza should be, is a metal ball about the size of a grapefruit. It's mechanical, looking much like a tiny "Death Star" from *Star Wars*.

The teenager sprints by outside the restaurant, shedding his kitchen whites and fleeing the scene as fast as his scrawny legs will carry him. Agent Bertram leaps from his chair, draws his pistol, and prepares to pursue, but is stopped when you yell, "Wait!"

The device has begun moving, rearranging itself like a Rubik's Cube, expanding in some places and contracting in others. There's a note beneath the device, and Agent Danly snaps it out from underneath.

The note reads:

"I thought we had a deal?"

It's written in a new, third person's handwriting. Maybe the teenager's?

"What the fuck is this?" Danly demands.

Bertram tries to answer, but his breath is *sucked out* of him by the device.

You feel it too, your insides collapsing as the tiny thing turns into something akin to a miniature black hole and sucks out all the air from the room. Windows shatter inward, the ceiling threatens to collapse, and every patron in the restaurant dies when the strange bomb implodes.

THE END

Double Back

Leaving the teenage drug trafficker in the broken home, you head back into the alley. It hasn't been too long since you abandoned your stake-out of the armored vehicle, so maybe it's still there? Detective Dos Santos tucks her service revolver into an ankle holster, then holds an open palm toward you.

"You don't want to get caught out in the open with a weapon. Elite Squad will see the AK first, then they'll notice you're American after they've shot you."

Can't argue with that; so you hand Irma the weapon. She dashes forward and hurls the rifle atop one of the buildings, then ducks into a different alley—trying to randomize her movements—and jogs back toward the main street. Through labored, running breaths, you realize that you no longer hear gunshots.

Every few steps, the Rio cop looks back to ensure you're still behind her. She suddenly stops, her running shoes skidding against the tiny mortar fragments that litter the ground. Then Irma turns back, whispers a husky, "Trust me," then presses you into a corner and slides her tongue into your mouth.

She takes your hand, guides it under her shirt and atop her breast, and with an amorous intensity, runs her hands over your body. Somewhere in the back of your mind, you notice two armed drug traffickers run past.

She continues to kiss you deeply and passionately. When she finally stops and pulls away, you open your eyes. You didn't even realize they were closed.

"That was a close one," she says with a sigh of relief.

Still in a daze, you blink and say, "Yeah."

"You can let go of my breast now."

Embarrassed, you quickly drop your hand. You try to apologize, but end up stammering. She smirks and says, "Come on."

You continue down the alleyway. Using a telephone pole for cover when you reach the end, you peer into the street. The armored car sits in the middle of the road, its engine turned off, a pair of Elite Squad members guarding either side of the vehicle.

The *caveirão* looks empty on the inside.

"Damn, where's Agent Danly?" you ask.

"They must be pursuing on foot."

"Let's go ask the guys where he went!"

She puts out a hand to stay you, then shakes her head fiercely, hoop earrings jangling. "I didn't bring my badge. To them, I'd look like some *favela*-girl coming out to harass them."

"They wouldn't recognize you?"

She shakes her head. "Elite Squad keeps to themselves. I just have my one contact and it's a big department."

A shout comes from the street. You look back to see one of the Elite Squad members walking toward you, his assault rifle raised and lethally aimed. Irma raises her hands.

Out of the side of her mouth, she whispers, "Run."

"What?"

"*Run.* NOW!"

- Turn and sprint, but keep an eye out for traffickers. Go to page 29
- Remember the "Lost Tourist" plan? Seems like a good time to invoke it. Go to page 70
- Try and weave past him—you've got to find Danly! Go to page 363

Dropped

With the quick severity that only comes from training, the two rush in and subdue you. Their movements are fluid, unconscious. "You an American?" the woman asks with a scowl. She's slammed you against a wall and handcuffs your arms behind your back.

"Are you guys cops?" you return.

"Lucky for you," the man answers. "Now why don't you tell us what the hell you're doing here?"

"I—I don't know. I was lost and….Look, I just want to leave," you say. "My friends will be wondering where I am."

"So will hers," the woman continues, indicating the body on the floor. "And I'm guessing once the consulate hears of this, you'll have some questions to answer. Muniz, call it in."

Muniz—the man with the teal shirt—nods, holsters his pistol, and takes out a cell phone. He steps out into the alleyway as he dials. Your heart sinks and you feel as though you might vomit.

The woman picks up on your distress, holsters her own weapon, and produces a badge. "I'm Detective Irma Dos Santos and that was my partner, Lucio Muniz. If you didn't do anything wrong, you should have nothing to worry about. Now, please, step outside so we can take you to the police station. We don't need you contaminating the crime scene further."

"You think I'm innocent?"

"We'll see."

➤ *Get escorted to the police station.* Go to page 65

Drug-addled

"Detective, can you translate? What happened here?" Danly asks.

Irma Dos Santos nods, then talks with the policemen in Portuguese. While they converse in the alien tongue, you look at the strict lines of cocaine. Three lines, perfectly set up, with a rolled-up Brazilian *Real.* It has the tell-tale red ink of an $R50.

"Looks like the door was kicked in," Irma says, directing your attention to the busted door jamb.

The wood is cracked and frayed out around the door latch, spreading forth from under the paint. The chain lock dangles higher up. Undamaged.

"They say there's no other sign of a struggle, which would lead to the conclusion that she was either passed out or they held her at gunpoint and she cooperated."

Danly shakes his head. "Anything else in the house?"

"No other illicit substances. Not much of anything, actually. Doesn't look like she spent very much time here—either that or she sold her personal belongings, spent her whole paycheck on cocaine, and was quite the housekeeper when she was high. She have a drug history?"

Through a frown, he says, "No. This amount of cocaine would affect someone's work performance and all of our employees are drug-tested. I don't like it."

"I know what you mean. I've seen a lot of users and their apartments are usually filthy."

"We'll look into her bank accounts, see if she had any outstanding debts or any savings. For now, this is the best lead we have." Agent Danly says. "I'll be by tomorrow to see about a trip into the *favelas.* We should get to the bottom of this drug angle."

"Okay, I'll see what I can do," she replies with a nod.

"Come on, Rookie, I want to get back to the hotel and review Ms. Nightingale's files."

Danly puts his sunglasses back on as you leave the apartment. Once you're in the SUV and driving back, he says, "Listen, you're doing great, but I'm not sure you should stay with me. I aim to get to the bottom of this, even if that means coming head-to-head with the drug cartels in the *favelas.* You can't even imagine what it's like in there—gangsters dance in the clubs while shooting AK-47s in the air. Even the kids are armed and they won't hesitate to shoot you if they think it's worth a laugh. I can't put your life in jeopardy like that.

"Tonight we'll meet up with Agent Bertram and decide how to proceed."

➢ *Head to the DSS hotel.* Go to page 36

The RSO gives a curt smile, then heads out. The other agents head to their respective interview rooms, leaving you with a junior agent—an office worker who looks young enough be an intern, though you're not sure if they have interns here. His hair is orange-red, parted to the right in a failing effort to hide a bright red blemish on his forehead. His freckled cheeks dimple with a smile.

The two of you introduce yourselves. He takes over the conference room computer, loads up a slideshow and powers up the projector. You make small talk. He asks how you like Brazil, that kind of thing.

"How long have you been an agent?" you ask.

"This is my first post," he admits. "I was a philosophy major in college and did some volunteer law enforcement work. Joining the State Department seemed like a great way to help the world in a real, tangible sense, y'know? Plus, I still have a lot of college debt."

Finally, the computer is ready. "Ah, here we go."

The first slide on the PowerPoint presentation reads, "Welcome to US Soil," with the subtitle, "Brought to you by the Bureau of Diplomatic Security."

He reads the next slide verbatim, "The Diplomatic Security Service, or DSS, is the Department of State's security and law enforcement arm. These quiet professionals do not dictate foreign policy, but rather provide a secure environment through which diplomacy may occur.

"Our 2000 Special Agents have myriad responsibilities, including providing security for embassies, ensuring border protection, investigating passport and visa fraud, performing high-risk search warrants, tracking and capturing known terrorists, and creating a protective bubble around foreign dignitaries and the Secretary of State.

"To uphold these enormous responsibilities, our agents receive Military Special Operations and Law Enforcement training, and many learn foreign languages. All of our Special Agents in Brazil attend a Portuguese language course. These highly trained and highly motivated men and women stay out of the public eye, but are ready for action at a moment's notice…."

He sighs. "You know, really, there's a program that the Military Channel did—you should check that out. It's a bit dramatized, but not bad. The rest of this stuff is pretty dry; talks about how we formed in 1916, officially cemented as our own organization in 1985, then expanded after September 11th."

"Give me the condensed version," you say.

"You've heard of the Secret Service? The guys who protect the President?"

You nod.

"It's basically a cross between that and FBI Agents, but don't tell the other guys I said so. Agents *hate it* when we're confused with Secret Service. Although when I was in training, one of my instructors said he used to hand out business cards with the SS phone numbers on it, so that way they'd get a call and have to say, 'Sorry, sir, you're thinking of the DS guys.' Hilarious."

He grins.

"Thanks, I think I get the gist of it," you say.

➢ *Meet up with the agents.* Go to page 175

"Good thinking," he says.

The two of you casually stroll over to the police barricade the policeman standing there puts out his hand to stop you. He says something in Portuguese while shaking his head "no."

"We're reporters," Viktor tells the young man, removing his notebook. "What's the going rate for an inside scoop? R$200?"

The man's eyes widen, and you think he might balk, but then he smiles. "R$300."

"R$350, you don't mention this to your supervisor, and I'll look forward to working with you again."

The policeman nods and accepts the bribe. He checks his watch, "The guys should be heading out to lunch in a couple of minutes. Just hang back until then."

This pervasive culture of corrupt officials sure does make things easy. Viktor steps aside, leading you to the parking lot, to an unassuming white sedan, tiny like many foreign cars.

"This was hers," he says. "So that means she was here at some point, but why? Sometimes she would park it here and take the bus so we could go out drinking, but—"

"Look!" you shout, spotting a phone on the ground near the car. "Is that...?"

The police investigators flood out of the apartment to lunch. The cop who was guarding the barricade signals you; it's time.

"Yes! That's her mobile—incredible. Grab it and let's go!"

Pocketing the phone, you head inside with the young policeman as your escort. The apartment is small, and it's the living room—where a coffee table sits midway between couch and television—that captures his attention. There on the table sits a stash of cocaine, several lines laid out neatly as if the party was just getting started.

"What's all this?" Viktor asks.

"Most likely a drug deal gone bad," the cop says. "Put that in your article."

You snap a photo with your digital camera. "You think she was taken from here?"

"Looks like it," the cop shrugs.

"We'll just have a quick look around, and then we'll be out of your hair," Viktor says with a warm smile. As soon as he turns away from the cop, his smile disappears and his jaw clenches. "This is all lies. My Jane would never..."

"And why would her phone just be 'dropped' in the parking lot?" you add.

He nods. "It's a setup."

Viktor moves on. Around the corner is an office nook. It's the kind of space-saving technique that an apartment like this, which can't be larger than 300 square feet, has to employ. You scan that area, but it doesn't look like Ms. Nightingale used that space much either. She doesn't have a computer, at least not here, and it seems like her main purpose for this nook was to display pictures.

Viktor reaches out for a photo of Jane; a picture of her up at the *Cristo Redentor* statue with her arms volant as if she's preparing to fly away. He pockets the picture and keeps walking. The rest of the house is nearly barren and nothing else interests him.

"She kept this apartment as her home-of-record for work, but she lived with me," he explains in a whisper.

Thanking the cop who let you in, you head back outside. The heat of the day is fully present now and the summer sun is warm and embracing. It's the kind of day meant for lounging poolside, not solving cases. You feel like it should be dark and drizzling, maybe with the occasional thunderclap.

"May I see the phone, please?" Viktor asks, interrupting your thoughts.

After he looks it over, he says, "It's off. We should check her messages and call log, but if they're tracking the number, then we probably only have a minute or two."

You nod and follow him over toward the dumpsters, a protected area behind the apartments. They're way in the back because, after all, who wants to look at dumpsters? So you're relatively hidden here.

"Here goes…" he sighs, powering the phone on.

It starts up, gets a signal, and synchs with the network. After waiting a few moments, a message comes through from a number called EMBASSY:

Format One Recall. Please Report To Nearest US Consulate Immediately. Call Back To Confirm.

Yesterday, 7:17pm

"Check her outgoing messages," you suggest.

There's one sent to him:

I HAVE WHAT WE NEED, BUT I THINK THEY KNOW. DATE FIRST.

Yesterday, 9:24pm

"The last message I got from her," Viktor says though a lump in his throat. "After that, I ditched my mobile because I knew they'd be tracking us."

"What did you need?" you ask.

"Evidence."

You wait a moment, but it appears as if he's not going to elaborate. "Of…?"

Deep in thought, he doesn't respond right away. "I just realized what this means. She said 'date first.' It's code: when we first met, my English was not so good. In Portuguese you say the descriptor after, so our 'first date' I called our 'date first.' She always liked that… I think she might have left something for me up on the hilltop where we had our first date. It's funny, I might have gone up there even without this message—simply out of longing for her."

"Viktor, how did you end up in that warehouse? Did you know she would be there?"

A sad smile appears on his face. "I got an anonymous call. I thought they might want to meet. Blackmail me, maybe. But I never imagined…"

Then, with a renewed determination, he separates the phone from its battery and tosses it into the trash.

"We've been here too long already," Viktor says.

He steps out from the refuse enclosure, but stops in his tracks. There, bearing down at you from across the parking lot, is death himself.

He's tall, well-built, his black hair close-cropped like a combat soldier's. Clean-shaven, but there's a thick scar along the front of his chin like you'd expect to see on someone who flew over the handlebar of a motorcycle. He wears aviator-style shooting-range glasses and his face is as pale as a skull sun-bleached in the desert. He wears all black—combat boots, tactical cargo pants, a vest to match, and skin-tight long-sleeved under-armor. He has dual-holstered handguns on the sides of his vest and wears black motorcycle gloves.

In short, he's terrifying.

"*Jesus Cristo,*" Viktor mutters.

The young policeman you bribed runs out toward this Man in Black, calling out to him in Portuguese, but to no avail. The man removes one pistol—and turns one eye—toward the cop and shoots him twice.

The other eye stays fixed on you, while the man goes for the second pistol with his other hand.

"Run!" Viktor shouts.

The brick enclosure near you explodes under the impact of a bullet from the man's gun—an impossibly close shot from that distance, especially with both shooter and target on the move. There's a declivity on the other side of the apartment building and Viktor sprints down it toward the next avenue below.

Back on the streets, you rush into traffic and crowds of pedestrians.

Viktor gets onto a bus and bids you to follow. With one final look back, you see your would-be assassin melt again into the shadows of the warehouse, his pistols still trained forward.

➢ *Get on the bus, quickly!* Go to page 95

Eavesdropped

Irma leans over the roof further, but stops abruptly when tiny bits of tar and pitch start to crumble over the edge. You both hold your breaths, but no one looks up. Once the cops are certain the payoff has left, they talk to one another in hushed tones.

"They're arguing about letting him go," Irma explains. "The younger cops seem to think they should track him down and kill him, but Lucio says the joke is on him. He just paid for the name of an informant where Elite Squad's doing their raid. If they're lucky, he might even get killed."

"He's headed toward Agent Danly?" you ask. "But why?"

"I don't know. He obviously has cash; he might be delivering hush money."

It makes sense, in its own corrupt and craven way. The Shadow Chiefs own that slum, they have the final say over who lives or dies. So if you kill someone on their turf—you have to pay for the privilege. And now the perp is headed straight for Danly. Hell, this might be the final part of his cover-up! All he has to do is square up with the Shadow Chief Mafiosos and he's in the clear. If only you had some way to warn Agent Danly…but would he even listen?

Irma nudges you, interrupting your woolgathering by drawing your attention towards the cops. Their sub rosa meeting over, they leave the scene.

"They mentioned something about a body. We can follow, but I'm not sure we should. This is starting to become very dangerous. Give me the revolver. I'll take you back to your hotel."

- "Okay. I'm ready to leave." Go to page 300
- "We've come this far… why stop now?" Go to page 181

"It shouldn't be all that bad," she says. "Elite Squad kicks down the front door—they go in with guns blazing. The drug traffickers probably won't even notice us with all they'll be dealing with."

"We do what? Investigate from the sidelines? Stay out of the line of fire?"

"Sure. Don't you want to see what Agent Danly sees, instead of waiting for him to tell you what he *wants* you to know in the morning?"

You don't respond.

"Give me a minute to change," she says. "I'm going plainclothes."

"Undercover?"

"Drug traffickers think of cops the same way young boys with rocks think of windows. If we get caught, we're going to pretend we're lost tourists."

You remember the role of lost tourist all too well. "And then they'll let us go?"

She smiles again. "No, but this way they won't torture us before they kill us. Be right back."

While she's gone, you find the restroom. Suddenly your stomach's not feeling very "strong and brave." After you come back, you see she's now wearing tight-fitting jeans, running shoes, and a banana-yellow Brazilian soccer jersey, her hair pulled back in a ponytail.

Time to head out.

From afar, the *favela* has a certain beauty. It lights up the hills like starlight, similar to the effect of photographs showing Earth at night as seen from space. It's too dark to make out individual houses, but the lights—white, green, yellow, blue—belie the presence of humanity on these jungle hills.

The *favela* itself is all brick and concrete. Detective Irma Dos Santos parks on the outskirts and together you head in on foot. The night is warm, and though the slums are never silent, there are no sounds of combat. Your heart thumps and your palms sweat from nervousness.

You don't see or hear a single person, but radio music fills the air. You look at graffiti-emblazoned homes, expecting one of the ramshackle doors or partitioned curtains to fly open at any minute to reveal a gang of thugs.

"Isn't it a little too quiet?" you ask in a whisper.

"Elite Squad announces which *favela* is scheduled for pacification. It's possible the tide is turning and the traffickers are starting to flee when warning is given."

Then there's a distant *crack,* like someone slapping a broomstick against a brick wall—the *crack, crack, crack* of gunshots. "Or not," she says. "Come on, let's go!"

With that, she's running down the alleys of the *favela.* The path between the houses is thin, made thinner by abandoned wooden pallets, heaps of trash, abandoned scrap, and other detritus. The slum is bathed in a ubiquitous orange from the cumulative glow of lights. Irma's running shoes scrape pebbles and dirt against the concrete as she flies toward the noise. You struggle to keep up, taking in deep breaths of foul air.

She suddenly takes a step back and slaps her arm against your chest to prevent you from going any further. With a great *crack* followed by a whining *ping*, brick gravel explodes out from the wall across the alley, the ricochet hitting you in the face. Images of a cruel child hurling sand on the playground are conjured up.

"Come on," Irma says, doubling back from the gunfire.

She pauses in the alley, looks up, and examines the nearest house. Satisfied, she turns back to the alleyway, claims a wooden pallet, and props it against the house as a makeshift ladder. One step up and she's pulled herself onto the roof of the building in a seamless, impressively athletic move.

She turns back to you with her hand extended. "Hurry!"

You scramble your way onto the rooftop as well, then follow her, squatting down and ducking past a wash basin and plastic chairs. She goes prone by the roof's edge and you lie on your belly next to her, looking out over the main street where the action unfolds.

What's spread out before you is something out of a war zone. The Elite Squad armored vehicle lumbers down the street, its metal surface singing out with rejected bullets. There are tiny portholes on the sides, just big enough for the barrel of an assault rifle to fit through. The portholes are presently being filled by the guns of Elite Squad members, who are firing haphazardly at the drug traffickers engaging them from the street.

Gunshots light up darkened doorways and windows. Two traffickers are perched on a rooftop across from you, but they're too focused on the armored vehicle to notice you. A lone young man, maybe a teenager, wearing a tank top and shorts and carrying an AK-47 sprints across the road toward you and into the nearby alley.

"Want to catch that one? Ask him some questions? Or stay here?" Irma asks.

Decide quickly; he's getting away.

- Grab the boy and question him. Go to page 161
- Stay where the action is. Go to page 3

Employees Only

"Okay, just give me your driver's license and I'll annotate it on the computer."

You know you can't do that, so your brain scrambles for a solution. "I…uh…that's in the car too."

"Are you new here? You don't look familiar."

"Yes! I'm totally new. Still figuring things out, making mistakes—like this one. Oh, you know, a typical new person and making mistakes. Yup, that's me!"

His eyes narrow. "Okay, give me the name of your immediate supervisor and I'll have him come out and vouch you in."

"No, no. Don't do that."

"Why not?"

"Because…I don't want to get in trouble."

He picks up a handheld radio and keys in the transmitter.

"Wait!" you shout. "The truth is…."

He stops, looking to you, waiting for your explanation.

- "I don't actually work here… but I met somebody who does at a club last night. Can I give you $100 to leave a note on the car for me?" Go to page 289
- "My friends dared me to see if I could sneak in. We're here on spring break, sorry. I'll leave now…." Time to steal a motorcycle and force my way in! Go to page 131

Endangered

You blast into the sugarcane just as the swaying grasses touch the barrel of your shotgun. The intruders scream out in animal screeches—literal animal screeches. A golden lion tamarin, a small jungle monkey with bright orange-red fur, and your would-be intruder, is instantly killed by the barrage of lead pellets. His family screams in fear and outrage.

"Jesus, Hotshot, cool the jets," Bertram says.

"They run from the fire," Maria explains. "Animals like this are endangered because over 85 percent of their forests have been destroyed."

You swallow, lower your shotgun, and take a deep breath. Then a new disturbance rushes through the sugarcane; this one is a much larger primate. Agent Bertram and Maria turn to face the new threat.

You pump your shotgun to load a new shell into the breach, but before you can decide whether or not to blind-fire again, the sugarcane erupts in gunshots. Your thigh explodes with stinging pain; you've been shot. Bertram and Maria fire into the darkness as you fall to the ground.

With a groan, Bertram falls to the earth next to you, motionless. Maria blasts round after round from her revolvers, until both of them suddenly click empty.

Now the *grileiros* arrive—more than a dozen of them—their hunting party has homed in on your shotgun blast. You can't be sure how many of them were shot and killed in the confrontation, but as they arrive to finish the job, you can be sure how many in your party died. Three.

THE END

Energetic

"If you go to the Energy Summit, you go as a private citizen, not as part of the US investigation team," Danly says, his voice stern.

"I know that."

"As in—you go there because you like science, and not because you're looking for a killer. Got it?"

"Yeah, I said I got it."

"You'll still have to walk through *Carnaval* to get there," Bertram says. "All the main roads are open to foot-traffic only. If I had to bet, you'll spend ten minutes at the conference, get bored, and then go party."

"Maybe. I'll take that chance."

Bertram grins. "One more piece of advice. If you're out there dancing *samba* and some sexy stranger wants to take you somewhere private, remember this: If it has an apple up above, it has a banana down below."

"Ummm, wow. Thanks…"

"Just go. Try to have fun," Danly sighs.

Bertram was right: it's a madhouse out here. Like Mardi Gras and Halloween rolled into a public party at the Playboy mansion, Rio during *Carnaval* is like no other place on earth. And the freak-flags fly like the color guard of an invading army.

Many of the revelers look as if they go to the gym all year just so they can show off their toned and sculpted bodies for these five days. Those who were born with more than their share of confidence now show it off in abundance.

The route is slow-going, but you're in no rush. It's the perfect opportunity to take in the scenery with your digital camera. You snap a picture of twenty people in green, scaled body paint as they snake through the crowd in a conga line meant to embody the visage of an anaconda.

The crowd makes way for the massive serpentine dance party, and you walk in their wake, traversing the crowd faster than you could snaking your way on your own through the multitudes. Eventually, you make it to the mega-conference grounds of the Energy Summit.

Once inside, you're greeted with a security line reminiscent of LAX or JFK. People are slowly shepherded through and you join this much-less-jovial conga line to wait your turn.

At security, you notice two pictures posted by the screening monitors. The first is a shot of Viktor Lucio de Ocampo, the man you haven't seen since he gave you the slip-up on the Christ the Redeemer statue. The second is the sketch artist's rendition of the mysterious man you saw at the crime scene. The drawing still doesn't capture the intensity of those blue eyes, which still seem seared onto your retina, the way the sun leaves an impression after you stare at it for even the briefest moment.

After the security line is a table with pamphlets and program schedules. You're looking through one when you hear a familiar voice. When you look up, you see Ambassador Mays coming down the adjoining hall talking with Agent Howard, the lead investigator on the replacement team.

"Have you been in touch with Agent X?" the Ambassador asks Howard.

"*Romeo Papa* is in place, Colonel."

When they spot you, Agent Howard says, "The cooperating witness."

"Ah, yes!" the Ambassador says, putting his hand out for you to shake. "On behalf of your country, let me thank you very much for all you've done. It's been an enormous help, I'm sure."

You shoot a look at Agent Howard. "Happy to do my part."

"What brings you to the Energy Summit?" Howard asks.

"Oh, just a love of science."

"Fantastic! We need more people with an interest in new energy. It's the future, you know," the Ambassador says, his politician's grin shining brightly.

"If you'll excuse us," Agent Howard says.

You nod and watch as they continue down the hallway.

Something else catches your attention. Even though you were expecting him, you're shocked that he's actually here. You rub your eyes, but there he is, in the flesh—the man with the shimmering, gunmetal-blue eyes.

The suspect doesn't see you just yet. When he spots Ambassador Mays, though, hatred fills his eyes. He slips his backpack off one shoulder and reaches into it—

"Look out!" you cry.

Howard and Ambassador Mays turn back to you as the suspect removes a small metal grapefruit-sized object from his backpack. He twists the device, *clicking* it into place, then throws it underhand straight at the Ambassador.

"Bomb!" Howard shouts, rushing to protect his boss.

The mystery man turns and sprints around the next corner while the DSS agent tries to shield the diplomat. The device flashes and rearranges itself like an automated Rubik's Cube before it finally detonates. But rather than exploding, it *im*plodes. The bomb sucks the air from the hallway like a black hole, and the change in pressure cracks and nearly brings down the ceiling.

Oxygen is ripped from your lungs and you fall to the floor like you've just been gut-punched. After an instant, you gulp air back in with the ferocity of a skindiver just returning from a record descent. You push off the floor on your hands and knees and move toward the Ambassador.

The devastation is immense; it's likely many of the people in the hall are dead. You're lucky to be so far away from the bomb—you're all lucky that the hallway was open; otherwise there'd be no air to breathe after the initial blast.

The suspect reappears briefly, to see if his bomb did the job. Upon seeing that you are up and able, he turns and runs. Without thinking, you grab Agent Howard's handgun from him as you go by and chase after the suspect, who flies down the hallway toward the emergency exit. You don't have enough energy to pursue him.

The hallway is clear.

- Shoot him in the back. Go to page 141
- Watch him go, then see if you can help the wounded men. Go to page 93

Escaped

The blue-eyed man outruns you, flees from the scene, and is never heard from again. The deadly assassination attempt was a failure and the Ambassador is still alive, but Jane Nightingale's killer will never be brought to justice.

You'll often think back, later in life, on that moment when you *almost* caught a killer.

THE END

Escape from Rio

You run back into the road, hoping you didn't lose much ground, but hoping in vain. As gunshots erupt, echoing off the brick and concrete around you, you turn back and see Viktor fire his AK-47 haphazardly at an Elite Squad policeman—sending the man diving for cover.

But you're not out of the woods yet. The assassin, the Man in Black who's been following you, is on a rooftop in this *favela.* You don't recognize him at first when you start shooting blindly at him, but then your brain recalls his creepy, independently-moving eyes as you escape around the next corner.

"Come on!" Viktor shouts. "We've got to bed down. We find Jane tomorrow!"

➢ *Follow Viktor to a safe house.* Go to page 284

Even the Odds

Catching your breath, you take a seat next to Viktor. Both of you watch out the bus window, waiting until the vehicle has passed safely out of view of the would-be assassin. You've escaped, for now.

"Who was that?" you ask.

Viktor shakes his head. "He must have been following us, waiting until we were alone and exposed."

"But he didn't look like a cop or an agent. He didn't even look Brazilian."

"I don't think he was." Viktor takes off his glasses and uses a handkerchief to wipe the lenses, fogged from sweat. "That man has the look of a professional hitman."

You're not sure how many "hitmen" Viktor has met, but you can't argue; the description is spot-on. Something about that terrifying man reeked of death and destruction.

"So what do we do?"

"What can we do? Dodge bullets and look over our shoulder—or we can fight back. I had hoped to do this like Sherlock Holmes, with brain over brawn, but it appears as if they see me as Jack the Ripper, so that is who I will become. That man, whoever he is, was hired to kill us, which means our enemy is afraid. Now is the time to push back."

"What enemy? Who is it that you think killed Jane?"

Viktor looks around the bus, but no one is paying attention to your conversation. Still, he remains tight-lipped. "I'll explain later, I promise."

You sigh. "Okay, what did you have in mind for the meantime?"

For the first time in a long time, Viktor smiles.

You stand before a storage garage in one of the more neglected parts of town. Viktor opens the padlock and rolls up the metal door to his unit, allowing sunlight into the dark recesses of the storage room.

It's a science lab. You'd expected some sort of weapons cache after the way he just talked about "pushing back," but no, instead, this is where he keeps his experiments. It kind of looks like a meth lab, maybe something out of *Breaking Bad*.

"We're gonna mix chemicals and try to blind the guy? Make pipe bombs?"

He huffs. "Ha! Not exactly."

Viktor steps into the unit, reaches beneath a workbench, and slides a small trunk out along the dusty concrete. He crouches to work the combination of the padlock. When he opens up the trunk, you see it's filled with…spheres.

Six spheres, packed in foam, fill the box from corner to corner.

"What the hell are those?" you say.

He reaches in and presents a sphere to you. It's a metal ball about the size of a grapefruit. It's mechanical, looking much like a tiny "Death Star" from *Star Wars*, but you've never seen anything quite like it.

"This is my own little 'Manhattan Project,'" he says. "I don't *want* to use it, but if things go badly…"

"It's a bomb?"

"In a manner of speaking, yes. But unlike a bomb, there is no explosion here. This device creates a rapid chemical reaction that consumes all oxygen, endothermically and not exothermically, essentially *sucking* the air out of a room. It minimizes damage to property, thus making for a rather clean kill."

"You… invented this?"

"More like *discovered*, but yes. Every new weapon was once a scientific discovery: metallurgy, gunpowder, even splitting the atom. I recognized the potential in militarizing this discovery, but I want to help people, not kill them. Well, maybe kill a few, specific people…"

You shake your head. "How about—I don't know—a gun?"

He nods. "Of course, but these can do in a pinch. In order to activate the weapon, you must rotate the top section, see? Left, right, then left once more. Remember that, okay? We'll buy guns in the *favela* tomorrow, but it's getting late and we don't want to go in there after dark. I've got something better in store for tonight."

Viktor packs a backpack full of the mystery objects.

After leaving the storage unit, you hike up to a secluded hilltop: a private clearing with a view of the city. The aureate clouds billow brightly in preparation for the dusky setting sun.

"What is this?" you ask.

"Something palate-uh—" he says, trying to find the word. "Something *pleasing* after such a bestial day. You are a tourist, yes? I don't want you associating my city with depressing sights. You won't find this spot on your map."

There's a naturally smooth and level stone, still warmed by the day's sun. It's perfect for sitting and enjoying the view. From your perch on the rock, your hand reaches into a crevice and your middle finger catches the lip of something. It's a rolled-up note!

"Viktor—look," you say, pulling it free and discovering the clue:

From the source of love to the source of hate.
Come and find me, before it's too late.

"What does it mean?"

"I'm not sure," he confesses with a grimace. "Jane must have left this here in case anything happened to her…."

"Maybe it's time to fill me in. I can't help you if I'm kept in the dark."

"Maybe it is, only… once you cross this line, you can't go back. They want me dead for what I know; that's my burden, not yours. If I fill you in, as you say, the only way out is through evidence and the press. Otherwise, you help me as much as you can, but you're wearing a parachute of deniability should they take us in. What do you say?"

- "Enough cloak-and-dagger stuff; I'm ready!" Go to page 256
- "Keep it to yourself. Your reasons are your own." Go to page 259

Evident

Viktor and Jane review several scanned documents on the laptop. As a layperson, it's hard to make out exactly what you're looking at, but from what you can tell, it appears to be official correspondence. If they've got the Ambassador's signature approving elicit dealings, and can reliably prove they weren't forgeries, Colonel Mays is in a tight spot.

"Couldn't he just claim you faked these documents?" you ask.

Jane smiles. "He ordered the originals destroyed, but they never were. I have them in a safe-deposit box."

"Smart," you say.

Viktor kisses her on the cheek. You're back in Rio before sunset and presently look out the window towards Rio's enormous crowds forming for *Carnaval* and the Energy Summit.

Viktor turns to you and says, "This is it, Tourist. The grand finale. Thanks to André, the police are looking for him rather than myself, and they think Jane here is dead, so we should be able to sneak in undetected."

"What about me?" you ask.

"You're still anonymous. After tonight, win or lose, the world will know who you are."

"Unless…" Jane says.

You look from Viktor to Jane and back again.

"Unless you're ready to retire," Viktor says. "You've done so much for us. This—tonight—is our fight. You don't need to risk your life any further."

"Look for us on the news," Jane says. "There should be live coverage. I'm going to upload the evidence onto the Energy Summit computer system and project it on the main screen during the opening ceremonies. Then Viktor will arrive on stage, proclaim his innocence, and condemn these two evil Kings while everyone is there to see it."

- "Okay… Good luck. I'll want to meet for champagne after you're successful." Go to page 263
- "Seriously? So close to the finish line? No way you're leaving me here!" Go to page 309

Facts & Food

"Ever have *churrasco*?" Agent Bertram asks when he picks you up. Before you can answer, he adds, "There's a great place near here."

Flames leap out from the kitchen, kissing the meat as the chefs rotate each skewer, trying to keep in as much of the juices as they can. You're in the *Churrascaria* now, a high-end restaurant dedicated to Brazilian beef. *Churrasco* is synonymous with barbeque in this country, and they have a specialized way of cooking it. The sizzling spit from the grill and the smell coming from the kitchen is intoxicating and on an empty stomach, you start to salivate.

"You're in for a treat, Hotshot. Good luck looking the same at steak back in the US ever again."

"Is that all they serve here?" you ask.

"What more do you need? You're an American, goddammit. Eat some red meat."

The server arrives wearing *gaucho* attire: wide pants tapered into boots, a flowing blouse beneath a tight vest, a red scarf about the neck, and a broad, flat-brimmed hat. Bertram banters with him in Portuguese and then orders for the two of you. Over a glass of red wine, you share the details of your respective oil company interviews.

"If anything, they're *excited* by the prospect of new energy—not threatened by the possible disappearance of fossil fuels at all," you say.

"Ditto," Bertram sighs. "I really thought we might be on to something with the Big Oil idea. I'm half-tempted to cancel with Volkswagen, but we've come all this way…."

"When do we see them?"

"First thing in the morning. I'm going to check in with good ol' Stewie Danly and see if he's got any better leads."

Agent Bertram starts thumbing away at his smart phone, leaving you with your thoughts. Feeling buzzed on red wine, you admire one of the folk paintings nearby. They've certainly done a good job romanticizing the *gaucho* South American cowboy.

"Jesus." He looks up from the phone. "He's going into the slums on a night Op. I may not like the guy, but that takes balls."

"To what end?"

"He doesn't say. He—" the phone buzzes in his hand and he looks down. "Sneaky bastard… Looks like our friend Viktor's been busy."

You take another sip of wine, waiting for him to continue.

After he finishes scrolling, he looks up. "Our guys on the background team double-checked his history. Pretty standard on high-profile cases to run it again, but this time certain facts have gone *missing*. The son of a bitch is erasing himself! Trying to delete his online presence so it's harder to find him."

"What's gone?"

"His university profile, gone. His employment history and resume, gone. If you look now, it's as if he was never on the Energy Summit lineup. Goddamned hobgoblin—no wonder we can't find any pictures of the guy; who knows how long he's been at it! I bet he's been holed up somewhere with a laptop for the last two days trying to cover his trail. It's not enough to physically disappear these days; now you have to hide from the Internet too.

"All right. Talk to me no more of murder," he says as the food arrives. "Tomorrow we're back on the case with VW—tonight? *Bon appetit*!"

After a night in a hotel much less posh than Rio's Copacabana Palace, you're up early for the meeting with Volkswagen. The drive to the plant is a long one. The hotel breakfast was traditional Brazilian: meat, cheese and bread, and coffee. São Bernardo do Campo is just outside of São Paulo, and once you free yourself from the city traffic, the distance between the two cities is not great.

Before you enter the front doors of—you guessed it—a skyscraper, Bertram says, "I want you to take lead on this one. I'd like to try and evaluate from the sidelines, see if I can increase my powers of perception. Think you can handle that, Hotshot?"

You say yes and proceed inside. The man who greets you is a middle-aged European with wireframe glasses. His head is shaved bald and he wears an expensive suit. With an accent befitting the German automaker, the man introduces himself as Heinrich Renfield.

"Renfield….Is that English?" Bertram asks.

"Indeed! My father is an expatriate, but my mother is full German."

"Convenient background for working at a multinational corporation."

"As you say, sir. How may I help you?"

Bertram nods to you.

"Your company was specifically mentioned by the Energy Summit chairman," you say. "Can you tell us why that is?"

"Ah, we have quite the reputation in Brazil," he replies with a proud smile. "The people here are pioneers of ethanol, and we're often credited with that breakthrough. Without a boring history lesson, let me simply say: Alcohol-powered vehicles were not very practical for city driving, as they took time to 'warm up.' In 2003, we developed the first practical flex-fuel engine and ethanol was finally able to take off. 85 percent of cars on the road in São Paulo are now flex-fuel and since *álcool* is cheaper than gas here, most go straight for the ethanol.

"Boring enough for you?" he chuckles.

"So you must be familiar with the work of Doctor Viktor Lucio de Ocampo?" you ask.

"Of course! We helped him with some of his energy grants in *Deutschland.*"

"Oh? Please go on."

"I can talk your ear off on the science he was working on, truly."

- "Skip it. Why was he important? Why was he banned?" Go to page 180
- "If it's relevant to the Energy Summit, we'd like to hear it." Go to page 114

Fanning the Flames

Viktor embraces you with surprising strength, pressing his lips to yours and sending warmth down into you like a rush of wildfire. For now, there is nothing but the two of you. You have no wine, but you do have the heat of the jungle and the intensity of the moment.

His hands knowingly explore your body with a practiced lover's confidence and before you know what's happened, your clothes and his have blended together to form a blanket, atop which you blend together in your own way.

You share a cigarette, sitting atop the rock and overlooking the city once more. The urban lights have replaced the sun, and shine out to match the radiance you feel within.

"Forgive me," he says, crushing the butt of the cigarette into the rock. "We *Brasileiros* are a passionate people and I let my passion get the better of me. We must focus on finding Jane's killer."

"Sure," you say, playing it cool. "It's good we got that out of the way. So what's next?"

"She left us bread crumbs, and if we can retrodict the facts with the evidence, then maybe we'll find the whole loaf. Once we have proof—then we go to the press."

"Not the police?"

"There's a long track record here of inconvenient evidence conveniently getting lost. Tomorrow we head to the *favelas*. With enough bribes, we may just be able to find the trail. Let's sleep here tonight. It's warm enough, and I'm a little worried about that assassin finding us if we go back to either the hostel or André's."

➢ *Get some rest and start fresh in the morning.* Go to page 215

Femme Fatale

Irma responds to your embrace with electricity and you soon find yourself entangled on the hostel bed. She straddles you, rising only long enough to pull the soccer jersey over her head, and then lowers herself upon you to please you with an intensity you've never known before.

Irma Dos Santos sits up in bed, smoking a cigarette. She offers it to you and you see a profound sadness come over her countenance.

"I'm sorry…" she says. "I have a confession to make, and I'm afraid you'll hate me for it. I never thought…I think I'm falling for you. That makes things difficult. I don't want to. Please don't hate me, okay?"

"What is it?"

She takes a deep breath and lets it out slowly. "The note missing from the crime scene. I—I took it."

All the post-coital relaxation is gone from your body and you're shot right back into stress. "Irma, why would you do that?"

"My chief knew it would be there; he told me to dispose of it. And he told me…" she looks at you with glistening seawater eyes, "not to solve your case."

You're stunned into silence.

"I took you out tonight because I thought you might spoil things for Agent Danly. I'm so sorry."

"Why?" you ask her.

"I love you, I know that now."

"No!" you jump out of bed. "*WHY!?* Why would you do all of this?"

Her lip quivers. "You don't understand how hard it is for a woman cop in Rio. Chief said he had his reasons, and that I would be rewarded for my loyalty. Sometimes you have to make sacrifices…"

"I thought your partner was the dirty one," you say coldly.

"He is," she responds with a sad smile. "But there's a difference between doing something for money and doing it out of loyalty; surely you understand that?"

You don't respond.

"Lucio doesn't know about the note. The Chief doesn't trust him because you can't trust a man who sells his loyalty. I could be chief one day! What is one little wrong if it sets me up for so much good in the future? I can make a difference as chief, clean things up… You're the only person I've told, and I only did so because I love you. I'm sorry. Please, say something."

- "I think it's time you take me back to my hotel." Go to page 300
- "I understand. I don't agree with it, but I understand…" Go to page 196

Field Day

The fresh smell of spring rain that greeted you outside the storage shed is long gone, replaced by the wet fart smell of mud and manure. You move through the sodden sugarcane, muck squishing underfoot, the wet stalks tugging at your clothes, seemingly sharpened by the rainstorm. At least the fire shouldn't pose a threat anymore.

Agent Bertram's satellite phone rings. You and Maria look to him.

"Turn that off, the *grileiros* will hear us!" Maria growls.

"Damn. They know I'm in the field; they wouldn't call unless it was an emergency." Then, opening the phone, he answers the call. "Agent Bertram… Negative, I'm still on scene."

Maria turns to you with eyes wide as the caller speaks. You can't hear the words, but you can hear the angry tone. The pilot draws her pistols, clearly on edge.

"Sir, all due respect, that's bullshit. I haven't even—"

He grits his teeth.

"Yes, sir… yes, sir." He hangs up and says, "We've got to go back."

"What? Why?"

"The official investigation team landed this morning. We're off the case."

"But we haven't even—" you start to say. His glare silences you.

There's a rustling in the cane and Maria takes aim. It's impossible to pinpoint the exact location of the sounds, almost as if they're coming from everywhere.

"We're too exposed," Bertram says, raising his rifle.

"We need to run!" Maria hisses.

- "Form up, make a triangle back-to-back on me! We shoot to kill!" Go to page 26
- "Let's high-tail it to the plantation! Shoot anybody in our way." Go to page 282
- "Lower your weapons. The only way out of this is surrender." Go to page 188

Flee the *Favela*

You peer out of the curtain beside Viktor, staring into the street with disbelief. What's spread out before you is something out of a war zone. The Elite Squad armored vehicle lumbers down the street, its metal surface singing out with rejected bullets. There are tiny portholes on the sides, just big enough for the barrel of an assault rifle to fit through. The portholes are presently being filled by the guns of Elite Squad members, who are firing haphazardly at the drug traffickers engaging them from the street.

Gunshots light up darkened doorways and windows. Two traffickers are perched on a rooftop across from you, but they're too focused on the armored vehicle to notice you.

"*Caveirão,*" Viktor informs with awed whisper. "We need to get out of here, but we can't just run…"

The battle rages on, gunshots pinging off the armored car as if lamenting their own inefficiency. A young drug trafficker steps out of a house and hurls a *grenade* at the vehicle. It's a quick movement, and he's safely back inside again before the police can shoot him.

You duck inside the hovel with Viktor just as the grenade explodes. After the dust settles, you check back and it appears the *caveirão* is unharmed. Not even the tires are punctured; this thing is a beast.

And now it's angry.

The tires screech as the thing darts forward under full acceleration. Since the front end is reinforced, covered with an extra-thick cattle guard, the vehicle doesn't feel much when it *smashes* into the building head-on and punches a hole through the poorly constructed brick and mortar. Pulling back with equal force, the vehicle retreats away from the damaged home as the roof collapses.

"If they bring that *caveirão* this way, we're dead."

"What we need is a distraction," you say.

Movement on the rooftop across the way catches your eye. There's another trafficker coming out, holding an RPG—the guy has a fucking *rocket launcher*! He crouches down on one knee, takes aim, and prepares to fire.

"Like that!" Viktor cries, "Let's go!"

As a testament to their skill, the top of the armored car flips open, and an Elite Squad member bursts forth from the cylindrical hatch, firing his rifle as he emerges.

No time to take aim, yet incredibly, he hits the RPG-wielding gang member. Only winged, the trafficker fires a wild shot; the rocket-propelled grenade flies off, spiraling out of control.

Viktor sprints out of the hovel just as the rocket *explodes* into a nearby building, the tremors on the street and the rain of debris buying you a momentary reprieve as both the drug lords and the policemen take cover. You're right behind him, but before you make it into the intersection across the street, you're spotted by Elite Squad.

With Viktor holding an AK-47 and you holding a sub-machinegun, you're taken as threats. Bullets scream out across the pavement—barely missing you as you run into the narrow road and away from the *caveirão*.

Viktor spots an open door and takes the opportunity to run in. You follow, only to find he's led you into a dead end. Clearly, he was hoping for a rear exit and not another home to get trapped in. He looks at you with frightened desperation in his eyes.

- Go back out and keep running through the street. Go to page 94
- Use the door for cover and fire at any Elite Squad that try to follow. Go to page 312
- "Let's get down and hide here!" Go to page 185

Flandering

He eyes you with suspicion. "You're American, no?"

"I'm studying at the university," you say, your mind racing.

"What are you studying?"

"Uh, Portuguese?" You wince inside as you say it.

"*Você fala Português, então*?"

"I, um, just started…"

Another cop walks over toward the barricade. "Hey, weren't you at the station tonight? What are you doing here?"

You're about to try and talk your way out of it, but the first cop leans forward, looking toward the back of the house, and says, "What the hell is going on over there?"

You see Viktor hanging out of the window, trying to push his way out. Apparently he's finished his part of the bargain, so time to finish yours—distraction!

- Kick the policeman in the groin and/or punch him in the face. Go to page 242
- Sprint inside a random apartment. The police can't follow without a warrant! Go to page 278

Floundering

"That's just crazy enough to work," he says.

Viktor sneaks around the periphery of the apartments, getting closer to the back of Jane's unit while trying to remain unseen. You casually stroll over to the police barricade the policeman standing there puts out his hand to stop you. He says something in Portuguese while shaking his head "no." Oh boy, here goes nothing.

"What's happened? Is everything okay?"

"Please don't worry. We have it under control," the policeman says.

Casting a sideways glance, you see Viktor slip inside one of the back windows. The policeman starts to follow your gaze, so you press forward.

- "Let me in, I can help! I'm her neighbor." Go to page 105
- "I'm with the American agents; they'll be joining me shortly. What have you found here so far?" Go to page 241

Forgotten

The man's smile disappears and Maria's revolvers rise. Before she has a chance to shoot the Sugar King, however, his security team opens fire, shooting each of you in the back and stopping the attack before it begins.

With a victor's smile, the man walks over toward where the three of you lie bleeding but not yet dead.

"How do you…expect to get away with…?" Bertram groans.

"I will make a call to the police soon. Did you forget that your helicopter had crashed? Surely no one could walk away from such an accident. The three of you are just walking ghosts."

"Bastard," Maria says.

"Do not worry, you will be returned to the aircraft and each of you will receive a warrior's burial—purified by fire. This way it's much harder to find any traces of the bullets. You will be identified by dental records; they'll know it was you. You will be mourned."

He signals for his men to finish you off.

THE END

Fox and Hound

You dash to the edge of the building and slide over the side, lowering yourself down. Irma is right behind you as you rush out into the street. Two Elite Squad members remain by the armored car and one shouts at you as you dash across the road. He brings his rifle up to his shoulder.

You make it into the alley. Jesus, was he going to shoot you? You keep running, afraid to look back and see if he's coming after you, praying he'll stay there to guard the vehicle.

"Keep going!" Irma shouts from behind. And though there's not enough air in the world to fill your burning lungs, you sprint on.

The mystery man steps out from one of the homes, an AK-47 pointed at your chest, his blue eyes glaring at you coldly. Your legs try to bring you to a halt before your brain processes what you see, but it's not quick enough. You plow into the rifle, the hard metal slamming into your sternum and taking away what little breath you had. You fall to the alley floor, wheezing.

The man, who looks more like a drug lord's accountant than one of their enforcers, shouts at you in Portuguese. Irma ducks down, ostensibly checking to see if you're okay, but uses you as a distraction to go for a handgun strapped to her ankle.

- Lunge at the bastard. Go to page 189
- Raise your hands and shout "Turista!" repeatedly. Go to page 57

Free as a Bird

On the rooftop, a welcome breeze helps wick the sweat from your skin. The sun shines brightly but your prospects do not. There's a fire escape ladder headed down, but when you get close enough to look over the edge of the roof, a hail-storm of bullets whips by your head. Well, you've certainly painted yourself into a pretty little corner, now haven't you?

With certain death coming at you from below, a concrete handi-capable ramp on the far end of the roof catches your eye. If you hit it fast enough, you could launch yourself over the guard barrier. And since your other option is bullets, what've you got to lose? Who knows, maybe that trash truck is still circling down below and you'll land amongst the cushy garbage. Or maybe you'll fall into the branches of a tree and *Tarzan* your way down.

Or maybe you'll crunch against the pavement.

Pushing the motorbike's engine to its limits, you smack into the base of the ramp, violently bouncing the shocks. But what immediately follows is a feeling of weightlessness. You sail over the guard rail, just like you hoped you would, and into the open sky beyond.

You're several stories off the ground and your outward velocity pushes you further and faster than the gravity trying to bring you down to the ground. In fact, you're going to smash into the office building next to the consulate long before you hit the street. Then, by some miracle of timing, you head straight for a large window.

With better luck than an action star could hope for, your motorcycle crashes through the window and into the office building. Using adrenaline-fueled reflexes, you swerve around cubicles and office workers, eventually crashing the bike into a water cooler.

You jump off the motorcycle and dash past the terrified office workers. There's an exit sign above the far door, so you sprint that way and slam into it. When you open the door, stairs—glorious stairs—are there. You rush down, unable to believe you made it through this thing in one piece, and run out the back of the building.

Time to go meet Viktor for pizza. And a beer. Yeah, you could sure use a beer…

➢ *Head to the restaurant.* Go to page 338

She looks from you to the agent.

Bertram sighs. "I'm in enough shit as it is," he says. "But I'd do the same thing for my family. If you want to go, I won't stop you."

Maria smiles and her eyes shimmer with emotion. She steps over to the security booth and returns with the second revolver and two sets of car keys. She puts a set in Bertram's hand and at the same moment rushes in for a kiss. Though it lasts only a fleeting instant, the passion is undeniable.

Without a word, she slips out the front door. Neither of you will ever see her again.

"Goddamn. I'm gonna have a hell of a time explaining this," Bertram says. "Come on, Hotshot. Rio's waiting."

- *Leave the jungle for the consulate.* Go to page 273

The Future is Now

The man who introduces himself is bookish, lean, in his fifties. He looks like he could've been a scientist once, but has evolved into a businessman over the years. He's certainly not the man you saw at the crime scene.

"Italo Fellini," he says, saying his first name with a soft 'I' (eee-tall-oh), shaking hands with each of you. "Welcome! I'm told you have questions about the Energy Summit."

"You're Italian?" Bertram asks, taking a seat.

The man sits as well. "That's my heritage, but I'm a born *Paulista*."

"So why's your conference in Rio then, Mr. Fellini?"

"Ah, you know how they can be—so tetchy. Please, call me Italo."

Agent Bertram nods. "Indeed, they can be. Just as *Paulistas* can be…a little elitist, no?"

The businessman laughs. "We had a drawing. Rio won this time around, but it'll be good for them. What with this, the World Cup, and the Olympics, they might just be a real, grown-up city when they're done."

"And the conference coinciding with *Carnaval*, whose idea was that?"

"*Brasileiros* like to mix business with pleasure. It's a wonderful opportunity for our foreign guests to get a taste of our culture—the Energy Summit will take place during the day, and we'll unwind in the streets of *Carnaval* at night."

"Makes sense," you say. "Many American businessmen meet their foreign counterparts in Las Vegas for the very same reason."

"Exactly," Italo Fellini responds. "So…questions?"

"Give us a brief overview of the conference, please," Bertram asks.

"I can give you our press brief, if that will help, but the short version is this: The world is growing while our energy supplies are dwindling. We need new, more efficient, cheaper, renewable resources for a sustainable future. *Brasil* is already the world leader in ethanol production, meaning we're less dependent on oil than other countries, but that's only a start.

"Our presenters aren't here just to 'go green' but to change the world! Top scientists from around the globe will present their research findings, propose new ways forward, and—unlike any other energy conference—receive direct corporate financial attention and grants. Our Energy Summit will be packed with investors, ready to grow rich by making the world a better place. There's been a lot of negative press about 'corporate greed' over the years, stories of heartless companies making profits at humanity's expense, but what if corporations could make money by *benefiting* mankind? It's the ultimate win-win, and it starts here."

"And who are your biggest investors?" Bertram asks, taking notes.

"Oh, we have many. *Petrobras*, of course. They're the largest energy company in South America and they were our first sponsor. We also have major interest from British Petroleum, and other multinational corporations."

"Wait…the oil companies are signing on for alternative fuel research?" you ask.

"Of course! The world is changing, my friend. Anyone who doesn't want to end up fossilized must change with it. Volkswagen is a great example. They're the very reason we can use ethanol so successfully in this country, and they're excited to be a part of our next step."

"Which leads us to Viktor Lucio de Ocampo," Bertram says. "What can you tell us about him?"

"The doctor is a brilliant inventor," Fellini says. "I sincerely believed he was going to be the one to change the world with his biofuel patents."

"*Was*," you reply. "Until he was crossed off the program lineup."

"Can you tell us why the doctor was blacklisted?"

Italo Fellini pauses for a moment, looking at his folded hands in thought. He rises, taking a moment to gaze out into the distance before saying, "I'm afraid I cannot."

Bertram leans forward in earnest. "Please, this is for a murder investigation. Whatever you can tell us could help take a killer off the streets."

"I'm truly sorry," he replies. "I'd love to help, but our sponsors have their reasons."

"We could return with a court order," you say.

"And you'd find the non-disclosure agreement I signed would stop your progress." He isn't being smug, he's just telling you where you stand. This is clearly a dead end.

"Which sponsor was it? Just tell us that," Bertram asks.

"Now, please," he says, shaking his head. "You're barking up the wrong tree, trust me. Go back to Rio and simply investigate from there. You're wasting your time here; as you say, there's a killer on the streets."

The gravity of his tone stuns you into silence.

"I must go now. I've told you all I can, and I'm a busy man."

"We'll see you at the Energy Summit," Bertram says.

Italo Fellini frowns, shakes his head in disappointment, and walks away.

You turn to Bertram. "The sponsors. We should check the press release to see who else is on that list, but he specifically mentioned the oil companies."

"Right, BP and *Petrobras*," he says, checking his notebook. "He also mentioned Volkswagen.

"All right, we're short on time and long on suspects. Only two days until the Energy Summit; I think we might need to split up. These corporations will all have someone who speaks English, so you'll be fine there. How about this: we each take an oil company, then meet up and talk with VW?"

- "I'll take BP. He said *Petrobras* is the state-run company, so I think you might be able to swing your diplomatic weight better there." Go to page 20
- "I'll take *Petrobras*—maybe I can play the role of tourist and catch them off-guard while you look into BP's dirty secrets." Go to page 248

Ganging Up

She asks, then interprets his reply. "Yeah, he says the Shadow Chiefs are involved in everything, but to me it just sounds like machismo. Then he says that he'll take you to the rest of the gang so you can ask them yourself. After that he talks about what he'd do to you if we didn't have guns trained on him, but I don't want to repeat that. It's…very explicit."

Bastard. He's stalling, you can tell that much without any need for translation. You probably won't get another opportunity like this and he's wasting it—your jaw tightens.

Through gritted teeth, you say, "Motivate him to be more specific."

Irma pistol-whips the young drug trafficker again and waits for a response. He spits once more, this time sending a tooth across the concrete floor. His only reply now is a string of swear words.

- "Keep going. Make him talk." Go to page 326
- "We don't need to waste our time on this punk. Let's go see what Agent Danly has found." Go to page 78

Geeking Out

"You asked for it!" he laughs. "Okay, so ethanol has long been touted as the 'fuel of the future.' In your country, massive subsidies for corn ethanol have tried, with little success, I'm afraid, to push ethanol to the forefront. But you see, even though corn ethanol is 22 percent cleaner than gasoline, a gallon of ethanol is only 67percent as effective as a gallon of gas and the energy gained is debatable. Best estimates give ethanol an energy input-to-output ratio of 1:1.3. That is to say, the energy it takes to produce one unit of ethanol will give you an energy output of one-point-three. Meaning you have only one-third of a unit of energy left over to use in your car or what-have-you, which is not very much, comparatively.

"Take ethanol compared to biodiesel, for example. Biodiesel is 86 percent as effective as conventional, fossil-fuel diesel, but the energy input/output ratio is 1:2.5, or *more than twice as effective* as corn ethanol. Additionally, biodiesel is 68 percent cleaner than diesel—compared to corn ethanol being only 22 percent cleaner than gas, if you recall. We use a lot of biodiesel in Germany, and have had some success with it, but *nothing* compared to what Brazil has done thus far.

"Here they use sugarcane ethanol, which is a big difference. Sugarcane has an input/output ratio of 1:8, that's *eight times* more efficient, and it's 56 percent cleaner than gasoline! They have government subsidies here too, which is why the ethanol is significantly cheaper than gas at the pumps; but the main difference is that sugarcane ethanol production is almost immediately profitable. Do you follow me so far?"

You look to Bertram, who has his notepad out. "Continue," he says with a nod.

"This is where Dr. Viktor Lucio de Ocampo comes in. He's a pioneer in cellulosic ethanol, which is the next step—the next *leap,* really. By some estimates, cellulosic ethanol has a production ratio of 1:36 and is 91 percent cleaner than gasoline. Which is incredible, but I've heard rumors that Viktor has even beaten these estimates in his breakthrough."

"What's cell-you…?" Bertram asks.

"Ah, do forgive me! Cellulosic ethanol is a fuel produced from *any* plant matter, even plant waste. You could use the cornstalks instead of the corn, you could use green waste from your citizens, recycled paper, wild prairie grasses, weeds, lawn clippings, anything!"

"That's incredible," you say.

"Truly. And when we were supporting Viktor's research, he was working on harvesting algae from smokestacks. Which would go further than just clean fuel for our vehicles—with this technology, we could greatly reduce the environmental impact of power plants: cleaning them with the algae and then harvesting the plant-scum for fuel afterwards. It's the closest thing to 'free energy' yet."

"So he's set to be a billionaire," you say.

Mr. Renfield smiles. "If successful, this technology would be needed worldwide and would pervade nearly every industry. We are talking about what might be the world's first *trillion-dollar* idea."

The room is silent for a moment, Bertram stops writing, and the three of you let that notion sink in.

"So why would he be banned from the Energy Summit?" you ask.

"There are always those resistant to change. While the potential of gain is obvious, you must ask yourself, who has the most to lose?"

"Like oil companies?"

He shakes his head. "If anything, they want control of such a commodity. Think of it this way—what does an oil company primarily set out to do?"

You say nothing, hoping the question is rhetorical, so it's Bertram who answers. "Sell oil?"

"Precisely. They're *sellers* of a commodity. If a newer, better commodity comes along, they'll just start selling the next big thing. What you need to look for is the *producers*—they're the ones who fear change."

"Those invested in crude oil production?" you try.

He bobbles his head uncertainly. "Perhaps. I'd say you were on to something if he was banned from an Energy Summit hosted by the Arab Emirates, but you're in Brazil. And in Brazil they're producing…?"

Then it clicks. *Sugarcane.* How much sugarcane must be produced and harvested annually if 85 percent of the vehicles run on sugarcane ethanol? And if suddenly sugarcane wasn't needed? If *any* plant would do? Who would lose indeed…?

"Dear God, sugarcane," Bertram says, reaching the same conclusion.

Renfield smiles like a professor whose pupils have finally solved the equation. "The fastest way to become a billionaire in Brazil is with sugarcane production. I don't want to bite the hand that feeds me, but—maybe you should pay a visit to a mill? The Governor of this territory, Mateo Ferro, owns every sugarcane plantation within five hundred miles."

"The so-called Sugar King?" Bertram asks.

"As you say, sir."

Agent Bertram closes his notebook, extends his hand, and says, "Thank you for your time."

Upon leaving, he adds to you, "If we were looking for someone who hates Viktor, we might have a motive, but why the girl? Something doesn't add up. Let's check in at the local consulate and see if Danly has reported in from last night. I'm afraid we might've hit a dead end with this whole Viktor thing. Hopefully Danly's got something."

➢ *Head to the consulate.* Go to page 314

A Gentleman's Agreement

The man takes pity on you and agrees to let you leave. The airlines charge you $300 to change your flight (greedy bastards), and you're off the next day. And not a moment too soon; the whole time it feels like you're being watched—and most likely, you are.

You return home and never hear the results of these odd events. Did they ever catch the killer? Did this man find his fiancée? You'll never know, but you'll always wonder—to your dying day—what would've happened if you'd stayed and helped.

THE END

Get to the Chopper

The fetching young pilot arrives, powers down the helicopter, bounces out in her uniform and aviator sunglasses, and stretches out a map before you to plan your trip into the jungle. The name "Maria" etched on her nametag glitters in the late afternoon sun.

"I will not lie to you, this trip cannot be cheap. Private charter never is, but the distance is great for such a journey," she says.

With a protractor, she draws a circle around your present location and adds, "This is how far I can take you because of fuel, yes?"

"We understand. Can you show us where the sugar plantation *Monopólio* is on the map?" Bertram asks.

Her eyebrows rise. "You have a meeting with the *fazendeiro*?"

Bertram nods, then turns to you and translates, "Plantation owner."

"Ah, yes," you say. "I'm an inspector and this is my bodyguard."

She looks at you, the expression in her eyes hidden behind her mirrored sunglasses and smiles coyly. "As you say. This is no problem; the plantation is within our fuel range."

Soon you're up in the air and on your way. Civilization turns to jungle almost immediately and the scenery goes by in a blur of emerald waves. The smallish helicopter is noisy, but the headsets you all wear make communication possible.

"We've got a problem," the pilot says. "See that up ahead? It's a fire. We're going to have to divert."

On the horizon, thick black smoke rises high into the sky. Maria consults a map strapped to her leg for an alternate route.

Bertram asks, "How far out are we? Is there a problem at the plantation?"

"I don't think so. It is likely because they are clearing forest for farm land. They destroy the land as if on accident, but then they clear it and pretend they owned it all along."

"So… they're stealing it. And they just get away with that?" you say.

"It's very common practice. *Grilagem*—ah, land thieves. There are only a handful of inspectors, and there is so much land, so they can get away with it. Governor Ferro, the man who happens to own *Monopólio* plantation, makes it very easy for such thieves because they make land cheap and available."

"Wait, the Governor? He's in on it?" you ask.

"Yes, of course. You do not know this? They call Mateo Ferro *O Rei do Açúcar*, 'the King of Sugar.' He owns over 350,000 acres of sugarcane land. You see that dirt road below us? It's called the 'Sugar Highway'– it may not be paved, but it's very wide and very long. It is an illegally made road for loggers, ranchers, soy and sugarcane plantation owners. Soon the Governor will have it paved. He grows rich in this way."

"To be honest," Agent Bertram says, "We don't know much about these land sharks. In truth, we're actually law enforcement investigating an American death. The inspector/bodyguard is only our cover story."

"I figured it must be something like this. You should be careful. They have a lot of money, yes? People disappear in the jungle all the time. If the *grileiros* think you are government officials, and that you are all alone, they will kill you."

"*Grileiros*?" you ask.

"*Grileiros* are the hired guns who work for these 'sharks' of land, as you say. They sell off the timber, then clear all remaining plants with fire to make room for cattle and farm owners, who they will sell the land to."

"How do you know so much about this?" Bertram asks. "I grew up here, but in the city I didn't see any of this."

"I did not 'grew up' in the city," she says. "Did you hear of the nun who was killed by *grileiros* when she was trying to stop them from taking land?"

Bertram snaps his fingers. "I do remember hearing about that. She was shot dead for defying them, then they killed the rancher who wouldn't give up his land, right in front of his wife and kids. It was a big deal. When was that? Almost ten years ago?"

She nods. "It was a big deal. I lived out on a ranch then with my family, when I was a little girl. My father did not want to sell, but it was too dangerous. Once they killed the Sister, my father feared we were in too much danger. To kill a nun, this is a great sin. They have no souls, these *grileiros*. My father sold our land and moved our family to the city. Both my mother and father worked two jobs so I could go to school."

"And after all that, you were going to fly us to a business meeting with the man responsible?" you ask.

"To survive in *Brasil*, you have to shut your mouth and play dumb," she says. "But now that I know you will help us, I want to do something. I will not take my fee—you pay for fuel only. I wish I could do more, but…"

"We can't promise anything," Bertram says. "But if the Sugar King is responsible for this girl's death, he will be prosecuted."

She smiles. "It's a good thing you aren't working with the local police, otherwise the *grileiros* would already know you were coming."

Just then you hear a series of metallic raps, the helicopter shakes, and a yellow light flashes on the dashboard. Notes and charts are sucked from their spots inside the aircraft toward three tiny holes in the floor—gunshot-sized holes.

"We've lost oil pressure!" she cries.

"We've been shot!" you call out.

"They must have hit the oil lines."

Then a red indicator goes off, accompanied by a high-pitched beeping. The language of aviation is English, so the two words you see illuminated in red on the dashboard display make your heart stop: "ENGINE FIRE."

"Hold on!" she cries.

Maria pulls on the controls, idling the throttle and effectively turning the helicopter into a brick, taking the nimble craft into a dive. With no throttle, only the air passing through the blades makes them windmill as you plummet toward the earth below.

"It's okay," Bertram calmly says to you.

Despite the confidence in his gravelly voice and saltwater eyes, your stomach turns and your heart rises into your throat. You're falling so quickly that you feel your weight in your shoulders, pressing against your seatbelt rather than against the seat. The blood rushes out of your legs and your body tingles. The ground is getting closer and closer, growing in relative size and proximity at what feels like an exponential rate.

Seconds before hitting the ground, the pilot pulls up on the stick using the rotational speed created by the wind blowing through the blades to create a last-second push of lift. In effect, the helicopter falls from five feet instead of five hundred feet as the rotational energy of the blades is depleted.

Maria may have just saved your lives, but you still slam into the ground with jaw-wrenching force and are momentarily stunned as a result. She took you to the largest clearing available—the middle of the Sugar Highway.

You look around the cabin, stunned. The other two shake their heads, in a similar daze.

"We're alive?" you say.

"Don't forget about those bullet holes, Hotshot," Bertram says, claiming his assault rifle. "Now let's go, they'll come to investigate soon."

"Maybe I can refund the whole trip after all! Hope the boss has *grileiros* insurance…" Maria says, popping open the canopy.

After you step out of the helicopter, you can hear a car engine approaching in the distance.

"We should get off the road," you say.

"Be careful of the sugarcane, that is a place for *serpente.*"

"Snakes?" Bertram asks.

"Yes, that is the word. Snakes are in the fields."

Great, you think.

"Okay, fuck that," Bertram says.

He drops to one knee in the road and wraps the strap of the rifle around his forearm. The agent puts the rifle butt snugly against his shoulder and takes aim down the road. From around the bend, two vehicles appear: the first is a jeep and the second is a light pickup truck. Both are overloaded with *grileiros* and you can see the silhouettes of the firearms they hold in the air.

Crack. Bertram takes a shot. *Crack, crack, crack*. He puts four rounds into the engine block of the jeep, disabling the vehicle with trained efficiency. Bertram rises and starts to walk forward, never lowering the weapon from his line of sight. Three armed *grileiros* exit the jeep, ready to do combat, but Bertram puts them down with one shot each.

The pickup truck does a quick u-turn and burns down the road, fleeing at top speed. The three of you walk over toward the jeep, Agent Bertram keeping his rifle at the ready.

"Dead," Maria confirms when you arrive. "All three."

"So's the jeep," Bertram says. "We'll have to walk."

You say nothing.

"They drew first blood with the 'chopper," Bertram explains. "Once shots are fired, deadly force is authorized."

"The world is better without scum like that," Maria says. She spits on the dirt for emphasis, then adds, "There will be more coming. The helicopter was meant to be a warning, I think. Next will be war."

You look down at the bodies of the three dead men. One had a pump-action shotgun and the other two each carried a revolver. They were probably used to intimidating locals without so much as a shot fired in resistance. Now, against an elite DSS agent, they didn't stand a chance.

"Arm up," Bertram commands. "Hotshot, go for the shotgun. You're on snake patrol."

Maria takes both revolvers, one in each hand. You and Bertram both look incredulous.

She smiles. "Helicopter piloting requires many tasks of our hands and we often become—umm—both-handed, yes?"

"Ambidextrous," you say.

She nods, pointing the pistols at the dead men. You look away, assessing the situation. The fire causes a ruby glow on the eastern horizon, and the setting sun brings a similar resplendent light to the west, so that the whole sky is bathed in red.

"It'll be dark soon," you say, adding:

- "We should hide out in the cane." Go to page 265
- "Let's seek refuge at the plantation." Go to page 260

The Getaway

You follow Agent Bertram as he jogs down the hallway of the Energy Summit conference grounds. He's constantly stopping, checking rooms, coveys, and alcoves for signs of the RSO or any other law-enforcement presence.

Then an explosion rocks the building.

Agent Bertram unholsters his handgun, carries it high, and sprints toward the chaos while terrified civilians run in the opposite direction. In the confusion, you barely notice one man fleeing—a bespectacled scientist wearing a backpack and running away from the explosion. When he throws a quick glance over his shoulder, you notice his haunting blue eyes.

"Stop right there!" Bertram cries.

Instead, Viktor crashes through an emergency exit and out of the conference grounds. Bertram barrels towards the suspect, flying down the hallway at top speed, ready to apprehend him and end this thing once and for all.

You're right behind him, losing yourself in the *samba*-fueled dance party that is *Carnaval*. People are everywhere—if Viktor gets even a ten-second lead on you, he'll be lost in the crowd and will most certainly escape.

People on the street don't seem to notice you, and those who do try their best to avoid the armed American and his prey. Except for one: a devil. A hulking man in glimmering black body paint, his body firm and muscular like an MMA champion fighter's. His face is painted white over black, like a bleached skull (the only color on his otherwise black painted body) and his shaved head is topped with long, twisted ram's horns. A thick scar covers his chin.

His great bulk and musculature first catch your attention, but the fact that he's jogging *toward* you is what keeps it. Then his eyes move in two different directions.

"Devil Ray!" you shout.

Bertram looks back. The assassin, who apparently takes his nickname quite literally, holds a pitchfork and removes the outer two prongs—which were actually affixed handguns.

Like an Old West draw in the crowded streets, there's a second-long eternity where the men size one another up, neither willing to make the first move. Then, lightning-fast, both gunmen go for the attack—Agent Bertram raises his handgun just as the assassin aims his own weapons. It's to be a photo-finish, and gunshots ring out in stereo.

Your mind dully recognizes the boom of the handguns, but no one's moving. They just stand there, pistols raised as if nothing ever happened. Did they actually shoot? Has time stopped? Smoke curling off the gun barrels belies the truth and the men fall to the ground in unison.

You rush over to Agent Bertram's side. He's wounded, but appears to be alive. *O Jamanta,* on the other hand, is no more. The assassin is dead. Bertram groans in pain.

Viktor—the *real* Viktor—has stopped and now looks at you. After a moment's hesitation, he takes off again, sprinting through the crowd.

- Take Bertram's handgun—go get the bastard! Go to page 151
- Stay to make sure Bertram lives. Go to page 267

A Ghost of the Past

Viktor doles out his first bribe and asks the question. Accepting the money, Tinho looks up at a crack in the ceiling, thinking before he answers.

"*Narcotraficantes,*" he says, "*de cocaína.*"

"Drug traffickers," Viktor translates.

"Ask him why," you suggest. "And ask how he knows."

Tinho explains to Viktor, but you see Viktor's brow furrow. "*Como*?" Viktor starts yelling, the conversation growing heated.

Turning to you, he says, "This guy's feeding us bullshit. I think he's pumping us for money and just making it up as he goes along. He says 'because her brother came looking for her.' Jane didn't have a brother. He doesn't know anything, let's go."

"Where to?"

"Well, I have an idea, but it's dangerous. Each *favela* has at least one cop on the payroll. We find out which dirty cop works the territory of the warehouse crime scene, and we bribe him for information."

"How do we find *that* out?" you ask.

"There are two professions here where paying off cops is part of their business insurance. Drug traffickers and prostitutes."

- "Wait, let's hear him out. Why does he think traffickers did it?" Go to page 173
- "I don't trust him, either. Okay, how do we find a drug trafficker?" Go to page 211
- "Yeah, this guy gives me the creeps. Let's talk to a working girl." Go to page 72

Viktor doles out his first bribe and asks the question. Accepting the money, Tinho smiles.

"He says of course they're after us. That we're smart to have bought weapons."

"Who? Who is after us?" you ask.

Tinho looks to the ceiling and scratches his chin before answering. Viktor translates, "Police, gangs, everyone."

"How does he know?"

Tinho explains to Viktor, but you see Viktor's brow furrow. "*Como*?" Viktor starts yelling, the conversation growing heated.

Turning to you, he says, "This guy's feeding us bullshit. I think he's pumping us for money and just making it up as he goes along. He says 'because 'the colonel' put a bounty my head.' But I called his bluff, he doesn't know who I am. He doesn't know anything, let's go."

"Where to?"

"Well, I have an idea, but it's dangerous. Each *favela* has at least one cop on the payroll. We find out which dirty cop works the territory of the warehouse crime scene, and we bribe him for information."

"How do we find *that* out?" you ask.

"There are two professions here where paying off cops is part of their business insurance. Drug traffickers and prostitutes."

- "Wait, let's hear him out. Why does he think there's a bounty?" Go to page 173
- "I don't trust him, either. Okay, how do we find a drug trafficker?" Go to page 211
- "Yeah, this guy gives me the creeps. Let's talk to a working girl." Go to page 72

The Ghost Yet to Come

Viktor doles out his first bribe and then describes your would-be assassin to the man. For the first time, Tinho's smile fades. "*Jamanta*?" he asks.

He shares a brief, impassioned conversation with your partner, and you wait for the translation.

"We're in more trouble than I thought," Viktor says. "This is a well-known assassin. Some say he's an American operative, some say he's former Elite Squad, some say both. The more superstitious think he's the Angel of Death. They call him the Stingray or Devil Ray, and they say once he has you in his sights, you're already dead—you just don't know it yet."

With a thick feeling of dread, you say, "Who does he work for?"

Viktor asks and soon gets an answer. "He says *Jamanta* is out for revenge, for what we've done."

"Which is…?

Tinho explains to Viktor, but you see Viktor's brow furrow. "*Como*?" Viktor starts yelling, the conversation growing heated.

Turning to you, he says, "This guy's feeding us bullshit. I think he's pumping us for money and just making it up as he goes along. He says 'because we killed that girl.' He doesn't know anything, let's go."

"Where to?"

"Well, I have an idea, but it's dangerous. Each *favela* has at least one cop on the payroll. We find out which dirty cop works the territory of the warehouse crime scene, and we bribe him for information."

"How do we find *that* out?" you ask.

"There are two professions here where paying off cops is part of their business insurance. Drug traffickers and prostitutes."

- "Wait, let's hear him out. Why does he think we did it?" Go to page 173
- "I don't trust him, either. Okay, how do we find a drug trafficker?" Go to page 211
- "Yeah, this guy gives me the creeps. Let's talk to a working girl." Go to page 72

Going Green

Bertram nods with a resigned smile and bids you goodnight. The next morning, over breakfast, you meet with the hotel's business relations manager. It's no coincidence that DS put you up at the Copacabana Palace, one of the most prestigious five-star hotels in the world. This is *the* spot for all visiting dignitaries, billionaire investors, and corporate CEOs who will be in attendance at the Energy Summit. Though the main conference center will be in a theater down the street, the Copacabana Palace's many ballrooms are reserved for "high-level" private presentations. Come Friday, the DSS agents will help provide security for these dignitaries—though the agents themselves must sleep in their own apartments or less exotic (i.e., less expensive) hotels.

"You speak Portuguese, yes?" the man asks.

He's middle-aged, well-dressed, with salt-and-pepper hair in a friar's crown, and has a pot belly despite his spindly arms and legs. Probably from all the drinks he shares with potential clients.

"I do. But my friend here does not," Agent Bertram replies.

"Ah, English it is, then. No matter, most of our clients don't speak the language. I don't often get to have a professional conversation in my own tongue, so I thought....Anyway, how can I be of help?"

"What can you tell us about the Energy Summit?"

"Oh, I could talk your ear off for days!" he chuckles. "What do you want to know? The Copacabana has made strident green energy efforts over the last few years to become the most modernly powered hotel in all of South America. It was the ideal choice to host this conference on new energy."

"So that's what this is all about? Use less water, make more efficient light bulbs, that kind of thing?"

"No, no, no. Think *bigger*, much bigger. Changing the world—that's the goal of this conference."

"Solar and wind power?" you ask.

"I'm afraid I don't know the specifics. I'm just the event coordinator; you'd need to talk with someone more involved in the conference itself."

Bertram readies his pen and paper. "Who's the man in charge of presentations?"

"His name is Italo Fellini and he runs a São Paulo based think-tank, *Futuro Verdejante*. The entire summit is his baby."

"Thank you for your help," Bertram says, shaking the man's hand. He then looks to you and says, "Time for a road trip."

With an overnight bag packed, and a quick call to Agent Danly to let him know you're headed out, you ride with David Bertram to the mega-city of São Paulo in search of answers.

If the murdered woman's fiance was banned from the Energy Summit, surely the conference chairman would know why. Perhaps the man even ordered the blacklisting himself. Maybe this Italo Fellini is the man you saw at the crime scene, exacting his final revenge for some (as of yet unclear) slight. If you want to destroy a man, taking away both his job and the woman he loves ought to do it. That would bring just about anybody to their knees. If this unknown enemy is willing to do that, while leaving the man unharmed, he must *really* hate him, and he must not be afraid of retaliation.

"I've got a good feeling we'll find the guy here," you say.

"Oh yeah? Why's that, Hotshot?"

"He looked like a scientist. It would make sense if he's somebody from the conference."

"We're only seeing the chairman today, but still—that's a good point. We should make it a priority for you to be at that conference. The subject would have a hard time skipping such an event. Most of these guys live for their work."

It's a fair point. There's no certainty that the guy is anything more than a fellow attendee. Yet this fiance—this Viktor—was blacklisted, so there must be an enemy in power. Sure, maybe the guy you saw at the crime scene was only an underling, but if that's the case, this thing must be bigger than one man…

"Hey, that's not bad," he says. "Hear me out. This guy was going places, right? His career was on a rocket's trajectory, but then *something* changed all that. Blacklisted from the Summit, and by association the entire green-energy industry, he's left more or less unemployed. An office tech can't support a family on her salary alone, so she dumps the guy. But he can't let her do that—some guys are just animals and won't let a girl walk out on them—so he kills her. Or maybe it was just an argument gone too far; that happens all the time. He kills her, accidentally or otherwise, then dumps her off to try and make it look like a mugging gone wrong!"

"Then who's the guy at the crime scene? It's not the fiance, so who is it?"

Bertram scratches his beard, thinking. Finally, he says, "It *is* another scientist, like you said. Somebody Viktor trusts and brought in to help him once he had killed the girl. BOOM—crime solved. All we have to do is ID the guy, and the nerd will crack in interrogation."

"Seems flimsy," you say. "He calls in a coworker to set up the body? Isn't that incredibly risky? Aren't there better dump spots in Rio?"

At length, Bertram says, "Okay, the ideal dumping ground is the landfills, but this guy is no repeat offender—he doesn't know the ins and outs of the criminal underbelly. Trust me, most of these book-smart guys have no street smarts. Nine times out of ten, the killer is the husband or boyfriend."

"Couldn't it just as easily be that she was having an affair with one of his coworkers?"

"Hey… that's not bad. But then which one killed her? The fiance or the fling?"

"Whichever one she was going to break off."

"Now you're thinking, Hotshot!"

You've made it to the outskirts of São Paulo. The last four hours were wide-open highway, similar to what you might find in the western United States. There aren't too many countries with massive swaths of unused land, but that's a feature your two nations share in common.

The transformation from rural highway to mega-city starts as you enter the suburbs. The highway goes to four lanes, and traffic flows in thick streams. When you drive out from under an overpass, you get your first skyscraper views. The billboards double and triple their population while traffic swells to levels seen in Los Angeles at rush hour, slowing your pace to a crawl.

A pleasant amount of greenery lines the side of the road, where cranes look for food in the flooded ditch, but just as many construction sites fill the scene. São Paulo is one of the world's fastest-growing cities (even though it's already the largest in the southern hemisphere) and there's hardly a mile stretch where you don't see some kind of development. It's enough of an effect that the city's official bird could be the crane—the construction crane, that is.

"Dammit, we'll never make it through all this," Bertram complains.

You look out the window. The skyscrapers of the business district seem like a distant mountain range. "Maybe he can come meet us halfway?"

With a *thud-thud-thud*, the rotors of a helicopter beat the air into submission above you. You can't help but duck forward to look up—there goes the aircraft, flying toward downtown.

Bertram spots something else outside the SUV and points a finger toward it to get your attention. It's a billboard, and the ad looks much like one for an airline back home. The well-manicured pilot with bronze skin, perfect hair, and a crisp uniform smiles at you with a bleached, toothy grin. There's a phrase in Portuguese and a phone number printed in the foreground, but behind him, where his open hand ushers you, is a helicopter, glorious and blue like the sky.

"Air taxi," Bertram announces.

- "Heli-yes! Does the guy's office have a helipad?" Go to page 298
- "Yeah, I was thinking maybe a public park or a café." Go to page 130

Good Cop

"Oh dear…." The man says, looking down and touching his forehead. "You know, Viktor had grown paranoid over the last few weeks—or at least I thought he was being paranoid. I guess he might have been right."

"Start at the beginning," you say.

"Well, he's done some visiting lectures here. Viktor is a brilliant engineer and researcher and I sincerely believed he would change the world." The word "believed" sticks out to you. Past tense. You make a mental note as the man continues, "He was selected to share his newest findings at the Energy Summit here in Rio. That's why I had seen him recently—normally he travels and maintains a lab in Europe. Germany, I believe."

"And when was the last time you saw him?" Bertram asks.

"Just last week. I had let him use some lab space. There are several algae cultures growing down there. Usually we let the students intern on such projects, but this time Viktor insisted—no one in or out but him."

You share a look with Bertram. "We'd like to see the lab," he says.

The professor nods, rising, and leads you out of the office.

As you walk, he continues, "His first concern was that someone had been hacking into his computer. He questioned me on our network security, and I assured him that a breach was impossible. As part of their curriculum, our Computer Science Department has students run an active network security protocol that is closely monitored by the professors. Our computer network is globally recognized as one of the most secure in *Brasil*.

"Still, he unplugged his LAN connection on all of the terminals and proceeded only to transfer data via hard disk. It seemed like a bit much to me at the time, but you know the old cliché about brilliant men and their eccentricities. That's how I knew I'd never be an Einstein; I'm not strange enough." He chuckles, amused by his little joke, then says, "Ah, here we are."

Professor Tavares-Silva checks the clipboard hanging by the door, then uses a key from his pocket to open the door. As he heads in, you check the clipboard: it shows Viktor's signature, signing in and out of the lab several times on the sheet. The last entry was six days ago.

"*Meu Deus!*" the professor cries from inside the room. "It's all gone!"

You rush in, eager to see what's happening, but all you see is an empty room. There's literally nothing in here.

"What? What *exactly* was in here?"

"I—I don't know. Big tanks of algae, computer terminals lining the walls, books, journals, printers. This was a fully functioning research lab."

"Who else has a key?" you ask.

"There are only two. I keep a copy with me, then the professor in charge of the project keeps another that students normally check out. In this case, Viktor kept the second copy."

"I think we'd better head to his apartment," Bertram says.

➢ *Get going!* Go to page 166

Gopher

You figure he's the boss, and for your first day you'll play nice. But he'd better not push it too much; you're not getting paid, after all. So you head out to the coffee station (which you passed on the way to the detective's office) to get Danly his coffee. You can hear him talking to Irma from within her office, but there are enough distracting noises from the cubicles nearby that you can't make out their words.

When you head back in, whatever conversation they were having is now over. Danly nods as you hand him the warm Styrofoam cup—that's all the thanks you'll get—and he blows against the lip of the cup to cool the beverage.

- *Continue the investigation.* Go to page 137

Grounded

Bertram calls the Energy Summit guy, talking to his secretary first. Eventually, he strikes a deal with the man and hangs up. He takes the next highway exit and, while traffic is still crazy, at least it slightly abates on the side roads.

"What'd he say?" you ask.

"*He's* going to take the air taxi. We're going to find a drive-thru coffee shop and meet him at a nearby park."

"They let helicopters land in parks?" you ask.

Bertram shrugs.

Using his smart phone's navigation tools, Bertram takes you through—big surprise—a Starbuck's. He orders a candied coffee mocha-chocolata-yaya for himself, and a venti green tea for the executive. After you place your order and pay, the agent drives the SUV to a large public park. He finds a shady spot to wait.

There's no helipad here, and Bertram just leans against the parked vehicle, taking sips of whipped cream without concern. It's not long before that thundering sound of a helicopter beating the air into submission returns. This time, it's headed toward you. You follow the aircraft with your head, over toward an unused soccer field, where it starts to set down.

"Come on!" Bertram yells.

He grabs the green tea and jogs toward the helicopter. It's not far, and you run to keep up. The rotor blade whips air at you, all the debris of the parking lot coming with it. You have to shield your eyes from the pebbles as the helicopter lands. If you were expecting something out of *Black Hawk Down,* this aircraft is comparably tiny; akin to a traffic helicopter you've seen on the news back home. It's almost all windshield and propeller, with just barely enough room for the pilot and three passengers. Slowly the blades slow their pace, and eventually the pilot comes out to greet you.

It's a woman. She wears an official uniform, just like the one on the billboard, but she's comparably tiny herself. Surprisingly petite, she must be just over five feet tall and maybe a hundred pounds. Yet she grins with confidence and her radiance is more than the man on the poster could muster at thirty feet tall.

"*Olá, bom dia,* I'm Maria Rodrigues Igor," she says, using the Portuguese greeting. "You are the Americans?"

You nod, and she hands you a business card.

"Call if you ever need a ride," she says with a wink. "I'll go fetch your associate."

Before you can answer, she's off and returning to the helicopter. You watch as she opens the door for Italo Fellini, your contact for the Energy Summit and head of *Futuro Verdejante.*

➢ *Find a picnic table for your meeting.* Go to page 111

GTA

There must be a helmet law in Rio, because even in their shorts and t-shirts, all the riders wear helmets. You've made out your mark—a man on a dirt bike with a package securely tied around the rear of the motorcycle. He puts the bike in neutral (you can tell this because he releases the clutch to put both hands on his hips at the stoplight) and now he's yours.

Coming from behind, you grab his shirt and pull him off the bike laterally. He's completely unsuspecting, so you easily pull him down in one clean jerk. He thuds to the pavement and his helmet bounces off the concrete road. Good thing there's that helmet law. This leaves him in a temporary daze, and provides you the opportunity to exit.

You leap on the bike, squeeze the clutch, and step into first gear. Cranking the throttle, you weave through the pylons toward the parking garage. The pedestrian traffic flees with screams of terror at your arrival. The guards, however, do not. Even as you're rocketing toward the garage, they're pulling out their sidearms. This is gonna be close.

- Punch it! Go to page 258
- Swerve toward the nearest guard. He can't shoot me if I'm running him over… Go to page 308

"Guests"

The rainstorm beats against the windows in great gales. You're in a private room on the second floor where, once disarmed, you were escorted and then left alone with a change of clothes. Maria and Bertram were shown to their own quarters, so you're here by yourself.

This isn't a fancy guestroom. No foreign dignitaries will be put up here. The Sugar King must have other lodgings for entertaining his friends and colleagues. If you had to guess, this might be where the security guards sleep. There's not much more than a bed and a television.

At length, you're summoned.

O Rei do Açúcar—Governor Mateo Ferro—is waiting for you on the main floor, just beneath the stairs. Bertram and Maria are right behind you as you begin to descend. The Sugar King brings a glass of red wine to his lips, then smiles. His teeth are stained crimson, giving him a vampiric quality.

"Ah, much better. Feeling refreshed, yes?" the man booms. "I should like to have offered you a feast, but I'm afraid you've caught me unprepared. I do, however, keep some fine wine on hand for when investors visit. It would be a pleasure to share my finest vintage with you."

He gestures to a servant who has three glasses on a tray. "As the saying goes, 'If you cannot serve good food, at least serve good wine.'"

He bellows in laughter.

- Might as well. Don't want to insult your host just yet. Go to page 179
- Refuse. You've got to keep your wits about you. Go to page 303

Gung Ho!

She looks at you with grave seriousness. "Okay, but know this—there is nothing more dangerous than trying to expose police corruption. If Lucio gets wind of it, next time he'll take you to the most violent slum he can find. Then he'll leave you there and pay a bounty for your head. That is, of course, if your hunch is right."

You nod in understanding.

"One more thing—just because we're not driving an armored car, doesn't mean we're not in danger. I want you to take this." She produces the revolver from the crime scene, the gun that originally sat by the *pick me up* note. You were already cleared of the crime, but the grave implications of possessing such a weapon can't be denied. Could she be trying to re-pin the crime on you? Why would she offer you their one lethal clue?

Seeing your eyes grow wide, she says, "This is a condition of my assistance. If things go bad, I need you to have my back. On short notice, this is the only gun I can get you—it's still checked out to me as evidence, so no one will miss it. What do you say, still feeling brave?"

When she says "still," it comes out with her accent as "steel," and that's what she offers right now: a cold, hard steel revolver, so dark and ominous you can feel your heat being sucked away by it.

- "I'm in. Give me the piece." Go to page 74
- "Never mind… how about dinner and you drop me off?" Go to page 301

Happy Reunion

Viktor and Jane walk through the village hand in hand, laughing, smiling, and enjoying a moment together. You watch as they stroll along the jungle's border, as do many of the villagers.

"It's nice, isn't it?" Dr. Susan Brandon says.

"What's that?" you ask.

"Love. Real, true love. I see it here in the tribe and it really shows you what's important in life."

She starts walking in the opposite direction as the happy couple, evidently expecting you to follow.

"How about a Brazil nut?" she says. "They come in plastic bags in the supermarket, but you might be surprised at how they look in the wild."

She picks up what appears to be a large coconut from a pile and cracks it open against a rock, revealing a cluster of Brazil nuts inside.

"Technically, this is a fruit and these are the seeds. Not a nut at all, in the true sense."

"Pretty big seeds," you say, taking one.

"Indeed," she laughs. "Sort of makes the fruit feel prehistoric, doesn't it?"

You look at the familiar "nut" in a new light. In the traditional American experience, the natural home for Brazil nuts was inside a Christmas stocking. She crushes one of the seeds between two rocks, taking out the white flesh from within and handing the rock to you. As you crush your own seed, you look out over the village. In a clearing, several children kick a soccer ball.

"Soccer all the way out here?" you say.

Dr. Brandon smiles. "Football, but yes. This is Brazil, after all. Want to see something you won't see the kids doing in the city?"

You nod and she leads you over to another group of children who appear to be playing with a kitten. They tap sticks on the ground, willing it to run, but when it does, you realize it's not a kitten at all. The children laugh and shriek, fleeing from a gigantic tarantula.

"Goliath birdeater," Dr. Brandon informs. "Commonly described as being the size of a dinner-plate."

You watch as the children dash to and fro near the enormous spider. Enjoying the game of cat and mouse; or, in this case, the game of spider and bird.

"Not venomous?" you ask.

"Oh, it is. But not deadly. Like a wasp sting."

A shiver runs down your spine. "I think it's time to go. The Energy Summit is tonight, and there isn't much time."

"I think I can help," she says. "Let's go find your friends."

➢ *Go get Viktor and Jane.* Go to page 283

Hard-boiled

Irma looks impressed. With raised eyebrow she says, "You ever consider a job as a Rio cop? Maybe you should stick around here when you're done."

Then she slaps her pistol across the teenager's face.

She asks him again, yelling now, her tones harsh and relentless. He spits once more, this time leaving a swath of red on the floor. This time, he talks.

"He says of course, they've all heard about her. The cops have already made their way through here with questions. What else do you want to ask him? We don't have much time."

- "Was it his gang who killed her?" Go to page 113
- "Let's just go. If they've all heard about it, we can ask someone else." Go to page 78

Hard Drive

You wait in the corner, on pins and needles, your head pounding and holding your breath. You can feel your heartbeat in your temples and you're so filled with anxiety that the room around you fades away until you see only the door.

A handgun with a long, black silencer breaches the doorway. Then comes the gloved hand carrying it, followed by a black suit-clad arm. Before you even know what you're doing, you swing the laptop toward where a face will appear.

Sunglasses, blood, teeth, plastic and circuitry explode in a grisly fireworks show. The man thuds against the wall and you swing what remains of the laptop toward his nose. This time you bring it in horizontally, unlike the broad swing you first took, so all the force you can muster will use the flat edge of the notebook. This time, you knock him unconscious.

There's nothing left of the computer; it's now either embedded in his face or spread around the room and covered in blood. Without a second thought, you claim his handgun. Your finger is tight around the trigger, with the weapon aimed at the door, when a second man in a black suit steps into the room and receives six holes in his chest, as you fire over and over again.

You quake with fear and adrenaline, unable to move and waiting for another target. What could be a few seconds or a few hours passes and eventually you move. These two men in black suits and black shirts almost certainly weren't police. Brazilian mafia, maybe.

And now they're both dead.

No one else remains in the duplex apartment, and what you came for is destroyed. Taking a towel from the bathroom, you wipe down the pistol to clear it of fingerprints—just like you've seen done on TV cop shows—and drop it on the floor between the two men. Time to go.

➢ *Meet Viktor at the restaurant.* Go to page 48

Hard Evidence

A policeman brings in a cardboard box, sets it on the desk, and Detective Dos Santos thanks him in Portuguese before he leaves. From within a drawer, she removes an evidence bag containing a revolver—the very same one from last night—and sets it on the desk in front of Danly. Your eyes focus on the blued steel as if magnetized. Something so small, yet so powerful….

"Serial number has been filed off, so we can't track it," she says.

"Mafia?"

"Or petty criminal. It's a common trick."

"Hmmm. What else have you got?"

She removes a few 8x10 sheets, photos of footprints in the dust, spreading them out between the two of you. "There were at least two different men, possibly three. But the woman didn't walk there—she was carried, alive."

"How do you know?" you ask.

"There aren't any traces of her flats. Bruising around her wrists, ankles, and mouth indicate she was bound and gagged and we know she was killed in the room because of the blood spatter. We also recovered the slug from the wall behind her; it was definitely fired from that revolver."

"So why bring her there to kill her and leave the body? Aren't there better dumping grounds?" Danly asks.

"Yes, we find most bodies from missing persons cases in the landfills. Well, the pickers find them, anyway. This room is new to us. It's abandoned, and I'd guess it used to be locked, based on the amount of dust."

"Okay, so who do we talk to? Is there a particular gang that controls that territory?"

"We? You want to go into the *favelas?*"

"What's that?" you ask.

"Slums. Very dangerous."

"Yes, very dangerous," the detective agrees. "Is this case personal to you, Agent Danly? Did you know the woman?"

"Anytime an American is killed on foreign soil, it's personal. I take it you weren't planning on questioning the druglords?"

"Drugs? You have reason to suspect it was drugs?"

"I didn't say that. What about Elite Squad? Will they go in?"

She sighs, then shakes her head. "I can put in a request."

"Elite Squad?" you ask.

"Basically police Special Forces. They're the only ones willing to go all the way behind enemy lines. Anything else you've got to show us?"

She shakes her head. "Not yet. We've got a team at her apartment, checking to see if the abduction might've taken place there. I'll let you know what they say."

"How about we go see for ourselves?" Danly says.

"Now? I was about to head over myself, but you can follow me or….?"

"You can ride with us if you'd like."

"Thank you."

Detective Dos Santos rises, shuts off her computer monitor, and gestures for you to leave. The revolver and photos remain on her desk, but she locks the office door after the three of you exit.

The apartment complex is located just about halfway between the police station and the consulate, so you're backtracking, but not too far. It's a little further inland than either of those two landmarks, and the three locations form a triangle, with the Olympic stadium as its center.

You can tell as soon as Agent Danly pulls up to the police barricade that this is the kind of place you'd live in only if you had to, if it were all you could afford. There's virtually no public green space, which says a lot in this country. It's not seedy per se, at least not in the bright sunlight.

Staying close to your law enforcement escorts, you duck under the police tape. There's the flush of *I'm in the movies*, a feeling that you can't quite subdue. Irma Dos Santos shows her detective's badge to the cop guarding the door and heads inside.

Agent Danly takes off his sunglasses and says, "I appreciate you not bringing up the drug angle. I want to look into it before we pin that as the motivation."

You nod. He heads inside and you follow.

The small apartment is gravid with Rio cops. It's the living room—where a coffee table sits midway between couch and television—that captures their attention. Police investigators flock around the coffee table, snapping pictures, taking notes, and collecting samples.

"Never mind," Agent Danly says.

There on the table sits a stash of cocaine, several lines laid out neatly as if the party was just getting started.

"Whoa," you breathe out.

"Yeah. Let's ask some questions," he says.

- "Okay, I'm right behind you." Go to page 81
- "Actually, I'm gonna take a quick walk around." Go to page 68

Here There Be Monsters

You stand by the railing on the port side of the barge, the warmth of the sun beating down upon you, and enjoy the cool mist that rises up as the boat surges through the river. The brackish water is dull and murky on the surface, but teems with life beneath. It's easy to think of the danger here, what with piranha, anaconda, and such, but what you soon see cruising through the water is truly shocking.

A large dorsal fin splits the surface, pressing up near the boat and rising high into the air. You see the dark outline of a creature swimming effortlessly, its tail a powerful paddle of swaying confidence. Easily ten feet in length, and probably 500 pounds of muscle and cartilage, the massive shark torpedoes downriver, unconcerned by the noisy engine of the barge.

You find your hands gripping the railing tightly out of fearsome awe, but you're able to control yourself enough to take out your camera and snap a picture.

"*Touro,*" a local Brazilian says to you. "*De bull.* Eh, shark. Bull, yes?"

He has his index fingers extended at his temples as makeshift horns.

You smile and nod. "Bull shark."

"Yes, bull shark. It is lucky to see her. At least from up here!" He laughs heartily.

"What is it doing here?" you ask. "Isn't this fresh water?"

He shakes his head and chops his hand across the air. "She does not care. The bull swims from the sea to be Queen of the River."

You frown. He frowns as he tries to think.

"I am professor, I study the animals. Hmmm, how to explain? She comes in, she goes back. River to sea, sea to river. This shark—it is the only kind like this, yes? *Especial.*" He pats his belly. "Keeps her salt."

Making a mental note to tell Viktor about the other professor onboard, you look back at the water. There's no sign of the shark.

Suddenly, from across the deck, a commotion draws your attention to the starboard side.

➢ *Go find Viktor and see what's going on.* Go to page 329

Here's Your Sign

The blaring T. Rex roar of the car horn sends the kids scattering, but once they realized you're nothing more than a wounded lamb bleating for help, they come back. You duck down out of view in the back seat, but you can hear muffled sounds from the feral children outside through the car window. Little hands try the door handles, tugging over and over in frustration.

You hear the *cluck, cluck, cluck* of the spray paint can being shaken, followed by a hiss as the ruffians tag the car. Muffled shouting, then the paint can sounds stop. Then there's silence. Maybe they're done? Maybe they've gone away? The silence lasts so long, you're about to leave the car and check to see if the coast is clear. Then you hear something metal in the lock and the door opens. You back away, ready to scream as the door opens—but it's Agent Danly.

"What the *fuck*? Look at this shit!" he screams.

He opens the rear door, allowing you out, and shows you the colorful mural that has been spray-painted over the entire length of the car.

"You did say stay in the car, boss-man," Muniz says.

"Do you have any idea how much paperwork will be involved? *Ugh*!"

Shaken, trying not to look like an idiot, you say, "Did you find anything out there?"

"No. Asshole here took us to a pacified slum," he says. Then responding to your puzzled look, he adds, "That's a slum that's been cleaned up. Christ, those kids would've had guns in any other slum. Come on, we're headed back to the station."

- *Return to the station.* Go to page 221

Hero

You lean against the wall of the long corridor to stabilize yourself, gather what little breath you can muster in your weakened state, and squeeze the trigger.

Just before he can reach the emergency exit, the man leaps forward, only to drop abruptly on the carpeted hallway floor.

That's it, it's over.

Now it's time for champagne. You've reconvened with Danly and Bertram at the hotel bar and the Ambassador and his team are with you. The Big Man thanks you personally for all your hard work.

"I'm going to nominate you for the Presidential Medal of Freedom," he says. "That's the highest honor that can be awarded to a civilian and I'm sure POTUS will approve. What you've done here is nothing short of miraculous. Unorthodox, maybe…."

The crowd laughs. Bertram blushes.

"I owe it all to the leadership of these two agents," you say, indicating your former partners.

Now Danly blushes.

Ambassador Mays continues, "And I won't forget it! You three brought a dangerous terrorist to justice and on behalf of a grateful nation, I thank you. Open bar tonight—on me!"

The room cheers. After shaking every hand in the growing party, you find a quiet corner to sit with the two agents.

"I thought you were just going to check out the newest scientific breakthroughs," Danly says.

The edges of his mouth curve up in a smile. You give a modest shrug.

"Man, I really had the fiance pegged for this," Bertram says.

"Still no ID?" you ask.

"They still need to run his prints and dental records, but we'll find out who he was soon enough," Danly says.

"What about that other assassin? The *Jamanta*?"

"You let us worry about that, Hotshot," Bertram says. "Enjoy your moment in the sun!"

"No kidding. There's always more police work to be done after a murderer is caught, but leave it to the police, for Chrissakes. Take comfort that you did your part."

"The biggest part!" Bertram says. "You were the only one to see this guy, y'know? You found him hovering at the scene of the crime, and he escaped, but then it's *you* that catches him later. I'd call that providence."

You nod in silence. It's hard to enjoy the party with so many loose threads. Just who *was* that guy? Why would he kill Jane Nightingale *and* make an attempt on the Ambassador's life? Could he be a terrorist after all? Was it just a simple hatred of America that motivated the mystery man? And what kind of crazy pressure-bomb did he use on you?

Well, at least he's dead. If nothing else, you can take comfort in that.

➢ Go to page 304

Hesitation

Waiting to see who it is you're firing at is an intelligent decision that just about any rational, level-headed, sane person would make in an academic, stress-free environment. Pat yourself on the back; you just performed well under pressure.

Unfortunately, the drug traffickers who enter the house are neither sane nor rational. They start shooting immediately, one gunning for you and the other for Irma. If that woman and her baby were still in the house, they'd be dead too—such is the indiscriminate way these men retaliate against the screams of their comrade. You don't have a chance. But at least the obscene amount of bullets they inject into you means yours will be a quick death.

THE END

Hide

The twin beds are bolted to the wall and there's not much else in the room that could serve as a barricade. Still, there's a lock on the door…maybe that will be enough? You secure the door and turn out the lights. Time to hide under the blankets until the monsters go away.

But there was one thing you didn't exactly consider in your plan. These pirates are here for money, and the private cabins are generally reserved for the wealthier passengers. So yeah, they'll be coming right for you.

The door explodes open as two of the pirates kick it in unison. The lights flicker on to reveal several young men with AK-47s and machetes tucked in their waistbands. Time to find out if they're here to rape and murder or just rob and murder.

"Enough is enough," Viktor says, his eyes glowing like cold steel.

The men shout at him in Portuguese.

"I'm sorry, Tourist."

Viktor slings off his backpack and removes one of the tiny metal orbs; his "Manhattan Project," as he called it. After twisting it a certain way, the device begins moving of its own accord. The pirates shout in nervous anger, punctuating their remarks with their weapons.

And then they can't shout anymore.

Their breaths are *drawn in* toward the device. The door slams shut. Then you feel it too. The device *collapses* the room in on itself, sucking the air out of the cabin, depressurizing the area and causing each of your internal cavities to crush inward.

THE END

It really isn't far, despite the city's constant, overwhelming traffic. Bertram skirts a highway, passing a massive soccer stadium and sports arena, and finally takes you to the university. At a traffic roundabout (sporting a modern-art totem sculpture in the center) you can see the first signs of the school.

It's impressive in size, but unfortunately, not in aesthetics. The building is gray, old, dusty, and square. If anything, it looks like a mega-apartment complex. From out your window, you'd guess it's maybe fourteen stories high and just as many city blocks wide. You can't help but be impressed by the scale; it's nearly as large as the soccer coliseum next door. Which, incidentally, is the largest in the world.

Bertram parks in a handicap spot, which you assume is another faux pas made kosher due to the diplomatic plates. There are hundreds, if not thousands, of students milling about the campus, which is called *Universidade do Estado do Rio de Janeiro* and abbreviated to UERJ on many t-shirts. Agent Bertram's Portuguese serves him well in this capacity, and after asking for directions, he leads you inside. To offset the bland buildings, there's a green courtyard at the entrance filled with lush jungle trees—palms flitting peacefully against the slightest breeze. Well, that's something.

The halls within are "tiled" with linoleum and bathed in fluorescent lights. Some of the classrooms are open and you can see students in connected chair-desks like those at grade schools back home. From here you move on toward the professors' offices and lab stations, taking an elevator up to floor six. Once you get to a section labeled "*engenharia,*" Bertram starts asking around.

He shows his badge to a secretary, a 40-something woman who tries her hardest in fashion and makeup to look like she's still college-age. Their words flow back and forth, unintelligible to you, but you're becoming something of a body language expert (as it's the only way to keep up with Portuguese conversation) and you can tell Bertram's getting frustrated. The only thing you pull out is "*Professor*" and "Viktor Lucio de Ocampo."

She shakes her head, her mouth in a frown, saying something that sounds like "now" over and over. He keeps asking, and so it's her turn to get frustrated. She picks up the phone, and he produces his badge to check her move. She puts it back on the receiver, but keeps shaking her head.

"Excuse me, you are American?" a voice calls from behind.

You turn around to see a man with square, black-framed glasses, grey hair thinning at the top where dark freckles announce the sun's conquest over his hairline. He's clean-shaven, with deep grooves on his face and brow. He wears a white sweatshirt with the school's logo—an Olympic torch, gold with a red flame, adorned with "UERJ" in royal blue.

"We're looking for Professor Viktor Lucio de Ocampo," Bertram says. "Maybe you can help us. I'm David Bertram, here on behalf of the US State Department with my associate here."

The man smiles. "Viktor is not a professor here. That's why Sofia couldn't help you."

"But you know him," you say.

"Yes, our paths have crossed professionally. Is Viktor in some sort of trouble?"

"Is there somewhere we can talk?" Bertram suggests.

The man leads you to the elevator, up to the top floor. The offices here are much larger, each with a view of the Rio skyline. Urban sprawl flows out nearly as far as the eye can see, but beyond that, lush green hills provide a pleasing backdrop. The man's desk faces the door, so that his back is to the window, and two chairs await you in front of him.

Once you sit, he says, "I'm Dr. Agostinho Tavares-Silva, head of the Engineering Department here at Rio State."

When he says his name, his words slur almost as if his tongue had suddenly swelled, but his English becomes flawless once more and you can tell he gets a kick out of Anglicizing the university's name.

"We need to ask you a few questions about Viktor. Your cooperation would be greatly appreciated, Doctor," Bertram says.

"Am I speaking to you officially—on behalf of the university? Or off the record, as his friend?"

- "Listen, your 'friend' killed his fiancée. You need to help us before he kills again." Go to page 13
- "We have reason to believe Viktor is in trouble. Anything you tell us could save his life." Go to page 128

In a private charter plane like this one, there is no stewardess to block your entry to the cabin—you're able to just walk right in.

Inside you find a lone pilot, a middle-aged, greying-at-the-temples man who wears jungle khakis and a US Air Force flight jacket with his old unit symbol and nametag still affixed to the aged brown leather.

"Everything okay?" he asks.

You nod. "Is it distracting to have me up here?"

"Not at all!" He shouts. "Take a seat and put on the headset."

That's much better. Over the radio, you can talk without the need to holler over the engine.

"So… do you know Viktor and Jane?"

"The other passengers?" he says. "No, but Susan and I go back. Well, actually, it's Renfield who got me this job."

"Renfield?"

He nods, then pauses to check his instruments. "He's the genius behind ethanol who works over at the VW plant. I used to fly corporate jets, but that lifestyle will kill you after a while. This is a much better gig—independent contracting—I get to be the boss rather than the sky-chauffeur."

"And Dr. Brandon?"

"Right, sorry. About a decade ago she and Renfield were pretty hot and heavy, engaged, I think, but she couldn't tear herself away from the field and he was already married to the lab, so work came first. Those two back there are involved in the future of ethanol, right? Dr. Brandon probably sees her past self in them."

You nod in silence. So that's why she's helping, to give them the chance at happiness she herself gave up.

"You guys are off to the Energy Summit, right? I'll call Renfield. I think he still has connections with the chairman."

"That's very generous," you say.

"I know he'd want to help…. We should be landing shortly, so can you head back and buckle up for me?"

When you make it back to your seat, Viktor turns to you and says, "This is it, Tourist. The grand finale. Thanks to André, the police are looking for him rather than myself, and they think Jane here is dead, so we should be able to sneak in undetected."

"What about me?" you ask.

"You're still anonymous. After tonight, win or lose, the world will know who you are."

"Unless…" Jane says.

You look from Viktor to Jane and back again.

"Unless you're ready to retire," Viktor says. "You've done so much for us. This—tonight—is our fight. You don't need to risk your life any further."

"Look for us on the news," Jane says. "There should be live coverage. I'm going to upload the evidence onto the Energy Summit computer system and project it on the main screen during the opening ceremonies. Then Viktor will arrive on stage, proclaim his innocence, and condemn these two evil Kings while everyone is there to see it."

- "Okay… Good luck. I'll want to meet for champagne after you're successful." Go to page 263
- "Seriously? So close to the finish line? No way you're leaving me here!" Go to page 309

Hospitality

Viktor falls to the ground—you got him! The taxicab peels out in response to the gunshot, the driver not wanting to be your next target. You cautiously approach the suspect, who writhes on the cobbled street, his blood mixing with the dank wetness of the road.

He bleeds freely from the shoulder and groans in pain.

"Well done!" a panting voice says from behind.

Turning, you see Detective Irma Dos Santos jogging to catch up.

"You're fast," she pants.

"I—I didn't have a choice," you say. "He was getting away."

Irma removes a switchblade knife and drops it in Viktor's palm so it looks like he's holding it.

"There, now you *really* didn't have a choice."

Viktor groans, tossing the knife away. "You… have no idea what's…."

Irma kicks the man, tells him to shut up in Portuguese, then wraps an arm around your shoulder and takes you away from him.

"You did okay, Americano, you know that? Come on, I'll call in back-up; let's go check on your friends."

Some time later, you're sitting in a hospital room at the bedsides of the two agents, both of whom are unconscious. Danly recovers from "decompression sickness" after Viktor's bomb nearly turned his insides out. Bertram nurses a gunshot wound from his encounter with the infamous assassin when he tried to pursue the scientist, but the agent came out on top and the Devil Ray is now dead.

Detective Dos Santos enters the room, quietly closing the door so as not to wake the resting men. "How are they?" she asks.

"The RSO came by earlier. The Doctors say they should be fine, they just need some time."

"Good. How are you?"

"Fine. Did you just come from Viktor's room?" you ask.

She sighs. "He was a bad man, you know that, right?"

You don't respond so she continues, "He murdered the woman who loved him and was about to do the same to your Ambassador before you caught him."

"I know," you say.

She puts a hand on your shoulder. "He's dead. He died of his injuries on the way to the hospital."

"Good," Danly croaks, going into a coughing fit.

"I knew it was the fiance," Bertram says with a grin. "I knew it was the Devil Ray too."

"But how?" you say, no longer whispering. "I only hit him in the shoulder!"

"It must have struck an artery, because he lost a lot of blood. Then the transfer didn't take at the hospital. It's rare, but it does happen," Irma explains.

Something in your gut twists. You just killed a man? You only meant to stop him….

"Forget about that scumbag, Hotshot. You did what had to be done," Bertram says.

You look at Danly. The agent nods his approval and smiles.

"Good work, Rookie," he says, his voice husky, like a chain smoker.

There's a moment of contented silence as the room basks in a feeling of victory. Everyone smiles, except for you. Something still feels "missing." You excuse yourself, and go off to search your conscious and ponder the deeper meaning of things. The events of these last three days will, without a doubt, forever change you.

➢ Go to page 304

Hostel Environment

The government SUV pulls up outside *Che Lagarto Ipanema*, the five-story hostel you're staying at with friends. The road is busy, even at this late hour, but the vehicle's diplomatic plates supersede any parking regulation. You are still, however, subject to honks from angry taxi drivers piling up behind you.

"Don't go far, okay?" Agent Bertram says, handing you a card of his own. "Call if you have any trouble, even if you think you're just being paranoid."

You nod.

"Goodnight," Agent Danly says, opening the door for you.

Trumpets, bongos, and revelry greet you along with the warm, summer air as you step outside the car. Sure, it's February, but this is the southern hemisphere, so the seasons are reversed from what you're used to.

The first floor bar is packed with drunken 20-somethings (mostly tourists) and a live band. When you step inside, the bartender nods to you in greeting.

The entire bar façade is bathed in red light, originating from the back shelf, giving the bottles stored there an ethereal glow of murderous intent. Still, a stiff drink could be nice after the night you've been through. But then again, so could sleep, although you're not likely to get much privacy in the shared dorm room waiting for you on the third floor.

You look back over your shoulder; the SUV is gone. So, what'll it be?

- I think I'll take comfort in friendship, time to head upstairs. Go to page 226
- I could use some time, and some libations, to process what happened tonight. Go to page 350
- I'm going for a walk. Go to page 238

Hot Pursuit

You rush after Viktor, the agent's handgun held tightly in your grip. The man runs like a wild animal fleeing from a predator and you chase him down like your life depends on it.

The man knows you're hot on his heels and does his best to place obstacles in your path. He knocks down bystanders, flings trashcans, even runs through a shop and out the back exit in an effort to keep you off his trail.

He leads you into the heart of *Carnaval,* straight to the *Sambadrome,* where gigantic parade flotillas, with hundreds of dancers on each one, are cruising. He leaps over the barriers and flees directly into the heart of the performance. You don't think twice—you follow him right in.

The music is deafening here, loud enough so that the vibrations could help pass a kidney stone, and with the bright colors and feverish dancing, this is sensory overload.

Viktor nearly smashes into a pregnant woman, her enormous belly on display for the world as she dances in a thong bikini and a few feathers, but he swerves out of the way at the last second, letting you gain slightly.

Security for the event rushes in to capture the two of you, and Viktor slips out the other end of the parade grounds. You just barely make it out yourself, but the security guards aren't ready to give up and now you've got your own parade sprinting across the pavement away from the show.

You turn back, flashing the handgun at the security guards. They stop and meekly tuck their pepper spray back into their belts before turning back to the event. These rent-a-cops aren't willing to get shot simply for parade security.

Once again, it's just you and Viktor. He's about to make it to a taxicab—if he gets in, you'll lose him for sure.

- You've got a clear shot—try to wing him. Go to page 148
- Watch him go, just like in the beginning. Go to page 93

You follow the agents, running to keep up, and cast a glance back over your shoulder to Viktor. He stands still, smiling, and gives a nod in recognition. Bertram disappears into the chapel, then Danly, then you.

"Everybody out, now!" Agent Bertram commands.

"*Vá. Deixar. Agora,*" Danly adds in Portuguese.

The inside is rather small, about the size of a master bedroom in an average suburban home, with two rows of seating on either side and an aisle down the center leading up to an altar covered in flowers. The ceiling is raised like a Roman dome, painted with a bright blue sky and wispy cirrus clouds swirling about in an inverted, cosmic whirlpool.

Once the five terrified tourists end their prayers and leave, the two agents sweep the room.

"Look for anything unusual, Rookie, but don't touch anything," Agent Bertram says.

"Like another note?" you ask.

"Or a bomb," Danly answers.

You check the altar… just flowers. The agents look under the seats, around the edges, in every crack and crevice. You look at the crucifix at the front of the room and the other fixtures. Still nothing. It doesn't take long to search the modest chapel, and there's nothing out of the ordinary.

"What the shit?" Bertram says, going over the sweep a second and a third time.

In a shared realization, the two agents rise from their hunched search, snap to attention, and run back outside the chapel. Again, you follow. They search frantically for Viktor, but he's nowhere to be found.

Then a whistle pierces the high altitude air and the three of you lock in on the source. There he is, leaning out of the red train car, just as it takes off for the return trip down the mountain. Viktor moves his hand away from his mouth and into a wave. "Then again, maybe I didn't leave something!" he shouts, "Good luck on the case!"

The train disappears behind the bend of the mountain trail.

"Goddammit, one of us should've stayed back here," Danly says.

"No shit, Sherlock. I expected you to back me up while I checked it out," Bertram growls.

"Back *you* up? You think you're lead on this investigation? That's rich."

"Blow me, Stuart."

"Ummm, guys?" you say, interrupting.

The whole mountain crowd stares at the scene they're making.

"All right," Danly says, composing himself. "Let's forget that crackpot; we've got work to do."

"That work includes looking into this guy. He's obviously a sociopath. His fiancée hasn't even been buried yet and the guy's all smiles."

"We follow the evidence, and if it leads to him, so be it."

"No way. We need to put this nut behind bars before he hurts someone else."

"Bertram, seriously, do I need to ask the RSO to officially assign one of us as lead?"

"You might."

"This might just be a naïve rookie talking," you say, "but couldn't you guys split up and cover more ground?"

They both look at you, blinking. Then they say in unison, "Yes."

"Okay," Bertram says, "Let's split up. I'll follow the fiancé, you work with the local police."

"Fine with me. Just make sure you file your reports so we can cross-reference one another's findings."

"You want some cab fare to get back to the garage?" Agent Bertram asks. "The car's checked out in my name, so…"

"I'll be fine," Danly says.

They linger for a moment, staring at one another, before Bertram offers to shake hands. "Good luck, and I mean that," he says.

"Don't shoot anybody," Danly counters, managing a slight smirk. "The paperwork involved is worse than death."

- "And I'll come with you, Agent Danly. I've always wanted to go behind the scenes of an investigation." Go to page 322
- "The fiancé might not be the guy I saw last night, but maybe he can lead us to him. Let's do it, Agent Bertram!" Go to page 320

Imploded

"I'll notify security," Bertram says. "You find the Ambassador."

"Right," Danly replies, taking off down the hall.

You follow, sticking close, and something ahead catches your attention. Even though you were expecting him, you're shocked that he's actually here. You rub your eyes, but there he is, in the flesh—the man with the shimmering, gunmetal-blue eyes. He doesn't see you just yet, as he's trying to blend in and look inconspicuous. You've got him now!

Except at this exact moment, the Ambassador steps out of one of the adjoining rooms, standing between you and the target. When he spots Ambassador Mays, though, hatred fills his eyes. He slips his backpack off one shoulder and reaches into it—

"Viktor!" you shout.

The man looks towards you, confused, but it's all the distraction you need. Agent Danly surges into action. Ambassador Mays' security detail doesn't register the threat yet, though they sense something is off and surround the important man.

Viktor removes a small metal grapefruit-sized object from his backpack. He twists the device, *clicking* it into place, then throws it underhand straight at the Ambassador.

"Bomb!" Danly shouts, rushing to protect his boss.

Viktor turns and sprints around the next corner while the men try to shield the diplomat. The device flashes and rearranges itself like an automated Rubik's Cube before it finally detonates. But rather than exploding, it *im*plodes. The bomb sucks the air from the hallway like a black hole, and the change in pressure cracks and nearly brings down the ceiling.

Oxygen is ripped from your lungs and you fall to the floor like you've just been gut-punched. Everything goes black with the swift certainty of death.

You're lying there, coming to terms with dying, when miraculously your breath comes back and your vision returns. Sweet, sweet air fills you up and you weakly push yourself up off the hallway floor. It's difficult to focus, but you will yourself to move toward Danly and the Ambassador.

The devastation is immense; it's likely many of the people in the hall are dead. You're lucky you were so far away from the bomb—you're all lucky that the hallway was open; otherwise there'd be no air to breathe after the initial blast.

You stumble over to where Agent Danly lies prone on his stomach and roll him onto his back. Danly's eyes are red and lifeless from burst blood vessels. He isn't moving. Suddenly, he spasms and coughs blood. His eyes dart toward you in recognition.

"Go," he croaks.

- Stay to makes sure Danly doesn't die. Go to page 267
- Pursue Viktor. Go to page 237

Instant Karma

You shoot the snake; the shotgun pellets leave little but mangled flesh. Then you look to Maria as if to say, *yep, that just happened.* The only good snake is a dead snake, *amiright?*

Her mouth hangs wide open, but upon seeing the smug look on your face, she raises a revolver to your head and pulls back the hammer.

Bertram bats her hand so that only a deafening explosion booms beside your ear and you're otherwise unharmed. You can't be sure if she intended to shoot you or if Bertram's blow caused her to pull the trigger, but before you can consider retaliation, he shoves the two of you apart.

Ringing like a telephone left off the hook, your hearing slowly returns.

"....I mean, seriously, you two. It's a goddamned snake. Christ, you're like toddlers with firearms," Bertram scolds.

Maria turns to you with narrowed eyes. "Asshole."

You shake off the concussive blast and head out toward the road.

A few minutes later, you exit the sugarcane field. Waiting for you are two carloads of *grileiros,* set up in tactical positions, using their jeeps for cover, weapons at the ready. They must've heard the gunshots.

"Fuck me," Bertram says.

Those are the last words you'll ever hear.

THE END

In Synch

Entering the consulate, you're greeted with familiar faces. The two Office Management Specialists look up from their desks hopefully. Everyone wonders if maybe you've brought some good news. If you've found her killer, they can move on….

Agent Danly shakes his head, communicating to the crowd that no news is, in this case, bad news. With a collective sigh, everyone's shoulders slump and they all go back to work.

Danly's first pit stop is the coffee station, where he refills the same paper cup he brought with him. The bald RSO, the agents' Regional Security Officer supervisor, steps out of his office and makes a high-pitched whistle through pursed lips.

"I've got ten, if you please," the man says.

Danly nods. "Can we get the conference room?"

His forefingers extended, the RSO points at a young office worker, points to you, then the conference room. He steps back into his office.

"Meet you in ten minutes," Danly says to you before stepping into his supervisor's office and closing the door behind him.

"Exciting case, huh?" the office worker asks.

"Oh, yeah," you say. "You wouldn't *believe* the night I had last night."

"I'll bet," he says, showing you into the conference room.

In quick, practiced moves he converts the room for video teleconferencing, wishes you good luck, then leaves you alone. A minute later, Danly arrives.

"We're going to the embassy in Brasilia after this," he says, logging into the computer.

"Why? I thought we were getting close?"

"We are, but the Ambassador wants a personal update. It's fine—I wanted to look into the drug angle and I'll need to review her records and talk to her supervisors there. But get ready for a long night; it's about a twelve-hour drive into the interior and I'm exhausted, so you'll need to take the wheel."

Great, you think.

Suddenly the large, flatscreen TV flickers from "no input" to a crystal-clear picture. Agent Bertram is on the screen in his shirtsleeves, larger than life.

"Are we live? Hello?"

"Good to go," Bertram replies. "Catch the guy yet?"

"Actually, I did have a major breakthrough last night, when I was visiting the *favelas.* We found—"

"Glad you're still alive, by the way."

Agent Danly's face frowns with impatience. "As I was saying. We found a drug trafficker who claims his gang was the one to kill Jane Nightingale."

Bertram's eyes pop. "Whoa, really? You make an arrest?"

"Not yet. The interesting thing is, they say she *wasn't* involved in drugs, even after what we found at her apartment. It looks like they were paid to kill her, plain and simple. It looks like…a hit. And—get this—I think I saw your 'merc; the Man in Black. I think he was tailing me."

"The same guy, are you sure? Think he was the one who pulled the trigger?"

Danly shakes his head. "The traffickers have their own hit-men. I talked with Elite Squad, and they recognized the guy. They call him *Jamanta.*"

"As in—The Devil Ray?"

"The same," Danly says. "A ridiculous urban legend, but apparently he's a platinum-level assassin, way too big-budget for this kind of thing."

"Fuck me," Bertram says. "The kind of budget you might have behind you if you were a rock-star scientist. I think the fiance might've hired himself some protection, and if you saw the muscle, that means we're getting close."

"Who is the *Jamanta*?" you say. "I'd like to hear the legend."

Bertram looks to make sure the door is secure, then leans in. In a low voice, he says, "Raymond Panoptes, AKA, 'Devil' Ray Panoptes, AKA, 'The Devil Ray', AKA, *'O Jamanta.'* He's supposedly an ex-DSS agent."

"Bullshit, it's just an urban legend," Danly says, waving the suggestion away.

"He started off as a helicopter pilot, and that's how you'll recognize him; he has those wonky eyes."

You scowl, so Danly elaborates. "Apache pilots' helmets have a monocle resting in front of their right eye that feeds them flight and weapon information. The other eye looks outside the cockpit, scanning for threats and watching the terrain, so the pilots develop the ability to use their eyes independently. That much is true."

"Right!" Bertram says. "I've even heard about some guys who can read two different books at once, so shooting at two targets is child's play for somebody like this."

"Apache pilots are real, and maybe he is one, but the Devil Ray doesn't exist," Danly says.

Bertram continues, "Supposedly, after he got out of the service, he joined the DSS. Many of our recruits are vets, so that much isn't farfetched. Legend has it, he was an agent back in the early '90s, when Ambassador Mays was an RSO, right here in Brazil, but Raymond had to be cut loose. He got a taste for killing and couldn't give it up. He would shoot a 'perp when he could have simply arrested the guy, and he would take the law into his own hands when he couldn't get a warrant. One day, when he was supposed to be tried for his illegal vigilantism, he just *disappeared.*"

Bertram waves his hands back and forth, his fingers waggling, as he says the final word.

"And… bullshit," Danly coughs. "I'll keep my ear to the ground on this Man in Black character, but he's an effect, not a cause. Let's stay focused on the case and the crime-world angle. I've got a real tangible lead here after last night."

"Did you get a name on who pulled the trigger?" you ask.

Danly looks to you. "No, but this is bigger than some petty crime. We'll get that lowlife, for sure, but what we really want to know is who ordered the hit. That's the million-dollar question, Rookie."

"We need tangible proof that the fiance paid somebody to kill his lady," Bertram says.

Danly looks back to the screen. "The informant mentioned that it was backed with 'sugar money.' As in, the sugarcane mafia."

Bertram pops out of his chair. "Jesus, we're slurping on the same spaghetti noodle here."

"What do you mean?" Agent Danly presses.

"As in, if we get any closer, we'll be kissing."

"No, what, goddammit, you know what I mean—what did you find?"

"Dr. Viktor, he's made some discoveries that could put sugarcane out of business. And sugarcane is in *big* business." Bertram scratches his beard. "Maybe our friend the good doctor made an illegal deal with the Sugar King, Nightingale got word of it, and he had to silence her before she reported him to the ol' U-S of A."

"Bingo," Danly says. "He plants the drug evidence in her apartment—he's no criminal, so it looks wrong—and the sugar lords agree to help silence his girlfriend. They hire drug traffickers to kill her, to keep the ruse, but they spend the *real* money on protection."

"So you're back on *Team Fiance*?" Bertram asks.

"I've always been on *Team Evidence*," Danly says gruffly.

"It's all connected…" you marvel.

Bertram puts his jacket back on. "There's a gigantic sugarcane plantation between us and you. If he made an allegiance for money, it's most likely there. That's what I'll check out."

Danly nods. "Be careful. I'm going to the Embassy in Brasilia to put to bed this whole drug thing once and for all, and to share what we've found with the Ambassador. He'll want to hear this."

"Perfecto, Dano. Bertram out." He severs the connection, and the screen goes back to blank.

Agent Danly shuts off the machinery on this end, then checks his watch. "You might want to grab some coffee. We'll gas up and grab some energy drinks too. If we drive all night, we should be there just in time for the embassy to open."

One of the few purpose-built metropolises in the world, Brasilia comes from nowhere—a modern city carved from jungle, built to be a utopia of logic and innovation. The periphery of the city struggles against the jungle's attempts to reclaim the territory with green vines strangling the white buildings.

You arrive at Brazil's capital just after sunrise, a soft light on the horizon and the electricity of the city still beaming. You're exhausted and stiff from your all-nighter spent behind the wheel, but fortunately Danly wasn't able to sleep much and offered to drive the last stretch while you napped.

Inside the über-organized interior of Brasilia, the city is sleek and clean, built from architecture that looks like 1950s sci-fi imaginings of the future. As part of this serial organization, a large chunk of the city is reserved for embassies and government offices, and that's where Agent Danly heads now.

But first—breakfast. You head into a Portuguese bakery, its shelves lined with what looks to be…

"Doughnuts?" you say.

"*Malasadas*!" Danly replies, far too excited after the night you just shared. "You can get plain, cinnamon, or get them filled with custard, chocolate, coconut, guava, fruits—you name it."

"So… jelly doughnuts?"

"Not hardly. You won't get *malasadas* this good outside of Leonard's in Hawaii. Go ahead, try one, you'll change your tune."

The fried bread is warm and rich, light and flaky on the outside, puffy just beneath the surface, and the gooey center sweet and creamy. From the look of seventh-heaven on your face, Danly says, "Told ya so."

He orders two dozen *malasadas* and, of course, an enormous coffee. The city lights are now extinguished, the morning sun hangs low in the sky, and palms sway as you ride in the SUV toward the embassy.

With white-washed walls reaching high into the sky and razorwire-topped fences, the embassy looks more like a federal prison than a place of refuge. You proceed inside, the barrage of security procedures going by in a blur to your sleep-deprived mind.

You snap wide awake as you go down a long corridor past armed marines toward the office of the Ambassador—the most senior US official inside Brazil at any given moment, short of a Presidential visit.

There's a large waiting room with several couches and a desk for the Ambassador's assistant, who is short and thin with prematurely grey-flecked hair. He is wearing a finely tailored suit and speaks with three other men—each dwarfing his own slight stature. They all look toward you as you enter.

"Well, well, Stuart Danly," the first of the three men says. He's tall and square-jawed, his blond hair meticulously combed to one side and pressed down at the ears where his sunglasses normally rest.

"Howard," Danly says in greeting.

The other men—both built like smokestacks—smile at Agent Danly's grimace. One is black and the other an islander; they both look like they dropped out of the NFL and into private security. Which is entirely possible.

"If you're done playing cowboy," the blond man says with mock hand-pistols shooting in the air, "time to let the professionals take over."

His two cronies chuckle. Danly does not.

"Are those *malasadas?* That's one way to make yourself useful...."

"They're not for you," Danly says, swinging the box away from the man's grasp like a spoiled child unwilling to share his ball.

"The Colonel will see you now," the assistant says, his arm open toward the door.

"Sure would've helped your career if you'd solved this case before we showed up, huh?" Howard says as a parting shot. "Too bad...."

The assistant shows the three men in, closes the door behind them, then returns to the desk. As he sits, he says, "It will be just a few minutes, Agent Danly."

You look to your partner for explanation. "Remember when I said there'd be an official investigation team here within 72 hours? Time's up."

"What does that mean for us?" you ask.

Danly sighs. "We'll find out soon, I'm sure."

"Maybe he'll let you stay on the investigation once you share how much we've found out."

"What *exactly* have we found out?" Danly snaps. He shakes his head. "I'm sorry, it just feels... over. Agent Howard is old Army buddies with the Ambassador, so he's going to be lead investigator for sure."

"Is that why they call him 'the Colonel?'"

Danly nods. "He retired as a full-bird from the Army before getting into the Foreign Service."

The assistant rises from his chair and says, "He'll see you now, Agent Danly."

"Stay here, Rookie. We'll call you in soon."

When the door opens, a voice booms out, "Paul, come take notes, will you?"

"And bring in those *malasadas,* Danly," Howard calls.

With stooped shoulders, Danly proceeds. Paul, the assistant, rushes back to the desk, grabs a pad of paper, and enters the office behind Agent Danly.

The door closes; you're alone. The Ambassador's office is thick and insulated; you can't hear anything above a murmur from within.

How to pass the time?

- Take a seat; just relax until I'm called in. Go to page 39
- Peruse the many plaques and awards on the wall. Go to page 352
- Take a peek at the assistant's computer screen. Go to page 45

Interrogation

Not for nothing, you're up and chasing a kid who wields an AK-47 while you hold only the knowledge that a child soldier typically has less remorse than a serial killer. You sprint away from the battle in the street, racing across the rooftop in an effort to catch up with a seventeen-year-old who spends his days and night fleeing from danger. So yeah, he's faster than you.

Without even thinking about it, you're on to the next rooftop as part of your pursuit. It's conjoined, like most of the buildings in the *favela*, and allows you a bird's-eye view of your prey. Even the buildings that aren't connected are so close that you can easily hop from one to another, as you're doing now. There are precious few streets as wide as the one behind you with the armored car in it.

Irma makes a leap across the alleyway—her legs outstretched like an Olympic hurdler's—in an effort to cut off the boy, should he veer to the right. But he veers left. The detective waves at you, signaling you to try and cut him off.

Pushing yourself to your limit, you dash across the rooftop in a diagonal line. Before you know what's happened, you've jumped off of the building and are careening toward the boy. You collide with him, both of you falling into one of the slum's many trash heaps. That does slow the force of impact, but *man,* does it stink.

His eyes wide and terrified, the boy freezes. There's an *explosion* from back in the street near Elite Squad and the armored car. You reflexively turn your head toward the sound, but you can't see anything from here. Sensing your momentary distraction, the boy elbows you in the face. Stinging pain rises through your nose and sends a rush of tears to your eyes. While you shake off your daze, he scrambles to claim his assault rifle, only to find it firmly pressed against the pavement under a woman's running shoe.

Looking past the shoe to a jean pant leg, then to a banana-yellow soccer jersey, he sees Detective Irma Dos Santos pointing a small service revolver at his head. The boy mutters something in Portuguese, then rolls back to sit up with his palms raised high.

"We need to get off the streets," Irma says. "I can hold him, but if his friends show up, we're in trouble."

You stand, shake off the garbage, and look inside the nearest hovel where a young woman holds her baby tight. She cries, silently sobbing and shivering. Her upper lip trembles, shiny with mucous. She rocks back and forth, unable to take her eyes off you.

Irma shoves the boy inside, instructs the woman to leave, waits as she flees with her child, and then hands you the AK-47.

"Hold onto this," she says. "Don't worry, I told her to go stay with friends."

She has a brief, impassioned conversation with the boy, who sits on the couch after Irma directs him to do so with her pistol. "His nickname is *Falador* —the mouth. If he got the name because he talks too much, you might be in luck. Ask your questions and I'll translate."

Another explosion rocks through the slums, this one even louder. You feel the impact; it's like the tremor from an earthquake; dust cascades from a crack in the ceiling.

"Be quick; we want to be gone before his friends come looking."

You nod. "Ask him if he's heard of the murdered American woman; that's a start."

She asks him in Portuguese and he answers. At the end, he looks at you and spits on the ground. Irma translates: "He says the only murdered American around here is going to be you when his friends show up."

- "Ask him again, more forcefully." Go to page 135
- "Tell him we're not after him or his friends; just the truth. He must have lost someone…." Go to page 313
- "I don't have the stomach for this; he's not going to tell us anything. Let's go before the others find us." Go to page 78

Intercepted

"Just tell the bus driver you need to go to the *Universidade do Estado do Rio de Janeiro,*" Viktor tells you. "My place is within walking distance of the University." After drawing a quick map and writing down the address for you, Viktor gives you the key to his unit and sends you on your way. It really isn't far, despite the city's constant, overwhelming traffic. Bertram skirts a highway, passing a massive soccer stadium and sports arena, and finally takes you to the university. At a traffic roundabout (sporting a modern-art totem sculpture in the center) you can see the first signs of the school.

It's impressive in size, but unfortunately, not in aesthetics. The building is gray, old, dusty, and square. If anything, it looks like a mega-apartment complex. From out your window, you'd guess it's maybe fourteen stories high and just as many city blocks wide. You can't help but be impressed by the scale; it's nearly as large as the soccer coliseum next door. Which, incidentally, is the largest in the world.

You exit at the bus stop, look around to get your bearings, and unfold the map Viktor gave you. It's written on that same checkered-green paper, and the boxes make his map uniform and—surprisingly—to perfect scale. Leave it to an engineer….

Using the soccer stadium as reference, you start on your route. Around the corner from the university, past the larger and more expensive houses, is a series of duplexes. They're off the main road and appear to be spacious and new enough to be expensive in their own right. Coupled with an ideal location (it was a rather short walk), and the visual appeal of a lush, forested backdrop, you can assume Viktor must have been doing something right to afford such lodgings.

You had expected to see the apartment complex surrounded by police tape, with federal agents swarming like an ant hill of investigators, but this isn't a television show. It's not "cue the crime…and cut to the investigation" in real life. It's probably too early for them to have pinpointed his address, but they'll be here soon enough, so you'd better hurry.

You walk past the units, looking for Viktor's. It's a quiet neighborhood; these duplexes should be beyond the price range for student housing. An old man in a suede tracksuit shuffles his way down the walk, stopping to pick up a receipt from the bushes and take it to the waste bin.

He smiles and waves, so you nod back, arriving on Viktor's doorstep. There's stillness in the morning air as you press the key into the lock, engage the latch, and turn the knob to let yourself in. Even though you know the man who owns this unit is across town, you feel like you're barging into someone's house and are half-surprised that an outraged tenant doesn't arrive to curse you.

The apartment is quiet and empty. Despite the glamor of the complex, the inside of his lodging is spartan. There are several bookshelves full of volumes both scientific and enlightening. The living room has a single chair with cushions that look well-worn and comfortable. There's a lamp on the end table and a dog-eared copy of *The Stranger* by Albert Camus.

The room opens into a kitchen with a bartop counter, a table with two chairs; across from the kitchen is a sliding glass patio door. No sign of the laptop yet, but you can see there's a hall leading into some back rooms. Most likely you'll find the computer in one of the bedrooms, especially if he has one converted into a office and….

Someone starts jimmying the front door behind you. Your heart jumps into your throat and every hair stands on end. Panic gives a necessary shot of adrenaline to your legs, which send you sprinting to:

- The back patio! Time to get outta Dodge! Go to page 281
- The kitchen nook. If I hide behind the bar-top counter, I can spy on the newcomer. Go to page 213
- The rooms. Snag the laptop, quick! Go to page 279

Interrupting POW!

You run back into the street, looking over your shoulder as you flee from the gun battle. Damn, another Elite Squad policeman comes, looking for his partner. You fire blindly at him and he hugs the side of the building for cover. While you've got him pinned down, Viktor comes out and offers a few shots of his own before turning to run. But then he goes down.

You look up at the rooftop just in time to see the assassin who's been following you. One of his pistols smokes from shooting Viktor, and the other pistol is trained on you—he watches Viktor with one eye, and keeps one eye focused on you.

He fires.

THE END

Into the Lion's Den

Around the corner from the university, past the larger and more expensive houses, is a series of duplexes. They're off the main road and appear to be spacious and new enough to be expensive in their own right. Coupled with an ideal location (one could easily bike or even walk to the university or stadium), and the visual appeal of a lush, forested backdrop, you can assume Viktor must have been doing something right to afford such lodgings.

Agent Bertram confirms the address on his phone, then parks the car a few units away from the home registered to Viktor Lucio de Ocampo.

Removing the car keys, he says, "Listen, if the guy beat us home, he'll be surprised to see us. He was cool and collected up by the statue, but that's because things were on his terms. When a criminal is surprised, that's when they become dangerous. Keep your wits about you."

You nod. Exiting the car, you slip in behind Bertram, your heart pounding with adrenaline. A woman walking two toy teacup pooches looks at you with suspicion, but you don't much care. When you get to the door of Viktor's unit, Agent Bertram slides to the side, up against the wall, and indicates with a nod that you should get off the porch as well. Maybe he doesn't want either of you to be seen through the peep-hole. As you move out of view, Bertram pulls out his sidearm, then knocks on the door with his fist.

Oh, you realize, he doesn't want you to get hit should this guy decide to shoot through the door.

No response. After a moment, Bertram bangs on the door again, this time with a few extra raps. He's got that "cop knock" down!

He shouts something in Portuguese, but still no response. After another moment of silence, he pounds once more and adds, "Viktor, we just want to talk!"

Nothing. Bertram turns to you and says, "I'm going in."

"Don't you need a warrant or something?" you ask.

He smiles. "This is Rio, baby."

Handgun raised, he kicks the door in. With practiced efficiency, Agent Bertram sweeps the house, looking in the corners and into each room before ducking back out to you.

"It's clear," he says.

You enter the unit, but it's as if no one lives here. It's completely empty: no furniture—nothing. It's not clean, like an apartment ready to be rented would be, instead there are the telltale signs of a human occupant. The carpet is dirtier at the entrance and near the rear patio. There are scuffs on the walls near doorways, and nails protrude from where pictures once hung, their ghostly impressions left in the dust.

"Damn, he's cleared out," Bertram says, holstering the handgun.

A barking dog catches your attention and you look out the rear window. The same woman from the front walks her teacup pooches down a path in front of the woods, pulling at their leashes to get them away from the woodline. Standing just at the forested edge is a man.

He's tall, well-built, his black hair close-cropped like a combat soldier's. Clean-shaven, but there's a thick scar along the front of his chin like you'd expect to see on someone who flew over the handlebar of a motorcycle. He wears aviator-style shooting-range glasses and his face is as pale as a skull sun-bleached in the desert. He wears all black—combat boots, tactical cargo pants, a vest to match, and skin-tight long-sleeved under-armor. He has dual-holstered handguns on the sides of his vest and wears black motorcycle gloves.

In short, he's terrifying.

"Ummm, Bertram?" you say, raising a finger to point out the window.

The agent rushes into action, removing his service weapon with one hand and slinging the glass door of the porch open with the other.

"Stop right there!" he shouts.

The man calmly shakes his head "no" and backs into the trees.

Agent Bertram sprints up the grassy hillside toward the trees; you're only a few feet behind him. In the green, there's no sign of the mysterious onlooker. The foliage is thick, but even so, it's odd for him to disappear without a trace.

"Who was that?" you ask.

"How the hell should I know?"

"Think he has anything to do with Viktor?"

"Again, no idea—but I'll tell you one thing, that was no innocent bystander. Pro-tip: when people run, it means they have something to hide. Keep an eye out for that guy, but let's go check in with the front office and see when Viktor moved out."

Paranoid and somewhat frightened, you follow Bertram and walk cautiously toward the rental office. Any tenant walking to their car catches your eye. No matter how innocuous they appear, they could be a threat; any movement could signal that it's the Man in Black.

You jump when a door slams, but it's just an elderly man with a sack of groceries. Something zips across the lawn—fast—and you duck, but it's just two kids playing soccer. To put it mildly, you're on edge.

You enter the rental office and find only a single attendant on duty, then lower your guard a little. The room is smallish—it could be one of the apartments furnished with office accoutrements—and the enclosed space is comforting. It'd be hard for the Man in Black to shoot you in here.

"Do you speak English?" Bertram asks the attendant.

Hesitantly, the woman shakes her head. She's in her mid-30s, somewhat overweight, and wears all black herself—a professional pantsuit and jacket with an orange blouse. Her hair looks dyed black, and she's painted her fingernails orange to complete the total coordinated look.

Bertram speaks to her in Portuguese and her face lights up. While he interviews her, you look about the office for anything that could prove clue-worthy. There are several information brochures, but none in English. Evidently this place is off the beaten path for tourists. There are three desks; the other two attendants are off-duty. You take a mint from a dish on one of the empty desks.

Pictures tacked to a corkboard show residents at a community picnic; you take the time to scan the faces—looking for the man from the incident, Viktor himself, or the Man in Black (just in case). Nothing catches your eye.

"All right, we're done here," Agent Bertram says. "Our guy has not officially moved out, as I suspected. His rent is still good and there's a deposit on hold. This reeks of premeditation. If he cleared his apartment in advance, it means he knew we'd come looking for him. He's most likely in hiding. He might've even hired that guy to see whoever came snooping around."

"The Man in Black?"

"Yeah. Looks like a classic 'merc to me—gun for hire."

Bertram's phone chimes and he checks the message. "Danly wants to meet up tonight for a progress report. Listen, if this Man in Black guy is paid to do more than just watch, things could get dangerous. I think it might be best if you hang out in the evidence locker with Agent Danly. Let's head back for now."

- *Head to the DSS hotel.* Go to page 36

Investigate

You're not sure if it's meant to throw off any possible tail, or if you're really just that far off the beaten path, but you've taken three different buses, then walked a few blocks between each one, and finally made it to the periphery of Jane Nightingale's apartment complex.

You can tell, even from a couple hundred yards away, that this is the kind of place you'd live in only if you had to, if it were all you could afford. There's virtually no public green space, which says a lot in this country. It's not seedy per se, at least not in the bright sunlight.

Her apartment is gravid with Rio cops.

"Damn," Viktor says. "No American agents, but the Rio police are here in force. I hadn't counted on that. How many young women go missing each year here? And yet one American causes all this uproar."

"Maybe they'll uncover the truth?" you ask.

He shakes his head. "They're just in the way. I need a distraction, I need a way in."

- "I'll provide a distraction; you go for a window." Go to page 106
- "Didn't we just learn that money talks? Let's try that." Go to page 83
- "How badly do you need us in there? Couldn't we come back another time?" Go to page 34

In Your Dreams

"You watch too many movies," Maria says with a smirk. "Good night."

She climbs into the cab of a tractor, curling up on the bench seat to go to bed. As soon as she closes the door, the windows steam up from the wet heat of her body. You look to Bertram.

He shakes his head. "I'm not that cold, Hotshot. Get some sleep."

➢ *Dream on.* Go to page 358

In Your Sleep

"Fine!" the governor bellows. "Have it your way."

He turns to his security guard and adds something in Portuguese. It's loud enough that Bertram and Maria can overhear, and they each protest.

"You're just going to lock us up?" Bertram says.

"I won't be your prisoner!" Maria cries.

"Relax… I'll return you to São Paulo in the morning," he says, a devilish grin on his face.

The security guards escort you back to the room where you cleaned up, locking the door tightly behind you. You try without success to communicate through the thick walls with Bertram or Maria.

Of course you can't sleep. You pace about the room like a caged animal when it dawns on you—the window! You rush over, release and pull up the latch, but it's sealed tight. Rain runs down the glass in serpentine trails.

The TV! You'll smash it through the window and escape! But just as you're about to, something glinting in the moonlight catches your eye. There, just below you at the rear of the house, is a man in a rain poncho.

He's holding a rifle.

They've actually posted guards outside your room in case you try to escape. A feeling of dread sinks in; there's no way out. You feel it deep down; you're doomed. It's as if you're trapped in a horror story. *It was a dark and stormy night….*

Then a key is inserted in the lock to your door. The Sugar King enters, with two of his thugs. The Governor sighs when he sees you.

"I had hoped you'd be asleep, so we could do this quietly," he says.

"Do what?" you say, hiding the fear from your voice.

"Kill you, of course. A pillow over the face would have been easiest."

"You're just going to murder us in cold blood?"

He smiles. "Once your helicopter crashed, you were dead anyway."

"They know we're here!" you bluff. "Agent Bertram called the consulate."

"Nice try. But I called in the helicopter crash and learned that your government hasn't heard from Agent Bertram since he left São Paulo. So I told them I found three bodies in the helicopter."

You try to run, but the two men grab you and force you onto the bed. The Sugar King picks up the pillow. "Now we just need to put the bodies back in," he says, lowering the pillow over your face.

THE END

It Sucks

After you *click* the device into place, it activates, rearranging itself like a Rubik's Cube, expanding in some places and contracting in others. You toss the grape-fruit-size object toward the men, who all dive out of the way as if you'd just thrown a grenade. The armed guards seek cover as well, buying you a few seconds' time.

You grasp Viktor and pull him out of the room, slamming the door behind you just as the air is *sucked* out of the room. The door cracks dully under the mounting pressure, and you can be certain they're all dead in there.

The "STAFF ONLY" door guard is dumbfounded, his face awash with horror at what you've just done. You punch the young man squarely in the jaw, sending him to the floor.

Viktor is still lost in shock and covered in blood, so there's no way you can just walk out the front door. Luckily for you, there's an emergency exit at every wing on the building. You rush out the nearest one, setting off the alarm system, and quickly get lost amongst the revelers of *Carnaval.*

Viktor is clearly in shock, unable to process what's just happened. So it's nearly two hours before he speaks, cold and devoid of emotion.

"Thank you for everything, Tourist. Because of you, justice has been served. The world is without three of its devils now. My patents are on that thumb drive, and I leave you to do what you will with them."

"You're not going to move forward with your discovery?" you ask.

"Be careful who you show that to; there are still many other devils in this world."

He walks off into the shadows and disappears forever. Maybe you can leave the evidence of corruption to the press, but Viktor's right, there are others who will rise up to take the place of those you killed tonight.

You may never know a feeling of safety again, but you've won…sort of.

➢ Go to page 304

Jacob Marley

Viktor sighs, and reluctantly prods further. With a confounded look, he says, "He tells us we'll understand why soon enough."

A sound like a thick chain scraping against concrete is suddenly interjected into the conversation. You all look at the door. The man who enters is pale, with blue veins just beneath the surface of his thin skin. Broken shackles, the remains of split handcuffs, are around each wrist, as if he either wants to wear them for jewelry or he's recently escaped from prison. From his pallor, you'd say he's been hiding out for quite a while.

He has an AK-47 assault rifle trained on you.

"What's this?" you say, but you already know.

Viktor nervously translates as Tinho introduces the man. "This is Marley, his business partner. 'What business,' you ask? The business of you. Us. He says, 'We operate right here, out of our money-changing hole. You see, we get plenty of referrals from around town, and the arms dealer will get his cut, but anyone not belonging to this *favela* must pay a toll. Give us your wallets and that backpack.'"

Closing his eyes and turning toward your robbers, Viktor simply says. "No."

Marley smashes the rifle butt into Viktor's gut, then turns back, points the business end of the weapon at you and waits to see if Viktor will comply. At length, he does.

Tinho goes through the backpack, removing one of Viktor's "Death Star"-shaped weapons and asks him just what the hell the object is. Viktor pantomimes a way to manipulate the device while explaining in Portuguese.

He turns to you and says, "See you in Manhattan, Tourist."

Tinho *clicks* the tiny thing into place and now the device has begun moving, rearranging itself like a Rubik's Cube, expanding in some places and contracting in others. Fearful, the two thieves shout to Viktor to explain himself, and now the AK-47 is pointed right toward the scientist.

Viktor tries to answer, but his breath is *sucked out* of him by the device. You feel it too, your insides collapsing as the tiny thing turns into something akin to a miniature black hole and sucks out all the air from the room. The walls, pictures, and television break inward, the ceiling threatens to collapse, and every person in the room dies when the strange bomb implodes.

THE END

You tear down the alley to the right, occasionally glancing to the rooftop where the assassin might be. Still, you have to be vigilant and focus on the here and now. There are plenty of recesses through which the blue-eyed man might escape. Irma doesn't follow you. She just shakes her head, backs into the other alley, and lets you go it alone.

Fear be damned; you're not going to let this guy get away again. There's a feeling of nakedness, being in this war zone without a weapon, but you know that the suspect left his AK-47 back in the previous alley, so he's in the same defenseless state.

Most of the shops are barred up or sealed with roll-away metal doors, so you keep running. The barred windows and barbed gates are evidence of the measures one is required to take to have safety in the *favelas*.

Up ahead, the alley snakes around two blind corners. After you pass the second one, you see you've caught up with the suspect! He's working on a gate and nearly has it open, but you arrive just in time to tackle him.

He tries wrestling free, but you've got him pinned. In an unconscious burst of excitement, you exclaim, "I've got you!"

He looks up at you, then past you, over your shoulder. The first thing you see are those blue eyes, which glow almost purple under the amber streetlights. There is the fear in his eyes and then, turning around, you see its source.

The assassin, the Man in Black, is there too. One of his handguns points at the suspect, and as you stand up, the other handgun rises to greet you. You see something else, something strange—he's looking at you, but he's also looking at the suspect…

Behind his shooting-range aviators, the man's eyes are moving independently of one another.

At first you think he's cross-eyed. But his right eye looks you up and down, scanning for threats, while his left eye is trained on your bespectacled rival, darting carefully over him as he stands with his hands raised in surrender. You lift your palms as well, his right eye watching as you do.

Seeing you're both unarmed, he smiles. In a simultaneous motion, he squeezes the triggers of each pistol and ends both your lives.

THE END

Jane's Addiction

The agents reconvene at the coffee station to fuel up before heading out. The coffee is tasteless and burnt, with powdered creamer, which means it's government standard, but the men drink it down in ample quantities nonetheless. There's a brief silent moment while the men prepare their coffee—Bertram takes cream and two sugars, Danly drinks his with the liquid hazelnut additive only.

"Find anything?" Bertram asks.

"Nightingale had a fiance named 'Viktor' with a 'k.' No last name yet."

"Didn't find a ring on the body, did we?"

"No, but it was a recent engagement, so the killer could have taken it without needing to cut off the finger," Danly says. Noticing your grimace, he adds, "Wedding rings tend to become permanent, as fingers swell up over the years. So when someone kills a married woman and steals her ring, the finger goes with it."

"Gross," you say.

Danly ignores the comment. "No idea where we can find the guy, but it's a good starting point. What about you?"

"Not much," Agent Bertram says. "She specifically asked for this post a few months back, but that's not unusual, especially if the fiance is from around here."

"We should check in with the police station. See where they're at in their investigation."

Using a red bought-in-bulk straw to stir his coffee, Agent Bertram turns to you and says, "Identify all the possibilities, all the 'what-if' scenarios, then rule them out one-by-one until all that remains is what actually happened—*that's* how we'll solve the case."

"No, it's not," Danly quips. "We'll solve the case by following the evidence. Standard police work, none of that 'gut instinct' crap."

Bertram looks at Danly, who blows on the edge of his Styrofoam coffee cup, cooling it. You can't be sure, but it looks like throwing the hot coffee into his partner's smug face is crossing Bertram's mind right now. Instead, the RSO's approach diffuses the moment. With no jacket on this time, he holds out a sheet of paper as if the document physically leads him to you.

"This fax just came in from Embassy records. Evidently your girl had failed a drug test."

The agents scan the paper, brows furrowed, heads shaking.

"Look into the drug angle," their supervisor continues. "Maybe she got in over her head?"

"Will do, sir," Danly says. "Do you think we should put the subject's sketch into the Rewards for Justice Program?"

The RSO shakes his head. "That's a big negative. He doesn't know we're onto him yet. The only witness he's looking out for is our new friend here, so we don't want to scare him off by plastering his face on matchbooks."

"In Rio, you might have better results just offering up a bounty," Bertram grumbles.

Danly glares at him.

"Listen up, boys. The new investigation team will be here before the opening night of the Energy Summit. That's Friday night, the start of *Carnaval*, when you guys will be transferred to conference security. That means you've got three days—seventy-two hours—and I want some results. The Ambassador has made a by-name request of the new investigators, so you can bet your ass he's going to be eyes-on this whole time. If you can solve it before they get here, I'll bake some goddamned brownies. Got me?"

The men nod in solemn understanding. The RSO leaves and the three of you do the same, walking back toward the parking garage and the government SUV.

"Since when do we give warnings for piss test failures?" Bertram asks.

"Good question. Might be worth a trip up there to talk to her supervisor."

When you reach the SUV, you find a note tucked under the windshield wiper.

"What's this, a parking ticket?" you ask, grabbing it. You open the note, which was folded into fourths, curious as to what it might hold. The paper is the color of pale chlorophyll and covered with cross-hatched lines. The effect divides the sheet into tiny, uniform boxes.

"Engineering paper," Agent Danly informs.

Written in the center, in a simple script very different from the note last night, is:

"No doubt you're looking for me.
Let's meet where we can do so with open arms."

"What does it mean?" you ask, showing the note to the agents.

Both men draw their handguns.

"It means he was *here*," Bertram says, looking everywhere but at you.

"Who?"

"The killer!" Danly hisses, sweeping over the SUV for bombs. "Jesus Christ."

There was no sign of the guy, nor of any tampering to the vehicle, so you leave the consulate security to sweep the garage and turn in the note to be analyzed by the FISH system: Forensic Information System for Handwriting—a database, Agent Danly explains, that the State Department keeps to compare every threatening note the US government has ever received.

Now you're riding in the back of the SUV.

"Where's a place where you can meet with open arms?" Danly asks.

"Certainly not a police station," Bertram says. "He'd be cuffed, for sure."

"It could mean something else, like maybe 'arms' means 'guns,'" you suggest.

"So 'open arms' means what? He wants to meet with guns drawn, like a shootout?" Bertram asks.

"Doubt it," Danly replies.

"Open arms means 'on good terms,' maybe," you try.

"Yeah, but where's that? It's not exactly like there's some kind of neutral ground we can meet on," Bertram says.

"He could be a—" you say, trying to think of the right term. Not quite "witness" or "informant," but… "source. The note was written in a different hand than the other one; it might not be the killer."

"What other one?" Bertram asks.

"The note I found at the crime scene."

"You mean the one that no one else saw," Danly says. "The one that mysteriously disappeared."

"It was *there*," you say.

You look out the window, watching traffic and the people walking on the streets. You see boutique shops/stands, created overnight from plywood and scrap metal in an effort to capitalize on the population boom that accompanies *Carnaval*. So many people, and one of them is the killer.

Finally, Agent Bertram says, "Okay, so you saw a note and it's different. But that doesn't mean anything. He could have written one or the other. Or neither. Or both—one with his dominant hand, one with his weaker hand, maybe even in all caps, to throw us off."

"The first note was in all caps," you admit.

"There you go. And an experienced killer, one who knows what he's doing, can distort his own handwriting. He could've even paid off one of the Brazilian guards to write and plant the note for him."

Danly shakes his head, then scoffs. "He was right there, right under our noses, maybe even following us! *Christ*."

Looking out the window again, you see Him—up on the mountainside. Christ, that is. All 130 concrete feet of Him, overlooking the city from His perch atop Corcovado Mountain, His arms widespread in a gesture of magnanimous acceptance.

"The statue!" you say. "Christ the Redeemer—a place with open arms!"

"Not bad," Danly says. "It's very public, and he knows we can't arrest him without cause."

"But what he doesn't realize, is that we've got somebody who can ID him. As soon as you say it's him, we take the guy in. Have you made it up to the statue yet?" Bertram asks.

"I have not."

"Cool, let's take the cog train. The guy can wait on us a bit."

"What are you, nuts?" Danly asks. "Let's just drive up there. It's time to nail the bastard."

"Hold on now. Have you ever taken the train? It's nice. And we won't spook the guy if we take the tourist route. But if we show up in a patrol car…."

"You're an idiot, the guy *invited* us, let's go!"

- "Hang on now, I think I'd like the cog train." Go to page 288
- "I can see the sights later, let's go!" Go to page 268

"**O**h! Of course. I'm so sorry." He hands you a press badge. Maybe you can keep it and use it on someone else later? You clip it to your collar. "So, where should we start?"

"I'm writing a piece on new energy," you say.

"You've come to the right place! Acting with social and environmental responsibility, to us, is a commitment to people and the planet," he says, reciting the company line.

His hands are folded in front of him and he practically beams with excitement. Espresso much?

"Meaning what, exactly?" you say. "That you try to keep your oil production as clean as possible?"

"Certainly, yes, but we have a whole branch dedicated to alternative fuels. *Petrobras Biocombustível* works with ethanol and biodiesel, both of which reduce our dependency on foreign oil."

"Then I assume you're familiar with the work of Dr. Viktor Lucio de Ocampo?"

The plastic smile falls away. "I can't say I know the name."

"Really? The foremost researcher, scheduled as the keynote speaker at the Energy Summit here in Brazil? I understand many of his patents could make him a national treasure—his name doesn't ring a bell?"

He picks up a manila folder from the lobby coffee table. "My schedule shows a different name for keynote speaker. We're actually really excited to hear the new updates on solar energy from Doctor—"

"Why did your company force Dr. Ocampo off the speakers' list? Had he pledged to share his results with foreign investors?"

"I'm sorry, but I have no idea—"

"Lying won't help!" you snap, trying to badger him into cooperating.

Your plan fails. He snaps the press badge back from you and points to the door. "Okay, this interview is over! I'll call your ride. Please wait outside or I'll be forced to call security."

- *Go wait for Agent Bertram.* Go to page 98

Jungle Fruit

The three of you each take a glass of wine and the Governor raises his glass in a toast.

"*Saúde*!" he says. "To your health."

The wine begins sweet, with a tangy, bitter, not unpleasant finish. The glasses are filled to the top.

"Now then," he continues. "Why are you here? Please, tell me quickly before we proceed."

Agent Bertram swirls the wine in his glass. "Honestly, Governor, I had only come as a curiosity. To ask you a few questions about the Energy Summit and Dr. Viktor Lucio de Ocampo. Things turned hostile when your men shot down our helicopter."

"That was unfortunate, but you should have called first. I would have gladly seen you."

"So you admit it!" you say. "Those thugs are on your payroll! Do you have the balls to admit you're starting these fires? Grilling up the rainforest to plant more farmland?"

The Governor smiles. "With pleasure. What do you think your early Americans did, hmmm? You cut down your forests for industry and now you're the wealthiest nation on Earth. We may be starting late, but why should we be the only ones with restrictions on our growth? If you want clean rainforests, pay us the same money we could make on sugarcane and I'd gladly let the toucans be."

Bertram stirs uncomfortably. His brow furrows and he says, "Why would you admit all this? Surely you wouldn't, unless…"

The agent looks at his wine glass.

"*Eu estou doente*," Maria says, just before dropping her glass and collapsing to the floor.

Bertram catches her right before she hits the tile, lowering her gently with one arm. He seems to have lost control of his other arm.

Then you feel it too. Cramps rip at the center of your body, more terrible pain than anything you've ever felt. You drop to one knee. You can't control your limbs anymore. The wine glass falls from your grasp, breaks on the floor, and bleeds out across the tile.

"You…you can't do this," you groan.

"Clearly, you don't know who I am. I can do anything I want."

Your vision fades to black, sounds go dull, and you slip into unconsciousness, never to awaken again.

THE END

Just the Facts, Ma'am, err, Sir

"Suit yourself," he says. "Suffice it to say this: Viktor has made incomparable leaps and bounds in the arena of new energy. He's found a way to make ethanol profitable without subsidies. Without relying on just one cash-crop to monopolize the harvest. Without the billionaire-owned sugarcane industry. Five percent of the population here owns eighty percent of the land.

"I can't say for sure because I wasn't involved, but if you want to learn who could possibly want to shut out the discoveries of a brilliant scientist—perhaps you should expand your *weltanschauung* and pay a visit to a sugarcane plantation. The Governor of this territory, Mateo Ferro, owns every sugarcane plantation within five hundred miles."

"The so-called Sugar King?" Bertram asks.

"As you say, sir."

"Why are you helping us?" you ask.

"Because first and foremost, I'm a scientist. I want to live on a planet where discoveries push mankind ahead, not where greed and corruption keep us back. But be wary, the deeper you press into the jungle, the further you'll be from the shelter of man's laws, and these plantations tend to 'crop up' very deep indeed."

Agent Bertram closes his notebook, extends his hand, and says, "Thank you for your time."

Upon leaving, he adds to you, "If we were looking for someone who hates Viktor, we might have a motive, but why the girl? Something doesn't add up. Let's check in at the local consulate and see if Danly has reported in from last night. I'm afraid we might've hit a dead end with this whole Viktor thing. Hopefully Danly's got something."

- *Head to the consulate.* Go to page 314

Keep Moving

With a good distance between herself and the three men, Irma Dos Santos follows the crooked cops across the street and over toward another alley. She stops, looking for a way to scale the wall.

"Another rooftop?" you grumble.

She smiles and finds an iron gate to climb. Shaking your head, you follow her up. This rooftop is higher than the last and you have to shimmy up an intermediary ledge before you make it all the way to the top. You try to keep quiet and to ignore the vertigo that accompanies the precarious handholds, only succeeding in the former goal.

Looking down the alley, you're met with a grisly sight. Even removed from it by height, it's all you can do not to gag. The alley is lined with old car tires and one of the cops is hunched over a stack of tires, vomiting into the center cavern. The other two cops look down at the blackened image on the pavement—as seared into the concrete as it is into your retinas.

Lying prone with arms outstretched in a permanent crawl for help is a skeletal body. This poor soul has been burned beyond recognition; only a charred corpse is left behind. You can't tell gender, age, or even ethnicity.

Detective Muniz and the strong-stomached cop are having a heated discussion. You look to Irma. "They're discussing whether or not to move the body. That guy is saying that it's already been called in. Lucio says unless they can solve the crime and arrest a suspect, they're better off dumping the body in a different precinct and letting somebody else deal with an unsolved murder on their watch."

"My God," you breathe out.

"I had no idea he was this bad, I promise."

Behind several gas cans, Detective Lucio Muniz finds a rolled-up tarp and spreads it out on the ground.

"*Merda!*" Irma says. "They're actually going to move the body."

The other cops help him roll up the corpse.

"Let's go, now! You need to forget what you saw here tonight, *Americano*. For the safety of both of us. Now come on, let's get out of here before he sees my car. Give me the revolver. I'll take you back to your hotel."

➢ *Leave the slum.* Go to page 300

Kick the Hornets

You scramble for something—anything—you can use to defend yourself from these pirates. A water hose? No, that won't do. A fire extinguisher? Maybe, but the reach is pretty short. A flagpole? It's about twice as long and thick as a broomstick. That might work.

Without any hint of irony, you remove the Brazilian flag and turn back to bash one of the pirates with the flagpole just as he makes it above the ship's side. You connect cleanly to the side of his head, sending the dazed man tumbling down into the river.

Now the other passengers are awake and come to see the source of the commotion. The boat's cook arrives with a kitchen knife held defensively, but clearly he's too frightened to help. Families hide behind the fathers, who in turn press back against their families. Looks like you're on your own.

You ready the flagpole for another strike just as two more angry pirates pop up with AK-47s aimed right at you. Uh-oh.

The passengers scream and hide as the two pirates blast apart the Brazilian flag and the brave tourist holding it.

THE END

Kiss Kiss, Bang Bang (In No Particular Order)

The revolver kicks back in your hands as the bullet explodes from its casing in a deafening echo. With trained proficiency, Irma, Lucio, and the two policemen all draw their weapons and take fire. In the span of three short seconds, a total of eighteen shots are fired and the three men lie dead. You can't be sure if the fatal shots were yours, Irma's, or a combination, but the outcome is the same.

Three cops are dead, and though the two of you are unscathed, you're responsible. Irma turns toward you, but instead of terror on her face it's a look you can't quite place.

She grabs you in a firm embrace, kissing you deeply and passionately, perhaps beyond what's merited for having just escaped death. "They were going to kill us," she says, panting as she pulls away.

"What do we do now?"

She steps forward into the alley with the burnt corpse and the three fresh ones. Without a word, she takes a gasoline can and pours it over the bodies. Taking a lighter from one of the dead cops, she sets all three of them ablaze.

"Never speak of this again," she says. "For our own safety, we cannot report them. Who knows what friends they have in the department?"

You nod your understanding.

"Give me the revolver. I'll take you back to your hotel."

➢ *Return to the hotel.* Go to page 300

A Key Piece of Information

Irma takes a step back when she hears his answer. She's dumbfounded. Her mouth hangs open and her eyes glitter with discovery.

"What? What did he say?" you practically shout.

"He says 'no.'"

That doesn't make any sense. "No? No what?"

"She didn't owe any money. She didn't deal in drugs," Irma says, her voice breathless. "No one has ever heard of her, he's sure of it. It's all they've been talking about—he says one of his friends knows one of the guys who pulled the trigger and he's *certain* that they never heard of her before the night she was killed."

"But that would mean…."

"It was a hit."

Jane Nightingale was targeted specifically…she was *assassinated.* But why? Who? "Who ordered the hit? Does he know? What's the name of the killer? If we can bring that guy in…"

The drug trafficker is already shaking his head. Detective Dos Santos asks, but he just shakes his head more firmly. "He says he cannot, no matter how much you pay him. They will kill him."

"Please!" you shout.

He shakes his head, raises three fingers, then opens his hand to receive his reward.

- Pay him the $R300. Then catch up to Agent Danly. Go to page 78
- Tell him his reward awaits him in heaven, then head out. Go to page 194

Knock, Knock

Viktor steps to one side of the doorway and you to the other. The unspoken hope you share is that police or drug traffickers might look inside, think the room was empty, and continue on their way. No such luck.

An Elite Squad member steps over the threshold of the doorway and is met by the unpleasant surprise of *both* of you bashing the butts of your weapons against his face. That was completely reactionary and unplanned, but it works splendidly.

The man crumples in a heap on the floor.

"Cover me," Viktor says.

The policeman wears protective body armor and is clad in black, much like the US SWAT teams. Viktor stoops and drags the body away from the door into the room proper. You point your sub-machinegun into the open air, silently praying this man was alone.

"Should we run?"

"I've got an idea," Viktor replies. "I'll get in his uniform, then escort you out as my prisoner."

"Why do I have to be the prisoner?"

"Because I'm the *Brasileiro*. You can't pretend to be a Portuguese-speaking cop."

- "Ummm, let's just run." Go to page 165
- "I'll stay at the door, hurry up and get changed!" Go to page 351

A Long-Awaited Discovery

"You don't know?" she says, not without a little indignation. "The professor had finally cracked cellulosic ethanol—the Holy Grail of biofuel production."

"Could you put that in layman's terms?"

"Sure. Right now ethanol exists only as a corn-based product in the US or a sugarcane-based fuel here in Brazil. It requires a rich, sugary pulp to be produced. But with cellulosic ethanol, you can use *any* plant—even plant waste—to produce ethanol. This would be a total game changer. Think about it; instead of harvesting food plants for fuel, you could feed the world and then use the leftovers—corn stalks, what-have-you, as the base for ethanol."

"Which, if the technology was yours, would make BP a fortune."

"It will make whoever gets it a fortune. Of course we want it! We've admittedly had some PR problems in the past and we're striving to get away from that and do real good in the world. If we could solve world hunger and the energy crisis in one fell swoop, well, I'm sure you can imagine—that would change the world."

You *can* imagine indeed. That technology would make a company billions of dollars; they'd become the world's number one energy *and* food producer overnight.

- "Do you know why he was blacklisted? Did BP have anything to do with it?" Go to page 280
- "Tell me more about BP's ethanol developments." Go to page 195
- "Thank you for your time, Marilyn. Would you mind calling Agent Bertram?" Go to page 98

The Long Night

You scuttle across the street, hurrying to get away from your pursuers. A surge of fresh panic rushes over you as you realize the door to the hostel is barred and locked. Irma feverishly shouts through the porthole and rattles the bars. A short, potbellied man with thin grey hair peeks out cautiously from within.

You remove what money you have left and shake it at him like you're bargaining for your life; which, in a sense, you are. He comes forward and lets you in, God bless him. Irma thanks him profusely, kissing both sides of his face over and over, which gets a smile from the innkeeper.

Irma looks back to you with tears of joy welling up in her eyes and a large smile parting her red lips. She negotiates the price for a room, then takes a key from the man, thanks him again and leads you upstairs.

The room is small, the floor is tiled instead of carpeted, and there's nothing more than a bed in the center, a floor lamp in one corner, and a faux plant in the other. A sliding door leads to a balcony, but neither of you are considering taking a stroll outside. Irma sits down on the bed, the mattress creaking in response, and lets out a long-overdue sigh.

Muffled gunshots continue from the streets beyond the hostel.

She runs her palms across the thighs of her jeans, her breasts swaying against her yellow soccer jersey, and finally looks up at you. "I'll get you back to your hotel before Agent Danly suspects you're gone, but we're staying here until Elite Squad finishes their operation and the drug traffickers go back into hiding."

You step over to the window and part the curtain slightly. An Elite Squad member combs the street below, moving in tactical fashion.

"That might be a while…" you say.

She rises from the bed and blinks at you through long lashes. "With all that's happened tonight, I don't know that I can sleep."

- "I'll just rest my eyes for a moment, if you don't mind. Then you can take me to the hotel when it's safe." Go to page 300
- Take her in your arms and kiss her passionately. Go to page 101

The Low Road

"**F**uck that," Bertram says.

"I'm with him," Maria adds. "They will kill us."

But when the first of the *grileiros* arrive, you make a show of throwing down your shotgun and raising your hands in surrender, and your companions have no choice but to do the same thing if they want you to live. Luckily for you, they do. Further compounding your luck, the *grileiros* don't kill you.

Instead, the men escort you at gunpoint to their waiting truck. They say something in Portuguese as you load up, then start the engine and drive down the road.

"He's here?" Maria asks Bertram in response to the threat from the men.

"Apparently," he says.

"Who?" you ask.

"The Sugar King. And he'd like to meet us, alive."

Must be your lucky day.

You half-expected something out of the pre-Civil War Southern states, like a giant manor from *Gone With the Wind,* but you're greeted with a much more utilitarian structure. This isn't a place where people live, it's a place where people work.

Still, it's a massive set of buildings. A cafeteria, several barracks for workers, washing and refining stations, and of course, the main house of the plantation.

"Hang on," Bertram says to you. "Do you think Maria should come? This man has done terrible things to her family."

"I can hear you, and I'm coming," she says firmly.

"Hmmm. I don't know…." you say, considering.

"No, I'm coming. This man is the devil."

- "Okay… Just so long as you're ready to meet him." Go to page 227
- "Which is why I don't want to put you through hell. I'm sorry, but I agree. We'll take care of it; you stay here." Go to page 270

Lucky Strike

With one final burst of energy, you take out the man's legs with your shoulders, chopping him down at the knees in a football tackle. It's not difficult; he's thin, and he certainly wasn't expecting that. Irma goes with your move and draws on him as gunshots ring out, but not from his AK.

There's another shooter, up on the rooftop. He's tall, well-built, his black hair close-cropped like a combat soldier's. Clean-shaven, but there's a thick scar along the front of his chin like you'd expect to see on someone who flew over the handlebar of a motorcycle. He wears aviator-style shooting-range glasses and his face is as pale as a skull sun-bleached in the desert. He wears all black—combat boots, tactical cargo pants, a vest to match, and skin-tight long-sleeved under-armor. He has dual-silenced handguns pointed at you and he wears motorcycle gloves.

In short, he's terrifying.

He fires with both weapons simultaneously, but hasn't gotten a clean shot with all the movement. You're not certain, but it looks like he's firing at all three of you, like he's targeting each of you at the same time with computer precision, à la *The Terminator.*

Irma returns fire with her handgun and the man you tackled takes the opportunity to flee down the alley, leaving the AK-47 on the ground behind him. The Man in Black on the rooftop ducks behind cover and out of sight, but Irma keeps firing just in case. You run down the alley after the suspect, as much trying to catch him as you are trying to distance yourself from the rooftop assassin.

There's still a deep burning in your chest from where the rifle barrel struck home, and your breath is labored. The suspect pulls away, expanding the distance between you. Looking back over your shoulder, you see Irma catching up to you.

You come to a tee intersection as the alley dead-ends. The suspect flees to the right. Irma points to the left. "*Jamanta*," she huffs. "This way; we must run away. That man—the assassin—*Jamanta*. He will kill us."

Her eyes are distended with terror.

- Ignore her. Pursue the suspect! Go to page 174
- Trust her instincts. Flee the scene. Go to page 71

You hold up the USB thumbdrive with the evidence that Jane nearly died to obtain and Viktor risked everything to get hold of. All eyes go to the device.

"This was given to me by the Energy Summit Chairman," you announce to the group. "I'm Doctor Clines and I need your help. There was a last-minute change to the program lineup and an update to the opening presentation is here."

"Come on, quickly," the computer technician says, waving you over.

The ruse works. You smile and move toward him as the rest of the room goes back to what it was doing.

"Cutting it down to the last minute," the tech says.

"Yeah, I know. Thanks for your help."

The "auto-play" window opens as the tech inserts the USB drive and double-clicks the notification to browse the contents. There's only one file on the device.

"That must be it," he says.

You nod. He opens the program and starts the presentation, which plays automatically.

"Dim the lights," you request.

The computer tech signals one of his co-workers, who dims the lights in the auditorium. Watching the security feed, you see scientists, luminaries, and members of the press take their seats and focus their attention on the screen.

The first slide fades in from black and shows, "Welcome to the International Energy Summit, with keynote Speaker Dr. Viktor Lucio de Ocampo."

There's some grumbling from the crowd, people no doubt wondering if there's an error in the program lineup. The brochures, of course, show a different speaker for the event.

"Imagine a world where harvesting energy and food are one and the same. Imagine a world with cellulosic ethanol: fuel based on waste. Food and energy for all," a man says over the PA system. You recognize the voice as Viktor's.

Then the screen flickers with distortion. You think it's an error at first, maybe some kind of interference, but when a red line creeps across Viktor's name on the slideshow, you realize it's an intended effect. After his name is "crossed off," it starts to fade away altogether.

Through the video feed monitors, you can see the astounded faces of the theater audience. All of this is being broadcast live on Brazilian television and international news outlets. The silence and rapt attention of those present says it all.

"This world could be a reality, but there are those who would keep it from you," Viktor continues.

The screen flashes police reports and news footage of Jane Nightingale's murder, all proclaiming Viktor as the killer and a wanted fugitive on the run. The audience is getting restless now, looking around for the authorities to see if this is some kind of hacker's prank.

With dramatic flair, the curtain flies open and Jane and Viktor come out hand-in-hand, arms held high, Viktor with a microphone.

"Get a spotlight on them!" you command.

The technicians comply. The DSS security agents jam their fingers against earbud microphones, desperate for guidance.

"These two men colluded against this new world for their own personal gain! Ambassador Peter Mays was willing to kill to protect corn ethanol and Governor Mateo Ferro did the same for sugarcane!" Viktor cries, pointing out the condemned men.

A camera films their reaction, which is nothing short of fury. The men sit side-by-side, their faces red with anger. They're shouting something, but with no microphone, are drowned by the clamor of the crowd.

The slideshow shows pictures of both men, then splashes to a scanned document ordering the young couple to be targeted as reward for their discovery. It's signed "Peter Mays" and you recognize the Ps and Ms as matching the handwriting on the "pick me up" note.

The presentation goes back to Ambassador Mays and Governor Ferro, but now both photographs have been doctored to give these Kings their rightful crowns and scepters.

"Cut the feed!" the lead agent says.

"Don't you dare—this is the most important moment in your life. Let it play," you tell the tech.

"Shut it down!"

One of the agents removes a pistol to intimidate the computer technician into submission. The man looks terrified but doesn't move. The third agent swoops in to shut the computer down himself.

"No!" you shout, blocking them with your body.

Trained and ready for resistance, the agents grab hold of you, restraining your protests and handcuffing you with ease. The agents are still trying to shut down the presentation when the door opens.

"Leave it alone!" a male voice shouts.

The man who enters is bookish, lean, in his fifties. He looks like he could've been a scientist once, but has evolved into a businessman over the years.

"Italo Fellini," he says, saying his first name with a soft 'I' (eee-tall-oh), "Chairman of the Energy Summit."

"You have no idea who you're dealing with," the blond lead agent says.

"I know exactly who I'm dealing with," Fellini replies. "I was intimidated into taking Viktor off the program lineup, but now I'm putting things right."

"Sorry, Doc. We take our orders from the Ambassador."

"Who has no authority here," a woman says.

Detective Irma Dos Santos, the Rio cop who interrogated you on your first night here, enters with two junior policemen.

"Step away from the computer terminal, or I will have you arrested," she says.

"You're all clueless, aren't you? Dumb bitch," the agent says.

The Detective punches the pretty-boy agent square on the nose. "Escort these men out."

Once the junior police officers comply, she turns to you and Chairman Fellini.

"It wasn't just a conspiracy between your Ambassador and our Governor," she says to you. "The Rio Chief of Police was in on it too. Luckily, I have proof of his assistance in the attempted murder of Jane Nightingale, the plot to frame

Doctor Viktor Lucio de Ocampo, and his efforts to cover up the identity of the true murder victim: Sarah O'Connor, an American tourist visiting Rio with her brother."

"The Ambassador must have paid the cops to dispose of the 'pick me up' note!" you say.

She nods. "We were told not to solve the case, and were threatened by the Chief, but now I'm going to 'blow the whistle,' as you say. We need to rid ourselves of police corruption, and what better time? Just as both our countries are now free of these corporate evils."

"It's over," Chairman Fellini adds. "The truth is out, and now progress can march on without further impediments from these deep-pocketed corporate criminals."

"All thanks to you," Detective Dos Santos says with a reverent smile.

Part of you can't believe you pulled it off; that this week's events have actually happened. With a sly grin, you pinch yourself to make sure you aren't dreaming. Yet here you are, seated in a private room at *Antiquarius*—perhaps Rio de Janeiro's most upscale restaurant and the preferred spot of monarchs, pop stars, and the Brazilian elite.

The champagne tickles your throat as it goes down, but honestly, you couldn't tell the difference between the $3,000 bottle and the $1,000 bottle.

"Guess you'd better get used to this, now that you're going to be the richest people in the country," you say.

Viktor and Jane smile from the other side of the table and then lean forward to claim their own champagne glasses.

"Just tonight," Jane says. "We're planning on investing in Brazil's future. Education, healthcare, infrastructure. There will always be a place for you here, if you want it."

Viktor raises his glass. "To you, Tourist."

You raise your own champagne flute, *clinking* the glass against theirs and say, "*Saúde!*"

➢ Go to page 304

The Main Stage

This is the primary auditorium of the Energy Summit. Thousands of people are sitting in rows upon rows of theater seating, all waiting for the presentation to begin. When it's not used as a conference site, this could be (and probably is) an opera house.

There are two main sections, split in half by a walkway upon which you now stand. Half the seats are to the right, down toward the stage; an upper section is to your left. Divided by aisles, these two sections are further split so that there are a total of six seating areas.

And that's just on this floor. There's a balcony with almost as many seats. It looks like the Dolby Theatre where the Academy Awards are presented in Hollywood.

You look to the stage, at the grand curtain where Viktor and Jane will swoop out and accept the Oscar for *Best Conspiracy*, but only if you find the control room in time and plug the evidence into the projector.

So what are you doing wasting your time here? You'd better rush over to the only room you've yet to visit in this wing:

- *Imprensa*. Go to page 252

Making Enemies

Falador is furious. What did he expect—honor amongst thieves? He jumps up, angry enough to attack you, but Irma waggles her revolver like a school marm might wave a finger at an unruly student. He stays back, and the two of you leave the teen alone in the house, with only hatred as his reward.

Detective Dos Santos tucks her service revolver into an ankle holster, then holds an open palm toward you.

"You don't want to get caught out in the open with a weapon. Elite Squad will see the AK first, then they'll notice you're American after they've shot you."

Can't argue with that; so you hand Irma the weapon. She dashes forward and hurls the rifle atop one of the buildings.

"Okay, now what?" she says. "Do you want to go see what else Danly might be up to, or head back to the hotel, or—?"

The brick wall nearest you suddenly explodes outward as a progression of bullets pushes toward you. Irma runs around the corner, grabbing your hand and pulling you with her. After the second burst of gunfire, you hear a teen's shouts echo through the alley.

"It's Falador," Irma explains as you run. "He's found some friends and has offered 100 *reis* for our heads. I think he's planning on using your money for payment."

Your legs windmill beneath you from pure adrenaline, and eventually you emerge from the alley into another wide street like the one where the armored car battle took place. Looking down each side of the road, you see several Elite Squad figures blocking each egress route. If those are traffickers bearing down behind you, you're about to get stuck in another gun battle.

"What now?" you ask in desperation.

She looks around, equally frightened. Then something catches her eye. She points ahead at a graffiti sign reading, *Albergue.*

"It's a hostel!" she cries. "Come on!"

- *Flee to the hostel.* Go to page 187

Making Green

"Our Biofuel Division is constantly expanding. Have you heard of *Tropical*, our sugarcane processing facility? Well, BP Biofuel is adding a further $350 million to *Tropical*, expanding our ethanol interests substantially. We plan to increase our harvest to 5 million tons of sugarcane per year, which would allow us to produce around 450 million liters of ethanol equivalent per annum."

"Sounds impressive."

She nods. "This investment will create almost eight thousand jobs for the construction and running of the mill, as well as sugarcane cultivation. Additionally, we'll be able to export approximately 340 gigawatt-hours of electric energy to the Brazilian national grid. We see a bright future for ethanol with Brazil."

"I'll say. It seems like this isn't just a one-time thing, then?"

"I should say not," she says with a smile. "In the last five years we've invested more than $2 billion in biofuel research."

- "Do you know why Viktor Lucio de Ocampo was blacklisted? Did BP have anything to do with it?" Go to page 280
- "What exactly was Viktor working on?" Go to page 186
- "I've heard enough. Thank you for your time." Go to page 98

Making Up

She wipes the tears away and her face beams with a new, radiant happiness. She kisses you again, in joy and love, arousing attraction within you once more. You make love again, this time with new understanding of one another, unlike the rushed frenzy of discovery that characterized the first time.

You're left out of breath but satisfied. Once again Irma smokes a cigarette, perspiration clinging to her naked body.

"We must keep our passion a secret," she says. "If the others knew, it could compromise the investigation. But maybe after the whole thing is over….?"

"We could go out on a proper date?"

She laughs. A warm feeling overtakes you as you look at her smile. "Come on, we'd better get you back."

➢ *Return to the hotel, your passion a secret.* Go to page 300

The Messenger

Viktor takes out a small notebook, the same journal you used to test his handwriting, and scribbles on one of the pages. He uses a handkerchief to tear the page from the notebook so as not to leave any fingerprints. With equal care, you receive the note. It reads:

"No doubt you're looking for me.
Let's meet where we can do so with open arms."

"Just a small riddle," Viktor says. "Where in this city are you always welcomed with open arms?"

He turns toward the sky, his body pressed against the railing, arms spread like he's "On top of the world!" in *Titanic.* Beyond him on the distant horizon is the statue of *Christ the Redeemer* with its arms open toward the city.

"What if they don't figure it out?"

Viktor shrugs. "Then they're not very bright. If that's the case, I'm not worried about them anyhow."

You're not sure you share his apparent lack of concern, but you don't argue the point. "So, what? I'm just supposed to go tape this on their windshield?"

"Pretty much. Here, I wrote down the license plate of their Land Rover when I was trailing you last night. Odds are you'll find it down at the consulate while they're talking to Jane's coworkers. Go downstairs, get on the red-line again, and tell the bus driver you're an American and you need to get to the consulate. That'll be easy. The hard part is avoiding detection at the garage. Good luck. We'll meet up at *Capricciosa*, a nearby pizza joint in Ipanema."

He was right; getting to the consulate wasn't hard. The bus dropped you off only a block away, a total of a thirty-minute ride, and now you're walking around the corner to the *Consulado Geral Dos Estados Unidos.*

It's kind of an odd sight. In the middle of a busy downtown intersection there's an office building with majorly restricted access. Foot traffic is constantly scrutinized by men in Security uniforms and Kevlar vests. The road out front is blocked from any would-be kamikaze car-bombers by rows of concrete pylons and a guard shack allowing entry only to those with proper identification.

The consulate itself is a palace-sized office building with a clear route to the parking garage. There's the ID station, and the path for approved cars is delineated by several neon-green and black-striped signs.

Traffic streams heavily past the consulate and there are plenty of pedestrians on the sidewalk. So…how to get inside?

- Talk to the guard, tell him I forgot my ID. He'll let me in; I'm an American. Go to page 6
- There's a trash truck and I'll bet anything it's about to head inside. Jump in the back! Go to page 325
- Plenty of motorcycles here in traffic; knock the driver off, swerve through the pylons, rush the gate! Go to page 131

Microwaved

"We were just looking around," you say, palms raised in supplication.

"For what?"

You gulp. "We didn't see anything."

Muniz draws his handgun. "Irma, I'm kind of freaking out. Talk to me."

The other two cops draw as well, whispering to Detective Muniz in Portuguese.

"It's okay, Lucio." Irma says. "The *Americano* understands how things work here."

"How long have you been following us?" he chambers a round. "*Why* have you been following us?"

"Agent Danly knows," you bluff. "He knows where we are, and he knows you met with the suspect. The jig is up."

Lucio Muniz's head cocks to the side, like a dog who's found something curious to play with. He says something in Portuguese to the men, motioning toward you. They step forward.

"Well then, boss-man's gonna want a report, right? He'll wonder what happened, no?"

"Lucio, please," Irma says, and a tear runs down her face.

"Once a witness, always a witness." Then, turning to you, he adds, "Do you know what the drug lords do to witnesses here?"

You shake your head.

"That's okay, I'll show you."

One cop grabs Irma and the other grabs you, pulling you into the alley with the burnt corpse. They take your weapons, toss them into a stack of tires, then line you up against the wall and wait for Detective Muniz.

"Please step into the tires."

He indicates a waist-high stack of tires beside you. At gunpoint, you follow the order. Another stack waits for Irma and she does the same, sniffling against freely flowing tears.

"The first step in any good cover-up is finding a plausible story. See here? You say you came to find the suspect, well, here you go—looks like you found him, just as he was about to kill again, but you were unable to save this poor girl. Instead, you became a victim yourself."

The men put another tire over your head, adding to the stack. One adds a tire to you, the other to Irma. One by one, growing the stack.

"Please," she sniffles.

"Sh, sh, shhh….It's okay, you get to die a hero, trying to stop the killer. And I tried to save you, only I got here too late."

They add another tire. The stack is up to your chest now.

"Agent Danly will never believe you," you plead. "You won't get away with this!"

"Hush now, you'll miss the best part. The drug lords, they load witnesses—squealers—into tires like this. This is called 'the microwave' and it's the only way to be sure you don't talk."

They put one more tire on you, this one over your head, so you can no longer see out. A moment later, liquid pours over the rubber rim, dousing and saturating the tire pile. From the smell, you can tell it's gasoline.

"Don't worry! We'll catch the murderer! He'll pay for all the girls he kills, and for all the Americans. A cop-killer cannot go free."

With that, the stack is lit on fire. Despite a pain like you've never experienced, you cannot free yourself from the tower of tires, struggle though you may. In a frenzy to save yourself, you're able to knock the tire stack on its side and you fall onto the alley floor, but the tires have fused together under the intense heat.

Soon you're unconscious. Soon after that, you're burned alive.

THE END

Mind the Car

Agent Danly and Detective Muniz leave you to twiddle your thumbs in the SUV. As soon as they close their doors, you lock them shut. You watch from the tinted windows as they head out through the hole in the broken wall, disappearing from view. Almost immediately you start to sweat. It's warm out, but Danly didn't crack the windows. Nor did he leave the keys. The air grows thick with humidity and the effect is like resting head-first under the covers in the heat of summer.

You're contemplating opening the door, just to get some kind of breeze, when you see several figures come through the wall. It's not your law enforcement friends. In fact, it's a gang of six young boys. They're all shirtless, save for two, who wear baggy tank tops. The one in the lead has a soccer ball and they're eyeing the SUV with great intensity. That's when you notice that the two at the rear are shaking spray paint cans.

- Jump out and scare the living bejeezus out of them. They're just kids, they'll go away. Go to page 25
- Honk the horn, hide on the floor, and hope they go away. Go to page 140

Money Talks

As Irma explains the concept to the drug trafficker, you see his expression change almost immediately. He smiles, nods, and says something to Irma, but you don't even need the translation. You pull out a $100 Brazilian *reais* note (the equivalent of $50 USD), flash the cool blue currency at the man, and then your own smile.

"Tell him this is just a taste."

She does so. The Mouth spills it to the plainclothes detective. His entire body language is different now, and he leans forward and nods eagerly as he speaks.

"He says everybody has heard of the American murder. He says 'killing an American is like bagging a jaguar,' then he offers that he doesn't mean any offense."

You produce a matching $R100 note, sliding them side-by-side, the bust of a Roman woman with a crown of bay leaves peering proudly out at him in duplicate from the banknote faces. This amount of money could change someone's life in a *favela*. He starts to stand up, but Irma shoves him back toward the couch.

"Tell him 'he makes me happy, I make him happy.' I want everything he knows."

You fan yourself with the $R200 while you await his answer.

"He says he wishes he knew more, but only that the order came from high up in the ranks of the Shadow Chiefs. Something about a colonel. Near the very top. 'She must have pissed off somebody,' he says. What else? We must go soon."

- "We know it's the Shadow Chiefs who ordered the murder. That's enough for now. Let's go before it's too late." Go to page 78
- "Tell him this next question is very important: Did she owe money? Did she buy or sell drugs? How was she connected? If he answers, I can make it $R300." Go to page 184

Monopólio

Like a giant mansion on some remote estate, so sits the sugarcane plantation *Monopólio.* The sun has long set and now a cloudburst erupts overhead, dumping buckets of warm summer rain atop the three of you as you stare up at the grand staircase leading to the main house.

"It is not likely we will see *O Rei do Açúcar,*" Maria says, one hand atop each revolver, "but if we do—remember that this man is *serpente,* and do not trust his lies."

Off to the side, at one of the annexes to the main house, a Range Rover arrives. Not full of armed *grileiros* like the others, this one carries cane cutters—the plantation laborers. When the first man steps out, you see he's clothed head to toe in gray cloth, like a padded ninja, a turtleneck pulled up over his face and a boonie hat pulled so low that only his eyes are visible.

The other cutters exit and their machetes glimmer in the moonlight.

- "We should infiltrate dressed as workers." Go to page 244
- "Let's go straight to the main house and get the jump on management!" Go to page 328

The Morning After

"What's the plan?" you ask, walking alongside Viktor as you leave the *favela*. "You said get the agents off our trail, but what do you propose we do?"

"I've been wondering that very same thing. But last night it finally dawned on me—if the Americans think I killed my Jane, then surely they'll be looking for me. I assume you gave my description to a police sketch artist?"

You say that you did.

"So let me ask you this: if you're looking for something, and you're truly dedicated, when do you stop looking for it?"

He sits at a bus stop and you take a seat next to him, pausing to think. But there's only one answer: "Once I've found it."

"Exactly. Which, if you'll follow the premise to its conclusion, means I have to give them…*me*."

"You're turning yourself in?"

"Of course not, no. Come, you'll see."

The red-line bus pulls up and Viktor tosses a few coins into the slot for both of you.

"Your English is excellent," you say once you're seated, making small talk.

"Thank you. I've spent so much of my life abroad, both in education and professionally, that often my instinct is to call myself 'a Brazilian,' as you say, rather than *'Brasileiro,'* as we say here. It's funny, really, but in spite of everything I still consider Rio my home."

He looks out the window and you do the same. Eventually, your companion indicates it's time to disembark. As soon as you get off the bus, you realize you're in a much nicer district.

There aren't any *favelas* near here—just skyrise apartment buildings. Viktor walks up to one skyrise and buzzes the intercom. "André! It's your old roomie, let us up."

After a moment, the door buzzes and you open it. The hall echoes as you step inside, announcing your arrival to the empty lobby. It's much cooler here inside this marble cave, and you can feel the slight bite of the conditioned air against your spine. You find the elevator and punch the "up" button.

After a short ride, you're on the sixth floor. A man whom you assume is André steps out into the hall to greet Viktor. Your assumption is confirmed when the two men embrace in a hug and slap each other on the back like long-lost brothers.

"Who's this?" he asks, looking at you.

The man is a handsome Brazilian, rugged and masculine. He's taller than Viktor by about two inches, his face is fuller, and his body is broader. He wears a ribbed sweater despite it being summer. Where Viktor is intelligent and agile, André is cock-sure, charismatic and powerful. His eyes are a creamy golden-brown, and he has a five o'clock shadow.

"*De boa*—it's cool," Viktor replies. "Can we go inside?"

André nods and waves you in. It's a plush penthouse with all the trimmings. The latest in modern décor and minimalist style. You don't have to be an ace detective to figure this one out: the man is wealthy. He goes straight for what looks to be an antique gun safe, and your first instinct is to bolt for the door, but when he opens the safe, you breathe a sigh of relief. The safe has been refurbished and now serves as his liquor cabinet.

"Can I offer you a drink?"

"You may want one yourself," Viktor says. "I have quite a story to tell."

"Lucky for you, I was already enjoying a *Canario,*" he says, claiming a cocktail from an end table. The table is an old wooden powder keg, emptied out and reclaimed. It still has the original label stenciled on the side. "Are you sure you won't join me?"

"We have much work to do, my friend. Our day has just begun."

"Of, course. Mine was just ending," André says with a smile, toasting the air with his glass.

"We're interrupting?" Viktor asks.

"No, no. Nothing of the sort. I only mean—my mind is prepared to receive your urgent news."

Viktor looks around the penthouse apartment with deliberate caution. "May we talk on your balcony? You have the most brilliant views of the rising sun."

Your host nods and leads the way outside. You're greeted with a slight breeze; the air is cooler up here than it was on the red-line and holds a peerless view of the city. It's stunning. Though you're only six stories up, the building sits on a hilltop and offers a panoramic vista of the coast.

Once the glass door slides closed, Viktor says, "I can't be too careful. I don't believe your home is bugged, nor do I think they'll link us together. I'm not sure the university keeps records of who shared a dorm room with whom, and you've got your stage name, in any case."

You share the same puzzled look as the man before you, but he's able to hide his grimace with a sip from the cocktail glass.

"Just—out with it already!" you blurt.

They both look to you and Viktor lets out a nervous laugh. "I'm sorry. I know each of you only know half the story. André here is one of the most talented actors in *Brasil*."

The man gives a dramatic bow.

"And I'm now one of the most wanted," Viktor continues. "So I need you, my friend, to perform the role of a lifetime. I need you to pretend to be me! To convince the American federal agents of my innocence and to throw them off my trail. I'd do this myself, but you can talk your way out of anything. I've seen that first-hand too many times to count. If they think you're me, I can blend in and travel unencumbered on the rest of my journey."

André taps his index finger on his lips, deep in thought. He sighs, then drains the rest of his cocktail, throws the glass over the balcony and firmly grips Viktor's shoulders with both hands.

"What do you get the man who has everything?" André asks with a playboy's grin. "Adventure! My friend, you're just what I need. I've been driven mad with these *television* roles. This—this is real acting."

"You'll do it?" Viktor asks.

"With pleasure!"

Viktor turns to you with a grin. "I'll fill André in. Time is precious, so I think we should split up for an hour or two. We need to leave a note on the agents' car so they'll meet André later today for his big show. I also need my laptop, and that's back at my apartment. We'll have to act with extreme care at either location: the former is the lion's den and the latter is their hunting ground."

- "I'll leave the note; just tell me what to do." Go to page 197
- "They'll be looking for you at your apartment; I'd better go instead." Go to page 163

Motorist

You walk along the edge of the road by the sugarcane, looking for headlights in the waning light. With your focus on the horizon, you accidentally kick something, but it's soft and loose and you don't tumble. Instead, it *bounds* away—croaking.

It's a gigantic frog, six inches across, thick and covered in warty globules of skin. There are a dozen toads at least, most likely fleeing from the fires.

"Don't touch," Maria says. "The skin has venom."

"Great," you say, and rub your shoe against the dirt.

"Cane toads," Bertram says. "That gives me an idea."

He removes a pair of thin shooting gloves from his pants' cargo pockets and dons them just as the headlights of a vehicle start to shine through the sugarcane. Maria takes a step back into the crop and you follow suit.

Bertram lifts two toads, one in each hand, and readies himself. "If either of you are an animal-rights type, you may want to look away," he says with a grin.

Just as a jeep rounds the corner, Agent Bertram hurls the toads at the vehicle's windshield, spattering them across the glass like they were water balloons. The jeep swerves wildly and finally skids to a stop.

Bertram rushes around to the driver's side and bashes the driver with the butt of his rifle, incapacitating him. Maria points a revolver at each of the passengers in the rear seat as you train your shotgun on the man up front.

"We've got another one!" you shout, spotting a second set of headlights.

Maria demands in Portuguese that the men exit the vehicle.

"Hop in back and fire a warning shot when they get too close!" Bertram commands, pulling the slumped body from behind the wheel.

As the rear passengers exit, you take a seat and ready the shotgun. Maria hops in front and Bertram peels out.

"Hotshot! We're gonna flip around. I want you to blast their tires."

Agent Bertram performs a flawless J-turn, flipping the jeep around 180 degrees just like he was taught in his DSS anti-terrorism driving course, and flies towards the oncoming pickup truck. You let out a shotgun blast from the rear of the jeep, easily turning the driver's side tire into Swiss cheese.

The truck crashes into the sugarcane embankment, flattening more toads, and leaving the *grileiros* in the ditch.

➢ *To the plantation!* Go to page 202

The Mouth

The child gang leads you through the slums, out into a wide and open street, and finally just outside a hovel. It would appear the man you seek is inside. The leader of the gang steps in front of the curtained doorway and holds out his palm expectantly.

"He wants his payment for bringing us here."

"But we don't have any money…." you say.

Viktor says something in Portuguese, then brandishes his pistol. Adrenaline shoots through you and you go for your own weapon in preparation for a firefight. At the last moment you stop, realizing that the children remain as placid and unafraid of Viktor as if the man had just pulled out a lollipop. Indeed, he announced his intent so that the gang wouldn't be frightened when he gave the teen leader his pistol as a gift, which he does now.

"What are you doing?" you ask.

"We can either give them something valuable or have them take our valuables from us."

You look at the boys, each of them eying you hungrily. The leader takes Viktor's weapon, passes it off to one of his lieutenants, then opens his palm to you.

"Go ahead, Tourist. This is our charge for transport and safe passage, and we each have to pay. Think of it as a ticket; time to pay the ferryman."

Reluctantly, you hand off your pistol. The leader of the child gang smiles, gives a slight bow, and with that the group disappears down the street. After they leave, you turn back toward the hovel. Here you are—hopefully. It suddenly occurs to you that you could've been led anywhere. Who knows whose home this is!

Viktor calls out and the curtain opens. There to meet you stands the next tier of drug lord—a young man of high-school age. Thin, baggy-clothed, and wielding an AK-47, he greets you with a suspicious scowl. You're not sure what Viktor says to him, but he opens the curtain and bids you enter.

The room is occupied by two other teens with AK-47s. The one who wears a tank top and looks about 17 introduces himself as Falador. He folds his spindly arms across his chest with an air of impatience.

"I'm going to try something," Viktor says.

As he speaks to the teens in Portuguese, your anxiety runs high. You feel powerless in this room, impotent and unarmed against three killers with assault rifles. You hope his "something" pays off.

Viktor grins. "I told them we talked to the bleach-haired detective and that in exchange for information, they don't have to pay him next month. I told them that the cop says if they refuse, they will pay double. Falador will gladly tell us what he knows."

Well, that was easy, you think as Viktor converses with the gangsters. These young men will be in for a rude awakening next month when the cops expect their regular tribute, but you won't lose any sleep over pitting crooked cops and drug traffickers against one another.

Viktor brightens. “He says he knows everything about the American girl! He says it was the Shadow Chiefs who killed her, and that the bounty for her life was paid for by the sugarcane mafia. It’s just as I figured; my new energy patents threatened the Sugar King’s empire and now Falador has confirmed that the order came from *O Rei do Açúcar*, himself!”

Then Viktor’s eyes darken and he adds, “I’m going to find the hitman who killed Jane, I will have justice against him, and then we will see Governor Mateo Ferro, the Sugar King.”

“But how?” you say. “How could you expect to take on an entire mafia with no money and only a single sub-machinegun?”

“You’re forgetting two things, Tourist: My determination and my ‘Manhattan Projects.’”

He speaks with the teen in Portuguese again, but soon becomes frustrated. “*No, no, no,*” he says, shaking his head.

“What is it?” you ask.

“He says they kidnapped her at sunset, near the consulate, when she was walking back from work….”

“So the scene at her house was a decoy? They didn’t get her from there?”

Viktor shakes his head. “He says he’s certain, but that’s impossible. I got a message from her just before…Here, I wrote down all my messages with timestamps before I ditched my mobile.”

He produces a sheet in his journal, then reads, “I have what we need, but I think they know. Date first. Sent Monday, 9:24 pm.”

Replacing the journal, he says, “See? Long after sunset. It doesn’t make any sense.”

That’s when it dawns on you: the timestamp! The very same thing that freed you from jail. You pull out your digital camera and flip through the pictures of the crime scene. The timestamp of your picture of the alley, the one with the glorious graffiti angel, reads, “8:57 pm.”

“Look!” you shout, showing him the camera. “She sent you that message nearly half an hour after I stumbled upon the body. You just didn’t check your phone until after you ran from me!”

Viktor’s eyes gleam, though he doesn’t share your full enthusiasm. “What does this really prove? That her phone was used later that night. Anyone can send a text message. Or maybe she was in an area without service when she wrote it and it didn’t send until later?”

“Listen to me! If this guy’s so certain they took her at sunset, then it’s possible they took a *different* girl. I know this sounds crazy, but what if Jane gave them the slip? What if she’s…still alive?!”

Viktor turns to Falador and asks him a new set of questions with fevered intensity. When the boy answers, Viktor shouts with joy.

“I asked him what the girl they took looked like. She was a young, pretty American and blonde like my Jane, but he said this girl had blue eyes—my Jane has green! He says she had a mole on her nose, and my Jane has no moles! What if you’re right, Tourist? What if she’s in hiding because she knows the only thing keeping her safe is the idea that they think she’s dead?”

"What if she claimed the evidence on her own and is leaving you clues so you'll find her?"

His bright eyes glitter with inspired madness. "The message could have a double meaning…I thought 'date first' was just a way to verify her identity—it's an inside joke of ours—but it could be telling me to check the date and time of the message! To see what happened first! And if she's alive… that would mean it is Jane who is in 'the place of hate.'"

"You know where it is?"

"Yes! If the men who tried to kill her were the Sugar King's men…"

He turns to leave, but Falador has blocked your exit to the door. The three young men all brandish their AK-47s. With a cruel smile, Falador shakes his head. You're not going anywhere.

"He says he knows who we are; knows I'm the fiance and that there is a bounty on my head as well. They have orders to kill us. 'No hard feelings,' he says. I'm going to offer him a bribe—go for my backpack."

Viktor talks to them in Portuguese while you:

- Offer them your passport. It's the most valuable thing you own. Go to page 337
- Remove one of the "Manhattan Projects" and hand it to Viktor. Go to page 262
- Slide the safety off the sub-machinegun and go to town. Go to page 287

Nailed

The two of you chase Viktor through the crowded streets. A few times it seems like he might have lost you, but then his glasses glint under the street lights and the chase will be on once again. Just when you think you can't run any further, Viktor makes a mistake.

He turns down the wrong alley and into a dead end. Seeing that he's lost, he turns back and shoves a hand into his backpack.

"Drop that bag, now!" Irma shouts, her revolver leveled at his head.

Viktor does so, his hands raised in the air. In one hand, he holds a small metal sphere.

"Drop the bomb, you son-of-a-bitch! One sudden move and I will not hesitate to kill you."

She pulls back the hammer on the revolver.

"Okay, okay!" the man says. "Listen to me, please. You don't understand."

"Shut up!" she cries.

He continues, "You have no idea what you're dealing with. The men you think are your friends, your bosses, everyone—"

The chamber starts to rotate as she depresses the trigger.

- Watch as she shoots him. Go to page 58
- Knock the gun askew—hear him out. Go to page 10

Narcotraficante

It's not hard to find a drug dealer in the slums. Just say the magic word, *narcotraficante,* and odds are whomever you ask knows a guy.

Back out into the *favela* proper, just around the corner from that open-air market, you get word that one such man is inside a nearby bar—still there from the night before, in fact. You enter the dump (which gives new meaning to the term "dive bar") and wait while Viktor asks the bartender for information on the drug trafficker you seek.

You look around, but don't see anyone else here. Indeed, you're surprised that the place is even open at this hour. It's the kind of establishment where you pay solely for the liquor, where you pay to forget that you live in the slums. Not the kind of place that serves patty melts in the daytime, in other words.

"Our guy's in the bathroom," Viktor says. "Too much to drink."

"Great. What now? Wait for him to sober up?"

Viktor's jaw tightens and something fearsome flashes in those ethereal blue eyes. The same look that stared you down over a dead body when the two of you first met.

"Not hardly."

Viktor turns and heads toward the restroom. You follow, gooseflesh appearing on your spine, tingling with anticipation. The doorjamb is broken so that not only is the bathroom door unlockable, you don't even need to use a doorknob to open it.

"Keep that pistol handy, okay?"

"Okay," you swallow.

Viktor opens the door casually, as if he were merely trying to use the restroom himself. Not rushed like a cop, or slow like someone frightened or nervous. It's a one-seater, with two things worth noting: the man hugging the toilet and his AK-47 leaning against the sink.

The man curses at you, telling you to get lost, but this just brings up a fresh round of vomiting. The stench of stomach acid, alcohol, and seafood burns your nostrils and makes your eyes water. While the drug trafficker is "occupied," Viktor slips out his money-clip, hands it to you, then claims the AK-47 and gives that to you as well.

"Give both of these to the bartender. He'll understand."

Moving quickly, you leave the restroom and make the handoff. Without a word, the bartender nods in understanding, stashes the rifle under the bar and pockets the cash. He then walks out the front door, closes it behind him, and locks the three of you inside—paid not to see whatever's about to happen.

You rush back toward the bathroom, where shouted Portuguese cursing is growing in volume. The man is standing up now, making threatening gestures toward Viktor, who is oddly calm.

"Tourist—step in, close the door, stand with your back to it, and let our friend see your pistol."

Nervously, you comply. The drug trafficker is taken aback for an instant and looks from you to Viktor, back and forth several times, sizing you up. Unimpressed, he starts cursing again, growing louder and angrier.

Viktor asks the man the name of his source in the Rio police force and a few words jump out at you: *polícia* and *narcotraficante*. But he isn't going to play ball.

Like a striking viper, Viktor snatches the front of the druglord's shirt and yanks him down toward the toilet. The man's sneakers squeal in protest against the wet linoleum. Once he has the man prone, Viktor shoves the drug trafficker's face into the toilet bowl, straight into the vomit floating there.

After a cacophony of thrashing and gurgled screams, Viktor lets the man up and asks him the identity of a dirty cop once more. It looks like he's going to cooperate, but then all at once he lunges toward you, ready to take your weapon.

Bang.

The man falls back onto the floor, holding his gut with red fingers. The pistol smokes in your hand. You look to Viktor, but he only asks the man a third time. The drug trafficker cries in pain, shaking his head, and refuses to answer. Strike three.

Viktor claims the plunger from the corner of the room and with the controlled calmness of a madman, presses his shoe firmly onto the drug trafficker's nose, his heel atop the crying man's lips and teeth.

The man grabs onto Viktor's leg, trying to get his foot off his face, just as the scientist hoped he would. Viktor carefully places the plunger against the bullet wound, steadies his feet, and begins to pump.

"Viktor!" you shout, but it's lost amidst the shrill cries of tortured anguish.

The drug trafficker wails with inhuman pain and now Viktor roars like a lion, shouting his questions at the top of his lungs. The man continues to scream.

"*Viktor*!" you shout again.

He stops, but not because of your pleas. Miraculously, the man is able to answer him.

"*Obrigado*," Viktor says, thanking the man for the information.

He releases the drug trafficker, drops the plunger atop his dying body, then removes his own pistol and shoots the man.

Looking to you, Viktor says, "You shouldn't use my name."

Too dumbfounded to speak, you simply follow him from the bar—despite your newfound fear of the man. Just who is this Viktor? Sure, he lost his fiancée, his job and his career, and the murder is pinned on him, but…that was insane.

- *Go meet the dirty policeman.* Go to page 224

Neither Fight nor Flight

You tuck yourself behind the bartop in the recesses of the kitchen, trying to flatten yourself next to the refrigerator. With hands over your mouth in an effort to muffle your terrified panting, you resemble a *Speak No Evil* sculpture. Using the strange image as inspiration, you keep stock-still and completely silent.

With wide, unblinking eyes, you watch as two men enter the house. They wear black suits and gloves and have handguns drawn, but these are neither American agents nor Brazilian police, you can tell that much. These men have the look of cold, hard killers. Brazilian mafia, maybe? They sweep through the apartment, scanning for intruders like you, but thankfully, they're looking for someone at eye-level and skip right over you.

The men come back and start to tear the house apart—overturn bookshelves, rip open seat cushions—and then they see you. They start shouting in Portuguese, guns drawn and pointed at you. One of them grabs your arm and yanks you up from your seated position while the other searches you. They find the map, the key to the unit, and your American passport.

The man searching you raises his handgun to your forehead. He marches you out in front of the house, where there's a moving van, its interior lined with plastic. It's the last thing you'll ever see.

THE END

The Net

Viktor sits down at the aged laptop, which has been glued to the table to prevent theft. There's a sign above it that reads, *Smile, you're on camera*, in several languages, though there's no security cam in sight. Could be a clever bluff?

He's silent as he pecks absentmindedly at the keyboard. You use the opportunity to delete any blurry pictures off your digital camera. Your most recent photo is from port, just as you embarked on the river. It shows the shore as the boat leaves, the first section of jungle just outside civilization.

But there's something else.

There's a box on the display, added atop the foliage. Your camera focuses on faces as part of its auto-optimized settings, which adds a box around portraits to ensure they're given due attention. But why is there a box around a tree? You zoom in. Is something there? You keep tapping the zoom toward the box, amplifying the picture. *Holy shit*, the camera is right.

It's a face. You see it now—it's the assassin, the Man in Black. He was watching you; he followed you to the port. He knows what boat you're on.

"Viktor..." you say.

"Oh, *merda*," he murmurs.

"What?"

Viktor's cursing grows more rapid, in tune with his newly frantic keystrokes. Webpage after webpage splashes across the screen with surprising speed for a jungle barge. He shakes his head in disbelief, mumbling inaudible slurs.

"What is it?" you press.

"My university profile is gone. I don't appear anywhere on the Energy Summit page—even though I was supposed to be the keynote speaker. At first I thought it was just PR, like they were trying to divorce themselves from controversy, but then my employment history is missing too. Even a simple web search shows nothing. No pictures, no records. It's almost as if I never existed."

"That might have something to do with this," you say, showing him the picture.

"Dear God, they aren't just going to kill us—they're going to *erase* us."

There's a sudden commotion over on the starboard side of the boat. Viktor logs off the computer, then rushes over to see what's going on.

- *Follow him!* Go to page 329

New Beginnings

Like a flower opening toward the sun, the shanty town stirs with first signs of life just after dawn. Right now it's the workers opening their shops and the elderly generation with their Copernican lifestyles (as informed by decades of rising with the first light) who roam the dusty streets. Soon the warm glow of late summer will emerge and, with it, the *favela* populace.

A bakery whose sole form of advertisement is an open window next to the oven catches your attention. You're famished. You're about to tell Viktor as much, but the gurgle in your stomach does so for you.

"Hungry?" Viktor asks with a smile.

He takes you inside the *padaria,* where the smell is even more intense. The small building uses 90 percent of its space for the kitchen, but there's enough room to stand and place your order in the doorway. Viktor orders for you in Portuguese, then steps out to the patio where white, mass-produced lawn furniture waits for you to sit down. It's silty from all the dust, and not very sturdy—about the quality you'd find at Walmart—but it'll do.

Viktor sets down two coffees on the plastic table as he sits, sliding one cup forward for you. He blows on the lip of his own cup, waiting for the liquid to cool.

"The note mentioned 'the source of hate.' What do you think that means?" you ask.

"I'm not sure," he confesses. "That's what we must figure out."

Your shoulders slump. This mission is getting more difficult—and with even bigger stakes—every time you hear a new detail.

Just as Viktor takes his first sip of coffee, the woman inside the restaurant hollers at him to come get his order. He rises and returns a moment later with your meal.

"*Bolinhos de bacalhau* and manioc fries," he announces, setting the tray down before you.

There's a circular dish with some kind of breaded, fried ball, similar to a hush-puppy, a dipping sauce that could be tartar in the center, and a basket of thick-cut fries.

"What is it?" you ask.

"Cod fritter; it's good, try it."

"Fish? For breakfast? And maniac…?"

"*Manioc*," he laughs. "It's similar to a potato."

When in Rome… you tell yourself, and dig in. You missed dinner last night, so this might as well be manna from heaven. The breading is light and slightly sweet, but the fish within is pleasantly salty. The fries are very much like farm-cut French fry wedges, but have a little more consistency. Before long, your belly is full and you're sated.

An old man with a cane shuffles down the street next to you; a dog in the same twilight of life is pattering along next to him. The morning stillness prepares to finally give way to city life.

"I don't get it," you say. "I know this is a poor neighborhood, and that poverty has a way of making people desperate, but it hardly seems dangerous. What's the big deal?"

Viktor doesn't answer right away. He lifts his cup and sips on his coffee, casually uncurling his index finger to point over your shoulder. "The rooftop, behind you."

Trying not to seem obvious, you turn and look back. An Afro-Brazilian sits up on the corrugated roof, smoking his morning cigarette. He looks right at you. He's shaved bald and wears an old bomber jacket with a fur-lined collar. Sitting across his lap, pointed carelessly toward you, is a sniper rifle with a ruby-red scope. The man raises his hand in the shape of a gun and lets his thumb fall as he "shoots" you.

You drop your coffee.

The man stands up, the golden wrestling singlet he wears beneath the jacket glinting in the morning sun, extinguishes his cigarette, slings the rifle over his shoulder, and turns to head inside.

"It's more than just poverty," Viktor says, eyebrows raised.

You look back to the rooftop, but the man is gone. Viktor drains the last of his coffee, tightens the straps of his backpack, and says, "Let's go buy some guns."

You reach down to grab the ghost of your coffee, unaware that it's making mud with the dust at your feet. Shaking your head to "snap out of it," you follow Viktor down the dirt road. Around the next corner, in a wider street, a market is just opening for business. Tarpaulin flaps are raised on stakes and anchored with nylon rope to the buildings behind them. The drone of conversation fills the air as people buy and sell fresh fruit, ice-packed fish, herbs and spices, thatched handicrafts, dry goods, and carved wooden wares.

Viktor smiles. "Looking for souvenirs, Tourist? You'll not find a cheaper price."

You shake your head. Near the end of the market, a hard-looking man with a pockmarked face chews coca leaf and eyes the two of you when you approach. Unlike the other vendors, he makes no sales pitch. He just stares. His posture stiffens and you see that his throat is tattooed with an ornate crucifix centered on the Adam's apple.

"*Armas?*" Viktor asks.

The man doesn't respond. Viktor flashes his money-clip at the shopkeeper, just long enough to catch the man's gaze. With the briefest cock of his head, the man motions toward the inside of the store, then ducks in himself.

"How did you know?" you ask.

Viktor runs a finger down the curve of a bowl on the man's stand, bringing it back up for inspection. His finger is covered in dust. "That man wasn't looking for customers," he says. "He was standing watch."

You follow Viktor inside the hovel, unsure what to think. Inside it's even smaller than his market-stand outside, but the man waits expectantly. When you enter, he pulls back a tapestry from the wall—a weaving of *Cristo Redentor*—to reveal a hidden staircase.

With a sinking feeling, you follow the men into the passage and up the stairs. Now there's a deep hum emanating from the building, a drumming from within the walls somewhere between a generator trying to start up and an underground rave. Every two or three seconds, an intense *thud-thud* rattles the building and causes the ceiling lights to flicker, as if the building's heartbeat is reflecting your own.

You walk past an open door and peer into a room bigger than you could've imagined. It's filled with a dozen gaming tables, six men at each, the patrons still gambling from the night before. How do so many people fit in here? Was that tiny shop the façade for this whole building?

The shopkeeper calls out to a man who shuts the remaining two doors in the hallway. This assistant opens a third door, the only one that was closed, and joins your pockmarked guide inside.

Staying close by Viktor's side, you step in. Each wall is mounted with the same pegboard panels a machine shop uses to organize its tools. Except here it's lined with weapons; assault rifles, handguns, sub-machine guns, an RPG, several types of knives, and a truck-mountable .50-cal machine gun.

The door shuts.

The assistant leans against the door, arms tucked behind his back, effectively sealing you in. You look to Viktor, trying to communicate, *Are they going to rob us?* You puff up, standing tall and trying to look unafraid. The hard man looks at the two of you, then nods toward the wall. Time to go shopping.

You linger near an AK-47, and Viktor says, "I like your style, Tourist, but let's take something we can conceal, hmmm?"

Nodding, you shift over to the handguns. A heavy revolver demands your attention, the weighty thickness of the gun potent with virility. You look it over—the serial number has been filed off. Hmmm, feels too much like the crime scene. Instead, you examine the room's semi-automatic pistols, searching for what feels the most natural in your hands.

Your eyes drift toward a section of grenades: standard military issue, tear gas, smoke, and flashbangs.

Viktor says, "Trust me, my friend, my little 'Manhattan Project' puts all of those to shame."

He selects his own handgun, each of you taking a spare magazine. *Whew*, this is intense. There's no going back, you know that, though you tell yourself it's just for defense. Viktor chooses special ammunition for your pistols: armor piercing rounds, aka, *copkillers*… but it's just for the assassin, right? You wouldn't shoot a cop, would you? They just think they're doing their job, right? I mean—

"How about a little something fun?" Viktor says, interrupting your thoughts as he claims a small black submachine-gun.

The unit is military grade, an H&K MP5, to be exact. Most likely lifted from a dead cop. The thought sinks in—all of these are stolen, for sure. Viktor slips off his backpack, puts in the weapons, and pays the shopkeeper. Then, with another bill lingering in his hand, Viktor says, "*Informação?*"

The shopkeeper shakes his head, then escorts you back outside. Returning to the fresh air, away from all the buzzing and thudding, you feel like you can breathe again.

Getting Viktor's attention, the hard man points across the way to an alley just outside the market. As you walk away, the man removes a cell phone and makes a call.

Viktor gives you your handgun and a box of bullets. He then proceeds to load his own weapons, right there in the open street in broad daylight. No one present so much as bats an eyelash, though they do intentionally avert their eyes. Once your handgun is loaded, you tuck the pistol into your waistband and follow Viktor toward the opposing alley.

Like the Cheshire cat, a grin emerges from the shadows when you approach. The man who materializes is a sinewy Afro-Brazilian, his unkempt hair just beginning to form dreadlocks. He's unshaven and his beard sprouts forth in tiny curls, giving a dark pointillism to his face and serving to emboss his grin and bright eyes.

He wears a hoodie, hands shoved into the pockets, the jacket unzipped to reveal that he is shirtless beneath. An outtie bellybutton presses proudly above his tattered cargo shorts. He says something to Viktor in Portuguese, his smile friendly and inviting.

"His name is Tinho. He says if we want to pay for information, he knows everything that happens in the *favela* and he'd be happy to help us."

A short woman with curly bleached hair approaches from the side and says something to Viktor. She looks dirty and tired, like someone worked to the bone, like a homeless person who can't quite open her eyes all the way. One word she says to Viktor sticks out: *Americano.*

Tinho shouts at her, trying to shoo her off. You look to Viktor, who translates: "She wants to know if we're looking for the dead American."

- "Of course we are! Let's see what she has to say." Go to page 249
- "I don't know…if Tinho is *The Guy* for information, maybe we should stick with him." Go to page 327

Nightcap

After a shower, a nap, and a bite to eat, you enter the hotel bar at sunset. The glint of waning light glimmers off the polished surfaces of the bar, focusing the rays at eye level, causing you to squint as you walk in. There's still champagne chilling on the counter, but it's still not time to celebrate.

As your eyes adjust to the dark covey of the bar, you find both agents waiting for you inside.

"Long time no see," you say.

"I'll drink to that," Agent Bertram says, signaling the bartender for a round of shots.

"So is it official, we're really off the case?" you ask, taking your seat.

"It's official," Danly says.

"What now?"

Bertram scoffs. "Didn't you hear? I'm on suspension, and Dan-O here starts the Energy Summit security detail tomorrow."

"You got suspended? For what?"

"Apparently my investigations out in the jungle weren't exactly orthodoxy."

"Orthodox," Danly corrects.

"*Orthodoxical*—who the fuck cares? I've got thirty days on the beach and I'm getting drunk!"

The shots arrive. Tequila. The three of you drink.

"And so, what, we all get fired and we're here celebrating?" you say through the bitterness of the alcohol.

Bertram swirls his finger around the bottom of the shot glass, scooping up any residue, then licks his finger clean.

"I believe it's called a 'wake,' when you're in mourning," says a man from behind.

You turn to see three agents in suits. It's the replacement investigation team, the men who've come from the States. The leader is tall and square-jawed, his blond hair meticulously combed to one side and pressed down at the ears where his sunglasses normally rest. The other men, both built like smokestacks, say nothing.

The blond smiles. "Mourning a dead career, right?"

Danly clears his throat. "Howard, don't you have—I don't know—a murder investigation to solve?"

"You know what? I actually do," the leader replies. "That's very perceptive of you; maybe you should be an investigator or something? Oh, wait…."

The two cronies laugh.

Bertram suddenly launches to his feet and his chair *screeches* against the floor before it slams against the wall.

"I'll drink to that. Round's on me, fellas, whaddya say?" he says.

"No… thanks. We need to get going. Duty never sleeps, right?"

Bertram and Danly say nothing. The three of you watch the three of them leave, but you can't help yourself.

"You don't want to interview me?" you ask. "Wouldn't that be part of a thorough investigation?"

Agent Howard's jaw sets. "Assuming these guys gave us a *thorough* report, we should have all we need. Just don't go far; we'll call if they missed anything."

And like that, they're gone.

"Assholes," Danly says.

"Speaking of which," Bertram says, turning to you. "What the hell are you doing hanging out with chumps like us? Go live your life! See *Carnaval.* Get back on vacation."

- "Well… as long as you guys don't mind. I probably should go see the parades at least!" Go to page 32
- "No way! There's nowhere else I'd rather be. Next round's on me." Go to page 317
- "You know what? I can still go to the Energy Summit. This doesn't have to be over!" Go to page 91

Nocturnal

"You can just drop me off out front," Muniz says when you return to the police station.

"It's okay, I wanted to come in anyway," Danly replies.

"Hey, if you want to go talk to the Chief, you go right ahead, Boss-man. You wasted the time, not me; you coulda talked with some guys in that *favela* if you wanted to. The slime is still there in a pacified slum, it's just hiding."

"Care to stick around and defend your case?"

"No can do. Night shift. Which should be an extra-long one, thanks to your dragging me out for tour-guide duty."

Danly parks the SUV without comment. The three of you walk toward the station, but Danly puts a hand out to stop you at the entrance. After Muniz is out of earshot, he says, "I'm going to find his beat from the Chief and I'm going to follow him tonight. There are only two reasons he'd take us on a wild goose chase like that. Either he's trying to keep us off the trail, or he really is a giant fucking pussy. We find out tonight."

Once you enter, Agent Danly tells you to wait for him in Detective Dos Santos' office while he gets the schedule from the Chief. When you go in, you're surprised to find Irma already there. She's dressed in a white blouse with a black jacket and black slacks; most likely what she wears when she's out interviewing possible sources and suspects.

"Hi there," she says, looking up from her desk with a warm smile. "I hear you guys went out to the *favelas* today. Find anything?"

"No," you say with a sigh. "Your partner took us to a pacified slum. Agent Danly's pretty upset."

She shrugs. "Lucio's not as brave as you. It takes guts to go into the *favelas* without Elite Squad, and it's suicide to go there at night."

She's still smiling, and looks like she has more to say, but her gaze goes past you to the doorway as Danly enters.

"Find anything new today, Detective?"

"Not on this case," she says. "There are a lot more murders here than there are cops."

"So you try to solve the easiest one, right?"

"Wouldn't you? Frees up more time for the others and gets the Chief off my back. Speaking of free time, you two still want to go to the *favelas*?"

"Tonight?" you gulp. "I thought you said it was suicide?"

"Not for someone brave and strong like you, right?" she says with a wink. "Elite Squad has an Op; I thought we could tag along. Believe it or not, a lot of the thugs are in school or working during the day, and the ones that aren't are off selling weed in the rich neighborhoods, so your odds of finding an informant go up when the sun goes down."

"Damn," Agent Danly says. "I sort of have an Op scheduled already."

"Does it require the both of you?"

You look up at him.

"Oh, hell no, Rookie."

"She's right," you say. "I'll go with Elite Squad. Don't worry, I'll be safe. You go put some surveillance on our suspected mole."

Irma looks at you when you say "mole." So does Danly. "I can see the headlines now," he says, chopping an open palm across the air to "print" the words out before you. "American Tourist Raped and Murdered in Rio; Responsible DSS Agent to be Crucified."

"Still, you bring up a good point," he continues. "Going out with Elite Squad should take priority."

"So what do you want me to do?"

He looks to Irma. "Detective, would you mind ensuring our Cooperating Witness here makes it back to the hotel room that has been so generously comped by the State Department?"

She nods.

"Rookie, go back to the hotel—eat something from room service, go for a walk on the beach. I'll let you play sleuth again in the morning. Now if you'll excuse me, I need some goddamned coffee," he says gruffly.

Irma smiles at you again as Danly exits the room. She flashes it so easily and yet each time it sends a flush of warmth radiating out from your belly. Her eyes, with what must be artificially long and lush lashes, flicker at you in a way that really does make you feel like you're some kind of superhero—like you could storm the *favelas* without fear of danger.

"What are you smiling about?" you ask.

"'The mole?' You wouldn't be talking about my partner, would you?"

Your mouth drops open. "How did….?"

"I've always felt something nagging about that note you found; the note that is now missing. I can tell about people in interrogation, and I believe you're telling the truth; it's a gift I have. So where did the note go? I doubt you'll find any connection between Lucio and the murdered girl, but I doubt even further that he cares who did it. His problem isn't that he's some kind of conspirator, out to foil your investigation, his problem is—he's not lazy—what's the word I'm looking for? Non-caring?"

"Apathetic, maybe?" Danly stands in the doorway, blowing on his coffee. "I assume you're talking about me, but don't take my decision as callousness, Rookie. I've trained specifically for urban combat like this, and so has Elite Squad. I hate to say it, but they make our SWAT look like police enthusiasts. These guys are so well-equipped, so battle-tested and hardened, they might as well be Seal Team Six."

You nod. At least he didn't overhear the crux of your conversation.

"Should I introduce you to the guys now?" Irma asks.

Agent Danly says that she should and you follow as she brings him to Elite Squad. He introduces himself (one sergeant has at least passable English) and they discuss the plan for the evening. Most of the jargon is lost on you, but the name "Shadow Chiefs" keeps popping up. It's the name of the faction that controls the *favela* they're set to start pacifying tonight.

You watch as they arm up for the evening—Kevlar vests, assault rifles, some with combat shotguns; everything in black. Elite Squad members wear berets with the symbol of a grinning skull, two pistols crossed behind it like a pirate flag, and a dagger plunged into the top. The skull is cracked open but couldn't care less.

The mocking grin invites pain. The unit's initials in Portuguese—B.O.P.E.—are emblazoned above the symbol.

Agent Danly leaves to retrieve a duffle bag from the SUV and changes in the bathroom. When he comes out, he's in khaki-cargo pants, desert issue US combat boots, a baby-blue oxford button-down with sleeves rolled-up and cuffed at the bicep, and a bullet-proof vest, tactical belt, and baseball cap all in matching tan. In addition to his sidearm, he now carries his own assault rifle. The look is completed by something out of the Old West—a badge pinned to his vest.

It's after sunset, so it's time for them to go. Danly loads up in his "battle rattle" with Elite Squad in an armored combat vehicle. Aside from being painted black, it's the kind of thing you'd expect to see patrolling the streets of Afghanistan. Judging by the spiderwebbed impact print against the bulletproof window, it's seen some action.

"Don't worry about me, Rookie." Agent Danly says, stepping into the passenger seat. "I live for this shit."

And then they drive away, off to conquer the slums.

Detective Irma Dos Santos looks to you. "Well?"

"Well, what?"

"What are you going to do?"

"Did I miss something?" you ask.

"He asked me to make sure you got back, but he didn't say when. I want to know what your plans are, so I can help."

Your eyebrows start to defy gravity. "You want me to disobey him?"

"That's not for me to judge. We have a saying here: *cada macaco no seu galho*—which translates literally to 'each monkey in your own branch,' but what it really means is 'each person is responsible for their own actions.' You do what you must, Agent Danly does what he must, and I do what I must. I think you're brave and honest, and I think Agent Danly is kind of an asshole, so the branch my monkey sits in is helping you."

She smiles. You try to think it over, but only one image comes to the surface: Agent Danly, a vein pounding on his forehead, his hands tightening into fists, the knuckles exploding out like newly white popcorn. If he found out you had disobeyed and followed him into danger, he'd kick you off the investigation for sure.

"Do you have any idea how angry he'll be if he catches us?"

She shrugs. "To be a cop in Rio, you must first be a master at keeping secrets. Ask yourself this: will he be happy if you find out something he misses? Maybe if you ID the guy? The case could be closed tonight."

- "Okay, I'm in. So what do we do? Follow Elite Squad into the slums? It's going to be a tall order to avoid being seen by both Agent Danly and the drug traffickers." Go to page 87
- "I don't think so. You'd better drop me off at the hotel. My monkey doesn't want to get raped or murdered." Go to page 301
- "Damn it if you're not right—and you were right about our suspicions of your partner: Danly wanted to follow Muniz to see if he's dirty. Will you help me do it instead?" Go to page 133

No More Easy Paydays

The sun crests over the Rio de Janeiro skyline, sending reddish-umber rays over the city. *Cristo Redentor* stands with arms wide as if pouring the crimson down upon you Himself. The Brazilian flag flutters in the breeze atop one of the broken rooftops of the pacified *favela.*

"You see my flag up there, Tourist? There are over 900 *favelas* in Rio, each an independent city-state controlled by the druglords—until now. When you see that flag, it tells you that government troops have reclaimed the territory in the name of *Brasil.*"

"So what?" you ask. "This *favela* is safe now that it's been pacified?"

He shakes his head. "The local police can be even more dangerous than the slumlords, because cops have law on their side. They can kill you with *carte blanche* authority and say you were a criminal, and if another cop stands up and says 'this isn't right,' they kill him too.

"Make no mistake, the druglords are still here, biding their time. They'll return after *Brasil* forgets about the World Cup and the Olympics, that is, unless the government succeeds in rezoning neighborhoods like this and wins their war on the poor. Look at these views, Tourist! This is prime real estate."

You look around, seeing the shanty neighborhood in a new light. If these crumbling buildings were replaced by high-rise apartments and ritzy hotels, this could be the new *Ipanema.*

Looking back at Viktor, you say, "But we're just going to pay off the cop, right? Bribe him for information?"

"That's the bad news. These venal police officers will do anything for a buck, true enough, but we've doled out so many bribes already…and after buying the guns? We're out of cash."

"So what do we do?" you ask.

Viktor shrugs. "We're supposed to meet up just after sunset, when the first street lights power on. I'm all for suggestions if you've got any."

You think for a moment. *Hmmm…*

- "Maybe we can strike a deal. Reveal who we are and offer to pay handsomely *after* this whole thing is resolved." Go to page 349
- "Before I came here, I read that people hold up ATMs all the time. Maybe we should 'get' some money before they arrive?" Go to page 239
- "Let's pretend that we're going to pay him off, then hold *him* up with that sub-machinegun." Go to page 14

No Thanks

"Well, then just go get me one," he says.

Before you can answer, Irma interjects. "I can have one of our new recruits grab you one, if you like."

"No, it's fine," Danly says in a tone that suggests otherwise.

He gets up and walks out.

"So, is this your first vacation in *Brasil*?" she asks you.

You laugh. "It's not much of a vacation anymore. I was here with friends, we were planning on doing *Carnaval,* but I guess they'll have to go without me. Is that picture from before you were a cop?"

"No," she replies with a frown. Then, in a flash of understanding, she leans forward and smiles. "In Rio, everyone participates in *Carnaval*—even cops. That was only last year. This year, I have to work. But you should go! The investigation will wait, *Carnaval* comes only once a year."

You realize her hand is atop yours. It's warm and soft. Seeing you blush, she takes it away.

"You are shy?" she asks.

Agent Danly re-enters the room, blowing against the lip of his Styrofoam cup to cool the beverage.

➢ *Continue the investigation.* Go to page 137

Not Much of a Comfort

You head upstairs to your room, only to find the lights off and the beds empty. Your friends aren't even here yet. It is pretty late, but not so late that the bars are closed. Your spot on the bottom of the third bunk bed is wide open, so you tuck in, ready for sleep. There'll be plenty of time to talk tomorrow.

It's a fitful night of sleep, plagued with nightmarish images of blood and bullets. A snake creeps toward you, a note affixed to its neck—the note—PICK ME UP. No matter how hard you try, you can't get away. The snake moves slowly, but it's like you're stuck in quicksand. You're frozen as the serpent crawls up your chest and coils around your neck.

- *Wake up in a cold sweat.* Go to page 230

Not so Sweet

If that man is the devil, she's ready to look in his face.

The main house of the plantation isn't opulent or gaudy. There is no parlor where you'll be served cognac. No great dining hall, no feast beside your host. This isn't where this man lives; this is simply where he conducts business. It's almost disappointing. Part of you wanted to see something out of *The Godfather* or *Scarface*, but you'll have to settle for substance instead of style.

A private security guard greets you: a thin, older man who requests that you leave your weapons and cell phones at a secure room in the front. The fact that he's not surprised in the least that you're armed serves as a not-so-subtle reminder that you're dealing with a man on a different tier than a mere farm manager. Maybe this will be interesting after all.

You give up the shotgun (not like it was yours to begin with), and Maria hands over a revolver, but Bertram refuses to leave his weapons at the front room. He shows the man at the security booth his badge, but the guy doesn't seem to care. He demands Bertram disarm, but the federal agent doesn't budge.

A pair of security guards arrive to settle the commotion and the hairs on the back of your neck stand on end. Bertram's right hand hovers ominously over his gun holster.

"Well, well, an American federal agent," a voice booms out from behind. "You three are a bit far from home, yes?"

You turn and see a large, middle-aged Brazilian man. Neither tall nor fat per se, but thick-limbed and possessing a sort of magnetic gravity you can't quite place. His full face is clean-shaven and has deep creases where a stark smile now finds perch. His eyes are dark brown, with an intense intelligence.

The man wears tight blue jeans tucked into black cowboy boots, dusty and grey with age. He wears a blue workshirt and an orange scarf tied loosely about his neck. Not exactly how you'd picture a billionaire. His short, jet-black hair is slicked back and neatly arranged in such a way that you can be certain he has a comb tucked in his pocket.

"To what do I owe the pleasure?" he asks.

You're about to speak when Maria steps forward. "I have a message from my father," she says.

The man's smile disappears, and he glances at his security. She's already given up the revolver, so the thin man nods to his boss. The Sugar King makes ready to speak, but Maria delivers the message before he has the chance.

There was a second revolver, you suddenly remember, and in an instant she empties all six chambers into the man.

The security men rush forward, but Bertram already has her covered. He raises his assault rifle and shouts at the men in Portuguese, then adds in English, "He's not paying your checks anymore. You don't want to die for a corpse."

Slowly, the men turn and then run out the front door.

Maria drops the revolver atop the dead Sugar King's chest. She turns and offers her hands to Agent Bertram to be cuffed.

"Your father didn't take your family from the jungle, did he?" Bertram says.

Her mouth pursed in a sad smile, she looks at the ground and shakes her head slightly.

"You know, it's funny," she says. "I hadn't planned on killing him. I only wanted to look in his face. But when I saw him, I only saw my father, and I couldn't abide that. Do you understand?"

"I could have stopped you," is Bertram's only reply.

She nods. "Now what?"

"I have to arrest you."

- "Do you have to? Can't you just 'phone it in' and say she escaped?" Go to page 110
- "A small price to pay for justice. Maria, you've just changed history. I'll never forget you, as long as I live." Go to page 339

Not White but Golden

You stand stock-still, shotgun raised and ready to pull the trigger. But instead of men charging in, you're met with a group of golden lion tamarins. The smallish monkeys screech in surprise at your presence, swerve around you, and continue fleeing into the sugarcane like a stampede of overgrown squirrels.

"They run from the fire," Maria explains. "Animals like this are endangered because over 85 percent of their forests have been destroyed."

You swallow, lower your shotgun, and take a deep breath. You're not sure what the bigger threat is: the bandits behind you or the burning jungle before you. The sun has now fully set, but there's an eerie red glow in the clouds above the sugarcane from the fires.

A new sound arrives—thunder—and with it rain, in a sudden and immediate cloudburst. The sugarcane canopy provides some protection, but if the storm doesn't break, you'll soon be drenched.

"Do these storms last long?" you ask.

"It's the start of the rainy season," Bertram says. "This storm could last for days. With any luck, the *grileiros* will abandon the search and seek shelter."

Maybe it's the constant brush with death, or simply the soaking rain, but you overflow with sarcasm. "Right, because that's what you do in a storm. Not, you know, hide out in some sugarcane field where jungle animals flee from an encroaching fire."

Bertram scowls. "Cool your jets, Hotshot. Let me check the GPS, see where we are exactly."

You sit in silence, heavy raindrops pounding down on your head. Maria sits close by, trying to stay warm. Bertram turns the waterproof GPS screen around so you can see.

"Here's us, here's the plantation. It's a bit of a hike."

"What's this smaller building here?" Maria asks.

"Most likely a storage shed. Could be barracks for the men, though."

- "Barracks? Sigh. Let's sleep out here." Go to page 264
- "It's worth checking out. Who wants to sleep in the rain?" Go to page 296

Now What?

The next morning, you're greeted with warm surprise once your friends realize you've rejoined them. They want to hear all about it, but first, breakfast. You head downstairs, all sunshine and laughter, but your face drops when you see the two agents waiting for you downstairs.

"Hey, guys. Is everything okay?"

"Just fine," the slim Agent Danly says.

"May we join you for breakfast?" Agent Bertram asks.

You turn to your friends and say, "I'll catch up."

The hostel transforms its bar into a continental breakfast in the morning, the highlight being the fresh fruit. You serve yourself up a plateful, then stake out a table on the outside patio. The agents join you with a cup of coffee each, Bertram with a Danish as well. Your friends take a table indoors and, save for the occasional outburst of laughter on their end, you cannot hear one another's conversation.

"So, what's up?" you ask.

Bertram says, "It's been confirmed. Our Jane Doe is now Jane Nightingale, an Office Management Specialist at the Rio consulate. I didn't know her."

Danly shakes his head; neither did he.

Agent Bertram continues, "She didn't hold a significant position—they're the ones that do the secretarial work—so we don't think the killing was politically motivated, but we won't rule out a terrorist attack until we know for sure."

"Most likely she was separated from the crowd, just like you, and it was a mugging turned sour. Who knows, you may owe the woman your life. It could have been you in there."

"It's even possible this is a serial killer—he's the right demographic, based on that sketch you provided—and you probably interrupted him during his rituals," Bertram says.

"I doubt it," Danly says. "Serial killers are extremely rare."

"In America, maybe. But with no extradition laws, Brazil is like a retirement community for criminals."

"And this guy has come out of retirement?" you ask.

"I don't buy it," Agent Danly says. "This was a first-time job, too sloppy to be a pro. Regardless, this is going to be a total shitstorm. We haven't had an American murdered in the Foreign Service since the Sixties, and that was at the hands of a coworker. So an American killed outside the line of duty by a foreign national? Shitstorm. Within 48 hours, a team will be dispatched by HQ, and in a couple of days this place will be crawling with feds from Arlington."

"But we know the first 48 hours are the most important, and we've been cleared to start the investigation."

"What about the local police?" you ask.

"It's their job," Danly says. "We're just going to do it for them."

Agent Bertram spreads his arms magnanimously. "Look, we're just going to do what we can before the trail goes cold, and the reason we're telling you is because we want your help. You're the only one who knows what the suspect looks like."

"What do you want from me?"

"Come with us and ID the subject. Help us find the goddamn murderer," Agent Danly says, leaning back and folding his arms over his chest.

- "Uh, no thanks. I'm here on vacation… I don't want to drag you guys down. Good luck." Go to page 353
- "I'm in. Do I get a gun and a badge? Or a pipe and a magnifying glass, at least?" Go to page 61

Off the Case

"Agent Danly!" you shout, waving your hands into the air. Detective Irma Dos Santos has already disappeared into the shadows.

The two Elite Squad members swing around, rifles pointed at you. You freeze. Agent Danly stops them just in time and they lower their weapons. With a smile, you jog toward him.

"Rookie?" he says in disbelief. "What the *fuck* are you doing here?"

You start to explain, to tell him all you've seen tonight, but he cuts you off. "That's the last straw. You've helped your country enough. Please detain my *former* Cooperating Witness, boys."

"Wh-What?" you stammer as one of the Elite Squad members zip-ties your hands behind your back. The other gags you and slips a bag over your head.

You squeal in protest and Danly says, "You have the right to remain silent."

There will be no charges levied against you the next morning, but you're quickly deported back to the USA.

THE END

Old and Experienced

The RSO smiles. "That's the spirit! See that, boys? You could learn something."

As he leaves, you turn to Agent Bertram. He smiles as well. "Welcome to the fold, Hotshot."

You follow the agent out and through the halls of the consulate. There's a private room set aside so Bertram can talk with the woman already waiting there.

"It's Karen, right?" he says, entering the room and finding a seat.

"That's me," says the woman across the table from Agent Bertram. Another Office Management Specialist; this one is a veteran secretary. Mrs. Karen Atwood has been through dozens of these question sessions over the years, although, admittedly, never as part of a murder investigation before. From what you can see on the surface, she's not touched by emotion in the least.

Her hair is a raised bramble of black and grey. Coarse, spindly strands escape her bobby pins by the dozen. She wears a blouse of deep lavender, coated in white floral patterns. She's bespectacled, though if you had to cast her in your own noir mystery, she'd be wearing cat's-eye glasses. Her voice has the husky rasp of a smoker, and her impatient air suggests she'd like to light up right now. She most likely would be, if it weren't for the regulations.

Her eyes, rheumy from decades spent under fluorescent lights staring at standardized forms and computer screens, flicker from his face to yours before resting back on Agent Bertram.

"Did you know Jane personally?" he asks.

"Only professionally. Nice enough girl, about as hardworking as the rest of 'em."

"Did she ever talk to you about her personal life?"

"No, sir." The "sir" is dragged out, making the statement one less of respect and more akin to "this is a waste of time."

"So you wouldn't know if she was having personal problems?"

The woman's eyebrows rise over the rim of her glasses and her mouth tucks back in a frown. She raises her hands as if to say, "I've got nothing."

"I see. Well then, professionally, did Jane have any problems at work? Any discipline issues?"

"As I said, she was a good worker."

"Did she ever seem tired or distant? Did you notice any changes in her behavior over the last few months, weeks, days?"

"No, sir," she says, with the same exaggeration.

"Anything you think can think of to help us?"

She shakes her head, mouth still in a frown.

Bertram, getting frustrated, says, "You know the woman was *murdered*, right?"

She sighs, pausing for a moment.

Then Mrs. Atwood says, "If I think about Jane, my biggest memory is that she requested to be at the Embassy most of the last year. We all cycle through the different consulates and sometimes the Embassy. People will ask to transfer to a different country, but usually the girls just go with the flow from consulate to consulate. Still, her request wasn't that odd. Embassy work is better for your résumé than consulate work. She asked for a transfer back to Rio almost a month ago, but again, it's not that strange. Carnival is pretty popular among the younger girls."

She says "Carnival" the American way, not *Carnaval.* The way Texans call the *Rio Grande* the "Rio Grand."

"Thanks, Karen."

➢ *Meet back up with Agent Danly*. Go to page 175

On the Road

The unmistakable sound of a chugging engine greets you as you approach the Sugar Highway. Bertram nods, raising his rifle. You and Maria get ready to do battle as you exit the sugarcane.

There, standing next to an idling jeep, a man holds a machete. He's clothed head to toe in gray cloth, like a padded ninja, a turtleneck pulled up over his face and a boonie hat pulled so low that only his eyes are visible. They're open wide, frightened at the sight of Agent Bertram's assault rifle.

The man in the driver's seat considers fleeing, but Bertram's persuasive Portuguese convinces him to stay.

"These are workers, normal men, not criminals," Maria says.

"They can take us to the plantation. Let's move, Hotshot," Bertram says.

As he's loading up into the jeep, Agent Bertram's satellite phone rings. You share a concerned look with Maria.

"Damn. They know I'm in the field; they wouldn't call unless it was an emergency." Then, opening the phone, he answers the call. "Agent Bertram… Negative, I'm still on scene."

Maria turns to you with eyes wide as the caller speaks. You can't hear the words, but you can hear the angry tone.

"Sir, all due respect, that's bullshit. I haven't even—"

He grits his teeth.

"Yes, sir… yes, sir." He hangs up and says, "We've got to go back."

"What? Why?"

"The official investigation team landed this morning. We're off the case."

"But we haven't even—" you start to say. His glare silences you.

Agent Bertram speaks to the men in Portuguese, but they shake their heads. He tries to emphasize his point by chambering a round in his pistol. The *click* of the slide springing into action sends a chill into your bones, but the men continue shaking their heads.

"Goddammit," Bertram growls.

You gesture for him to elaborate.

"I told them—just bluffing, mind you—that I'd kill them if they took us there. Didn't matter. I can only imagine what they're afraid of. The standard crime lord threat seems to be 'I'll kill your family,' but they might do something even worse than that."

"He's here in person? The Sugar King?" Maria asks, a mix of excitement and fear in her voice.

"Apparently," Bertram says.

You half-expected something out of the pre-Civil War Southern states, like a giant manor from *Gone With the Wind*, but you're greeted with a much more utilitarian structure. This isn't a place where people live, it's a place where people work.

Still, it's a massive set of buildings. A cafeteria, several barracks for workers, washing and refining stations, and of course, the main house of the plantation.

"Hang on," Bertram says to you. "Do you think Maria should come? This man has done terrible things to her family."

"I can hear you, and I'm coming," she says firmly.
"Hmmm. I don't know…." you say, considering.
"No, I'm coming. This man is the devil."

- "Okay… Just so long as you're ready to meet him." Go to page 227
- "Which is why I don't want to put you through hell. I'm sorry, but I agree. We'll take care of it; you stay here." Go to page 270

On the Run

Claiming Danly's pistol for your own, you offer a quick promise to the fallen agent that you'll nail the bastard, then sprint down the hallway of the Energy Summit in pursuit of the *real* Viktor Lucio de Ocampo.

You round the corner just in time to see the suspect dash out the emergency exit, with Agent Bertram hot on his heels. Flying down the hallway, you slip through the door and into the warm summer night in pursuit. *Samba* and humidity weigh heavily upon you and you can just barely spot Bertram in the crowd.

Seemingly from nowhere, a barrage of gunfire erupts and the crowd scatters, leaving Agent Bertram on the ground. The body of a costumed devil lies just beyond him. Before you have time to process this image, you see Viktor look back.

He sprints away once more.

- Check on Bertram. Go to page 267
- Follow Viktor! Go to page 151

On a Walkabout

The night is warm and the city is loud, but alone with your thoughts, you feel cold and isolated from the world. That poor woman, gunned down in some back alley. You'd heard Brazil could be dangerous, but you're in *tourist* Brazil, not the deep slums of some *favela.*

Part of you wants to hop the next plane to the US, get in bed, and pretend tonight was just some distant nightmare. But another part of you—a part that *scares* you—is excited. What if it's a serial killer, and you brushed into him? What if you had taken that gun and dealt some justice? What if this ride has only just begun?

You loop back to your hostel just as the adrenaline finally wears off and a deep primal need for sleep sets in. Your feet guiding you on autopilot, you head up to your room, only to find the lights off and the beds empty. Your friends aren't even here yet.

Not giving it much thought, you lie down in your bed and close your eyes.

➢ *Fall deeply asleep.* Go to page 230

One More Easy Payday

Looking forlorn, Viktor simply nods. With a hand on his pistol, he points to an ATM just down the street. You walk, nervous as to what you're about to attempt, but trying your best to look nonchalant.

A woman stands at the kiosk, three children in tow, and presently removes a large stack of bills from the machine. With nightfall approaching and the police soon to arrive, this might be your only chance. Viktor nods at you once more, uncertainty in those icy-blue eyes.

He's going to make you do it.

You pull out the handgun, drag the slide back to chamber a round—more because of the intimidating sound it makes, not that you'd actually shoot the woman—and shout for her to give you the money. She speaks no English, but understands the pistol clearly enough and screams in terror.

Viktor translates your threat, telling this mother to pay up in front of her children. She shakes her head and pleads with him, but now Viktor brandishes his own pistol, and, once he points it at the crying children, she complies.

With her month's paycheck in your hands, the woman tucks her children tight and escapes down an alley.

"Think this will be enough?" you say, counting the money.

Viktor looks extremely disturbed. Eyes skyward, he recites, "'They shed the blood of innocents… and the land became polluted with blood.'"

He's almost on the verge of tears. You snap your fingers in front of his face. "Hey, hello in there! Remember Jane? C'mon, we've got a job to do."

"I don't know your background, Tourist. But for me there is a clear line between revenge on criminals and becoming a criminal yourself."

Okay, so you just stole the bread money from a poor slum family with at least three young mouths to feed. This is clearly something he needs to come to terms with if you—

"*Pare aí mesmo!*" comes a shout from down the road. Huh?

Two uniformed policemen and one in plainclothes run toward you with weapons drawn.

- Hands up! Go to page 261
- Shoot first, questions later. Go to page 297
- Take cover, but hold your ground. Go to page 246
- Run! Take the alley your victims took. Go to page 359

Only Fools Rush In

You bum-rush the computer terminal, slamming the technician out of the way, knocking the roller-chair wildly across the room, and shaking the computer desk. You plug the USB drive into the computer and as the "auto-play" window opens, you're tackled and slammed to the ground by DSS agents.

A stunt like that wasn't smart, and now you're in handcuffs. Due to your haste, the evidence will never see the light of day. Later, when Viktor is killed "making an attempt on the Ambassador's life" and Jane mysteriously disappears, you'll be tried and found guilty of treason. The rest of your life will not be pleasant.

THE END

The Other Guys

The policeman scowls, looking you over. "You're law enforcement?"

"I didn't say that, I said I'm working *with* law enforcement," you say.

"I need to call this in to my superior."

"Wait!" you cry.

You're about to try and talk your way out of it, but another cop walks over toward the barricade. "Hey, weren't you at the station tonight? What are you doing here?"

"See? I'm the—I'm the star witness!"

The young man scratches his head while the first cop leans forward, looking toward the back of the house, and says, "What the hell is going on over there?"

You see Viktor hanging out of the window, trying to push his way out. Apparently he's finished his part of the bargain, so time to finish yours—distraction!

- Kick the policeman in the groin and/or punch him in the face. Go to page 242
- Sprint inside a random apartment. The police can't follow without a warrant! Go to page 278

Overconfident

Police brutality doesn't hold the same meaning here as it does in the US. In Rio, it's the name of what you just did by socking the cop in the nose and going for his nards. And the response? When the other policeman draws his handgun and shoots you, his actions will be not only justified, but he'll be rewarded with praise. You don't attack cops and get away with it; not here.

Bang. *Bang bang bang.*

THE END

Pacification

He sighs. "Fine, just stick close. If you get shot…." Danly shakes his head. "Don't get shot, okay?"

"You people are crazy," Detective Muniz says, stepping out of the SUV and slipping on his black suit jacket over his purple shirt.

You walk atop the dirty and dusty clutter of broken mortar, back out through the wall and into the populated area of the *favela*. You go past a "bike shop," which has an odd amalgamation of old and repatched bicycles for sale. Best case, it's a used shop. Most likely, they were all stolen. On the flat rooftop, laundry dries on wires under the hot summer sun.

A woman with an exposed midriff and frayed cutoffs sees your group, panics, and turns away into one of the houses. In an alleyway between units, a group of young boys plays ping-pong on a homemade table. It's an overturned door with a board propped up for a net. For paddles, they use pieces of tile. They wear Nike shorts and sandals and laugh, enjoying the game.

Old men sit together in plastic chairs, listening to soccer on the radio. You nod toward them as you walk by; they stare back as if you just landed and stepped out of a UFO.

"What—or who—are we looking for?" you ask.

Muniz shrugs. "You'd have to ask boss-man here."

Agent Danly stays silent. Around a corner are four men in Kevlar vests—maybe it's Elite Squad? They wear olive-green, short-sleeve, collared shirts adorned with unit patches and black tactical pants.

"Maybe we should ask them?" you suggest.

Looking to Danly, you notice the man is fuming. His face is red, and a large earthworm-like vein throbs on his forehead. He takes off his sunglasses, and you see his eyes are nearly bloodshot and are wet with anger.

"You son of a bitch," he says to Muniz through gritted teeth. "You took us to a pacified slum."

Muniz smiles. "Did I?"

"What does that mean?" you ask.

Danly looks at you, then back to Muniz. "You think I'm stupid, that I wouldn't notice?"

"I don't know, boss-man. What did you want to do? Roll up in your big, bad truck and slap the druglords around with your dick? I did you a favor! They would eat you alive. But hey, we're here—go ahead and ask around."

"What's a pacified slum?" you ask again.

"It's a goddamned waste of time. It's a *favela* without criminals," Danly says. "In prep to host the World Cup and the Olympics, they went through and cracked down on the high-visibility slums."

"Isn't that a good thing?"

"Not when we're here to talk with criminals, fucktard. They'll reclaim this area in a couple of years anyway. We drove all the way out here for nothing."

Muniz looks at his watch. "Yeah, we'd better head back. It's getting late."

"Okay," Danly says, his rage soaked into an eerie calm. "Let's head back."

➢ *Return to the Station*. Go to page 221

Padded Ninjas

In combat, there is no "rock, paper, scissors." There is only knife beats fist, gun beats knife, the end. So when Agent Bertram points his assault rifle at the farm crew and demands in Portuguese that they drop their machetes, they comply without hesitation. These are low-wage workers and they have no stake in the Sugar King's security.

When Bertram demands they disrobe, however, all eyes go to Maria. Good Catholic men such as these have their modesties, and disrobing in front of a young Brazilian woman is a bridge too far.

"We'll wait outside," she says, placing a hand on your shoulder.

"No, you won't," Agent Bertram says. "There should be a locker room inside."

He's right and the men change while Agent Bertram watches to make sure no one has a cell phone or triggers a silent alarm. A bit paranoid, perhaps, but caution is the better part of valor, as they say.

The agent escorts the men through the annex to a room with large double doors, pulling them open to reveal a cafeteria.

"Perfect," Bertram says.

He ushers the cane cutters into the room, assuaging their fears in Portuguese, and assuring them that everything will be fine if they stay in here until morning. Once the men are inside and the doors swing closed, Bertram removes a pair of handcuffs from his vest and cuffs the door handles to one another, effectively locking the farm workers inside.

"What about windows?" you ask.

"Locks only stop honest men, Hotshot. This is a mental barrier. They'll heat up some coffee, eat, and eventually fall asleep. C'mon, time to suit up."

The three of you don sweaty, grimy, stinky cane cutter uniforms. The padding is thick, meant to protect the wearer during cutting duty and from snakebites, but that also means the uniform is hot and stuffy.

It's hard to breathe with a turtleneck up over your nose, but it's the only way to blend in. The cutters use them in the field to protect against aspirating fertilizers and pesticides, but it should work just as well to protect your identity. Your breath leaves condensation on the mask, mingling with whatever residue was already there.

Bertram left his assault rifle in the locker room (and you left your shotgun), but the agent still has his service pistol concealed under the disguise. Maria gave you one of her revolvers, which presently rests coolly against your skin.

You walk toward a uniformed security guard, the first you've seen since entering the main house through the side door. Moment of truth: time to test your disguise. He's an "official" hired gun (unlike the *grileiros* from outside, who aren't officially on Mateo Ferro's payroll) and the man looks up briefly, but then goes back to playing Angry Birds on his iPad.

It worked! Ruse successful! You resist the urge to give your companions a high-five, but the smile hidden beneath your mask disappears when a voice booms out in Portuguese from around the corner. You creep forward to catch a better look.

"The Sugar King," Maria says breathlessly.

There before you stands a large, middle-aged Brazilian man on the telephone. Neither tall nor fat per se, but thick-limbed and possessing a sort of magnetic gravity you can't quite place. His full face is clean-shaven and has deep creases where a stark glower now finds perch. His eyes are dark brown, with an intense intelligence.

The man wears tight blue jeans tucked into black cowboy boots, dusty and grey with age. He wears a blue workshirt and an orange scarf tied loosely about his neck. Not exactly how you'd picture a billionaire. His short, jet-black hair is slicked back and neatly arranged in such a way that you can be certain he has a comb tucked in his pocket.

"He's asking someone the status of 'their problem,'" Bertram whispers. "He's probably too smart to go into details over the phone, but we might get lucky."

The man slams the phone against the receiver, then turns to you. His eyes dart from the hulking Bertram, to the petite Maria, to you. The three of you stick out like sore thumbs. Not too many Americans or women on the farmhand payroll.

"*Guardas!*" he shouts.

Security is on you in an instant, forcibly patting you down and taking your weapons. Maria gets thrown to the floor as she tries to brandish hers.

"So you're the ones causing all the trouble," the man says in English.

"Agent David Bertram, Diplomatic Security Service," your partner replies, fearsome gravity in his words. "Order your men to stand down, right now."

"An American federal agent? So far from home?"

"Order your men to stand down!"

"No, I don't think I will," the man grins. "You're inside my plantation, without proper clearance. Isn't that correct, Agent…Bertram, is it?"

Bertram gulps hard, doubt flowing into his hard eyes.

"That is what I thought, but don't worry yourselves. You three will be my guests. I offer you no ill will; I don't even know what brings you here, dressing up in costumes like this," he laughs. "Such theatricality! Change into something presentable, and then we can talk like civilized men. There is no need to come barging onto my property."

Not much of a choice here…

➢ *Get back into normal clothes.* Go to page 132

Pays Off

You tuck into the same alley where the mother fled with her children, shielding yourself and peering out behind your pistol at the cops. Viktor uses the ATM for cover in a similar way. The cops continue to shout, guns drawn down on you, but you don't budge.

Once they get close enough, you actually recognize the plainclothes policeman—it's Detective Lucio Muniz, the bleach-blond policeman who interviewed you on the night you were detained. Is he the one you're going to bribe?

"*You?*" he says.

"We're looking for the truth," you say coolly. "If you can help us, we can help you."

"You're the ones that called?"

Viktor nods.

Detective Muniz smiles and holsters his handgun. "Well, then, we're all friends here."

He waves the other cops down and they become calm with understanding. You put away your weapon and so does Viktor.

"Let's get down to business," Muniz says. "What information would you like to buy?"

"The murder I stumbled upon, what do you know?" you ask.

"More than you could imagine," he smirks.

Viktor steps forward. "Do you know who's responsible? Who the killer is?"

Muniz carefully considers the question. Seeing him waver, you flash the wad of money you pilfered from the ATM.

"Okay, I'm a fair man. And if you know my reputation, you know that I do what I'm paid to do, and I do it well. I do know who's responsible, and since you're a paying customer…" he smiles with a cocky confidence.

You hand over the cash.

"You've heard of the Shadow Chiefs? You know which *favela* they control?"

Viktor nods.

"Good. They're the ones who did it. We don't have a name, but we know it was their enforcers. Word has it someone high up—one of their colonels—ordered the hit." He looks through the wad of bills. "*Meu Deus*… Look for someone named *Falador*. He's our informant there, he'll talk."

"Thank you," you say.

"No, thank you," Muniz says, waving the bills. Then to Viktor, he adds, "And if you give me that watch, I'll forget I saw the pair of you when I meet up with the American agents."

Viktor looks at the watch for a long moment. He sighs. "Please, my Jane gave me this."

"I doubt she'll mind."

While he looks at you, he knows it's for the best. With great pain, Viktor gives the watch away.

"C'mon, let's go find Falador."

"Pleasure doing business with you," Detective Muniz says.

➢ *Go to the* favela *controlled by the Shadow Chiefs*. Go to page 294

Pedestrian

You jog toward the plantation, racing against the waning light and the thick black clouds overhead. Drops of water start to fall and a deluge is surely imminent. A pair of headlights illuminate the sugarcane so that shadows seem to reach out at you, much like in a haunted forest.

The three of you rush to the side of the road and hide in the crop. It works, and a jeep rushes past you. You start back toward the road, but something squirms over your feet. Something *alive*. Maria puts out a hand to still you as another set of headlights appear around the bend.

You hold your breath and look down: It's a gigantic frog, six inches across, thick and covered in warty globules of skin. There are a dozen toads at least, most likely fleeing from the fires.

A pickup truck rushes by. After it's out of view, you let out your breath.

"Don't touch," Maria says. "The skin has venom."

"Great," you say, and rub your shoe against the dirt.

"Cane toads," Bertram says.

Maria stops, unloads one of her revolvers, and crouches down. She strokes the bullets against the backs of the frogs, coating their tips in venom. "I'll catch up," she says.

"That's fucked up," Bertram mumbles, shaking his head.

You continue down the road, the sprinkles of rain giving way to heavy droplets. Soon, Maria catches up and the plantation comes into view.

- *To the plantation!* Go to page 202

Petrol-fied

Though it's getting later in the afternoon, both companies are able to meet with you. Bertram drops you off and tells you to have your contact's secretary call him when you're ready to be picked up.

Before you sits a tower of a building—the biggest in the area—with an impressive mirrored façade that launches into the sky at a dizzying, convex angle. It's almost like an optical illusion, but no, the building *really is* slanted.

With the possible exception of its neighbor two doors down (which pushes away from the street like an exponential curve), or perhaps the bank behind you (whose name is carved into the first four stories like a boastful monolith), the *Petrobras* building is the most eye-catching sight around for miles. The point being, it's not what you'd expect from a government building. It may be state-supported, but this is surely no post office.

Once inside, there's a young man immediately ready to greet you. He's either an intern or an extremely junior staffer, but either way, you're bombarded with the pungent energy of youth. His silver nametag is inscribed with the name MATIAS AZVEDO, which he says to you, with his hand extended.

He nods at your own introduction with a practiced smile. "You'll have to forgive me, my notes don't have anything but your name. You're here with….?"

Thinking quickly, you say:

- "The *New York Times*. You're prepared to answer a few questions?" Go to page 178
- "I represent your top shareholders in the US. Just a few concerns for you to address…" Go to page 295
- "I'm a fixer. The CEO tasked me to come in and get a few things straight." Go to page 44

Picked

Despite Tinho's objections and some sort of "you'll be sorry" warning (to you, or to her?) you're off with the young woman, riding on a city bus toward the dump site. She identifies herself simply as Isis (pronounced *eee-sis*) and through Viktor's translation you learn that she's employed as one of Brazil's "pickers"—a profession in which she spends her days wading through landfills, sifting through the garbage to remove recyclable materials for resale.

"She says the body was found last night, but the police haven't come by to take it away. It's probably still early enough that we can get a good look at it before they arrive," Viktor says.

Soon the bus drops you off. You're greeted with a cyclone of birds circling above a great mountain of trash. The landfill is massive, the fetid mounds similar in scale to ski resort slopes. A hundred workers roam the trash heap, looking for diamonds in the rough.

"Be careful of drug needles," Viktor warns.

The smell is, of course, pervasive and overwhelming, but eventually you don't notice it anymore. You're not sure if that's a good thing or a bad thing. Even the shrill squawks of the birds fade into the background. Isis explains that 9,000 tons of refuse arrive daily and, along with her fellow workers, she's able to reclaim 200 tons of recyclable material each and every day. The reclaimed garbage is the equivalent mass to all of the trash in a 400,000-person city, she says as a point of pride.

"This is a good job?" you ask. It's intended as an aside to Viktor, but he translates it to her before you can stop him.

"It's better than the other job a *favela* offers a woman," he says.

"What's that?"

He shoots you a look. "What do you think?"

Without further explanation, she leads you to the body. This area of the landfill has been all but abandoned by the pickers; most of them have already seen the twisted limbs coming from the trash and stay clear, waiting for the police to arrive.

She points to the corpse but will go no further. You can see that none of the pickers want to be near the body, but they're not particularly terrified by its presence, either. They simply go about their job, pretending that nothing has happened. Pretending that this spot doesn't exist.

"Do you often find…bodies here?" you ask.

Viktor translates, gets an answer, then says, "When there are wars between the *favela* gangs, yes, quite often. These last few months the factions have been united against the police and their pacification efforts, so people have enjoyed a period of relative safety."

You nod and continue toward the body without Isis. When you arrive, you're in for a shock. A gray hand reaches up to the sky to a salvation that will never come. Viktor sweeps the refuse away, revealing the face. You cover your mouth—it's *not* Jane Nightingale; it's not even a woman. The man lying there before you, pale and anemic, looks up with dead eyes.

And you recognize him.

"I guess 'dead American' wasn't specific enough," Viktor sighs. "I don't know what I expected to find. Jane is in the morgue, the police saw to that the night you stumbled upon her."

"I know this guy."

"What? Who is it?"

"I saw him at the police station the night they brought me in. He looked like he'd been crying. I think he was looking for someone." You strain to think, trying to remember through the blur of events. "He spoke English, so he caught my eye. It reminded me that my friends would be worried about me, and now…here he is."

"You're certain?"

You nod.

"Come on, the police will arrive soon. Ready to get off this trash heap?"

"Where will we go?"

"Well, I have an idea, but it's dangerous. Each *favela* has at least one cop on the payroll. We find out which gang holds territory over the crime scene, then we find out which cop they're paying off, and we bribe him for information."

"How do we find *that* out?" you ask.

"I'm sure someone here knows, or at least knows where we should ask. Or we can contact that 'other' type of woman who works the *favelas*. Paying off cops is part of their business insurance."

- "Okay, let's go to the cathouse. Has to be cleaner than here." Go to page 72
- "We're already here. Couldn't hurt to ask." Go to page 9

Predator

Agent Bertram grits his teeth and moves toward the Man in Black. Bertram shoots blindly into the jungle with his assault rifle, releasing a bullet every other second, hoping to flush out the man or maybe strike him, with pure luck. It's possible; the greenery is thin and the bullets penetrate deep.

After about thirty paces in, Bertram stops, pops out the rifle's magazine and slaps in a fresh one. "Come on out, you son of a bitch! We're right here!" he shouts.

The jungle is silent, as if in fearful awe of this man and his weapon.

Then, with a hot explosion, a bullet burrows deep into your chest. You fall onto your back, are forced to look up, and there he is, the Man in Black, perched high up in a tree. One smoking pistol is aimed at you and another bears down right on Agent Bertram. With three shots, the DSS agent is dead on the jungle floor.

The assassin rappels down from the tree. You look up in terror, and with no other option, you raise your hands. Maybe since you're unarmed, he won't kill you?

Nope.

The man's eyes, working independently, like a chameleon's, take in your supplication and Bertram's prone position on the ground at the same time. He raises one handgun toward you and fires.

THE END

Pressroom

When you arrive, you see a young man wearing a navy-blue shirt with yellow block letters, much like the "EVENT STAFF" shirts you'd see in the United States. This one reads, "*PESSOAL*," and you can be fairly certain it means the same thing.

"I am sorry, authorized personnel only," the young man says in English.

Oh, boy…This must be it! You remove the USB, hold it up, and in your most professional, do-not-trifle-with-me tone, you say, "I need to load this onto the projector before the ceremony begins."

"May I see your press pass?"

"No, you may not. I'll show it to you after. We literally have about three minutes until showtime. If you want to get paid for this event, you'll open that door!"

"I am sorry…" he begins, but then the door opens.

From inside, the Rio Chief of Police steps out.

"It's okay," he says to the doorman, then turns to you and says, "We've been expecting you."

He pushes the door fully open and you see Ambassador Mays, Governor Ferro—the man known as "The Sugar King"—and several armed men pointing sub-machineguns at Jane and Viktor. Your heart falls into your stomach.

"Please, come in," the Police Chief says.

The door closes behind you as you enter. Despair washes over you, and you know from the very core of your being that you are in deep, deep trouble.

"You must be the American traitor I've heard so much about," Ambassador Mays says. "You really spoiled everything from the get-go, you know that?"

"I'd say it's you and your cronies who've tried to spoil things for the rest of the world," you say, feeling that you haven't much to lose.

The Ambassador laughs along with his cronies.

"Things are not so simple," he says. "If the good doctor here would have just sold us his invention, all of this could have been avoided. It's not that we don't like progress; we really do, whether you believe it or not, but there's a natural way to these things. You can't just go flipping the social order overnight. Do you know what the world would be like if suddenly everyone were rich? If no one had to worry about where their next meal came from or how their kids would get to school, or hell, if you never had to *want* for anything ever again? The population would simply *revolt.* No one would work; there'd be chaos in the streets. Anarchy, that's what I'm talking about here. The people need order."

"Bullshit," you say.

"How do you think men like us get to our positions?" the Police Chief asks. "Through hard work, yes, but through understanding the hearts of men and how society functions. In the areas I control, crime is nearly zero. It's safety that we offer."

"In exchange for freedom?"

Governor Ferro sighs. "We don't expect you to understand, but it's been this way as long as there has been civilization. The Greek symbol for fascism was a bundle of sticks. One could be broken, but there is strength in unity."

"But toss a match on the bundle and watch as the whole thing comes ablaze," you say. "Toss a match on a single stick, and the others are safe. You're breeding extremism, not safety. Look around; you have three innocent people at gunpoint."

"Fire is a natural cleansing agent. It purifies," the Ambassador says.

"So, what, now you're a fascist?"

He shakes his head. "We're businessmen."

At this, all three men smile, like a trio of schoolboys about to pull some prank.

"Then let us do business now!" Viktor protests, moving forward. "Let the others go; this is between you and me."

"It's too late for that," the Sugar King says.

"I know you will kill me, and take my patents for your own, but please—I beg of you—let my Jane go."

"You still don't get it, do you?" Ambassador Mays says. "We've won. We have everything we need, and now we can tie up the loose ends. It's over; you've lost."

Viktor's composure disappears. His face flushes red and spittle flies from his mouth as he yells a string of Portuguese curse words. He rushes forward, only to be detained by the guardsmen. He's all tendon-strained muscle.

"*Cachoro!*" He screams, "You are an *evil* man! You are *merda. Caganita!*"

The Ambassador takes a step forward. "No, I'm just a man." He pauses, putting a hand inside his suit jacket before continuing, "Sometimes I'm nice, and sometimes I'm not; just like any man. Look, I can be nice—"

Ambassador Mays removes a handgun.

"You said she has nothing to do with this?" With cold indifference, as if he were merely crushing a spider, he shoots Jane in the head. "Now she's no longer involved. See how nice I am?"

You can barely hear the Ambassador over Viktor's guttural scream. The doctor falls to the floor, cradling Jane, her blood spilling out over him.

"On to business, then," the Governor says to one of the armed guards. "Bring me his book-bag."

"Wait—It could be dangerous. Let the Tourist do it," the Police Chief says.

The Ambassador puts away his handgun. "Good idea. Show us what's in the bag."

Viktor's jaw quivers, but he manages to whisper, "Remember 'Manhattan'? Do it."

You reach into the bag, removing one of the tiny bombs…Do you remember how to use the device?

- Yes. Go to page 172
- No. Go to page 364

Prey

Figuring bullets to be more dangerous than fangs, you run into the marsh. The anaconda is nowhere to be seen. Somehow, the entire length of its gigantic body has been submerged in the translucent, tea-colored water.

Avoiding the exact spot where you saw the snake, you run into the sludge, sending spray everywhere and feeling much like a wildebeest rushing into the jaws of death on a nature program. Isn't this exactly the kind of cue a predator picks up on?

Bertram is right behind you, sending out warning shots back into the trees as you cross the clearing. Maybe the anaconda is frightened by the bullets? Maybe it's *not* hiding, waiting to strike and constrict you? Or, maybe you'll make it across safely?

Miraculously, you do. As you step onto high ground and into the jungle, a wave of relief washes over you. Now you pray that the snake might make a meal of this assassin and take care of your problems for you, *Deus ex Machina* style.

Another hundred yards and the jungle gives way to an enormous agricultural field, where sugarcane stalks tower nearly twenty feet high. You must be getting close to the plantation. The stalks of the plant are segmented like bamboo and grow out in thick bunches from the ground. They're spaced about two feet apart, which gives you just enough room to run into the field.

Agent Bertram's satellite phone rings.

"Damn. They know I'm in the field; they wouldn't call unless it was an emergency."

- "Call them back when we get somewhere safe." Go to page 5
- "Go for it, I'll cover you. Give me that pistol." Go to page 31

Private Quarters

Viktor shows you to your cabin, then bids you *adeus*. The interior is small and windowless, with a pair of twin beds stacked like bunkbeds and bolted to the wall. There's a chamber pot in the corner (gross) and a curtained partition leading to a single-stall shower, such as you might find at a military deployment base. A pair of plastic-wrapped flip-flops wait by the shower—the height of luxury and hygiene.

It's been a long time since you've showered, and it's tempting. Then again, so is that bed. Who knows when will be the next time you'll have an opportunity for either?

- Shower first, then bed. Go to page 343
- Bed, zzzzzz. Go to page 365

"Okay, then, here goes. I'm at the forefront of a new technology. I never thought it would be dangerous, but I'll explain that too. First, the discovery. I've potentially cracked the world-wide energy crisis, and I don't say that lightly. I'm sure you've heard of alternative fuels—biodiesel and their ilk. Many have thought ethanol was the wave of the future, but ultimately the conversion of corn or sugarcane has proven too costly and not abundant enough a resource to completely overtake fossil fuels."

He begins pacing across the hilltop, lost in his own thoughts, pontificating like a mad scientist explaining his foolproof plan to the captive hero. "With my revolutionary methods, I was going to show the world something truly novel. Save for—I don't know—cold fusion, there's nothing that would change the world like this. I have perfected…" he pauses, his arms raised theatrically like an orchestra conductor's, "*Cellulosic ethanol.*"

You blink. "What?"

He shakes his head. "Not to drag you into the specifics of the science, but the long and short of it is this. With corn or sugarcane, you must use the nutrient-rich parts of the plant; that is to say, the part normally used for food. I found a way to use the *waste* as the basis for ethanol, and at an efficiency *four-thousand percent* more effective than gasoline! Do you know what that means?"

Trying to wrap your head around what he's saying and where he's going, you answer, "The end of fossil fuels?"

"Yes! And so much more than that. If we can grow plants to use their waste for fuel, what can we then use the main plant for?"

You shrug.

"Food! The end of world hunger! The end of deforestation! This new technology will be the marriage of environmentalism and commerce, thus quelling the feud between their two houses. We could use land unsuitable for crops—prairie grass, even—as fuel. We could recycle and pulp paper to power our autos! Any organic plant matter. I was going to be the next Edison, the next Tesla, and the next Henry Ford all rolled into one, except with clean, renewable energy."

"So you were going to be a billionaire, and someone wanted the technology for themselves, is that it?"

"Not remotely. This day and age, you don't steal technology, you race to invest in it."

"Then what? Big Oil wanted to shut you down?"

"A good guess," he says, "but wrong again. Only after much ratiocination was I able to decipher the true nature of my attackers. Except…"

"Except what?"

"This is where Jane comes in. I was afraid of *Brasileiro* crime syndicates. The fastest way to become a billionaire in *Brasil* is with sugarcane ethanol production. Five percent of the population owns eighty percent of the land here. If we no longer needed obscene quantities of sugarcane—because, let's face it, there are better food sources—then that industry dries up. Money will always defend itself."

He looks you squarely in the eyes, his own eyes shimmering in the starlight.

"What happened to her?"

"She was going to speak with her Ambassador, to present the evidence we'd found—actual correspondence from Governor Mateo Ferro instructing his forces to shut me down—and to seek help or asylum, but the sugarcane mafia must have gotten word. The American presence works closely with local law enforcement, and Rio cops are just criminals on the city's payroll. So they killed her and tried to pin it on me, only somehow you spoiled it for them."

You're stunned into silence. He waits, allowing you to digest what you've just heard. At length, you say, "But if she's dead, where's the evidence? Do they have it?"

"Good question, but if there's an assassin after us, I'd say not. If you hadn't been there, I might be dead too. Would I have picked up that revolver, with my Jane lying next to it? I can't say…"

A chill runs over you, like someone is stepping on your grave. "If the local police are in on it too, it wouldn't matter. They could have arrived, killed you, then set the scene however they pleased."

Viktor nods, the realization of his own mortality and the weight of Jane's murder appearing as heaviness in his blue eyes. He looks out over the city, then back to you. As he speaks, his smooth accent is caramelized with wistfulness.

"This is where I took my Jane on our first date. We shared a bottle of red wine, a block of fine cheese, and summer sausage, sliced one bite at a time. On a blanket, we made love under the warm embrace of starlit autumn."

In fact, as the sun begins to set and color pours out over the city, you can already feel the romantic appeal. Viktor's azure eyes glitter with something ephemeral and he puts a hand on your shoulder. "Sit with me a moment."

Out across the green expanse rises the great city, close enough to be stunning, but far enough away so that you hear the forest singing over the noise of cars swimming in concrete rivers. The skyscrapers shimmer, golden in the waning light.

In a husky voice, he whispers, "You look like you want to be kissed."

- "Umm… what?" Go to page 259
- "You look like just the man to do it." Go to page 100

Punch Out

You pull the throttle back as far as it will go, and, in first gear on this dirt bike, that means you're pulling a wheelie. You stand up on the pedals to keep an eye on the garage and lean forward to keep your balance while trying to force the bike back down onto two wheels.

Over the roar of the engine, another sound erupts—gunfire. This is the moment these bored security guys have been waiting for. *Hooray! Someone tried to run the gate. Finally, a chance to use our training!*

Well, at least you went out with style. And you'll probably make the news.

THE END

Putting out the Fire

"You're right," he says. "I'm sorry. We should focus on the mission at hand. Sometimes my passion spills over…."

"Yeah." It's all you can say. You shake your head. "So what's next?"

"She left us bread crumbs, and if we can retrodict the facts with the evidence, then maybe we'll find the whole loaf. Once we have proof—then we go to the press."

"Not the police?"

"There's a long track record here of inconvenient evidence conveniently getting lost. Tomorrow we head to the *favelas*. With enough bribes, we may just be able to find the trail. Let's sleep here tonight. It's warm enough, and I'm a little worried about that assassin finding us if we go back to either the hostel or André's."

➢ *Get some rest and start fresh in the morning.* Go to page 215

Quick Decision

"I'm a bit disoriented. I think it's this way, but the fire makes it hard to tell," Maria says, pointing in the direction the pickup truck fled.

"That would make sense," you add.

Bertram nods and removes a handheld GPS from his utility vest. He slings his rifle over his shoulder, freeing his hands to manipulate the device. "She's right. Let's get moving; it's going to be a bit of a trek."

- "In that case, let's hijack a vehicle." Go to page 206
- "Fine, but let's stay hidden." Go to page 247

Quietly, or With a Murmur and Not a Bang

You're arrested, taken into custody, and charged as an accomplice to murder. Sure, there will be a trial, but good luck defending yourself in Portuguese. And even if you do get a bilingual public defender, that's where your luck ends. You'll be convicted for sure, and there are no bilingual prisons.

THE END

Quite the Cocktail

You dig through the backpack, removing one of Viktor's "Death Star"-shaped weapons and hand it to him. He seems shocked that you decided to go this route, but simply nods like a man grimly accepting his fate.

The three young men, however, are anything from calm, and angrily demand an explanation. Viktor turns to you and says, "See you in Manhattan, Tourist."

He then *clicks* the tiny thing into place and now the device has begun moving, rearranging itself like a Rubik's Cube, expanding in some places and contracting in others. Fearful, the three gangsters shout to Viktor to explain himself, and now the AK-47 is pointed right toward the scientist.

Viktor tries to answer, but his breath is *sucked out* of him by the device. You feel it too, your insides collapsing as the tiny thing turns into something akin to a miniature black hole and sucks out all the air from the room. The walls, pictures, and television break inward, the ceiling threatens to collapse, and every person in the room dies when the strange bomb implodes.

THE END

Quitter

You shake hands, which quickly turns to hugs, and then say your goodbyes. The Energy Summit is right outside the *Sambadrome*—ground zero for *Carnaval*—but something in you just can't party tonight. Instead, you check into a hostel and watch the news.

It's not long before you see the report.

The broadcast is in Portuguese, but there are English subtitles. "BREAKING NEWS: Disgruntled scientist and engineer, Dr. Viktor Lucio de Ocampo, allegedly made an attempt on the US Ambassador at the Energy Summit in Rio de Janeiro. Authorities have stated that the Doctor, who was gunned down by American Diplomatic Security, was the prime suspect regarding the murder of his fiancée, who was found dead earlier this week…."

So that's it. You can't be certain they would have succeeded with your help, but they've certainly failed without it. Odds are, Jane was also killed with a cover-up after the fact. The thought nagging at the back of your mind right now, though, is: Did Viktor mention you? Could he and Jane have been caught and interrogated first? Is the Man in Black coming for you?

You'd better get back to the States, fast. Time to live the rest of your life looking over your shoulder and jumping at every shadow.

THE END

Rain of Terror

The rain has become a deluge of drops that are invisible in the black of night. The three of you spoon for warmth, Maria taking the middle because her pilot's uniform is thin and offers little warmth. She's soaked to the bone and you can see right through her white garments.

Sleep comes fitfully. Every time you start to nod off, a raindrop lands on your eyelid, instantly waking you. The soil around the sugarcane becomes a muddy soup and the fertilizer stinks something fierce. At one point during the night, the sprinkler system comes on.

"Seriously?" is all you can say, suppressing a laugh.

Eventually the rain stops, just as morning comes.

"Can we leave now?" Maria asks.

Bertram rises, his clothes as drenched as if he had jumped into a lake, and marches silently out to the road. You offer Maria a hand, then follow in Bertram's muddy tracks, the sludge *squishing* with each step.

"Shotgun!" Bertram hisses.

There before him is a coiled snake seeking shelter amongst some fallen leaves, but the golden color has given the creature away—it's too bright against the water-darkened environment.

"It's a lancehead," he says. "One of the most venomous snakes in the Americas. Very fucking deadly. Shoot it."

"Wait!" Maria shouts. "This is a jungle snake. It's not his fault he was forced from his home. We can walk around it; leave it be."

- Shoot it. Go to page 155
- Whisper words of wisdom, *let it be*. Go to page 235

Raising Cane

The sugarcane creates a vast forest of grass, much like the ubiquitous cornfields of Iowa, except much higher and thicker. The stalks of the plant are segmented like bamboo and grow out in thick bunches from the ground. They're spaced about two feet apart and meet high above your head, converging in a leafy canopy that blocks out the last rays of the setting sun. Some of the stalks are as much as three times your height.

Odds are no one will find you if you go deep enough into the crop, but then you put yourself in serious risk of getting lost. The sharp elbows of the segmented plant tug at your clothes and sting your exposed skin with tiny cuts.

You freeze—someone is coming. More than one someone, from the sounds of it. The others hear the sounds too and stop dead in their tracks, weapons raised. The shuffling of sugarcane grows louder and louder until they're almost right on top of you.

- Shoot blindly into the cane. Go to page 90
- Wait until you see the whites of their eyes. Go to page 229

Rattled

That's not quite how it works here. The last lesson you'll learn about the Rio slums, a lesson learned too little too late, is that each of the kids see themselves as future lords of the *favelas*. Just like any kid in the US could grow up to be President, each of these boys could one day rule their slum. In their minds, they've only yet to prove themselves.

Well, as you pull out your pistol and gun down the leader, that's a dozen more young boys all ready to take his spot. And how will the new Lord of the Flies take control of the group? By killing you, of course. The one who avenges the former leader is the obvious choice.

The only problem? They all shoot.

As you and Viktor are riddled with bullets, the sound rattles your skull with a cacophony of booming explosions. The shots enter your flesh with a hissing stab, like venomous fangs sprung forth and delving deep into flesh. It lasts only long enough for you to realize you're dying.

THE END

Recovery

Some time later, you're sitting in a hospital room at the bedsides of the two agents, both of whom are unconscious. Danly recovers from "decompression sickness" after Viktor's bomb nearly turned his insides out. Bertram nurses a gun-shot wound from his encounter with the infamous assassin when he tried to pursue the scientist, but the agent came out on top and the Devil Ray is now dead.

Finally, they both stir.

"What the hell…?" Danly asks.

"Hotshot—tell me we got him…"

"We got him," Detective Irma Dos Santos says as she enters the room. "He was shot as he fled, and he died of his injuries on the way to the hospital. He's dead."

"Good," Danly croaks, going into a coughing fit.

"Take it easy," you say. "It's over."

"I knew it was the fiance," Bertram says with a grin.

Danly just shakes his head, weakly taking a cup of water from his bedside tray. He sips it through a straw.

"I knew it was the Devil Ray too," Bertram continues. "But now it's all over. Viktor must've been a wealthy bastard. He was involved in some illegal, under-the-table shit, and Nightingale didn't like it. She told the Ambassador, so he killed her, hired an actor, hired an assassin, and hired the mafia—all to confuse us until he could finally kill the Ambassador himself. It wasn't just business; he took it personal."

"Sounds right to me," Detective Dos Santos says.

"I don't know…what about that note?" you say. "Who was that meant for?"

"The only man who knows for sure is dead," Bertram says. "Sure, there're a few unanswered questions, but you're a national hero."

You look at Danly. The agent nods his approval and smiles.

"Good work, Rookie," he says, his voice husky, like a chain smoker.

There's a moment of contented silence as the room basks in a feeling of victory, but something still feels "missing."

Finally, Bertram says, "You better let us get some rest, Hotshot, and you might want to get some sleep yourself. I bet the Ambassador will have a medal for you in the morning."

You nod and shake hands with both men.

"Thank you," you say, "for letting me be a part of this. It was truly an honor."

They both grin and wave as you leave. Detective Dos Santos follows you into the hall. "Maybe you want to grab a drink?" she says. "I'm buying."

You smile and think, *being a hero sure has its perks.*

➢ Go to page 304

Once you arrive at the base of the statue, you're greeted with throngs of excited tourists, most of them non-locals, save for a busload of schoolchildren on a field trip. And they're all doing one of two things: either looking up at the towering monolith or posing with arms spread wide before Him. Once they're done, people generally crowd by the stone guardrails that overlook the city.

You snap a few pictures, and you're just about to ask Agent Bertram to take your portrait in the same mock-pose as the others, when you're approached by a man.

"Excuse me, gentlemen. You are the federal agents, yes?"

Both your companions stiffen, prepared for the worst.

The man raises his hands. "Please, let's be civilized." His accent is thick, and it sounds as if he says, "*sieve*-ilized."

"Is it him?" Danly asks you.

It's not. This man wears glasses, true, and he's a handsome Brazilian, but he's not the man you saw last night. His face is fuller; the man as a whole is broader and he has a five o'clock shadow. He's rugged and masculine with rakish good looks. The man you saw last night looked deft, intelligent and agile, whereas this man is cock-sure, charismatic and powerful.

And this man's eyes are a creamy golden brown, not the ice-blue of the man from the murder.

"No," you say.

"Who are you? Let me see some ID," Bertram says.

"I'm sorry, sir. The only thing in my pockets is a *Real* or two. You'll find I'm unarmed and I only want to talk with you and your partner. My name…is Viktor Lucio de Ocampo."

He smiles warmly—the man could be Javier Bardem's Portuguese cousin, he's so handsome—and slowly lowers his hands.

"You seem awfully smug for a man whose fiancée was just murdered," Bertram says. "You call us here to brag about it? Gloat that you'll get away with it?"

The man's brow furrows, as if he'd never considered this, and he looks past you in introspection.

"You're right. I'm… I must just be nervous. Let's try again," he says.

He lets out a sigh, then slowly passes his hand over his face, from top to bottom, and his countenance changes drastically. His strong jaw now quivers and his eyes well with tears.

"My Jane was my everything. If I do not look destroyed by this, it is only because I now cling tightly to my *Saudade*—the memory of her, you Americans might say. Though Jane is gone, my love for her remains."

"Then come with us, we only want to help find her killer," Agent Bertram says, reaching a hand out as if the man might take it.

Tsk, tsk, tsk, Viktor clicks his tongue against the roof of his mouth, shaking his head slightly. "The question is not who killed Jane, but *why* kill Jane."

"But either way, the answer doesn't involve you, right?" Danly says, not buying it. "Got any proof?"

"If I had, you'd be reading about it in the papers. But there is proof, should you like to find it. I—as you may know—am a man of science. In fact, I'm here for the Energy Summit, but someone doesn't want me to share my findings."

"What findings?" Bertram asks.

"Still not the right question."

"Still" rolls off his tongue like "*steel.*"

"Who?" you say. "Who doesn't want you sharing your findings?"

"There we are. You gentlemen have a smart friend here. Find the *who* and you'll find the *why,* which will lead to the girl. Otherwise, you're just shooting in the dark."

"Enlighten us," Bertram says. "Give us a name."

He smiles again, thinking for a moment. "I am not at liberty to say," he replies, stretching out "liberty" to three distinct syllables. "Perhaps, once you solve the case, we can talk again."

"I don't think we're done with you," Agent Danly says.

"No, I wouldn't think so. Which is why I might have left something for you agents in the chapel at the base of the statue."

He looks at his watch, then back up, and smiles.

Bertram turns and sprints toward the chapel, already removing his badge, ready to clear the building of tourists in case of a bomb, crime scene, or any other evidence. Danly hesitates a moment, but then chases after his partner.

Viktor watches you to see what you'll do.

- Follow the agents into the chapel! Go to page 152
- Stay here, keep an eye on the man while they check it out. Go to page 23

The main house of the plantation isn't opulent or gaudy. There is no parlor where you'll be served cognac. No great dining hall, no feast beside your host. This isn't where this man lives; this is simply where he conducts business. It's almost disappointing. Part of you wanted to see something out of *The Godfather* or *Scarface*, but you'll have to settle for substance instead of style.

A private security guard greets you: a thin, older man who requests that you leave your weapons and cell phones at a secure room in the front. The fact that he's not surprised in the least that you're armed serves as a not-so-subtle reminder that you're dealing with a man on a different tier than a mere farm manager. Maybe this will be interesting after all.

You give up the shotgun (not like it was yours to begin with), but Bertram refuses to leave his weapons at the front room. He shows the man at the security booth his badge, but the guy doesn't seem to care. He demands Bertram disarm, but the federal agent doesn't budge.

A pair of security guards arrive to settle the commotion and the hairs on the back of your neck stand on end. Bertram's right hand hovers ominously over his gun holster.

"Well, well, an American federal agent," a voice booms out from behind. "You two are a bit far from home, yes?"

You turn and see a large, middle-aged Brazilian man. Neither tall nor fat per se, but thick-limbed and possessing a sort of magnetic gravity you can't quite place. His full face is clean-shaven and has deep creases where a stark smile now finds perch. His eyes are dark brown, with an intense intelligence.

The man wears tight blue jeans tucked into black cowboy boots, dusty and grey with age. He wears a blue workshirt and an orange scarf tied loosely about his neck. Not exactly how you'd picture a billionaire. His short, jet-black hair is slicked back and neatly arranged in such a way that you can be certain he has a comb tucked in his pocket.

"To what do I owe the pleasure?" he asks, then adds something quickly to the security team in Portuguese that causes them to back down.

"We're here investigating a murder," you blurt, trying for a reaction.

He shakes his head. "Way out here in the jungle? I'm sorry to disappoint, but I know nothing of the Nightingale girl."

"I didn't say the victim was a woman," you say. "And they haven't released her identity to the public. Tell me, how did you hear her name?"

He throws his head back and lets out a booming laugh. His grin widens, like a man who's truly enjoying himself. "There will be no such *'gotcha'* moment. Of course I know of the dead secretary. This is a 'big deal,' as you say in America. You think a man such as me gets his information from the news?"

"No, of course not," Bertram says. "You're the Sugar King,"

He chuckles once more, but this time it seems forced. "I'm just a businessman. A governor. A man of the people. That is only a silly nickname. You activist types are so terrified of corporations these days, but this country grows strong because of sugarcane. I employ ten percent of the nation!"

"We're not here to discuss politics," Bertram says.

"Indeed not. May I see your badge, sir?"

Agent Bertram considers this for a moment. At length, he steps forward and gives the man his badge.

"My RSO knows we're here," Bertram says. "I just spoke with him via sat-phone."

Governor Ferro's smile fades. He's quick to bring it back again, but it's enough lapse that you notice. He falters with his words for a moment, then finds his stride.

"I'm certain that he does. Because you strike me as a good agent, one who would not come all the way out here without permission."

You see the bearded man's Adam's apple bob up and down as he suppresses a gulp.

"Agent David Bertram. I'll remember the name next time I speak with your Ambassador. Colonel Mays has helped facilitate business relations between our two nations, and I'm looking forward to seeing him this week at the Energy Summit."

The Governor hands back Bertram's badge and continues, "I completely understand how thorough you need to be in your investigations. Please tell me if I can be of any help, Agent Bertram. I should want nothing more than to help you catch the murderer. With the Energy Summit, the World Cup, and the Olympics, we need foreigners to feel safe in our country—Americans, especially. This could be a great economic boon for our people."

"You'll be in Rio?" Bertram asks.

"As I said, for the Energy Summit. I owe the Ambassador a box of cigars." He laughs again. "Cubans."

"If the investigation team has any questions for you, would you be available in Rio?"

"Of course. Anything to help, really."

"I'll let them know," Bertram says.

"Very good. Anything else?"

"We seem to have lost our transportation," you say.

"You must be careful way out here in the jungle. There are thieves and dangerous men."

On your payroll, you think. *What a slippery man. Just like a politician….*

"Perhaps I can help? I can have a driver take you back."

"If you can spare a car, we would be in your debt, Governor," Bertram says.

"Done. Glad to help."

➢ *Drive back to Rio.* Go to page 273

Respect for Authority

Agent Danly's jaw tightens, and then your head erupts with splitting pain. The punch was lightning-fast and completely unexpected, so it doesn't even register until he's already throwing you against the wall and cuffing your hands behind your back.

"Wrong, jackass. You're not in America. No Miranda rights, got it? I don't know what your role is in all of this, but I don't have time for it. You better hope to hell you're not an accomplice on this thing or so help me God, I will see you *rot.*"

Holding you prone against the wall, he removes a radio and calls for backup. The blood from your broken nose drips down over your chin and onto your shirt.

Security soon arrives and Agent Danly instructs the cop to "keep an eye on" you. Later, when Viktor is killed "making an attempt on the Ambassador's life" and Jane mysteriously disappears, Agent Danly will make good on his promise.

You'll be tried and found guilty of treason. The rest of your life will not be pleasant.

THE END

Return to Rio

After exchanging the Sugar King's loaner Jeep for Bertram's government SUV, you head straight to Rio. You don't even stop by the consulate in São Paulo—the agent's supervisor, the RSO, is in Rio and he wants to see Bertram ASAP.

It's late afternoon when Bertram pulls into the parking garage at the Rio consulate. Though you're hungry, groggy, and seriously in need of a shower, it appears there's no time to waste. After going through the security protocol, you head inside.

"Stay here," Bertram says.

He steps in his boss's office and you hear, "Well, it's about fucking time. Shut the *goddamned* door."

You cringe as the door slams shut.

"So… going to *Carnaval*?"

You turn around. You think you recognize the guy—a junior agent who was here when you first visited the Rio consulate. He's a classic ginger, with his pasty, freckled skin and his bright carrot hair.

"What?" you ask.

"*Carnaval.* It starts tonight. You should go, there's no other party like it on Earth."

"Are you going?"

"I wish," he says, grinning. "I'm working security on the Energy Summit; that starts tonight too. Maybe when things close down. The *Sambadrome* is nearby the conference grounds, so we'll see. Hopefully I don't have to escort somebody through the crowds. As an agent, you have to concentrate on protection, so you don't get to focus on all the fun. It's the worst."

The way he keeps smiling, though, tells you he thinks it's the best. Humble-bragging at its finest.

His eyes dart toward the muffled shouts that come through the door of the RSO's office. You're able to pick up words like "sugar" and "fiance" and "jungle" and "scientist," but most of what you hear are words like "goddamned" and "fucking" and "bullshit."

"Good luck with that," the junior agent says.

He shakes his head and walks away as the door opens and Bertram steps out.

"We're not done yet!" the RSO shouts.

Bertram wipes a weary palm down his face, sighs, and turns around. "I'll give a full report to the new team when they get here, okay? Just give me a day to get cleaned up."

"Oh, you'll have all the time you need. That stunt out there in the jungle? You just earned yourself 30 days on the beach."

Bertram's body tenses, but he bites his tongue.

"And lucky for you, the investigation team is already here."

"Come on, boss. Just give me a couple of hours."

"You know there's no time," the RSO says. "Conference room, now."

"They need our cooperating witness?"

"Not right now, but make sure your 'little partner' doesn't go far."

Bertram comes over to you, the strain of a browbeating clear on his face, and says, "I'll meet you back at the hotel in a bit, cool? I need to debrief, but let's grab a drink in the bar after."

"That's it? We're done?" you ask. "What about the Sugar King?"

He sighs. "Come on, Hotshot. Not now."

"We were so close, can't you feel it? That guy was up to something."

"Look, I agree, he was a bad guy. I just don't think he's *our* bad guy. My money's still on the fiancé but—ah, shit, what does it matter? Did you forget? We're off the goddamned case!"

You say nothing.

"Look, I'm sorry. It's just…first round's on me, okay? You got money for a cab?"

"Sure," you say. "Good luck in there."

➢ *Head to the hotel.* Go to page 219

Rio's Divine Comedy

With Agent Danly's reluctant blessing, you pair up and return to the police station the next morning. Once inside, you're greeted by the bleach-blonde Detective Lucio Muniz, Irma Dos Santos's partner. He wears black slacks with a silken purple shirt. His ears are pierced and he has a diamond stud in each earlobe. He waves at you when you enter.

"Where's Detective Dos Santos?" Danly asks.

"She's out. What's new, boss-man?"

"We're ready to check out the *favelas*. Did our Elite Squad request come through?"

"Sorry, chucky. You're on your own for now. Elite Squad only goes in once there's a lead or a target. Which—I believe—you don't have, no?"

"*We* don't have," Danly corrects. "So let's go find one. You're coming with us."

"Whoa, whoa, whoa! I'm not Elite Squad." The detective backpedals, palms raised, head shaking furiously. "No way, no how, man."

"Yes way," Danly counters, stepping forward. "This is still your show, did you forget that? I can do all the investigating I want, but you need to make the arrest if it's going to stick. Last time I checked, the *favelas* were on Brazilian soil."

"Yeah, well. Check again, boss-man. That's a fucking war zone. Maybe you don't know how it works, but cops don't go into the slums, ever. These kids, they kill cops for sport. It's like a manhood ceremony, *entendeu?* You're asking me to commit suicide here."

"I'm not asking. Would you prefer I talk to the Chief, and see how much he'd like your precinct—and you specifically—splattered all over international news for refusing to aid the United States in their investigation of the highest profile murder case our two countries have ever shared?"

Detective Muniz's chest sinks and his eyes fall to the floor. He heaves a heavy sigh, then pulls out a cigarette and lights up. A junior policeman complains that he needs to smoke outside, but Muniz curses at him in Portuguese, then slaps him on the back of the head as if he were addressing a wayward nephew.

After taking a deep drag on the cigarette, he says, "We're not staying out after dark."

Danly nods, then offers to shake hands with Muniz. If an actual Rio cop is this rattled…then what are you getting yourself into?

"Hey, you know—I bet Irma will be back soon. Wouldn't you rather—"

"We're leaving now. The three of us. Shake."

Lucio Muniz shakes Agent Danly's hand.

"Now come on, we're just going to ask a few questions. Think of yourself as a translator. Don't be such a coward—this tourist here is braver than you are."

"Ignorance is not bravery," the detective says, looking at you.

As you descend into Rio de Janeiro's underworld, you expect there to be some kind of physical barrier separating the city from the slums, like the border between the US and Mexico. You try to remember which bag contains your passport, just in case, but no such threshold ever comes. Instead, the streets simply become narrower, the shops become smaller, and the buildings begin to stack up atop one another.

From a distance, it looks like they're mining the mountains—so sharp is the contrast between the tree cover and the barren earth. Where once the rolling hills were green and lush, they are now covered with acres of tool-shed-size housing; a ramshackle mess of temporary structures now permanently cemented and crushed together.

The *favelas* are all brick and concrete. Without exception, each structure was built by hand and not by professionals. Those who occupy the shanties either erected them themselves or simply moved in, taking over like a hermit crab once the original occupant died. Lifespans are short and there are no property deeds in the slums. Real estate is plentiful, the wait isn't long, and you simply take what you want.

Instead of billboards and signs, the shops here use graffiti. The Portuguese words for "liquor," "bakery," and "barber" are spray-painted on nearly every corner. Most of the shops have metal gates for doors, the kind you roll down and lock at night, retracting them in the morning when it's time for business as usual. Residences use concrete walls and iron bars with spear-tipped zeniths intended to keep out thugs and rapists.

Crumbled brick crunches beneath the tires of your government SUV. Large, new, and black—you stick out like a sore thumb. Bare-chested men stare at you warily from the periphery of the street. Children running barefoot pick up their soccer balls and instead chase you, trying to get a glimpse of which celebrity might be inside the SUV.

Agent Danly pulls through the opening of a collapsed wall, parking atop a disintegrated building. He turns off the engine, then looks at you. "Listen, if we ask the wrong question to the wrong guy, things could get dangerous. I think you'd better stay in the car."

- "No way! Aren't I here so I can ID the guy? How will you know it's him without me?" Go to page 243
- Nod, pat the seat, and say, "I'll keep her safe." Go to page 200

Roadblock

You try to stare at the wallpaper as you walk back past Agent Danly, willing him not to see you, but no such luck. It's his job to see you.

"Where the hell have you been?" he asks. "I thought you were dead! You just up and disappeared—we've been looking all over for you."

- "I think you have me confused with someone else." Go to page 47
- "Get bent. I was partying. It's a free country; I can go where I please." Go to page 272
- "Oh, thank God you found me!" Go to page 306

Roaming Charges

Like a rabbit, you go from frozen to bolting in the blink of an eye. The young policeman sprints after you while his partner runs to catch Viktor. Where the hell did you hear that you can't be followed into a house without a warrant? That's ridiculously false, on so many levels. You try the first apartment and are fortunate enough to find the door unlocked. You burst in, surprising an older woman who just came out of the shower.

The woman drops her towel, revealing nothing more than her country's eponymous grooming technique. She probably in her sixties, and it's not a pretty sight. The cop apologizes to her in Portuguese before he eagerly subdues and restrains you.

It's over. The murder will be pinned on Viktor, and you'll be sentenced as his accomplice. Foreign prison isn't fun, but apparently Rio has started a new program where you can run a stationary bike to generate electricity in exchange for a shorter term. Don't worry, you'll have plenty of time to work out the details.

THE END

Room to Think

You slip into the hallway just as the front door opens. Whoever it is shouldn't have seen you duck back here, but you get the feeling you didn't buy yourself much time. The hall is carpeted, so your steps are silent. You move with urgency.

You're in luck; the first room is his office. There's a drawing desk covered in figures and sketches, mountainous piles of books and journals, and acres of that chlorophyll-green grid paper tacked to the wall. Unlike the neat and orderly nature of the rest of the house, this particular room looks like the lab of a mad scientist.

And there it is—the laptop.

You can hear them coming (there are at least two, from the sound of it) as they whisper to one another in Portuguese. Well, they're certainly not the American agents. Brazilian police? Do the police here just jimmy the door and let themselves in? Hard to say.

There's one coming your way.

- Hide behind the door. If the guy's a threat, he's getting a laptop in the face.
  Go to page 136
- Try to reason with him. Pretend you're Viktor's lab assistant or something.
  Go to page 334

She chuckles. "I'm afraid you've got the wrong impression. We were excited to hear from the professor, and whatever personal problems he's been going through are unfortunate."

"So you follow his work?"

"Of course, who doesn't? He's making major ripples in the clean energy world."

"But isn't that counterproductive? You're an oil company; this is like a snake eating its own tail."

"Hardly," she says. "You're viewing things in black and white. If certain sectors of industry are moving toward clean energy, we'd be foolish to turn our backs on them. It's not like gas is the only alternative; there are people who will keep using oil so long as it benefits their bottom line. Those who wouldn't use it anyway are the ones we're trying to entice. There's no reason we can't sell oil to company A and ethanol to company B. I'm sorry, but if you're looking for some kind of conspiracy, you won't find it."

"Why would anyone want to silence his work?"

"I honestly don't know. Rumors say it was a personal problem, he's a superstar professionally. His technology is ten years ahead of everyone else, but it's the way we're moving. If he can't figure it out, someone else will."

- "What exactly was Viktor working on?" Go to page 186
- "Tell me more about BP's ethanol developments." Go to page 195
- "I've heard enough. Thank you for your time." Go to page 98

Run Away, Run, Run Away

Before you can even see who's opening the door, you fly over toward the back patio, skipping across the carpet like a basilisk sprinting on water. You tug at the glass door frantically, but of course it's locked shut. While letting out a barely audible moan of terror, you fumble with the latch.

The front door opens behind you just as you slip out and close the sliding glass door. Your legs haul you up the rear hill and into the woodline behind the apartments. From your vantage point in the foliage, you watch the patio, trying to catch a glimpse of the intruders through the glass.

It appears as if you made it out unseen, because no one comes looking for you.

You watch in silence as a bookcase is overturned and an avalanche of books spills toward the patio door. A torn-open pillow from the reading chair flies into view, the stuffing floating over the books like new snow. From your hillside perch, you see two sets of boots move throughout the apartment, though you cannot see who they belong to.

Well, that was close. Better not press your luck: time to get out of Dodge. Here's hoping Viktor was more successful on his mission.

➢ *Head to the restaurant.* Go to page 48

The Running Option

Not waiting for consent, you sprint into the cane, nearly tripping as the mud sucks at your feet in cobbled holes and pools. Bertram and Maria run after you, one on either side and back slightly, so that the three of you move like a flock of birds in a "flying-V" formation.

A flash of red catches your eye and you look ahead to see a *grileiro* in a red scarf coming your way. You blast a warning into the cane with the shotgun, pumping another round into the breach as the man ducks for cover. Your partners shoot into the field as well, keeping the men in the cane at bay.

Suddenly the thick sugarcane ends and you make it into a clearing. *The* clearing.

You half-expected something out of the pre-Civil War Southern states, like a giant manor from *Gone With the Wind,* but you're greeted with a much more utilitarian structure. This isn't a place where people live, it's a place where people work.

Still, it's a massive set of buildings. A cafeteria, several barracks for workers, washing and refining stations, and of course, the main house of the plantation.

"Hang on," Bertram says to you. "Do you think Maria should come? This man has done terrible things to her family."

"I can hear you, and I'm coming," she says firmly.

"Hmmm. I don't know…." you say, considering.

"No, I'm coming. This man is the devil."

- "Okay… Just so long as you're ready to meet him." Go to page 227
- "Which is why I don't want to put you through hell. I'm sorry, but I agree. We'll take care of it; you stay here." Go to page 270

Rush Back

"I'm sorry," you say, "but none of us will be safe until we share your evidence."

"You're right," Viktor replies. "Let's go."

Dr. Brandon steps forward. "If I may, I'd like to help. I know the pilot of a seaplane that can pick you up on the river and take you into Rio. He's my ride when I'm done here."

"I don't know that I can ever thank you enough, Susan," Jane says.

"If your fiance really has cracked the ethanol code, how can I not help? He's our best chance at preserving this ecosystem and these people."

"Thank you," Viktor says.

The older woman removes a satellite phone from her gear. "Just say the word."

"Let's do it," you say.

Having said goodbye to Dr. Susan Brandon and the villagers, the three of you fly high above the jungle in the seaplane. Jane Nightingale presents a laptop to Viktor—presumably the location of their evidence—but worry covers her face as the computer boots up.

"What is it, my love?" he asks.

"It wasn't Governor Ferro," she says.

"What?" you both say in unison.

She shakes her head. "He's part of it, but he's not the one calling the shots. There are two kings. The King of Sugar…and the King of Corn. Ambassador Mays is one of the top three interest holders in corn ethanol in the United States."

"The US Ambassador to Brazil?" you say, dumbfounded.

She nods. "Corn already has lobbyists against it what with high-fructose corn syrup, and if they lost their foothold in ethanol as well…"

"*Cabrão*," Viktor says. "The Ambassador couldn't get his own hands dirty, so he farmed out the job to the crime lords. He'll pay for this, if I have to kill him myself."

"No need, my love. I have a document—direct correspondence between Mays and Ferro— proof that they conspired to keep the most important scientific discovery of the last half-century away from the public."

Viktor smiles. "Then let's work on my presentation for the Energy Summit, shall we?"

He turns to the laptop. While they go over the evidence, you:

- Take a nap. You'll need your strength. Go to page 49
- Talk to the pilot. Who is this Dr. Susan Brandon, and how is she involved? Go to page 146
- Listen closely as Jane and Viktor compile their presentation. Go to page 97

Safe/Deposit

The next morning you're stiff, achy, and still tired. Without money to pay for a hostel, you're forced to spend the night in one of the abandoned hovels of the *favela*. A mattress stained gray with age sits in the corner, surrounded by used needles and condom wrappers. Despite the sleepless night, you know that drug traffickers, Elite Squad officers, and an assassin are all looking for you.

"Up and at 'em, Tourist," Viktor says. "We have many kilometers to travel today and time is not on our side. The Energy Summit kicks off tomorrow night and if Jane has the evidence to clear my name…."

You yawn and stretch, and then look at him expectantly before he elaborates:

"In order to find Jane, we must leave the city and travel by river out into the jungle. But first, we must sell off the guns and gear to buy passage on a river barge."

"We're getting rid of all of it?" you ask.

"All but my little inventions. It's illegal to carry weapons on the river, so we'd have to leave them anyhow."

Following the drone of merchants haggling with their new customers, you easily find an open air market. It's just like the one where you bought the guns yesterday—perhaps all *favelas* have one of these?

Asking "*Armas?*" over and over, Viktor finds a man willing to buy your weapons. And just like that, you sell your guns back on the black market. Easy as pie.

Risking the few *reais* for bus fare, Viktor brings you to the port, where you'll find passage into the Atlantic rainforest. There are dozens of ships offshore, waiting for the opportunity to edge their way to the front of the line. The port is large and extremely unorganized. Many of the vessels are private fishing ships available for charter—the kind you might rent out to go deep-sea fishing off the coast of California—though, of course, you can't afford that.

The boat for you is the mega-barge. Being the largest commercial venture in port, the barge has a permanent space cleared where it can dock. Viktor pays your passage and the two of you board. The boat is all-metal, with paint chipping everywhere it's been applied. Gigantic tires are tied along the sides of the vessel to act as rubber bumpers in case it bumps against anything.

The bottom portion of the barge is full of cargo: metal shipping containers, an SUV being shipped, crates of produce. The upper deck is for passengers. Though there are a few Brazilian tourists using the barge as a cheap "booze cruise," the majority of the passengers are traders and merchants traveling with their goods, helping to stock the mini-marts of the interior.

There's a flat roof on top, protecting most of the seats of the upper deck from the brutal summer sun, save for those by the rail. Soon the boat's engines fire up and, snapping one last photo of the shoreline, you say goodbye to the city.

The river is wide and expansive. Although the *Amazon* gives Brazil worldwide fame, the *Fingido* is not to be underestimated. Too far south to be part of the biggest waterway on earth, this river is massive in her own right. Brazil becomes connected like so many aqueducts during the rainy season, but major trade routes such as the *Rio Fingido* are formed from perennial water sources and remain traversed year-round.

"So where are we headed?" you ask Viktor.

"It's easier if I show you," he says with a smile. "Go have a look around. I'm going to use the shared computer terminal to see if I can find anything new. I rented us a sleeping cabin. It will be a long journey, and after last night we need the rest."

- "I'll just hang out with you, see what we learn." Go to page 214
- "Yeah, I'm going to go check out the cabin, maybe take a nap." Go to page 255
- "I think I'll just watch the river go by; clear my head a bit." Go to page 139

Safe… For Now

He nods. "We'll have to work together, and two light sleepers are better than one."

The blue-eyed man pays in cash, then you're shown up to your room, which is not more than a bed and a bathroom. The entire hostel is tiled, to include the bedroom floors. Most likely to ease the cleanup after drunken patrons, or perhaps to clean up any other…messes. The image of the woman lying in a pool of her own blood flashes in your head.

"Get some sleep; we've got a busy day tomorrow."

"What's your name?" you ask.

He looks at you and something flickers behind those fierce eyes as he wonders if he can trust you with his real name. You can't be sure what he decides upon, but the name he tells you is, "Viktor."

The next morning Viktor wakes you early. The street light outside your window is no longer illuminated but the sun hasn't risen yet.

"What time is it?" you ask.

"Time to go; get dressed. There's some fruit and toast downstairs, then we must be on our way."

➢ *Break your fast, then be on your way.* Go to page 203

Say Hello

They want to play games? Okay. They want to play rough? Okay. You grab your "little friend" from the backpack, safety off, trigger finger ready to go. They never even see it coming. You fire as soon as your aim is clear of Viktor, mowing down the young men with ease. As you kill one, then the second, Falador stumbles backwards out of the curtained doorway. You follow him with your stream of bullets but as the curtains flutter in your lead breeze, you're not sure if you've connected or not.

The sound of frantic sprinting outside tells you he's alive. Viktor stares at the carnage with disbelief, eyeing the bodies of the two dead youths.

"It had to be done," you say.

More gunfire erupts from outside—a lot more. Viktor cautiously peers out from behind the curtain and ducks back inside, his face deathly pale.

"It's Elite Squad," he says. "Pacification. They're taking back this slum, to-night."

"Elite Squad?" you parrot.

Viktor claims one of the dead men's rifles. "Police special forces. Easily one of the most extreme combat forces on the planet. We need to get out of here, now."

- *Escape the slums!* Go to page 103

The Scenic Route

The cog train runs every thirty minutes, and luckily for you (and Agent Danly's thinning patience) the wait is only five minutes for the next carriage. Red, about the size of a city bus, and packed with tourists, the train car runs on rails powered by electric wires from above. This mars your views, so you have to use your camera's zoom if you want any good pictures.

The train begins moving, and soon you pass from rows of houses into the forest. Agent Danly stews in a seat next to a Korean woman while her child and husband sit in the row in front of her. The three of them chatter away, with the angry American hopelessly caught in their midst.

It's obvious this sort of mawkish tourism is killing Agent Danly, but Bertram enjoys pissing off his partner and acts as your tour guide in the seat next to you.

"Those trees were imported from Asia," Bertram says, pointing out a variety that contains large green pods about the size of pineapples—if the fruits were missing their shock of green and were hanging from old US Army surplus bags in the tree. "Jackfruit."

Just about everybody has a camera, videocamera, or cell phone capable of filling the role. You pass another train car coming downhill and notice a flash from within as someone takes a picture. As the train car ascends, the cameras in your car uniformly point to the righthand side, where there are breathtaking views of the city.

"The statue sits atop the highest point in Rio de Janeiro, so you won't get better views than this." Agent Bertram looks back at Danly, just to ensure the man is listening, then goes on in a mock tour-guide tone. "The statue was erected between 1920 and 1930 and weighs over 1,000 tons."

Soon, the train docks at the top where others await, ready to take your seat for the return trip.

- *Disembark and check out the statue.* Go to page 268

The Schmoozer

The gate guard smiles and leans back in his chair. This is your chance!

"You know how it is…you meet a sexy stranger, dance the night away, everything is magical—but you forget to get a phone number. Come on, can't you see yourself in my shoes?"

"I've been there," he says.

"I mean, I don't want to put you out," you say, removing your wallet and slipping a $100 bill under the glass. "But it was love at first sight."

"And the note?"

You pass him both the note and the license plate number. He reads it, flips the note over to check for more, then looks up at you. "Arms wide open?"

"Sure, who doesn't like a little mystery in their romance?" you reply, passing another $50 through the slot. "I'd appreciate if you didn't mention me to anyone. It's best if they solve my riddle for themselves."

"Of course."

You smile, give your thanks and turn to walk away. Whoa, what a rush! Time to go strut your stuff like you own this city and brag to Viktor over pizza.

Yep, you're awesome.

➢ *Head to the restaurant.* Go to page 338

Security

Viktor and Jane wait for you inside, near the metal detectors. You rush in and say, "He's—"

But Viktor silences you with a finger pressed to your lips. Man, Brazilians have no concept of personal space. His eyes slowly move over to the security line and you follow his gaze.

There's a table with nametags, beyond which official personnel check purses and briefcases like the TSA lines at the airport. No one gets through without the proper credentials.

In a sudden burst of inspiration, you claim three nametags, clip one to your chest, and pass the others to Viktor and Jane. They both grin and don the badges in understanding. Once you clear security, you can be sure that the only threat will come from law enforcement. No assassins, no *favela* druglords, no Sugarcane mafia. Just Rio cops and DSS agents.

You move toward the metal detectors, but Jane stops Viktor at the last second. She reaches up, takes his eyeglasses, then turns them around and puts them on the bridge of her own nose, giving her a bookish, librarian appearance. Viktor smiles, blinking to let his eyes adjust.

"Let's do it," you say, stepping forward into the security line.

You leave your metal objects in the bin, and progress through security without incident. That's when you hear the *beep* behind you.

"Is this your bag, sir?" one of the security agents asks.

The man holds Viktor's backpack. From your vantage point on the other side of the metal detectors, you can see the x-ray image of his bag and the tiny "Manhattans" held within. Viktor acknowledges that the backpack is indeed his.

"Please step to the side. I'm going to search your bag now, okay? Can you tell me if there are any sharp or hazardous materials inside that I need to be aware of?"

Viktor shakes his head. You look up at the security monitors as Jane passes through. There's a photograph of André, Viktor's actor friend, taped up there with the word "BOLO" printed beneath it. Next to that photo is the sketch of Viktor you helped create at the Rio police station the night this all began.

Hopefully they won't recognize him without the glasses…

"What's *this*?" the security agent asks, reaching a gloved hand around one of the small *Death-Star*-esque objects.

"*Careful*… please," Viktor gulps. "It's for my presentation. It's… a new form of battery I've patented. In a few years, these will be installed in every electric vehicle in the country."

The security agent looks incredulous. Viktor smiles and adds, "With any luck."

The security agent waves a gloved hand over to a coworker, then removes a cotton swab and rubs it along the small device. The agent looks up and stares Viktor down. These few seconds feel like an eternity.

Another security agent arrives with a German shepherd, which sniffs the backpack. This agent keeps a wary hand near his Taser gun.

"Okay, Dr. Vanderschmidt. Thank you for your patience."

Viktor's brow furrows, and his mouth opens like he's going to say something, but then he looks down at his nametag. "Right!" he says, "Thank you."

Grinning like a car salesman, Viktor dons the backpack and eagerly leaves the security line.

"That was close," Jane says.

"Too close," you agree.

"We don't have much time," Viktor says. "The opening ceremony should be starting soon; this is our best window of opportunity. Find the audio/video control room where they run the projector." He takes the USB drive from his pocket and passes it to you. He shakes your hand and adds, "Think you can handle it?"

The USB drive weighs heavy in your palm.

Jane leans in, gives you a kiss on the cheek. "For luck," she says.

With that, they're gone. You pocket the device, then look about—just in the nick of time. At the far end of the hall, Agent Danly, the DSS agent who met you at the police station, comes around the corner.

He hasn't seen you yet. You turn your back on him and walk away, trying not to appear in a rush. At the end of this hall is a four-way intersection, but the directional sign is written in Portuguese. *Damn*, you could really use a translator right about now, but there's no time.

Agent Danly is coming. Where to?

- Left—*Apoio*. Go to page 311
- Straight ahead— *Salas de Conferências*. Go to page 46
- Right—*Banheiros*. Go to page 16
- Back past Danly—*Entrada/Auditório Principal/Imprensa*. Go to page 277

Seek

Viktor nods in agreement and rushes out of the sleeping cabin to find the captain. You're quick on his heels, but it's not long before you hear a commotion on the top deck. Men shout out over the cries of women and children.

Then you're on the bridge, where you find the captain at the helm. Viktor pleads with him in urgent Portuguese and, just as your companion predicted, the captain goes for a hidden compartment. He produces an old Luger pistol. The thing looks ancient; you'd believe him if he said he bought the gun off a WWII expat who had fled to Brazil for fear of extradition.

"That's all he has," Viktor explains by way of translation.

The captain, evidently not a brave man, hands you the pistol. You look at the heavy weapon with the tapered barrel, then back to Viktor.

"I'll be bait," the scientist says. "But don't be afraid to shoot. These pirates will not hesitate, and no one will miss them way out here. Let's go."

Viktor leaves the bridge and immediately raises his hands. He perfectly blocks the doorway so you can't see what's beyond him, but they can't see you, either.

"Get ready, Tourist."

You raise the pistol, curl your finger around the trigger, and point it at his back. Viktor sidesteps to the right to reveal a pirate just beyond the door. The pirate's AK-47 follows Viktor as he steps away, but your Luger does not.

With a deafening explosion, the pistol kicks back in your hand, though not after filling the pirate with 7.65mm parabellum and dropping him in one shot.

As you linger with smoke curling off the handgun's barrel, Viktor scoops up the pirate's rifle and sends a burst of fire into the men who rush in as backup.

You now find yourself moving, ready to face more pirates. Viktor, out on the port side, makes a left turn and shoots another burst from the AK-47. You step out and look right. Before you even register the pirate raising his rifle, your hands have shot him twice.

The boat is silent now; there appear to be no more pirates. That's it; you've won. The other passengers and crew sheepishly appear, the ship's captain the first to congratulate you. He asks for his pistol back.

Viktor translates, "He says he's surprised it worked. It was his father's, and it's never been shot."

Glad I didn't know that beforehand, you think.

The crew starts dumping the pirates' bodies overboard, letting the river take care of burial. Everyone goes back to their corners; even the captain disappears. You win, but you're not a hero. The only thanks you'll get is the passengers keeping their mouths shut if questioned about this night.

"Come on," Viktor says, tossing the assault rifle over the rail. "Let's try and get some rest before tomorrow."

➢ *Head to the cabin and lock the door.* Go to page 52

Separate but Equal

He frowns. "I don't think we've been followed… unless it's me you're afraid of. I understand your hesitation, though you need not fear me. Perhaps with time we'll learn to trust one another."

The blue-eyed man pays in cash, then you're shown up to your room, which is not more than a bed and a bathroom. The entire hostel is tiled, to include the bedroom floors. Most likely to ease the cleanup after drunken patrons, or perhaps to clean up any other…messes. The image of the woman lying in a pool of her own blood flashes in your head.

"Get some sleep; we've got a busy day tomorrow."

"What's your name?" you ask.

He looks at you and something flickers behind those fierce eyes as he wonders if he can trust you with his real name. You can't be sure what he decides upon, but the name he tells you is, "Viktor."

The next morning, Viktor wakes you with an early knock on your door. The street light outside your window is no longer illuminated but the sun hasn't risen yet.

"What time is it?" you ask.

"Time to go; get dressed. There's some fruit and toast downstairs, then we must be on our way."

➢ *Break your fast, then be on your way.* Go to page 203

Shadow Empire

Viktor takes you to the primary *favela* controlled by the notorious Shadow Chiefs. As he explains along the way, this is the most powerful gang in all of Rio and their slum is the largest. The only reason it hasn't been pacified, he says, is because it's the most dangerous. There is no head of the snake to chop off; this beast is more akin to a *hydra*—kill one druglord and two more will spring up.

Instead, the government has decided to sharpen its sword against the lesser gangs, building up for the big takedown. At some point, the nine hundred *favelas* will be run by nine *thousand* little tyrants, and the *hydra* will collapse under the sheer weight of all the heads.

This *favela* is anything but quiet. Clubs and discothèques cry out into the night air. Radios blare and passionate arguments echo in squabbles. Despite all these sounds of humanity and civilization, you feel like you're headed into another planet. A planet far more deadly once the sun goes down.

A chicken shrieks its shrill squawk and bursts forth from an alley in a flutter of feathers, the terrified bird desperately trying to evolve into a hawk and fly away. The animal's pursuers come out of the alley—a gang of children and young teens. The leader, an Afro-Brazilian with a mouthful of tangled, overgrown teeth, grins and shouts something in Portuguese.

"He tells us to grab the chicken," Viktor translates. "Please do."

You look up from the bird to the child gang and notice for the first time that snaggle-tooth is armed with a *Dirty Harry*-sized revolver. Several of the other boys are openly armed as well. You crouch down, arms spread so the chicken won't run past you, but the animal is so blinded by terror it runs straight into your arms.

"Now what?" you say, holding the squirming bird, trying to avoid its talons.

Viktor thinks for a moment as the boys approach. Reaching with one arm to the pistol tucked in his waistband under his backpack, he says something to them in Portuguese.

You recognize a key word: *Falador*. The name of the informant you seek. A knowing glimmer spreads through the gang members like electricity. They know exactly who you're talking about and now their playful devil-may-care tone has changed to fear.

A juvenile rattlesnake is more dangerous than an adult because, in its inexperience, the young snake will inject you with its full load of venom, whereas the adult knows to gauge a threat and keep something in reserve. More important yet, the adult knows how to pick its battles and when to slink away. So too is a frightened child with a gun and something to prove far more dangerous than a hardened, experienced criminal.

The leader raises his pistol and the others follow suit.

- Shoot the leader. The others will cower before you. Go to page 266
- Draw your pistol, hold the chicken hostage. Go to page 362
- Do nothing. Let Viktor handle the situation. Go to page 340

Shares of Information

"Oh my, I had no idea! Would you like to see our newly updated prospectus?" he says, reaching for a manila folder.

"No, that's not where our concerns lie. What we'd like to know is, what are you doing to curb the appeal of so-called 'new energies'?"

"'Curb the appeal'? We've invested heavily in new energy; it's one of the fastest-growing economic sectors in the country."

"Sure, sure. That's all fine and good. But we want to make sure oil remains number one, don't we? And part of that is keeping researchers like Dr. Viktor Lucio de Ocampo and their findings out of the spotlight, am I right?"

He looks at you with a new degree of suspicion. "Who did you say you represent again?"

"Your top US investors. What is the status of *Petrobras* blocking the doctor from the Energy Summit? Did that go okay? Any hitches?"

His mouth opens slightly and he shakes his head in squinting disbelief. "I don't know; we had nothing to do with it. What firm are you with?"

"Dewey, Cheatem, and Howe. Thanks for the information—I'll see myself out."

➢ *Go wait for Agent Bertram.* Go to page 98

Sheltered

You trudge through the rainy night toward the small building halfway between your location and the plantation. Perhaps the *grileiros* have given up; you don't see another soul on the journey. When you make it to the aluminum building, you're fairly certain it's a farm shed and not anywhere people live, but you proceed with caution nonetheless. With a storm like this, who knows who or *what* might be sheltered within.

Bertram points his rifle at the large barn-style entrance and nods at you to slide the door open. When you do so, you're greeted by tractors, combines, and other farm machinery.

"Just as I thought," Bertram says, lowering the rifle.

The three of you seek shelter inside the empty building, stalking along the vehicles in search of a warm spot to bed down.

"I guess this is goodnight?" Maria says.

You suddenly realize you can see right through her white garments. The pilot uniform is thin and wet, clinging to her tight body.

- "Maybe we should take off our clothes and spoon for warmth?" Go to page 170
- "Goodnight." Go to page 358

Shootout

You open fire, taking down the first uniformed man. A barrage of noisy gunfire rings out as Viktor and the remaining two cops join the firefight. The second uniformed officer goes down just as the plainclothes policeman finds cover.

"We've got him pinned down!" you shout excitedly.

"He's no good to us dead," Viktor reminds you.

After exchanging a few more shots, an idea strikes you. "Get out that sub-machinegun! We'll scare him into submission."

Viktor nods and slips off his backpack. Just as he removes the powerful weapon, he falls to the ground, but not from the cop in the road. Gunshots ring out from a rooftop across the way and you look over to see Agent Danly and Detective Irma Dos Santos.

There's a flicker of recognition, but that doesn't stop them from firing. Both you and Viktor die in a hail of bullets.

THE END

Sky Cab and the World of Tomorrow

With a giant grin parting his beard, Agent Bertram mashes the phone number into his cellular and makes the call. After a quick conversation in Portuguese, he takes the next exit off the highway.

"Where do we have to meet them?" you ask. "Will it take long?"

"They're coming to us," he says with awe in his voice.

He turns off the access road, pulling the SUV into a mega-mall parking lot, and proceeds to one of the far corners to wait. It's not long before that thundering sound of a helicopter beating the air into submission returns. This time, it's your helicopter.

Your body surges with excitement at the prospect of a helicopter ride. Your mind races: how is this possible? What manner of city is this?

As if reading your thoughts, or more likely sharing them, Bertram says, "São Paulo has the largest number of registered helicopters of any city in the world!" He has to shout to be heard above the sound of the mechanical bird. "New York City has maybe a dozen buildings you can land on in a 'chopper. This place has over three hundred!"

The rotor blade whips air at you, all the debris of the parking lot coming with it. You have to shield your eyes from the pebbles as the helicopter lands. If you were expecting something out of *Black Hawk Down,* this aircraft is comparably tiny; akin to a traffic helicopter you've seen on the news back home. It's almost all windshield and propeller, with just barely enough room for the pilot and three passengers. Slowly the blades slow their pace, and eventually the pilot comes out to greet you.

It's a woman. She wears an official uniform, just like the one on the billboard, but she's comparably tiny herself. Surprisingly petite, she must be just over five feet tall and maybe a hundred pounds. Yet she grins with confidence and her radiance is more than the man on the poster could muster at thirty feet tall.

"*Olá, bom dia,* I'm Maria Rodrigues Igor," she says, using the Portuguese greeting. "You are the Americans?"

Like a great forest razed by fire, with ashen wood reaching high to the heavens, the skyscrapers of São Paulo reach out to touch you as you fly above the buildings. And yet there is nothing dead or dying about this vibrant city, the sheer scale of which takes your breath away. It's as if all the skyscrapers were taken out of Chicago, Los Angeles, New York, Dallas, and Austin, then deposited in this one urban downtown. There truly are tenfold more colossal towers of industry than in any other city you've seen.

You're in the front seat with the pilot, looking out on this alpha city. You can feel the heat coming off her as she maneuvers the aircraft. Amongst the megastructures stands a tall and glittering beacon. It's the building you fly toward now and its mirrored windows reflect the helicopter back at you.

"Here it is, the headquarters of *Futuro Verdejante,*" she says to you through the intercom. "We'll be touching down in five minutes."

The building grows larger and larger until you're on top of it. Maria sets you down with a deft touch and after winding down the controls, hands you a business card.

"Call if you ever need a ride," she says with a wink.

Before you can reply, Agent Bertram squeezes your shoulder from his seat behind you. "Let's go!"

Standing at the base of the helipad, a young office worker waits to take you to Italo Fellini, your contact for the Energy Summit. With a final look back at the helicopter and the pilot, you head inside and are shown to the man's office. Even though he has a capital view of the skyline, it's nothing compared to the views you just got flying above the city. Still, the room is impressive.

➢ *Sit down for your meeting.* Go to page 111

A Sleepless Night

What a night. It's late when Irma pulls up to your hotel. Or, rather, it's early. The sky holds the pre-dawn glow of impending sunlight. She idles the car out front, but you don't leave. Some part of you doesn't want to go inside.

You're not *afraid*, that's not it. It's a near-certainty that you haven't been missed—what with Danly assuming you've been asleep all night. It's more that you can't process all you've seen and heard. All you've *done* tonight. Looking over at Irma, you can see she's having similar thoughts.

"We have to forget about tonight," she says.

"What about all we've learned?"

"Do you think Agent Danly would accept any of that? I don't. I'll remember what we've learned, and I'll use it in my personal investigation, but don't expect me to talk about it."

"Irma…"

"That's the way it is. Do what you want, but don't drag me into it. I'll deny it if you do." She looks cold now, like she's distancing herself.

"If that's the way it is," you say, feeling your own spine stiffen. "Goodnight."

You step out of the car, your mind swimming with a thousand thoughts. As you walk to the hotel entrance you feel dizzy, almost as if you've been up all night drinking and are only now exchanging insobriety for exhaustion.

"*Americano*, wait!"

You stop, turning to see Irma Dos Santos get out of her car and walk towards you.

"Maybe 'forget' is the wrong word. I'll never forget this night, nor will I ever forget you. But we do have to keep it a secret. Can you do that for me?"

Not waiting for a response, she kisses you. It's brief, but passionate. With a smile at her own impetuousness, she ducks back into the car and speeds away.

What a night, indeed.

Fortunately, Agent Danly sleeps in well past lunch and you're able to fib that you were "only taking a nap" when he calls your room just after 2 pm and finds you asleep as well. He bids you to meet him down in the lobby. You find him nursing a cup of coffee when you arrive.

"Any luck last night?" you ask, keeping coy.

"Actually, yeah. We're going to go to the consulate and do a video conference with Agent Bertram, and the day's already half over, so I'd rather not share it all twice."

"Okay…"

"Sorry," he sighs. "I'm just tired. How was your night?"

- Risk it—say, "Don't be mad, but I found out some pretty interesting things myself…" Go to page 19
- Keep it to yourself—say, "Just fine. Quiet night alone, like you suggested. To the consulate?" Go to page 156

Sleep Tight

Detective Dos Santos drops you off in front of your hotel, declining the invitation for dinner. "I have to get some work done," she says with a weak smile.

You mumble your understanding, shake hands, and exit the car. After she departs, you step through the lobby and find a "happy hour" sign beckoning you to lounge poolside and await the sunset in luxury. Sounds good to you.

Someone left a paperback on one of the deck chairs, so you thumb through it while you wait for the sinewy young Afro-Brazilian waiter in the immaculate white polo shirt to bring the cocktail special out to you.

The book is a detective-thriller about two FBI agents who work to track down a serial killer in Nebraska. The cover shows bloody footprints in the snow. It looks interesting, but hits a little too close to home after all you've been through.

Putting it down, you let out a relaxed sigh. As the sun sets, the patio lights come on, illuminating the water like so many diamonds shimmering on the surface. The waiter arrives with your drink—a coconut full of liquor, the fruit balanced inside a bamboo cradle—and bends down to allow you to easily accept the libation.

The alcohol acts quickly on your empty stomach, and soon all your cares melt away and you feel like you're on vacation again, at least temporarily. The choices you make tonight will only be as difficult as what to order from room service and whether or not you'd like a massage.

For a fleeting moment, you enjoy yourself.

The next morning, you breakfast alone while waiting for Agent Danly to wake up from his long night out in the *favelas*. Then you have lunch by yourself. Finally, he calls your room just after 2 pm and bids you to meet him down in the lobby. You find him nursing a cup of coffee when you arrive.

"Any luck last night?" you ask.

"Actually, yeah. We're going to go to the consulate and do a video conference with Agent Bertram, and the day's already half over, so I'd rather not share it all twice."

"Okay…"

"Sorry," he sighs. "I'm just tired. How was your night?"

"Just fine. Quiet night alone, like you suggested."

"Great. Let's go."

➢ *Head to the consulate.* Go to page 156

Snapped

Something inside you snaps, and you can't take it anymore. Breaking into a clockwise arc, you push back to where you first saw the Man in Black, ready to catch him unawares. There on the ground is the metal rod that served as the base of the pitchfork. Lacking any other weapon, you pick it up.

There's surprising weight to the piece; this is no Halloween prop. That's when you notice that the barbed end of the rod isn't cosmetic, either. It's a knife-tip, sharp enough to shave with. You sprint through the wake the assassin left—people flee in all directions and the path to the devil is fairly clear.

You can see his horns bouncing above the crowd. He's taller than most of the population, and he runs confidently, scanning the crowd for you and your friends. With a hate-fueled burst of adrenaline, you sprint forward, with the pitchfork-rod at the ready. As you get closer, you get a good look—his back is covered in long raven feathers, like a devious sort of hedgehog.

Using the rod as a spear, you plunge the weapon deep into his back. The man doesn't even scream, he just drops. The knife tip sticks through his chest, perfectly skewering him through his heart. Hubris was his downfall. So sure he was the predator, he easily became the prey.

One eye looks up, the other looks down. He doesn't move, he simply bleeds out. The crowd stares at you—hell, some people are even *cheering,* but there's no sign of Viktor or Jane. Up ahead, the Energy Summit awaits.

- *Head inside.* Go to page 290

Sobriety

The Sugar King glowers. "You might have told me that before I went through all the trouble of opening such an expensive and rare vintage."

He sets his own glass down upon the tray and dismisses the servant.

"I had set up a show for us while dinner is prepared. Many of the farm workers here practice *capoeira,* an elaborate performance that combines dance and martial arts. But now I have half a mind to send you to bed without supper, if I need to treat you like spoiled children!"

- "Hey, not everyone drinks. Let's go watch the show and relax." Go to page 27
- "Gee, dad, are you gonna *ground us* too?" Go to page 171

SOLVED

That's it! You've won. You've helped bring justice to Brazil and made the world a better place. Few can brag of this accomplishment, and you are one of those few. Well done, but know this: the path you chose was only one of many. There are other ways, and in that vein, other clues you may have missed…

MURDERED has three unique storylines with over 50 possible endings, but only one *best* ending. So, if your gut says there's more to explore, go back and try again.

If you enjoyed the book, it would mean a lot to me as an author if you were to leave a review on Amazon or Goodreads. As an indie writer, word-of-mouth is the only clue some people see, and reviews are the #1 way to help Amazon promote a book to new readers.

When you're done, don't forget to check out the other exciting titles in the Click Your Poison multiverse!

INFECTED—*Will YOU Survive the Zombie Apocalypse?*
MURDERED—*Can YOU Solve the Mystery?*
SUPERPOWERED—*Will YOU Be a Hero or a Villain?*
PATHOGENS—*More Zombocalypse Survival Stories!*
MAROONED—*Can YOU Endure Treachery and Survival on the High Seas?*
SPIED (coming in 2019)—*Can YOU Save the World as a Secret Agent?*

** More titles coming soon! **

Sign up for the new release mailing list at: http://eepurl.com/bdWUBb
Or visit the author's blog at www.jamesschannep.com

Stigmata

He shakes his head and whimpers a sniveling response. She yells and he recoils, but only shakes his head more resolutely. Blood, mucous, and sweat fly off in generous beads. He tries to pull away, but her grip on his wrist is ironclad. So he tries to bring his hands together in a prayer instead.

"He says if he tells us, they will kill him."

You look at her and nod. You've come this far….

With a squeeze of the trigger, she blows a hole through the palm of his fresh hand—now both are split open. He screams, staring at his open hands, and you can see *through* them, the boy looking at you through hellish binoculars. Irma ducks down and presses the handgun atop his left foot. She's paying a vicious game of "hangman," it would seem. Answer wrong? You lose a hand. Then the next hand, a foot, the other foot—but what's after that?—in "hangman," it would be the head. She pulls back the hammer on the revolver, lining up the chamber with a fresh cartridge.

The boy screams. The door to the house swings open….

- Use the AK-47, point and shoot! Go to page 21
- Duck back and see who it is. Go to page 142

Stockholm Syndrome?

"He said he would kill me if I tried to run away. He made me help him…and…and…."

Agent Danly puts a hand on his sidearm and says, "Where is he now?"

"That way," you say, pointing the opposite direction Viktor actually went. "Hurry, please!"

"Come on, show me."

You burst into sniveling tears. "No! I can't. I can't go back there!"

"Ah, Christ!" Danly mutters. "Don't go anywhere, understand?"

You nod emphatically and Agent Danly turns and runs, already removing his radio and calling for backup. You bought yourself a little time, but not much. After he rounds the corner, you quickly move in the opposite direction.

"*Entrada*" points to the building's entrance, where you already made it through security. That leaves two choices:

- *Auditório Principal*. Go to page 193
- *Imprensa*. Go to page 252

Suicide

Back on the bike, you gun the engine. The tires squeal against the parking garage's paved surface and you slide around the corner to bum-rush security. Your bike shudders violently as you feel a punch to your shoulder. That's when you realize you've been shot. This time around, you're not nearly so close to your targets and there's nothing between you and them but air. Question: Which moves faster, bullets or a motorcycle?

Well, at least you went out with style. And you'll probably make the news.

THE END

Suicide Mission

In your effort to run the guard down, you've saved yourself. Sort of. Instead of shooting you, the man dives out of the way of your oncoming bike. The other guards, unable to get a clear shot for fear of hitting their comrade, instead curse and move to regroup behind you. You're free to enter the garage, but rest assured—security isn't far behind.

Shifting to second gear as you enter, the dirt bike's engine echoes throughout the parking garage. Bad news: just about every car looks the same. You cruise by, trying to read the plates and find the one that matches the paper scrap Viktor gave you.

As you turn to go to the second level, a bullet *twangs* from a nearby concrete pillar. That was close, too close—they're coming for you. You move through the second level, trying not to think about the consequence of missing the car. Time for level three.

There it is! You look at the license plate a second time just to ensure it's the right one. Yep, it's a match. You step off the bike, hurrying to remove the note (and careful not to get your fingerprints on it) and tuck it under the passenger-side wiper blade.

Done—missions accomplished. But how do you get out? The security officers will soon be on this level, and they've proven to have itchy trigger fingers.

- Trying to ram my way through their lines worked once. It'll work again. Go to page 307
- To the roof! I'll find a way out, even if I have to fly away. Go to page 109

Summited

"Listen up and listen well," you say. "I saw that dead woman. I know you're overjoyed she wasn't Jane, and I am too for your sake, but *someone* loved her. I could have just as easily been killed for finding her body. What's going on here with the Ambassador and the head of the Sugarcane Mafia isn't right. It has to be stopped, and we can do it!"

Jane and Viktor smile brightly, motivated.

"Besides," you say with a grin of your own. "Won't it be more dramatic to see the two of you walk out on the stage together, arm in arm, to reveal that Jane is alive and to clear your name? *I'll* upload the evidence onto the mainframe."

Outside the airport, you look for a taxi. There are plenty of cabs, but it appears that none of them are operating. The nearest taxi driver says something in Portuguese while shaking his head. Viktor translates, "The road ahead is blocked because of *Carnaval*. We'll have to walk the rest of the way."

After rounding the corner beyond the airport, you see that the cabbie wasn't exaggerating. People are *everywhere*. In the distance, gigantic parade floats crawl slowly through the street, readying themselves for the Big Show.

Most of the crowd hovers around these floats; teams of dancers are climbing aboard or preparing to *samba* around the base, all of them in matching costumes aligned with the theme of their particular floats. That's not to say there aren't other revelers in full regalia; nearly everyone is costumed. Throngs of people dance, drink, and otherwise party through the crowded streets of Rio.

You see a woman in a skin-tight leopard suit gyrating past you; her costume flows perfectly in tune with her body. Wait, scratch that, she's completely nude. That's her body flowing. There's no costume; it's all body paint.

And she's not the only one. A group of naked men and women, painted to look like marble sculptures, walk past you on their way to the parade grounds. They have enough modesty to wear thong underwear, but their costumes leave little to the imagination.

Another costume catches your attention: it's a devil. A hulking man in glimmering black body paint, his body firm and muscular like an MMA champion fighter's. His face is painted white over black, like a bleached skull (the only color on his otherwise black painted body) and his shaved head is topped with long, twisted ram's horns. A thick scar covers his chin. The paint is all-encompassing, and with his carved frame and intricate costume, you'd think he would be at the *Sambadrome*, leading an underworld team.

Then his eyes move in two different directions. They flick back and forth, looking, searching for prey. When he sees you, the teeth painted atop his lips part to reveal the real teeth in an impish grin. He holds a pitchfork, and you realize with horror that the two outer prongs on the pitchfork are actually handguns, long and slender, with silencers on the barrels.

Without a doubt, this is the Man in Black. The devil-costumed assassin pulls the two handguns off his pitchfork, as the center rod falls to the ground with a *clang*.

"It's him!" you shout. "Run!"

Viktor and Jane make a break for it, and in a flash, the fearsome man's handguns rise up, ready for the kill. You grab the leopard by her crimped, curled hair and fling her toward the devil.

It's enough of a distraction. The three of you push into the crowd, keeping your heads low and trying hard to put as many people as you can between that horror and yourselves.

A loud *crack* permeates the air and with a scream, a bedazzled woman falls behind you. This is bad. He doesn't care if he shoots innocent bystanders. You sidestep, plunging yourself into a thicker throng of people, rushing forward as fast as you can. Where are Viktor and Jane? You don't see them anywhere.

Up ahead, like a glittering beacon, sits a mega-conference center that must be your destination.

- ➢ Run for the Energy Summit! Go to page 290
- ➢ Enough is enough—Double back and attack. Go to page 302

Support

You push open the door, revealing a large control room, complete with police officers watching security feeds and technical experts monitoring everything from audio levels to air conditioning temperature. In the corner of the room, a computer tech loads up a PowerPoint slide that reads, *Please Find Your Seats, The Presentation is About to Begin*, in both English and Portuguese. As soon as he flips it on, you can see from the security monitors that the text is indeed projected on the mega-screen of the auditorium.

This is it, you've found it! Now to load the USB thumbdrive on that computer….

The heavy door *slams* shut behind you and suddenly all eyes turn your way. There are three American DSS agents in suits, none of whom you've ever seen before, hovering near the security monitors. The lead agent is tall and square-jawed, his blond hair meticulously combed to one side and pressed down at the ears where his sunglasses normally rest.

The other men—both built like smokestacks—turn their stone faces to examine you. One is black and the other an islander; they both look like they dropped out of the NFL and into private security. Which is entirely possible.

In fact, everyone's watching you, not just the three agents. The whole room is waiting to see what you're doing here.

- Make a break for the computer. Once the files are uploaded, they'll be powerless to stop you! Go to page 240
- You're wearing scientist credentials. Use that name badge to your advantage. Go to page 190

Surprise Attack

You lean hard into the doorway, take aim, and see a lone Elite Squad member charging toward you. The policeman wears protective body armor and is clad in black, much like the US SWAT teams.

Once he's lined up in your sights, you fire. With a controlled burst, the man goes down in the street. You can't be sure if your shots went through all that bulletproof padding, but either way, he's incapacitated.

"Got him!" You call to Viktor, stepping out into the street.

Viktor follows you out and looks down at the felled policeman, only to collapse to the concrete under a barrage of bullets himself. You look up at the rooftop just in time to see the assassin who's been following you. One of his pistols smokes from shooting Viktor, and the other pistol is trained on you—he watches Viktor with one eye, and keeps one eye focused on you.

He fires.

THE END

Sympathy is for Suckers

She conveys your message and Falador —*the mouth*—opens wide and laughs. He responds to her, using his hands in dramatic gestures, and laughs again before waving you off and folding his arms across his chest.

"Well?" you ask.

"He says of course he lost someone; who hasn't? Then he goes on about 'you think you know pain' and ends with 'just because you lose someone, doesn't mean you have to be a pussy.'"

This is going well....Maybe they call him "The Mouth" because he likes to shoot his off?

"What now?" Irma says. "We don't have long to waste."

Time to try a new tactic.

- "Ask him again, only this time, more forcefully." Go to page 135
- "Tell him, 'In America, we reward our informants.' Tell him I can make him a rich man." Go to page 201
- "We're wasting our time. Let's go back to Agent Danly." Go to page 78

Synching Up

The São Paulo consulate is very different from the one in Rio. Palm trees whisper secrets in the warm breeze while purple flowers invite bees with their fragrant smell. Rio was downtown, nestled amongst skyscrapers, but this consulate stretches out over a large swath of land, surrounded by trees and green lawns. Where Rio went *up*, the Paulistas built theirs *out*. It's still in town, but it's not competing for attention. Across the street sits a quiet café, waiting for those on break.

The inside has a relaxed atmosphere as well. People still scurry about, working hard, but you get the impression they *like* working here. Agent Bertram leaves you in a conference room with a promise to return shortly. There's not much of a view outside the window, but it's shaping up to be a warm, sunny day.

Once he returns, Bertram closes the blinds and dims the lights. He sets up a video teleconference, takes off his suit jacket, and within a few minutes, Agent Danly is on the screen, larger than life. "Are we live? Hello?"

"Good to go," Bertram replies. "Catch the guy yet?"

"Actually, I did have a major breakthrough last night, when I was visiting the *favelas*. We found—"

"Glad you're still alive, by the way."

Agent Danly's face frowns with impatience. "As I was saying. We found a drug trafficker who claims his gang was the one to kill Jane Nightingale."

"Whoa, really? You make an arrest?"

"Not yet. The interesting thing is, they say she *wasn't* involved in drugs, even after what we found at her apartment. It looks like they were paid to kill her, plain and simple. It looks like…a hit. And—get this—I think I saw your 'merc; the Man in Black. I think he was tailing me."

"The same guy, are you sure? Think he was the one who pulled the trigger?"

Danly shakes his head. "The traffickers have their own hit-men. I talked with Elite Squad, and they recognized the guy. They call him *Jamanta.*"

"As in—The Devil Ray?"

"The same," Danly says. "A ridiculous urban legend, but apparently he's a platinum-level assassin, way too big-budget for this kind of thing."

"Fuck me," Bertram says. "The kind of budget you might have behind you if you were a rock-star scientist. I think the fiance might've hired himself some protection, and if you saw the muscle, that means we're getting close."

"Who is the *Jamanta*?" you say. "I'd like to hear the legend."

Bertram looks to make sure the door is secure, then leans in. In a low voice, he says, "Raymond Panoptes, AKA, 'Devil' Ray Panoptes, AKA, 'The Devil Ray', AKA, *'O Jamanta.'* He's supposedly an ex-DSS agent."

"Bullshit, it's just an urban legend," Danly says, waving the suggestion away.

"He started off as a helicopter pilot, and that's how you'll recognize him; he has those wonky eyes."

You scowl, so Danly elaborates. "Apache pilots' helmets have a monocle resting in front of their right eye that feeds them flight and weapon information. The other eye looks outside the cockpit, scanning for threats and watching the terrain, so the pilots develop the ability to use their eyes independently. That much is true."

"Right!" Bertram says. "I've even heard about some guys who can read two different books at once, so shooting at two targets is child's play for somebody like this."

"Apache pilots are real, and maybe he is one, but the Devil Ray doesn't exist," Danly says.

Bertram continues, "Supposedly, after he got out of the service, he joined the DSS. Many of our recruits are vets, so that much isn't farfetched. Legend has it, he was an agent back in the early '90s, when Ambassador Mays was an RSO, right here in Brazil, but Raymond had to be cut loose. He got a taste for killing and couldn't give it up. He would shoot a 'perp when he could have simply arrested the guy, and he would take the law into his own hands when he couldn't get a warrant. One day, when he was supposed to be tried for his illegal vigilantism, he just *disappeared*."

Bertram waves his hands back and forth, his fingers waggling, as he says the final word.

"And... bullshit," Danly coughs. "I'll keep my ear to the ground on this Man in Black character, but he's an effect, not a cause. Let's stay focused on the case and the crime-world angle. I've got a real tangible lead here after last night."

"So who ordered the hit?" you ask.

"That's the million-dollar question, Rookie. He mentioned that it was backed with 'sugar money.' As in, the sugarcane mafia."

Bertram pops out of his chair. "Jesus, we're slurping on the same spaghetti noodle here."

"What do you mean?" Agent Danly presses.

"As in, if we get any closer, we'll be kissing."

"No, what, goddammit, you know what I mean—what did you find?"

"Dr. Viktor, he's made some discoveries that could put sugarcane out of business. And sugarcane is in *big* business." Bertram scratches his beard. "Maybe our friend the good doctor made an illegal deal with the Sugar King, Nightingale got word of it, and he had to silence her before she reported him to the ol' U-S of A."

"Bingo," Danly says. "He plants the drug evidence in her apartment—he's no criminal, so it looks wrong—and the sugar lords agree to help silence his girlfriend. They hire drug traffickers to kill her, to keep the ruse, but they spend the *real* money on protection."

"So you're back on *Team Fiance*?" Bertram asks.

"I've always been on *Team Evidence*," Danly says gruffly.

"And what we're seeing, is that everything's connected," you say.

Bertram puts his jacket back on. "There's a gigantic sugarcane plantation between us and you. If he made an allegiance for money, it's most likely there. That's what we'll check out."

Danly nods. "Be careful. I'm going to the Embassy in Brasilia to put to bed this whole drug thing once and for all, and to share what we've found with the Ambassador. He'll want to hear this."

"Perfecto, Dano. Bertram out." He severs the connection, then looks to you. "You may want to stay here. This is not the 'jungle tour'—I'm prepared for these gangsters to come for me, and come *hard.*"

"Suppose the guy I saw at the crime scene is a 'sugar lord'? I'm ready for this," you say.

"Okay…" he sighs. "The way I figure, we can take a riverboat—that's the common method and they won't see us coming—or we can take a helicopter. You still have that business card, right? I'm gonna go get geared up, so you think about it."

Bertram leaves. Your two options, as you see it, are stealth or speed. A boat will take a while but you'll get the drop on them, and be able to sneak in and out. Maybe access some files, who knows what? *OR…* You can swoop in on a helicopter, kicking in the front door. You could always pretend to be some kind of investor or something. Bertram can play your bodyguard, maybe. Hmmm…

Your thoughts are disrupted when the agent returns. He's in olive-drab cargo pants, US-issue combat boots, and a navy-blue polo shirt with a bullet-proof vest and a tactical belt, both in matching tan. In addition to his sidearm, he now carries an assault rifle. The look is completed by something out of the Wild West—a badge pinned to his vest.

"You ready for this?"

- "Riverboat. Stealth is the underdog's greatest ally." Go to page 354
- "Well, if it isn't my private security! Care to escort me as I 'chopper in'?" Go to page 117

Team America

"You know what, Hotshot? I knew you were good people. Old Stewie didn't believe me, but—"

"Oh, shut the hell up," Danly says.

Both agents laugh. It's good to see them getting along, even if it's only under the threat of a common enemy.

"Order it up, just none of that sugarcane stuff. Gives a wicked hangover. Or get whatever you want! You're buying. But seriously."

Left with that cryptic message, you go order a round from the bar, pay, and return to the table. There's a moment of silence as the three of you wait for your drinks. One of those inevitable conversational pauses where no one quite has anything to say until one person finally tosses out a new topic.

"I'm really sorry you guys got knocked off the case," you say. "I know it doesn't affect me as much, but it sure would've made your careers if we would have solved it before the replacements came in."

"Fuck off, ass hat," Bertram says.

"Yeah, what the hell? You think that's all we care about? This isn't about our careers, this is about a dead American," Danly says.

"Sorry…." you mutter. "I didn't mean it like that."

"You're buying the next round too," Bertram says, shaking his head.

Now there's a reason for the silence: you and your sudden onset of foot-in-mouth disease. Out of sheer embarrassment, you look away. The next round of drinks finally arrives and Agent Danly takes the black stirring straw from his empty glass and adds it to the fresh one.

Noticing your eyes on him, he explains, "It's so I remember how many I've had."

You go back to drinking in silence. There's not much in the bar to capture your attention, save for a few TVs, so you idly watch the Brazilian programming up on the tube.

On now is a hidden camera prank show, and while the volume is set too low for you to hear, you can read the English subtitles and follow along fairly easily. The current prank involves a fake job interview where applicants come into a fake office building and are shown into a fake elevator. Then, as the elevator doors close and the 'lift' prepares to rise, the power goes out, leaving the unsuspecting victim in complete darkness.

Through a night-vision camera the audience witnesses a hidden panel open, where a young girl made-up to look like a ghost sneaks into the elevator. She's pale with disheveled hair, wearing an old-fashioned nightgown and clutching an antique doll. Once she's in place, the lights flicker back on and the 'ghost' screams like a banshee while the frightened victim wets themselves and/or has a heart attack for the audience's amusement.

The program cuts back to the show's host, who howls with masochistic laughter. You could pinch yourself with disbelief, but…you recognize him. Dear God, it's Dr. Viktor Lucio de Ocampo, the man who met you up on the *Cristo Redentor* statue before giving you the slip.

Jane Nightingale's fiance is on Brazilian television hosting a hidden camera show.

"What the…?" you say dumbly. "It—it's *him.*"

Both agents look up at the TV just in time to see the man in question before the camera cuts to another victim climbing aboard the sham elevator.

"Was that…?" Agent Danly asks, stunned.

"Yes!" you shout, pounding your fists on the table and rattling the drinks.

"There's no fucking way," Bertram says.

After the ghost-girl screams and the Brazilian woman in the elevator falls to the corner, crying and crossing herself in timorous prayer, the show brings us back to Viktor's grinning face.

"How the hell does a doctor who's wanted for murder have a reality TV prank show?" Bertram asks.

"Because he doesn't," Danly says. "While he was busy erasing himself online, the real Viktor hired an actor to portray himself in the real world. *That's* how he's given us the slip."

"Yeah, that does make more sense," Bertram says.

You look up at "Viktor" on the TV, and it's almost as if his maniacal laughter is directed at you. In a way, it is. This guy has just pulled the ultimate prank, and you're the unwitting victim. A flush of anger wells up within you.

Leaping from your chair, you shout, "So they're looking for the wrong guy!"

Agent Danly jumps to his feet as well, pulls out his cell phone, and rushes over to the bar. He grabs the bartender by the shirt and pulls him forward.

"What's the name of this show?" he demands.

"*P-programa Pegadinha,*" the man stutters.

Now Bertram is up and dialing his phone. "Bertram here, where's the RSO? Well, try to bring him up anyway. We've got the wrong guy! Activate the crisis center. I'll dial back with ID."

"This is Agent Danly, US Diplomatic Security. I need Detective Irma Dos Santos," he pauses, waiting to be transferred. "Detective? Turn on *Programa Pegadinha.* I need an ID on the host. We've been spoofed—Doctor Viktor Lucio de Ocampo hired an actor to portray himself. I'd bet anything the real Viktor is the guy our witness spooked at the warehouse. Get the sketch artist's rendition out with a BOLO alert."

He hangs up, then turns to Bertram, who says, "I got somebody back at the consulate, but everyone's at the Energy Summit and they can't get a hold of anyone."

"The Energy Summit!" you shout. "Disgruntled scientist gives us the slip and masks his appearance—where do you want to bet he'll show up next?"

"Let's go! The conference grounds are only a few blocks from here. We'll have to run; the streets are shut down for *Carnaval,*" Danly says.

Bertram shrugs. "I'm just drunk enough to where that sounds like a good idea."

The three of you sprint through the crowded Rio streets, weaving through costumed dancers and shoving drunken revelers out of the way. *Carnaval* is often referred to as "The Biggest Party on Earth," and they might be right. Picture *Mardi*

Gras on steroids, except no beads are required—nearly one out of every three women wears bodypaint in lieu of a shirt, or nothing at all.

Even in your panicked state, it's hard not to stare. It's such a foreign concept for an American. Gorgeous, topless women with their bare breasts, in public, swaying in tune to the music. The men are distracting as well with their bare, hairless chests, sculpted abdomens, and anatomically-correct speedos. *This* is the reason people exercise in Brazil; to show off their bodies during *Carnaval.*

You shake your head and focus on the agents up ahead. Not a hundred yards further awaits the enormous Energy Summit conference grounds. When you arrive, you find Detective Irma Dos Santos at the entry, a manila folder in hand.

"His name is André Nascimiento da Silveira, host of *Programa Pegadinha.* Theater actor by trade, he took the hidden camera variety show after a painful divorce wiped out his bank account."

"The kind of guy desperate enough to do anything for money," Bertram growls. "Son of a bitch!"

"Let's go," Danly says. "We need to find who's in charge, activate emergency plans, alert host nation personnel, and see about a mobile security deployment."

The four of you push through the front door and into the massive building's lobby. The entrance is cordoned off by a security line, complete with metal detectors and bomb dogs. Danly and Bertram show their badges.

"These two are with us," Bertram says, indicating the detective and you.

Irma shakes her head. "I'm going to monitor the exits."

- Stick with Detective Dos Santos. Go to page 56
- Stick with Agent Danly. Go to page 154
- Stick with Agent Bertram. Go to page 121

Team Bertram

The two of you rush down to the lower cog station, but when Bertram questions the witnesses in Portuguese, he finds nothing but frustration in their answers. He makes a quick phone call with his cellular phone, then comes back over to you, shaking his head.

"Our guy jumped out of the train about a mile back, up where it goes through a neighborhood. He's definitely gone by now. C'mon."

The two of you get into the SUV and drive away from the rail station.

"Good call on splitting up, by the way," Bertram says. "That asshole is so goddamn annoying."

You just nod. "What's first?"

"I put in an address request and a background check for one Viktor Lucio de Ocampo. The address should be in shortly, but the background check could take a couple of days. Maybe faster; murder makes it priority one."

"Kind of convenient that he gave us his last name, wouldn't you say?"

"Could be. Or he could have thought we already knew it, or that we'd find out soon enough. You hungry?"

Without waiting for a response, he pulls over in front of a food cart, the angry honks of other vehicles punctuating the impetuousness of the decision. Bertram exits and you do the same. The SUV is still in a traffic lane and motorists have to swerve around you to continue down the road.

"I don't think this is a parking spot," you say.

"Diplomatic plates. You ever have a-car-jay?"

Again not waiting for you to answer, Bertram moves around to the front of the food cart. The middle-aged Afro-Brazilian woman working there looks concerned at your parking job for about two seconds, which is how long it takes Bertram to get his money roll out of his pocket. She's wearing a white, billowy muumuu with layered, flowing sleeves and a turquoise head scarf.

He says something to her in Portuguese and she smiles through missing and rotted teeth. A food cart career doesn't come with a dental plan, it would appear. You're not sure what he said, but she laughs, and the two fingers he raises make it obvious he's ordered lunch for you as well.

"How much do I owe you?" you ask.

"Don't worry about it. They're only a couple of *reais* a piece."

It's only a few more moments before she's done, and he claims the food and thanks the woman. A park bench waits a few paces away and the agent stakes it out. Once you sit, he hands you your lunch. It basically looks like Pac-man OD'd, choked on his own vomit and died.

Noticing your look, Bertram says, "When in Rome—eat up."

The dish, which is actually called *Acarajé* (despite the agent's pronunciation of 'a-car-jay'), is a ball of mashed black-eyed-peas, rolled, deep fried, then split open and filled with a paste consisting primarily—in this case—of shrimp, bread, and coconut milk.

You dig in and are pleasantly surprised at the taste. It's kind of like something you might find in Creole New Orleans. During the shared moment of chewing and contemplative silence, you're able to get a good study of Agent David Bertram.

He's still quite young, and from either love of simplicity or a desire to save money, it appears he uses his own clippers on his beard and his buzzed, auburn hair. Black sunglasses and a suit complete the no-frills look, and by most estimates, he fits the "fade-into-the-background" appearance his job demands.

"Where did you learn Portuguese?" you ask.

"Here. All the agents have to go through a language course, but my Pops worked in the consulate and I grew up in São Paulo. Made it pretty easy to snag a job working in the State Department, but I didn't want to be stuck in an office, so I went to the law enforcement side. Believe it or not, speaking the language doesn't help much on the job. I rarely talk while on a security detail. But when ordering lunch…."

His cell phone chirps and Bertram checks the message. "We've got an address; let's roll."

"Close?" you ask.

"Fifteen, twenty minutes away. He lives within walking distance of the State University. Makes sense; we know he's some kind of scientist, so he's probably got connections there. We'll want to check that out too."

- "To his house! Hopefully we can get a look around before he gets back." Go to page 166
- "It's still early. Let's check in at the University during business hours." Go to page 144

Team Danly

Paired with Agent Danly, you take a cab back to the consulate garage. The whole trip is spent in silence, and it isn't until Danly checks out a second car that he finally speaks.

"All right, Rookie," Danly says with a sigh. "We can team up—but no more tourist crap. We're all business. Lest we forget our roles, I'm investigating a murder and you're my Cooperating Witness."

"Aye, aye, Cap'n!" you say with a salute.

Danly glowers. "Mock professionalism is not professionalism. Agent Bertram gave you the wrong impression of the DSS, but we'll soon remedy that. Now, c'mon. Daylight's wasting."

The agent tunes in the vehicle's police scanner and you ride in silence toward the police station. You look out the window and take the time to soak up some scenery. It's a nice day—the sun is shining, the sky is blue, and the foliage is green. You're near the ocean for the first part of the drive, but not close enough to see it. Instead, you're greeted with construction and traffic. The city's still trying to give itself a facelift for the Olympics, and the city workers are toiling around the clock.

You drive through a corridor where traffic thins, abating only momentarily, and high cinderblock walls box you in on both sides. Graffiti flows not as murals but simply as gang territory delineation, and the overall effect is mildly depressing. As you come to a stop light, you see a hansom cab pulling tourists in its horse-drawn carriage. That could be you right now, enjoying the sun and seeing the sights, but instead you're here—ready to track down a killer.

Danly pulls into an inner-city neighborhood, complete with marketplaces, corner shops, a McDonald's, and supermarkets with sky-rise apartments on top. You pass through a roundabout so large, it holds a city park in its center.

The precinct is in the midst of a housing area but evidently, living near a police station doesn't do much for security. Even the neighboring apartment units have bars on their windows and barbed tips atop their fences. You can't even fathom the level of crime that goes on here. The last time you visited this police station you were a little preoccupied with other thoughts and it was dark out, so you're just now getting a good look at the neighborhood.

The precinct itself is rather striking. It sits raised off the street on a verdant, groomed lawn. Opposite the flowing flags at the entry, a palm tree waves its branches in greeting. A pleasing feat of architecture amongst the drab concrete jungle, the façade of the building is a false wall. As you walk along the path and step through the opening, you see the real wall up ahead—which has an impressive glass entrance.

Once you're inside, the beauty fades and the "real" Rio meets you face-to-face. All those criminals you remember from your first time are still here—hell, even that poor tourist looking for his sister is still here. If you want to lose your faith in humanity, spend a few minutes in a metropolitan police station's waiting room.

Detective Irma Dos Santos waves at Agent Danly and then leads the two of you into her office. Today must be some kind of "casual day," because she wears jeans and a navy blue polo shirt with the precinct logo embroidered on the left just above her breast-line. Her office is small. Another police officer helps her wheel in two chairs for Danly and you.

She sits behind her desk, which is neat and sparse, with only a computer, a printer, and a single photograph. It's of her in full *Carnaval* getup—that is to say, not wearing much more than a smile, bedazzled jewels, and feathers. In the photo she's pert, ready for fun, and…rather attractive. Her computer mouse pad is a novelty custom-print of her and a young girl. Could be a daughter, could be a niece. She wears no wedding ring.

"Have you got anything for me?" Danly asks, sitting down.

"Not much, but some things. What about you?"

"Tit for tat?" he replies.

She raises an eyebrow. "No, professional courtesy. We have our own investigation."

"Well that's a relief. We were approached by the subject, who of course proclaims his innocence."

"Really? We should—how do you say?—compare notes. Where was this?"

"He left a letter on our car," Danly says. "I'll have our office fax you over a copy. We ended up meeting him at the Redeemer statue. Rookie here figured that one out."

"And?"

"And what? That's all we've got."

"He gave us the slip," you say. "The other agent is tracking him down; we're going to help you focus on the crime scene evidence."

She nods. "Grab a cup of coffee, I'll have the evidence brought in."

"Rookie—liquid creamer, sugar-free syrup, if they've got it."

- "I'm still good from breakfast, thanks." Go to page 225
- "Suuuuure. I'd love to get you some coffee." Go to page 129

There's Always Backup

"No!" Viktor shouts, too late.

You gun down all three policemen in cold blood. Your sub-machinegun sends wisps of smoke into the night air. Then you realize you're not alone.

Gunshots ring out from a rooftop across the way and you look over to see Agent Danly and Detective Irma Dos Santos.

There's a flicker of recognition, but that doesn't stop them from firing. Both you and Viktor die in a hail of bullets.

THE END

This Stinks

You maneuver toward the street corner in an effort to cut off the dump truck at the pass. It has its blinker on as if it is going to turn toward the consulate; so far, so good. Jaywalking is common here, so you don't arouse suspicion when you step out into the street between the lines of the cars. However, you do get some interesting stares from the car behind the trash truck when you jump in the back amongst the wet and fetid garbage.

If there is one repulsive substance in this world, it is trash juice. The collection of rotting food leftovers, tobacco spittle, diapers, and used condoms forms an unholy salve that coats the inside of the truck. You doubt if it ever gets washed—just dumped and reloaded.

You plug your nose and settle deep amongst the bags so you won't be spotted. As the truck turns right around the corner, you can see the consulate disappear behind you. They didn't turn inside. Damn!

Time to hop out and try it again, albeit a little smellier this time around. A banana peel rests comically upon your shoulder.

- Talk to the guard, tell him I forgot my ID. He'll let me in; I'm an American. Go to page 6
- Plenty of motorcycles here in traffic; knock the driver off, swerve through the pylons, rush the gate! Go to page 131

Time Bomb, Ticking

She nods, then turns back to the trafficker, ready to do her grim duty. She says something to him that you can only assume means "last chance," and as he starts cursing at her again, she presses her revolver into the palm of his left hand and pulls the trigger.

The gunshot is deafening, but the ringing in your ears soon merges with the sounds of the teen's screams. The detective shoves the hot barrel of the gun into his right palm and calls for him to answer your question. His wounded left hand gropes to get her away, but is powerless.

He's in *your* hands now.

"He says he doesn't know anything; all he knows is, the order came from way up the chain of command."

"Why?" you say. "Ask him *why* she was killed."

She does so. He shakes his head; he's crying now.

"She must've pissed off somebody high up, a colonel in the organization. Something like that. Says that's all he knows."

- "Did she owe somebody money? Drugs? What?" Go to page 305
- "All right. Time to go." Go to page 78

Tiny Tinho

"He says he's taking us to a place where we can talk," Viktor explains. "I don't trust him, but it can't be worse than rooftop snipers and assassins, right?"

Tinho pushes aside a draped rug that covers a hole in a wall, and leads you inside someone's makeshift house. Possibly his. Most likely it's where people come to get high and congregate with hookers. Tinho offers you a seat on a dingy sofa, the fibers matted down from years of body oils, lotions, and God-knows-what-else, so you opt to stand.

Viktor speaks in Portuguese and you watch the body language of the two men. Tinho is thin, confident, ever-smiling, even smug, and doesn't balk at the topic of murder. Such is life in the slums, you suppose.

"He says he knows everything about Jane and that all we have to do is ask… and pay."

- "Okay, ask who killed her." Go to page 122
- "See if he knows who the assassin is." Go to page 124
- "Let's see if we're in any danger. Has he heard of anyone looking for us?" Go to page 123

Too Much Sugar Can Make You Sick

You climb up the stairs to the landing and the main entrance. The wide double doors creak open when you push against them.

"Let's try to keep in mind we're entering the private property of the Governor of this territory," Bertram says.

Despite his words, he keeps his assault rifle at the ready.

It's dark inside. There are dull, umber-colored lights, but the generators must be straining to power such a large structure, and the effect illuminates the house like candlelight.

The interior, while certainly impressive, proves that the house isn't a mansion after all. Everything here is utilitarian—serving a purpose instead of just putting on a show—as this is a modern place of business and not merely another display of wealth.

Two paces in, there's a security guard in a booth, and upon seeing your drawn weapons, he activates an alarm. He's enclosed in bullet-proof glass, so there's not a damn thing you can do about it. Soon, a security team arrives, shouting in Portuguese, with sub-machine guns aimed at you.

Bertram and Maria shout right back and the three of you draw down on the half-dozen guards in a Mexican standoff.

"So you're the ones causing all the trouble," a voice booms in English.

You turn and see a large, middle-aged Brazilian man. Neither tall nor fat per se, but thick-limbed and possessing a sort of magnetic gravity you can't quite place. His full face is clean-shaven and has deep creases where a stark smile now finds perch. His eyes are dark brown, with an intense intelligence.

The man wears tight blue jeans tucked into black cowboy boots, dusty and grey with age. He wears a blue workshirt and an orange scarf tied loosely about his neck. Not exactly how you'd picture a billionaire. His short, jet-black hair is slicked back and neatly arranged in such a way that you can be certain he has a comb tucked in his pocket.

"Agent David Bertram, Diplomatic Security Service," your partner replies, fearsome gravity in his words. "Order your men to stand down, right now."

"An American federal agent? So far from home?"

"Order your men to stand down!"

"No, I don't think I will," the man grins. "You're inside my plantation, without proper clearance. Isn't that correct, Agent…Bertram, is it?"

Bertram gulps hard, doubt flowing into his hard eyes.

"That is what I thought. Order your friends to turn over their weapons, do the same yourself, and we can talk as civilized men. You three will be my guests. I offer you no ill will; I don't even know what brings you here, but I cannot abide people barging onto my property."

The man waits while Bertram considers it.

"Don't listen to him!" Maria hisses.

"Please don't think you have any room to bargain. That would be a mistake."

- "Let's give up our weapons." Go to page 132
- "Tell him to go to hell." Go to page 107

Trespassers

Along with a dozen other passengers, Viktor leans over the railing. When you call out to him, he looks back and waves you over. "River kids," he says.

You look out over the river where several wooden canoes push toward the barge from shore. The boat is moving substantially faster than the tiny canoes, so they have to time it well in order to intercept her course.

As the first canoe makes it close, you see it's actually piloted by two *children.* Somewhere between nine and twelve years old, the boys paddle alongside the barge and the older of the two launches a grappling hook into one of the tires hanging from the side, effectively tethering the canoe to the larger ship.

Two children in another canoe do the same thing. These "river kids" are intentionally attaching their craft to the barge. Then you see why: The older child from the first boat scales the side of the barge with the practiced skill of a howler monkey. When he makes it to the top, the passengers pay him for his wares; the canoes are full of fresh fruit and jarred preserves.

Viktor gives the boy a *real* in exchange for a jar of candied sugarcane stalks. Once he's paid, he pops the lid, pulls one out just like a pickle, and hands it to you. The treat is sweet and crisp.

There are shouts as a third canoe attempts to gain perch and fails. The two children in this vessel are pulled to the rear of the barge, where the surge from the engine sucks down their canoe and chews it to pieces. They jump out just in the nick of time.

"Not an easy way to make a living," Viktor says, biting into one of the stalks.

There's no time, no way to help the boys out. Their heads bob up and down in the water next to supplies and planks from the canoe. Within a few minutes, they're out of sight.

Viktor licks sugarcane juice off his fingertips. "I'm going to head down below to get some sleep. Come wake me around midnight and we'll switch."

Before you can respond, he disappears below decks. Turning back, something catches your eye near the front of the boat—several white hammocks swaying under the sun. Yep, a nap sounds pretty good to you too.

You awaken under a cloudy sky in the dark of night. It's chilly, despite the warm summer evening; your lingering afternoon sweat has cooled under the breeze of the speeding boat. Your eyes immediately adjust to the dark and you see that the other hammocks nearby are occupied by whole families bedding down for the evening.

Clunk. Something slams against the starboard side of the boat. Out of curiosity and the need to stretch your legs, you go investigate. The canoes are long gone but under the dim night you see that another boat has attached itself to the side of the barge. Only this one is much larger, and instead of children with groceries, this skiff has a dozen masked men wielding firearms.

- Run! Go find Viktor. Go to page 342
- Untie that tire they've grappled onto. Go to page 333
- Look for a weapon. Knock them off as they pop up. Go to page 182

Trust

You hand her the rifle, hoping you're not about to become the fourth body on the floor of this shanty home. It seems your faith is to be rewarded. Irma turns to the interrogated drug trafficker, placing the AK-47 back in his bloodied hands.

"There," she says. "They all killed each other, case closed. You and I both share in the guilt, so we know I can trust you and you can trust me. Right?"

"We've both got blood on our hands," you say.

She looks at her palms; apparently the idiom doesn't translate. You take her hands in yours and she looks up. "It means I trust you."

"Okay, but we'd better get out of here fast; the cover story only holds up so well when I'm standing here with three spent casings in my revolver."

You nod; time to go. Stepping over the bodies, you make your way back into the alley. There's something ironic about killing three people while trying to catch the murderer of one person—even if the three were drug traffickers.

As if reading your mind, Irma says, "They would have killed us if we didn't get them first, you know that, right? The world is better off without scum like this in it."

Without response, you walk with her through the *favela,* still somewhat numb from the experience. Your trance is quickly broken by shouts and footsteps thundering down the alleyway.

Irma takes off running and you follow. You emerge from the alley into another wide street like the one where the armored car battle took place. Looking down each side of the road, you see several Elite Squad figures blocking each egress route. If those are traffickers bearing down behind you, you're about to get stuck in another gun battle.

"What now?" you ask in desperation.

She looks around, equally frightened. Then something catches her eye. She points ahead at a graffiti sign reading, *Albergue.*

"It's a hostel!" she cries. "Come on!"

- *Flee to the hostel.* Go to page 187

Uncovered

You shiver under the dim glow of the city lights, though it's plenty warm outside. *This is a mistake,* a voice inside whispers again and again as you walk the five minutes down to the shore. Eventually the walk is over and you stand at the border between concrete and sand, hesitating.

Like you're crossing a portal into another world, you force yourself through the perceived threshold and onto the beach. You're hardly alone. Couples walk hand in hand down the shoreline and a few homeless sleep under the stars. It's a bright night, made even brighter by the city lights behind you.

"Do you know who that girl was?" a voice from behind asks.

You turn to see the man from before, from the crime scene; the man with the beautiful blue eyes. Masking your apprehension, you simply shake your head "no."

"Didn't you see her? I couldn't see her face, but I'm afraid… afraid it was my Jane." He speaks fluent English, with barely the hint of an accent. He's Brazilian, the kind with light, almond-colored skin and black hair, the kind whose Portuguese ancestry shines through with little hint of Native or African intermingling. His blue eyes glitter with sadness and starlight. "My fiancée, my… everything. I was going to meet her there, but then…"

"Why there? What was that room?"

"Just a room. I thought they wanted a peace offering, to meet and…but it was all bullshit. I think they meant to kill me. I think they…I think she…" He's rambling and his voice cracks with emotion.

"I'm sorry," you say. "I just don't get it. Who is 'they'? The agents?"

His eyes narrow. "Who *are* you? What were you doing there?"

You hesitate, then decide to be honest. "Wrong place, wrong time. I'm just a tourist."

"Hmm. I…shouldn't have contacted you. I'm sorry. Goodbye, Tourist."

"Wait!" you shout, stopping him as he turns away. "Tell me what this is all about—please."

"I was hoping you'd be able to do the same. I thought you were there on purpose, that you spoiled things for them, that you were…a player. I was hoping you could lead me to Jane's killer."

"They think it's you! Let's go tell the agents, or the police. I'm sure they could help."

He smiles a sad, feeling-sorry-for-you smile, then shakes his head. "You really are clueless, aren't you? If you get in the way, they'll kill you too. And the police? Corruption is part of everyday life here."

You stand in stunned silence, trying to process what he's saying. Then you see his face fold in thought, those blue eyes flickering back and forth over an internal argument.

"I'm sorry," he says, adjusting his glasses. "But I cannot let you tell them you saw me. Too risky."

You see him put a hand into his coat pocket and grab something within. Raising your hands to plead with him, you say, "Whoa, whoa, whoa—hold on there."

"I'm not a killer, not yet. But I will kill for Jane. I will find out who did it, I will find proof to clear my name, then I will kill them. And if you try to flee now, I'll kill you too. I'm already wanted for murder, so what have I got to lose?"

- "Please, we're in this together. If they want to kill you, I'm not safe either. I can help you find your fiancée." Go to page 347
- "I'll head back to the States, never to speak of this again. I swear it." Go to page 116
- Lie. Tell him what he wants to hear, then tell the agents the first chance you get. Go to page 76

Undone

Thinking quickly, you rush over to the side and look to untie their anchor point. Bad news: all you find is smooth rope. The rope must be knotted down by the tire itself, and so you've got no way to untie it.

You turn, looking to run, but you're met by alarmed, panicky faces. Now the other passengers are awake and come to see the source of the commotion. The boat's cook arrives with a kitchen knife held defensively, but clearly he's too frightened to help. Families hide behind the fathers, who in turn press back against their families. Looks like you're on your own.

You reach out to get the knife from the cook, but he recoils in fear. You mime sawing using the edge of a flattened hand against your opposite forearm, then point to the rope. Cookie gets it and hands you the knife.

There isn't much time. You slide down against the rail, sawing furiously at the rope. The knife is dulled from overuse, but the rope is brittle. Strands leap away from each other as you set them free, one by one.

The first pirate makes it to the top, smiling greedily at the throngs of terrified passengers. It's their eyes that give you away. They can't help it; they all look to you, sawing away at the rope.

The pirate looks down, curious for an instant, but then screams at you in words you don't understand. Just as he raises his AK-47, the rope finally gives and yanks him off the rail just as it snaps off the boat.

There's a large crash below, and looking over the side, you see that you didn't just cut off one tire, but the entire set that hung on this side. Ropes and tires and an anchor all crash onto the pirate skiff, ensnaring the smaller boat and crippling it long enough to prevent further pursuit.

The angry pirates fire their rifles at the barge, but the cheering of the passengers drowns them out. You look back; the terror of the growing crowd is now completely replaced by joy. You step forward to give the cook his knife back, but instead the man crushes you in a bear hug.

You're a hero.

The Captain arrives, all smiles, congratulates and thanks you in Portuguese and offers a hearty handshake. The ship's crew rushes in and raises you on their shoulders. Cheering and jubilation begins as *samba* music blares over the ship's radio and bottles of liquor are opened and passed around. Babies are placed before you to be kissed. People reach out and touch your clothes, just to be part of the moment.

At length, Viktor arrives. "Way to go, Tourist, you've saved the day. But you may want to wear a cape and a mask next time; we're trying to lay low, remember?"

All you can do is grin.

"I suppose we might as well enjoy ourselves," he says.

Viktor finds two glasses overflowing with *caipirinha,* puts one in your hand, and toasts to you.

➢ *Drink down the sugarcane liquor and dance the night away.* Go to page 52

Unreasonable

You tuck the laptop under one arm, scoop a stack of papers under the other, and let out a hesitant, "H-hello?"

A man swoops into the room, handgun raised and pointed at you. *Gulp.* He shouts in Portuguese and another man appears in the doorway behind him. They wear black suits and gloves and have handguns drawn, but these are neither American agents nor Brazilian police, you can tell that much. These men have the look of cold, hard killers. Brazilian mafia, maybe?

While the first man keeps his handgun trained on you, the second searches your pockets. They find the map, the key to the unit, and your American passport.

"I'm Viktor's lab assist—"

The one searching you slaps his pistol across your cheek, silencing you. He takes the laptop and the papers. The other man raises his handgun to your forehead. He marches you out in front of the house, where there's a moving van, its interior lined with plastic. It's the last thing you'll ever see.

THE END

(Un)Resolved

You rush back to the hotel bar, flying through the streets and zigzagging past revelers. When you burst through the front door, Danly and Bertram are still here; the table is covered in empty glasses.

The two look up at you, their eyes glassy from booze.

"They're here," you say.

"Who?" the agents ask in unison.

"The suspect…and the *Jamanta,*" you huff out.

The men shoot to their feet and Bertram removes a set of car keys from his pocket.

"Whoa, you're not good to drive," Danly says. "Let's take a cab."

"We'll never get through the crowds without the sirens. Hotshot?"

You feel a cold sweat clinging to your spine. Despite having tossed a few back tonight, you were stone-cold sober the minute you saw the blue-eyed suspect run through the crowd. You put out your palm for the keys.

"This will get us more than suspended," Danly says, yet he doesn't resist.

In an instant, the three of you are out the door and piled into the SUV with diplomatic plates. Bertram flips the sirens on and you drive through the crowd in the direction you just came from.

"Just don't hit anybody," Danly says.

People yield to the vehicle, but it's very slow going, sort of like fording a river on horseback.

"Can't you just shoot in the air or something?" you ask.

"Ummm, no. We still need a job after this," Danly says.

Finally, the road clears, and you start to get excited—until you see why it's open up ahead. The road ends with a brick wall as its backboard, and there's already a crime-scene barrier in place. A dead body lays in the center—a man. Without a doubt, it's the suspect. His blue eyes are now a pale, ghostly white.

The three of you get out of the SUV and approach the police tape. Detective Irma Dos Santos of the Rio police comes over to greet you.

"What's happened?" Danly asks.

"It's him," she says, looking to you. "We got him."

"You shot him? What about the assassin?" you ask.

Her eyebrow rises in confusion. "The other American agents, they…."

She points back to the rear of the crime scene, where the replacement investigators, led by Agent Howard, mill around the body.

"Christ," Danly mutters.

"The killer made an attempt on the Ambassador's life," she continues. "They pursued him from the Energy Summit, cornered him down here, and when he hit a dead end, he drew on the agents."

"He was alone?" you ask.

The detective nods.

"And we still don't have an ID?" Agent Bertram asks.

"We'll run his prints and dental records. We'll find out who he was."

"Thank you, Detective," Danly says.

She nods again and steps back into the crime scene, leaving the three of you alone.

"Damn, my money was on the fiance," Bertram says. "But he just disappeared after we saw him up by Christ the Redeemer."

"I don't get it," you say. "Where the hell did *Jamanta* go?"

Danly shakes his head. "The other agents must have spooked him. Their first fucking night here and they solve the goddamned murder…"

"That's it? Case closed?" you say.

"What more do you want?" Danly replies. "You all but caught this guy red-handed; now he gets caught again, only this time the good guys win."

"It must have been politically motivated. Most of our training deals with terrorist threats like this," Bertram says. "This guy kidnapped and interrogated Nightingale, found out where the Ambassador would be at the Energy Summit, disposed of her, and waited until tonight to go for his real target. I'd say we got lucky, Hotshot."

You shake your head. "That doesn't make sense. What about Viktor? Where does he fit in? And why was an assassin—lying in wait in costume, no less—chasing the bad guy? Isn't *Jamanta* a bad guy?"

"The Devil Ray goes where there's money," Bertram says. "You don't know he was chasing him; maybe he was protecting the subject? Or, if he really was chasing him, maybe the guy tried to back out and stiff *Jamanta* on his fees. Who knows?"

"Listen up, Rookie. I've never worked on a case that doesn't have some loose ends. Justice was served; that's the end of it as far as we're concerned. The official investigation team will still scrub the case file, find out who this guy was and what motivated him, and we'll learn from it for future ops. Other than that, job well done."

"I guess so…" you say.

"Know it," Bertram adds. "You're a hero."

You nod, but it feels like a hollow victory.

➢ Go to page 304

Value

The three drug traffickers look like you just handed them a bar of gold bullion, and in a sense you did. A cheap passport forgery will cost about $300, while a high-quality job can run as high as $5K. But a used, already-in-the-system, genuine article? You might have just given these teens a year's salary in the Rio drug trade.

Your passport will most likely be used by terrorists or…yeah, let's just stick with terrorists, BUT—you just handed something so valuable over that the criminals are now debating whether or not to let you go. You can always claim you lost it, and you may have just bought your life back.

Suddenly the three men turn silent, looking toward the curtained door. Then you hear it too—a powerful engine growling close. One of the teens peers out.

"*BOPE! Tropa de Elite!*" he reports.

"Elite Squad," Viktor translates. "Police special forces. Easily one of the most extreme combat forces on the planet. They're pacifying this *favela*! We need to get out of here, now."

The three young drug lords are equally terrified. With a great *BOOM,* the *favela* is rocked by an explosion. In panic, one of them flees. The other two watch him go, deciding if it's a worthy choice, and eventually decide that it is.

You pounce on Falador, ready to attack and get your passport back, but the young man is so frightened that he drops not only that, but his AK-47 as well. He trips over his own feet running out of the hovel, leaving the two of you alone.

As you pick up your passport, Viktor claims the assault rifle. He checks to see if it's loaded, then gives you a knowing nod. You put your passport away and claim the sub-machinegun from Viktor's pack.

➢ *Escape the slums!* Go to page 103

Victory Pizza

The restaurant's red flag sails above the entry to hail your arrival. You find Viktor in a rear booth, waiting for you. The building's exterior walls are all glass, giving a panorama of street life while saving you from the sounds of traffic and the smell of the street vendors' food offerings.

You sit down across from Viktor, feeling the smooth pleather/vinyl seat beneath you, its surface polished by a thousand rear ends. The waiter gives you a menu and a glass of water, then leaves.

"How did it go on your end?" Viktor asks.

You grin, lean back, and tuck your hands behind your head. "Nothing to it."

"Deposited the note and nobody saw you?"

You shrug. "How'd your side go?"

His shoulders sink. "'I was too late. Mafia cleanup crew was already packing the place up. It would have been nice to have my laptop, but it's not essential. They'll never crack my computer security. The garage was the important step; well-done."

"So what's next?" you ask.

"Lunch. Take a look at the menu; everything's good here. I recommend the Gino's Combo if you're torn."

The waiter returns and you order a pizza and a pint of their finest beer on tap. After a moment, you ask the burning question in your mind. "So who do you think killed her, and why?"

He looks around. "I'm sorry, Tourist, I can't say just yet. The people we're dealing with… Later, I'll tell you later."

You nod but say nothing.

Viktor continues, "I must confess—I had one of my students follow you today—because I wasn't sure if you'd go through with your end. I thought maybe you'd get cold feet… I'm sorry I doubted you; I won't again. Still, I cannot tell you any more here. If I had you followed, it's possible we're not alone."

"Okay… then, aside from eating pizza, what are we doing?"

"Nothing," he says, his brow raised. "Have to eat, don't you? But after…."

He clears his throat, then downs the rest of his beer. "Afterward, I think we might find something at Jane's apartment, but we're not going to get it with those agents prowling nearby. André will send me a text when they've arrived, far out of our way."

He holds up a disposable cell phone, showing it off just as the waiter arrives with your pizza. The crust is thick and doughy, the cheese perfectly melted and browned, and the aroma makes your mouth water. You dig in, enjoying the pizza with Viktor, but after you pick up your second slice his phone buzzes.

After checking it, he looks up to you. "Finish up, it's time."

- *Follow Viktor to the evidence.* Go to page 169

The Vigilante

Maria turns to Bertram, again offering her hands to be cuffed. He *clicks* them around her wrists.

"Let's go, Hotshot. Grab a set of jeep keys from that security booth. We need to drop her off at local law enforcement, then I need to get straight to the Rio consulate. I can only imagine the fallout from this shit."

"Local law enforcement?" you say. "What if there are cops on the Sugar King's payroll? Won't she be in danger?"

Bertram says nothing.

"A small price to pay, indeed," Maria says. "My family will be remembered for standing up to Mateo Ferro, not as people who folded before such a tyrant. Maybe others will be inspired?"

Then she steps over to you and gives you a quick, if not impassioned, kiss on the lips. "You know, in another life…" she says.

➢ *Part with Maria, then head to Rio.* Go to page 273

Viktor's Way

In a calm voice, Viktor says, "I want you to throw the chicken at them."

Unsure how a chicken can compete against firearms, you hesitate. But the man is insistent. "Do it now, Tourist."

You throw the chicken. It shrieks through the air, talons wildly seeking purchase. The flailing bird has the intended effect on the group, and in the chaos, Viktor grabs one of the small children, holds him tight and puts his pistol to the boy's head.

After the chicken is subdued, the gang looks back at you. The leader's eyes grow cold when he sees Viktor and the boy. Shockingly, without a second's thought, the leader shoots the kid. In the immense silence that follows, he says something to Viktor in a strong yet emotionless tone. You think you're about to be executed, but he seems to be waiting for a reply.

"What is it?" you ask.

"He says he will never be blackmailed nor manipulated. He says if we want information, we simply must pay for it."

Viktor says something in Portuguese, and the leader bids you follow him with a wave.

"What did you say?"

"I told him we'd pay."

"With what?"

Viktor shakes his head. "I haven't thought that far ahead."

Oh, boy…

- *Follow them to the informant.* Go to page 207

Visitors' Entrance

"Ah, I can get you your press badge." He removes a clipboard and clicks the mechanism on a ballpoint pen, ready to check you off. "Name?"

"Sam…" you say, trying to make up a name on the fly. "…Adams."

You wince, but he doesn't notice. He scans his sheet. *Come on…*

"You're not on the list."

Damn.

You rack your brain, trying to think of a good add-on to the story. In a moment of inspiration, you say, "It was a last-minute addition. My editor is always doing this…*sigh.*"

"Well, give me the name of your point of contact and I'll have him come down here and vouch you in."

"No… I don't want to waste his time. Really, I'm late. Can't you just let me in?"

The guard shakes his head and says, "Protocol."

"What? That's ridiculous! I demand to speak to your supervisor."

"Really?" he says. "Very well."

The guard sets down the clipboard and picks up a radio. Wait—what are you doing? You're supposed to be *incognito.* If you get discovered and the agents get wind of what you're doing—helping the number one suspect in a murder investigation—this won't be good. Best case? You'll be deported back home, with a lifetime supply of no-fly orders. Worst case? Jail time.

"Hold on!" you say. "I'll…I'll go make a call."

He sets down the radio, watching as you step away. There has to be another answer….

You look over to the long line of cars waiting to enter the parking garage. Each one stops at the guard shack to show proper identification. There's one about two-thirds of the way down that sticks out—because it's a pizza delivery guy. How the hell does he have proper credentials?

Wait, that's it! All you need is a delivery. You don't actually need to get inside; you just need your letter delivered. You pull out your wallet (since you don't have a phone) and pretend to talk into it, keeping it pressed to the ear facing away from the guard shack.

"Just give a note to Agents…Bertram and Danly. Okay, will do!"

You turn back to the guard shack, quickly tucking your wallet away.

"Hi! I just need to leave a note for a couple of the agents. That okay?"

The guard says he can do that and proceeds to write down the agents' names. You pass him the note and thank him.

"Sam Adams, right?"

"Yep, that's me!" you say with a smile.

"Okay, I'll get this to them right away."

You thank the guard, then turn and leave. This had better work….

➢ *Go meet Viktor at the restaurant.* Go to page 338

Waking the Dead

Before the first of the armed men begins to climb the rope, you run to the back staircase, down to the mid-deck, and toward the passenger cabins. Hoping you've got the right cabin, you burst through the door.

Viktor immediately shoots out of bed, panting heavily. He grabs his glasses and looks at you with wild eyes.

"A boat—boarding us," you huff.

"Is it the assassin? The Man in Black?"

You shake your head. "I don't think so. Looks like hijackers or something."

"Pirates," he says knowingly.

"What do they want?"

"Usually it's a robbery. We could try and wait them out, see if they'll leave us alone. Or we could try and warn the captain. It's illegal for merchant ships to carry weapons, but most keep a shotgun or at least a revolver just in case."

- "Let's barricade the door and wait it out." Go to page 143
- "There's still time! Let's warn him." Go to page 292

Washing over You

Who knows when you might get a rinse-off again? Save for a dunk in the river—where there are piranhas, anacondas, camen-alligators, and countless microbial predators—this is it.

You turn on the shower, step in with your flip-flops, and as the water wets your head, you look down to the drain. Sticking out are two twisted, spindly strands of golden brown; either a clump of hair, or a pair of legs from a massive spider reaching out of the abyss. As water starts to run down the drain, they move slightly, but you're still not sure what you're looking at. It could be that the legs are recoiling from the wetness or simply it's a clog moving with the current. The more you stare, the more you try to convince yourself you're looking at hair in the drain, but your body tells you to flee.

As those prehensile locks of foulness reach toward your toes, you decide you've had enough. You flee the shower stall, back out into the room to towel off away from the hellish nightmare aborned from the drain.

Well, so much for sleeping. You dress and return out to the main deck of the boat, just in time to catch a major commotion on the starboard side.

➢ *Go find Viktor and see what's going on.* Go to page 329

Welcome to the Jungle

It's nearly noon and you've finally arrived. The boat is tied securely to the dock, a small wooden walkway that floats just offshore. The whole world is wet from the previous night's downpour, with humid raindrops clinging to every surface like a bathroom mirror after a steamy shower.

Someone has built a hut on the nearby riverbank and the collected fishing nets, clotheslines, and canoes tell of a family living off the land here—attached to the dock like a barnacle in the sea. Two small boys come out of the hut, blinking at you curiously as you step off the boat and onto the wooden panel. You have a feeling of vertigo when you go from the oscillating craft to the firm boards that are anchored to underwater pylons.

Agent Bertram steps off the boat as well, offering a wave of greeting to these river children. They duck back inside, only to return an instant later with fresh jungle fruits and jars of preserves ready to sell to the crew. With their bare-chests, bronze skin, obsidian hair, and broad features, they look much more like members of an Amazon tribe than the city dwellers of Rio or São Paulo, though their cargo shorts (and the *New York Yankees* cap the older one wears) show they're a few generations removed from tribal life.

The growls of some great behemoth make the lot of you turn back toward the river, where another boat putters and churns straight for the dock. It looks like another fishing charter, ready to unload supplies—only it's traveling far too fast. This is not docking speed; this is full cruising speed!

The crew of the *Navio Destino* shouts at this newcomer, waving frantic arms in gesture, desperately telling them to slow down and veer off their collision course —but it appears as if the new ship has neither crew nor passengers.

In a final realization that it's a ghost ship headed for impact, the crewmen grab hold of their docking poles and use them as lances in an effort to deflect the projectile ship away. Father and son together on one beam, cookie and deckhand on the other, they brace for the inevitable. Both poles snap under the force, but they succeed in their mission—at least partially.

The new ship doesn't collide into them; it simply glances off the side of their boat, rocking it back and forth and sending the crewmen tumbling: three onto the boat's deck and young Neto into the river. For an instant, the image of a baby bird falling into a piranha feeding frenzy flashes through your mind.

Now the ghost ship heads on a new course: straight at you, full speed ahead.

"Look out!" Bertram shouts, running toward the boys to get them away from the collision.

You run down the dock, boards exploding into splinters behind you as the boat crashes through the wood and heads for your heels. In a dramatic leap, you make it to shore just as the ship crashes into the hut, demolishing the dwelling and running itself aground.

Cookie pulls Neto back aboard the ship, his father there to ensure he's still in one piece. The deckhand is already aboard the empty vessel, shutting down the engine as fast as he can. You simply stare at the wreckage.

"I think I recognize this boat from port back in the city," you say.

"So do I," Agent Bertram replies. "But didn't it used to have a lifeboat?"

"Think they abandoned ship?"

"Let's find out," he says, raising his weapon.

Trailing behind your comrade as he searches the ghost ship for any sign of life, you explore the vessel. There's no evidence of a struggle, and yet there's no sign of the people who navigated the ship so far downriver either. It's like they all simply vanished.

Until you make it to the helm.

The captain stands at the wheel, still piloting the ship—eternally, it would seem. His throat has been slit and his lifeblood coats the floor around you. The captain had tied himself to the steering wheel, a rosary crucifix clutched tightly in his dead hands.

The crewman from the *Navio Destino* crosses himself and mutters a prayer in Portuguese.

The three of you, bewildered by what you see, step out of the helm and climb up to the highest point of the boat to get some fresh air and to get a better look at the ship as a whole.

"I guess… they were all killed?" you say.

"Or jumped overboard," your partner adds. "All except for the captain."

"But why?"

As if in answer, the crewman's head snaps back, a crimson bullet hole suddenly in his forehead. As he falls dead into the river, you dumbly look across the way, not comprehending what's happened. There on the opposite bank rests the ship's missing lifeboat, and up in a tree above that, the Man in Black mercenary-assassin reloads by pulling back the bolt of his sniper rifle.

"Hit the deck!" Bertram shouts, blind-firing across the way with his own rifle before jumping.

You're off the roof, then you're off the boat, running down what remains of the dock. Keeping the boat as an obstacle between you and danger, you sprint into the jungle.

Agent Bertram moves fluidly despite the bulk of his bulletproof vest and tactical gear. You run just ahead of him, pushing apart the wet jungle foliage. Last night's rainstorm has completely drenched the forest, and it's a bit like forcing your way through a wet plastic bag.

Soon you're fully ensconced in the rainforest, with no signs of civilization around you. The jungle is immense and breathtaking, like entering a sauna with a green filter over your eyes. Each step crunches the thick layer of decomposing plant matter, and you move forward with countless foreign smells confounding your senses. A group of monkeys calls out to one another in the trees.

"Hold up," Bertram says as you enter a clearing.

He removes a handheld GPS unit from his vest and powers it up. You wait while he gets a fix on your position and finds a heading toward the sugarcane plantation.

The area before you sinks down into an open prairie, with bugs hovering just above the grass, but then suddenly the ground *shifts*. It's not grassland at all, but a marsh. There is an acre of grass, to be sure, but no firm ground. Not anymore.

The field has flooded after last night's downpour and the deluge has transformed the sunken area into a grassy lake.

It shifts again.

You focus on the ripples of water, which surge in more than one spot but originate from the same, uniform serpentine motion. It's as if a telephone pole was weaving through the muck. That's when you see the dark, amber eyes of an anaconda.

It's swimming toward you.

"We're actually not far off," Bertram says, still looking at the GPS. "There's a road only a quarter-mile west of here that will take us straight to the plantation."

You step back, trying to find enough saliva in your mouth to say, "Sssssnake!"

The tree behind you explodes with splinters of bark, right where your head was, as a bullet just misses you. Bertram instinctively turns and fires back toward the direction of the attack. You look back just in time to see the assassin-in-black slip out of view.

"Run!" Bertram shouts.

- "We can't go into the field!" Go to page 251
- Snake be damned. Run! Go to page 254

We're Not So Different, You and I

"I don't understand," he says. "Why would you want to help me?"

It's a fair question, and one you're not sure how to answer. All you can see, seared into the retina of your mind's eye, is the body of that poor woman. And if she's this man's fiancée, unable to grieve because he's in danger of sharing her same fate... how can you *not* help?

"Do you have a pen?" you ask.

He looks at you, something boiling deep within those azure eyes, curious as to your intentions. But he reaches into the breast pocket of his thin coat without protest and produces a pen and a journal. He holds the pen out to you, but you don't take it.

"Write down 'pick me up.'"

"Pick you up? Pick you up what?"

"No, literally write the words, 'PICK—ME—UP.' As you would in your own hand. Please, just do it."

His face is a study in confusion, but he complies, opens his journal and uncaps the pen. It's a leather-bound notebook and as he opens it, you see the pages are scoured with equations, notes and diagrams. He must be some kind of scientist. He scrawls the phrase and hands it over to you:

"Pick me up."

There you go; his handwriting is nothing like the note you found last night. The paper is the color of pale chlorophyll and covered with cross-hatched lines. The effect divides the sheet into tiny, uniform boxes.

You hand the notebook back to him. "I believe you. I don't think you did it, which means that this thing is far from over. And if I'm witness to a conspiracy, I won't be safe until it's resolved. *That's* why I'll help you."

"All right, Tourist. I hope you know what you've signed up for, because there's no going back. You can't even go say goodbye to your friends. Most likely, you'll end up in a missing person's report. Hell, they might even pin your 'death' on me, but we'll have to risk it."

You nod solemnly.

"Our mission will be three-fold. First, we'll need to get the American agents off our trail. Then we must find Jane's killer and clear my name. Third? I'll have my revenge on those responsible and you'll be free. Come, I've got a safe house where we can rest until morning."

As you turn from the beach and head up the hillside, you see the tell-tale buildings-stacked-upon-buildings look of the slums. This is the place where *The Incredible Hulk* laid low in one of those movies. So, yeah, you're going to hide where Hulk hid out, except when criminals attack, you won't turn into an invulnerable green monster. You'll turn into a dead body.

"We're going into the slums?" you ask.

"The *favelas,* yes. Don't worry, it's just one night, and we should be arriving late enough so as not to attract any attention."

Should be? Greeeeeaaattt....

Streets give way to alleyways and everything gets more compact. This is where the crush of humanity manifests itself. There is so much noise—music, laughter, shouting arguments, television—it's overwhelming. You don't say anything to your new friend, in part because it's hard enough to hear yourself think, but also because you're hoping not to attract any attention from would-be muggers.

This area used to be a public park, wide and open and green (there are still trees around every corner), until one by one the squatters put up their shacks. The police are beset in this part of the world, and so they choose their battles. They abandoned this park, until it grew into a city for the homeless and for those who wish not to be found.

Those like you.

You head up poorly-constructed concrete steps, graffiti welcoming you at every turn, as the mystery man leads you deeper within. You're starting to feel like you've returned to the crime scene from earlier tonight—as if inside any one of these shacks could be a dead body with a cryptic note.

"Hey, whatever happened to that note?" you ask. "The one that was in the room."

The man looks at you and shrugs. "I don't claim to have all the answers. But think—if something is missing from there, maybe it's important. Who had access? The American agents and the Rio police. Whoever took it must be hiding something."

You make it to *Pousada Favela Cantagalo*, your hostel for tonight. You know you're there because the establishment's name is spray-painted above the doorway. It's late, the gate is closed, and the doors are barred. Your escort kicks his shoe against the gate in three quick *clangs*. A young woman shows up, but doesn't open the barred door. Your companion speaks to her in Portuguese and she nods, but disappears. A moment later, she arrives with a man who lets you in.

As they lock you inside, you notice the place is surprisingly clean.

"One room or two?" your new partner asks. "One is safer."

- "But two is smarter." Go to page 293
- "I'll take safer." Go to page 286

Whatcha Gonna Do When They Come For YOU?

The street lights flicker on and you wait for the corrupt policeman to arrive. Soon he does, but it's not what you expected. First, he isn't alone. The man is in plain-clothes, but he keeps two uniformed officers as his escort. Second, he knows you are.

In an instant, you recognize the cop. Incredibly, it's Detective Lucio Muniz, the bleach-blond policeman who interviewed you on the night you were detained. Is he the one you're going to bribe?

"*You?*" he says.

Viktor steps forward and you can tell the detective recognizes his face from your sketch. Explaining everything in a long, impassioned appeal, Viktor begs Muniz to help him find Jane Nightingale's killer.

Detective Muniz listens carefully until Viktor is finished, then smiles and rubs his fingers together in the universal sign for money. Clearly, he's waiting for his bribe.

"I'm sorry," you say, "we don't have any money."

"You came to bribe me without money?" He laughs.

"Just think! With this new information, if you cracked the case, you'd be a hero!" Viktor says.

An evil grin appears on Muniz's face. "You're right, you *are* helping me. Here's some free information: I'm being paid *not* to crack the case. And guess what? When I arrest you and bring you in—I'll be a hero, you're right about that too."

- Go quietly. Go to page 261
- It's a double-cross! Draw and open fire. Go to page 297

What's Black and White and Red All Over?

The bar. Most of the room is constructed from a honeyed wood, offset by deep espresso barstools. The counters are smooth, white-marbled granite, and globe lamps suspended from the ceiling help break up the red light that pours from behind the bottles.

The bartender uses a rag to clean a glass, never taking his eyes off you as you approach. Once you sit, he places the glass before you, scoops five ice cubes in, and pours a generous serving of *Cachaça*—sugarcane liquor—from a bottle whose label looks like an Wild West wanted poster.

"Thanks," you say, bringing the glass to your lips.

"Rough night?" he asks.

"You don't know the half of it."

"Why don't you tell me about it?"

Another patron tries getting his attention from further down the bar, but the bartender ignores him. He keeps his focus on you, smiling warmly.

Your eyes narrow involuntarily. Why's this guy so curious? What about you holds his attention?

"Saw something you shouldn't have, right?" he continues.

It makes sense that a man who works at an international hostel speaks English, but his Brazilian accent is thick, and so is your suspicion. Downing the rest of the drink, you toss a bill on the table and get up to leave.

"Wait," he says, sliding a note your way. "This is for you."

The message is scrawled on a napkin and, most notably, was not written by the same hand as the note with the revolver—the now-missing note. This one reads:

"Let's talk about the girl from Ipanema.
No tricks, no cops, just a walk on the beach."

"Who wrote this?" you ask.

"It was called in," the bartender responds with a shrug, pouring the other patron's order.

"Your handwriting?"

He nods. "You're supposed to give me 50 *reais* for the delivery."

That's the equivalent of around $20.

- Call the agents! Go to page 50
- Take another drink for courage, then walk the five minutes down to the sand. Go to page 331

Who's There?

Dressed as an Elite Squad member and wielding the policeman's automatic rifle, Viktor looks surprisingly authentic. You wouldn't think this bookish engineer could pull off the look of hardened killer, but he stands at ease in the armored uniform.

"Drop your weapon," Viktor says with a wry smile.

You play along, tucking your arms (and the sub-machinegun) behind your back and step outside with Viktor escorting you, your gut full of nervous anticipation.

Just outside the doorway, not ten yards from you, another Elite Squad member approaches—looking for his partner. Viktor nods to the man and you feel his grip tighten around your arm. The cop looks at Viktor, unsure what to think. He squints, looking hard…

Then he raises his assault rifle. You close your eyes and grimace, ready to take your fate. Your last thought before you hear the gunfire is, *We've been made.*

But you're not dead.

You open your eyes and see the Elite Squad policeman shooting *above* you, onto the rooftop. You look up above just in time to see the assassin who's been following you. He has one pistol—and one eye—trained on Viktor, with the other on the Elite Squad member.

The Man in Black ducks out of the way, narrowly escaping the gunshots, and Viktor takes the opportunity to flee down the street. You both run as hard as you can, rushing around the corner and into the next alley.

"Come on!" Viktor shouts. "We've got to bed down, I need to ditch this gear. We find Jane tomorrow!"

➢ *Follow Viktor to a safe house.* Go to page 284

Window Dressing

"The Colonel" has a long and storied history, the highlights of which are detailed for you on the walls of his waiting room. Photo ops with visiting dignitaries: the Dalai Lama, former President George W. Bush, actor Cuba Gooding, Jr., and many others. A diploma from VMI, the Virginia Military Institute. A group photo from an elite Army Rangers unit, his youthful face, from before he learned to smile, tucked under a beret. A family photo with his government-issued wife and two kids. A graduate degree from Harvard Business School. A promotion ceremony where he pins on rank. Plaques extolling his meritorious achievement. A ribbon-cutting in front of a Monsanto logo and a golden mountain of corn. Another military unit photograph, this one where he's in command—you actually recognize a few of the faces: Howard, the blond agent, and at least three other men that you think you saw working at either the consulate or the embassy. They all have cold eyes. One man has a nasty scar on his chin.

And then there's the centerpiece: A triangle-folded American flag with a label explaining that this particular Old Glory has been flown over Ground Zero, the White House, and Bagram Air Base, Afghanistan.

The door opens behind you.

➢ *Turn to meet the Ambassador*: Go to page 39

Would-a, Should-a, Could-a

You decline. They get it, or at least they say as much. Most likely, they think you're a coward. So you eat the rest of breakfast in relative silence, Agent Bertram offering an olive branch by suggesting some sights you should see on vacation.

Then you meet up with your friends, continue your trip through Brazil, and enjoy the nonstop party of *Carnaval* and the rest of your time here. You take lots of pictures, eat plenty of good food, and fly home.

In the end, your name becomes slang for a witness too craven to help a DSS investigation. That and cold sores are your only lasting legacy from this trip.

You don't hear anything about the case in the news, and you don't know if they ever managed to catch the guy. To your dying day, you wonder what life would have been like if you had helped out those two agents on their murder investigation.

THE END

A Wretched Hive

Agent Bertram drives to the port outside São Paulo where merchants dock to unload their cargo, resupply, and embark upon the mighty *Rio Fingido.* Wooden gangplanks float in the shallow waters just off the muddy shore. Some of the fishermen set stands to sell their fresh catch and so the concrete parking lot around the dock is somewhat of a marketplace as well.

"Keep your wits about you, Hotshot," Bertram says, smoking a cigar, looking and feeling like a badass with his black sunglasses and even blacker assault rifle. "This is no place for a tourist."

The river is wide and expansive. Although the *Amazon* gives Brazil worldwide fame, the *Fingido* is not to be underestimated. Too far south to be part of the biggest waterway on earth, this river is massive in her own right. Brazil becomes connected like so many aqueducts during the rainy season, but major trade routes such as the *Rio Fingido* are formed from perennial water sources and remain traversed year-round.

Cigar smoke billowing out in the windless air, Bertram says, "You familiar with *Star Wars*? This is the alien bar where we hire the *Millennium Falcon.* Time to find us a ship."

Several young boys run up and down the docks wearing nothing but tattered pairs of shorts. When they spot the obvious foreigners, they head your way. One of them steps forward and asks something of Bertram in Portuguese.

He takes a long drag from his cigar, blows smoke in the boy's face, then with a voice made hoarse by tobacco he says, "*Vai tomar no cu, garoto.*"

The boy swats at the smoke but persists in his request, leaving an open palm and chattering at the agent. Bertram steps forward and raises his arm as if he's going to swat the kid and finally they take off down the dock.

"What was that all about?" you ask.

"It's a scam. They ask for change for a twenty, then they give you a counterfeit note in return. Or, if they think they can outpace you, they just grab your wallet and go."

"What'd you tell 'em?"

He shrugs. "To get lost. Now c'mon, let's find us a boat!"

The smell of fish fills the air and makes you a little seasick, even though you're still on terra firma. One nearby fisherman bails water into a bucket, flushing out his deck of guts from the previous day's catch. The birds love it.

A larger boat sits in port; looking much like an old river barge you might have seen traversing the Mississippi in an 1800s black-and-white photo—that is to say, large, multi-decked, flat on top, and tapered on each end. The only thing missing is the waterwheel churning in the back. Instead, this one has a lifeboat. You can't be sure if it's a passenger barge or if just runs supplies, but most likely it does both.

Agent Bertram stops by a man who's loading crates of fruit, bottled water, and other supplies onto his vessel. The seaman wears a sleeveless *Pink Floyd* t-shirt as his uniform, the Dark Side of the Moon just enough to cover his potbelly.

He has the sinewy limbs of a sailor and walks barefoot on calloused feet. He smiles through missing teeth, stopping his task when Bertram calls to him in greeting.

While the agent talks to the man in Portuguese, you take the opportunity to look at the boat in more detail. It's a medium-sized transport, about the size of a deep-sea fishing trawler, like that of the *Orca* in the movie *Jaws*. This one certainly has spent a fair time on the water and her once-white paint is now faded and chipped. Stenciled on the stern is the name *Navio do Destino*.

While they chat, a teenage boy comes from inside the boat's cabin. He's thin and shirtless and resembles a younger version of the proprietor. He looks at you and smiles with a few more teeth than his father.

"Hell-o," he says in a stilted, unsure tongue. "You talk English?"

You nod. Bertram takes note of the boy, and assessing no threat, turns back to speak with the ship's owner.

"You are looking for passage, yes? How you like my boat?"

"Your boat?" you say.

The boy smiles. "One day, yes. It is my family."

"Heirloom?" you try. "Inheritance?"

He looks at you blankly, not understanding..

"Never mind, I think I know what you're saying."

He nods cautiously. Unsure what else to say, you break eye contact, awkwardly pretending to inspect the ship. Finally, your eyes go to Bertram, and so do the boy's.

"What are they saying?" you ask.

"He wants to know is she fast ship."

"Well?" you grin. "Is she?"

The boy leans forward and says, "She's fast enough for you…old man."

Bertram snaps out of his conversation and turns your way. "What did you just say?" he demands.

"From the movie! Eh… *Guerra nas Estrelas*."

"*Star Wars*?" you say.

"Yes! That's the one."

Bertram grins. "This is destiny. It's our ship; our *Millennium Falcon*."

"Just like that?"

"Just like that. Plus, his father quoted us passage for two at a rate within our budget." Bertram explains. "This is the captain, Bruno. That's his son, Neto. There are two more crewmen who're filling up the gas cans right now. They're headed into the interior to sell supplies, and our stop is on the route."

"How long until we leave?" you ask.

"Not long. But the journey will take us overnight and I don't think we should both sleep at the same time—just in case. So the question I have for you is this: would you rather sleep right away, hang out while I'm asleep, then snag another nap in the morning, or…the opposite of that?"

- "Ummm, I'll sleep first, if it's all the same." Go to page 63
- "I'll take the opposite. One sleep chunk sounds lovely." Go to page 41

Wrong Time, Wrong Place, Wrong Everything

You head back to the scene of the bribery. *What was in his other pocket?* You wonder. *A gun? What about that backpack?* The boldness of paying off the cops when you yourself are a wanted man, not to mention the effrontery it would take to pull it off, is staggering. This certainly is a dangerous man.

With your own weapon—the murder weapon—pressing tight against your hip, you lean against the threshold that leads to the street. You slink out into the street, heart pounding in your ears. Hard to believe you're stalking the detective who showed you around earlier today. Harder still to believe, you're frightened of him.

"They're gone," you say.

"What?" Irma asks, looking out herself. "Damn. Maybe still close by? Keep sharp."

Moving forward, you stay quiet, all too aware of the crunching grit beneath your shoes. Up ahead there's the muffled echo of speech, blurred by footsteps and shuffling. You look to Irma—it's them, but she can't make out what they're saying. She signals you to move to the alley to the right. You continue on with caution.

"Irma?" calls a voice from behind.

You turn back to see Lucio Muniz and the two policemen in the alley behind you. The echoes have betrayed you, carrying the sounds of these men into the alley across the way, and now you've stepped out into the open.

"And the American witness?" he says, dumbfounded.

The alley they stand in is bordered with old car tires and several gas cans tucked in one corner. Your eyes focus on the ground where the two cops roll *something* into a tarp. All three men turn red with guilt when they see your gaze, and the two uniformed officers stand up, hands on their guns in fear. The tarp unfurls and you see why they're worried.

Lying prone with arms outstretched in a permanent crawl for help is a skeletal body. This poor soul has been burned beyond recognition; only a charred corpse is left behind. You can't tell gender, age, or even ethnicity.

"Holy…" you mutter.

"They were moving the crime scene," Detective Dos Santos says, just loud enough for you to hear. "This is not good."

"Irma, what are you doing here?" her partner says, the calm in his voice straining.

He puts his hand on his pistol.

- Talk your way out of it. Go to page 198
- Shoot first, questions later. Go to page 183

X-Rated

"I hope you're joking." Viktor blinks at you in disbelief, but the prostitute is unfazed.

She starts rubbing your thigh.

"Hold on!" Viktor says. "Listen, Tourist, you want to come back here on your own time—have at it—but right now we're on time I paid for, and this is not what I'm buying."

"Come back to me once you finish with your friend," she purrs into your ear. "I'll help you celebrate."

Viktor swears to himself in Portuguese and the working girl just giggles. She removes her hand from your lap, leaving you with only a wink.

➢ *Arrange the meeting with the dirty cop.* Go to page 224

Yep, Still Wet

Well, at least you got some sleep, even if you're still a soggy mess. Agent Bertram looks like he just jumped in a lake and Maria look equally haggard in her muddy pilot uniform.

"The plantation isn't far," Bertram croaks.

"Back to the road or straight there?" Maria asks.

- "Let's get to the road. After that storm, the fields will be a swamp." Go to page 235
- "The fields. We're still avoiding people, remember?" Go to page 102

You Can Run, BUT—

You turn and sprint into the alleyway, Viktor following close behind and the cops just beyond him. Soon, the old woman and her children are within view and they all look back once they hear the pounding of your feet and your labored breath behind them.

The eldest boy, who looks to be around nine years old, is the only one who doesn't run. Despite the shouting pleas of his mother, he stands his ground. Even as you fly through the alleyway, you can see it—something has snapped within the boy.

He moves toward the alley wall as you approach, and you assume he's doing so to get out of your way, but you'd be wrong. He finds a loose board on one of the pallet crates propped up against the wall around every corner in these *favelas,* and before you realize what he's done, he swings the plank at your shins.

Pain erupts from your leading leg and you sprawl out along the alley floor. Even as you hit the pavement, the young boy takes out a lifetime of frustration—kicking you hard in the chest and face. Viktor pulls the boy off of you and extends a hand to help, but then gets tackled by the cops.

Better call your lawyer; Brazilian prison isn't supposed to be fun.

THE END

Young and Vulnerable

The RSO smiles. "That's the spirit! See that, boys? You could learn something."

As he leaves, you turn to Agent Danly. The man looks none-too-happy to have you tailing along, but makes no objections. With a quick snap of his head, he bids you follow. There's a private room set aside so Danly can talk with the young woman, and she's already waiting inside. He stops at the door.

"You ready for this, Rookie?" Danly asks.

Ready or not, you nod in acceptance of your duty and head inside behind the agent.

The woman in question is a twenty-something petite blonde with hair pulled back so tight, it's almost like she's wearing a swim cap. Her face is unremarkable, she wears no rings, and only studded earrings, but she obviously put effort into her makeup. Most likely, she was overlooked in college and joined the ranks of the Foreign Service to see new places. Well, she ended up in Brazil, so it must've worked out. Though it appears, right now at least, that this conference room is the last place on Earth she wants to be.

"Thanks for agreeing to talk to us, Miss Tompkins," Agent Danly begins. "How long would you say you've known Miss Nightingale?"

The secretary looks a lot like a scared rabbit. "Well, I've worked here three months. She's been here the whole time I was."

"All right. Did you see Miss Nightingale socially?"

"Sure, sometimes. We were friends. She spent a lot of time with her fiance, when he was in town, but there were nights out at the bars… sometimes."

"You never met this fiance?"

"No, I did. But he traveled a lot, so when he visited they were pretty cozy. She just mostly joined in for 'girls' nights' when he was away."

"And what did he do? For work."

"I'm…not entirely sure," she says, her eyes tilting back, searching for the right memory inside her head. "Some kind of scientist or engineer, I think. Smart guy. Handsome."

"Glasses?" you ask.

"Yes," she replies, looking to you, thrown off-guard.

Agent Danly glares at you, but you try to convey *this could be our guy!* through your own stare. "What's his name?" Danly continues.

"Viktor something, I don't know. He's not on Facebook or anything."

"Miss Nightingale doesn't have him listed in her personnel file. Please try to remember his full name; it would be a big help."

"They were dating for a while, I think, but only recently got engaged. Maybe she hadn't updated it yet? I think it was something Brazilian, though. He's originally from here, I think. I know it was Viktor with a 'k' though. He said it like '*veek*-tor.' I don't know, I'm sorry."

She looks like she might cry. Like she's already been crying all morning.

"Okay, all right. Just a few more questions. Do you have any reason to believe someone would want to hurt Miss Nightingale? Any love affairs? Local ex-boyfriends? Maybe this fiance has a jealous girlfriend?"

"No, nothing like that. She is…was…a really nice person." Her lip quivers.

Then the levies finally break and a flood of grief comes pouring out of the woman. She's an inconsolable sobbing mess in less than five seconds.

"That will be all," Agent Danly says, dismissing her curtly.

➢ *Meet back up with Agent Bertram.* Go to page 175

You're Hilarious

You bring your pistol to the side of the bird, looking as menacing as you can, ready to turn the chicken into a cloud of red mist and feathers. The kids watch you with true menace in their eyes. Then the leader laughs, and so they all laugh.

"He says you're funny and he likes you," Viktor translates for the leader.

"They'll take us to Falador?"

The leader nods, giving a wide, toothy smile, and bids you to follow him with a wave of his hand.

➢ *Go see the informant.* Go to page 207

Your Partner

You get across the street despite the angry protests of the Elite Squad members guarding it. A bullet *explodes* across the brick near your head. That must have been a warning shot; they wouldn't have missed if they didn't want to. Guess you won't be going back that way.

Irma runs behind you, her eyes wide, shaking her head in disbelief. You make it up to a corner and peer out. In the connecting alley ahead, you see Agent Danly and two Elite Squad members sweeping an open courtyard. You're about to shout out to him, but the detective puts a hand on your shoulder.

"I don't recommend it, but if you choose to contact him, you do so on your own. I'm not taking responsibility for bringing you here, do you understand? You must tell him you followed without my help."

- "I understand. Thank you Irma, for everything." Go to page 232
- "He won't be too happy to see us here, will he? This is ridiculous—let's just go back to the hotel." Go to page 300

You Suck

You turn the device, but it just makes a dry "click," like a bicycle lock on the wrong combination. Nothing happens; that wasn't the right order.

Viktor closes his eyes and slumps, nearly collapsing in on himself with despair.

Then, in one final burst of effort, he leaps up from the ground and grasps Ambassador Mays by the throat. He actually gets a good grip on the man, but a second later, the armed guards in the room shoot Viktor, killing him and freeing the Ambassador.

In the confusion of the violence, you're shot too.

THE END

Zzzzz…

Fluorescent lights flicker on, searing your eyes. What time is it? The haze of sleep is thick, and you can't tell if you've been sleeping for minutes or hours. Blinking through the harsh light, you see a man standing by the bed. When his voice registers to your mute ears, you know it's Viktor.

"What?" you say.

"I said we've been boarded by pirates. Get up!"

Now you're awake. "What do they want?"

"Usually it's a robbery. We could try and wait them out, see if they'll leave us alone. Or we could try and warn the captain. It's illegal for merchant ships to carry weapons, but most keep a shotgun or at least a revolver just in case."

You will your brain to think.

- "Let's barricade the door and wait it out." Go to page 143
- "Is there still time? Let's warn him!" Go to page 292

The Book Club Reader's Guide

If you want a Monet Experience (no spoilers), avoid these questions until after you've read through the book several times. Take 1-2 weeks, progress through as many iterations of *MURDERED* as you can, while keeping the following questions in mind. Then, meet up with your reader's group and discuss:

1) Was your first inclination to pick up the revolver? Why or why not?

2) Discuss your impressions of Agents Bertram and Danly. Compare and contrast the two men's styles.

3) What was the first ending you discovered? Share your experiences with the group.

4) What would you say was the "best ending" you found? Talk about solving the mystery.

5) There are certain expected norms in mystery fiction. To what extent did MURDERED uphold these traditions? Has Schannep added anything new to the genre?

6) Both the villains and heroes in this story work outside the confines of the law. What does this say about the value of the organization vs the individual?

7) There are several vignettes off the beaten path. What was your favorite "hidden gem"?

8) A major theme in MURDERED is that of environmentalism versus commerce. Is it possible to find a happy medium? Or will these two values always be at odds?

9) In what ways does the lawless aspects of Brazil impact the story? Did you get a dark or "noir" feel (much like 1950s LA where detectives worked outside the law)?

10) How did you feel about being "in control" of the story? Did you feel more or less involved than you do with traditional books?

11) Did you feel you were rewarded for altruistic or selfish actions? For reserved or brazen choices? Defend your positions.

12) After reading this book, are you more or less likely to visit Brazil? Why?

Made in the USA
Middletown, DE
12 February 2021

33608497R00220